The Winning of Barbara Worth

By HAROLD BELL WRIGHT

Author of "The Calling of Dan Matthews," "The Shepherd of the Hills," "That Printer of Udell's," "Their Yesterdays," etc.

WITH FOUR ILLUSTRATIONS
BY F. GRAHAM COOTES

A. L. BURT COMPANY

PUBLISHERS   NEW YORK

More to regain his composure than because he was thirsty, helped himself
from the earthen water jar

ACKNOWLEDGMENT

While this story is not in any way a history of this part of the Colorado Desert now known as the Imperial Valley, nor a biography of anyone connected with this splendid achievement, I must in honesty admit that this work which in the past ten years has transformed a vast, desolate waste into a beautiful land of homes, cities, and farms, has been my inspiration.

With much gratitude for their many helpful kindnesses, I acknowledge my indebtedness to H. T. Cory, F. C. Hermann, C. R. Rockwood, C. N. Perry, E. H. Gaines, Roy Kinkaid and the late George Sexsmith, engineers and surveyors identified with this reclamation work; to W. K. Bowker, Sidney McHarg, C. E. Paris, and many other business friends and neighboring ranchers among our pioneers; and to William Mulholland, Chief Engineer of the Los Angeles Aqueduct.

I am particularly indebted to C. K. Clarke, Assistant Manager and Chief Engineer of the California Development Company, and to Allen Kelly, whose knowledge, insight and observations as a journalist and as a student of Reclamation in the Far West have been invaluable to me.

To my friend, Mr. W. F. Holt, in appreciation of his life and of his work in the Imperial Valley, this story is inscribed.   H. B. W.

Tecolote Rancho, April 25. 1911.

"Give fools their gold, and knaves their power;
   Let fortune's bubbles rise and fall;
Who sows a field, or trains a flower,
   Or plants a tree, is more than all."

CONTENTS

CONTENTS

The
Winning of Barbara Worth

CHAPTER I.

INTO THE INFINITE LONG AGO.

JEFFERSON WORTH'S outfit of four mules and a big wagon pulled out of San Felipe at daybreak, headed for Rubio City. From the swinging red tassels on the bridles of the leaders to the galvanized iron water bucket dangling from the tail of the reach back of the rear axle the outfit wore an unmistakable air of prosperity.

The wagon was loaded only with a well-stocked "grub-box," the few necessary camp cooking utensils, blankets and canvas tarpaulin, with rolled barley and bales of hay for the team, and two water barrels —empty. Hanging by its canvas strap from the spring of the driver's seat was a large, cloth-covered canteen. Behind the driver there was another seat of the same wide, comfortable type, but the man who held the reins was apparently alone. Jefferson Worth was not with his outfit.

By sending the heavy wagon on ahead and following later with a faster team and a light buckboard,

Mr. Worth could join his outfit in camp that night, saving thus at least another half day for business in San Felipe. Jefferson Worth, as he himself would have put it, "figured on the value of time." Indeed Jefferson Worth figured on the value of nearly everything.

Now San Felipe, you must know, is where the big ships come in and the air tingles with the electricity of commerce as men from all lands, driven by the master passion of human kind—Good Business— seek each his own.

But Rubio City, though born of that same master passion of the race, is where the thin edge of civilization is thinnest, on the Colorado River, miles beyond the Coast Range Mountains, on the farther side of that dreadful land where the thirsty atmosphere is charged with the awful silence of uncounted ages.

Between these two scenes of man's activity, so different and yet so like, and crossing thus the land of my story, there was only a rude trail—two hundred and more hard and lonely miles of it—the only mark of man in all that desolate waste and itself marked every mile by the graves of men and by the bleached bones of their cattle.

All that forenoon, on every side of the outfit, the beautiful life of the coast country throbbed and exulted. It called from the heaving ocean with its many gleaming sails and dark drifting steamer smoke under the wide sky; it sang from the harbor where the laden ships meet the long trains that come and go on their continental errands; it cried loudly from the busy streets of village and town and laughed out from field and orchard. But always the road led toward those mountains that lifted their oak-clad shoulders and pine-fringed ridges across the way as though in dark and solemn warning to any who should dare set their faces toward the dreadful land of want and death that lay on their other side.

In the afternoon every mile brought scenes more lonely until, in the foothills, that creeping bit of life on the hard old trail was forgotten by the busy world behind, even as it seemed to forget that there was anywhere any life other than its creeping self.

As the sweating mules pulled strongly up the heavy grades the man on the high seat of the wagon repaid the indifference of his surroundings with a like indifference. Unmoved by the forbidding grimness of the mountains, unthoughtful of their solemn warning, he took his place as much a part of the lonely scene as the hills themselves. Slouching easily in his seat he gave heed only to his team and to the road ahead. When he spoke to the mules his voice was a soft, good-natured drawl, as though he spoke from out a pleasing reverie, and though his words were often hard words they were carried to the animals on an under-current of fellowship and understanding. The long whip, with coiled lash, was in its socket at the end of the seat. The stops were frequent. Wise in the wisdom of the unfenced country and knowing the land ahead, this driver would conserve every ounce of his team's strength against a possible time of great need.

They were creeping across a flank of the hill when

13

the off-leader sprang to the left so violently that nothing but the instinctive bracing of his trace-mate held them from going over the grade. The same instant the wheel team repeated the maneuver, but not so quickly, as the slouching figure on the seat sprang into action. A quick strong pull on the reins, a sharp yell: "You, Buck! Molly!" and a rattling volley of strong talk swung the four back into the narrow road before the front wheels were out of the track.

With a crash the heavy brake was set. The team stopped. As the driver half rose and turned to look back he slipped the reins to his left hand and his right dropped to his hip. With a motion too quick for the eye to follow the free arm straightened and the mountain echoed wildly to the loud report of a forty-five. By the side of the road in the rear of the wagon a rattlesnake uncoiled its length and writhed slowly in the dust.

Before the echoes of the shot had died away a mad, inarticulate roar came from the depths of the wagon box. The roar was followed by a thick stream of oaths in an unmistakably Irish voice. The driver, who was slipping a fresh cartridge into the cylinder, looked up to see a man grasping the back of the rear seat for support while rising unsteadily to his feet.

The Irishman, as he stood glaring fiercely at the man who had so rudely awakened him, was without hat or coat, and with bits of hay clinging to a soiled shirt that was unbuttoned at the hairy throat, presented a remarkable figure. His heavy body was fitted with legs like posts; his wide shoulders and

deep chest, with arms to match his legs, were so
huge as to appear almost grotesque; his round head,
with its tumbled thatch of sandy hair, was set on a
thick bull-neck; while all over the big bones of him
the hard muscles lay in visible knots and bunches.
The unsteady poise, the red, unshaven, sweating
face, and the angry, blood-shot eyes, revealed the
reason for his sleep under such uncomfortable circumstances. The silent driver gazed at his fearsome
passenger with calm eyes that seemed to hold in their
dark depths the mystery of many a still night under
the still stars.

In a voice that rumbled up from his hairy chest—
a husky, menacing growl—the Irishman demanded:
"Fwhat the hell do ye mane, dishturbin' the peace
wid yer clamor? For less than a sup av wather I'd
go over to ye wid me two hands."

Calmly the other dropped his gun into its holster.
Pointing to the canteen that hung over the side of
the wagon fastened by its canvas strap to the seat
spring, he drawled softly: "There's the water. Help
yourself, stranger."

The gladiator, without a word, reached for the
canteen and with huge, hairy paws lifted it to his
lips. After a draught of prodigious length he heaved
a long sigh and wiped his mouth with the back of his
hand. Then he turned his fierce eyes again on the
driver as if to inquire what manner of person he
might be who had so unceremoniously challenged his
threat.

The Irishman saw a man, tall and spare, but of a
stringy, tough and supple leanness that gave him the

look of being fashioned by the out-of-doors. He too, was coatless but wore a vest unbuttoned over a loose, coarse shirt. A red bandana was knotted easily about his throat. With his wide, high-crowned hat, rough trousers tucked in long boots, laced-leather wrist guards and the loosely buckled cartridge belt with its long forty-five, his very dress expressed the easy freedom of the wild lands, while the dark, thin face, accented by jet black hair and a long, straight mustache, had the look of the wide, sun-burned plains.

With a grunt that might have expressed either approval or contempt, the Irishman turned and groping about in the wagon found a sorry wreck of a hat. Again he stooped and this time, from between the bales of hay, lifted a coat, fit companion to the hat. Carefully he felt through pocket after pocket. His search was rewarded by a short-stemmed clay pipe and the half of a match—nothing more. With an effort he explored the pockets of his trousers. Then again he searched the coat; muttering to himself broken sentences, not the less expressive because incomplete: "Where the divil—— Now don't that bate—— Well, I'll be——" With a temper not improved by his loss he threw down the garment in disgust and looked up angrily. The silent driver was holding toward him a sack of tobacco.

The Irishman, with another grunt, crawled under the empty seat and climbing heavily over the back of the seat in front, planted himself stolidly by the driver's side. Filling his pipe with care and deliberation he returned the sack to its owner and struck

16

the half-match along one post-like leg. Shielding the tiny flame with his hands before applying the light he remarked thoughtfully: "Ye are a danged reckless fool to be so dishturbin' me honest slape by explodin' that cannon ye carry. 'Tis on me mind to discipline ye for sich outrageous conduct." The last word was followed by loud, smacking puffs, as he started the fire in the pipe-bowl under his nose.

While the Irishman was again uttering his threat, the driver, with a skillful twist, rolled a cigarette and, leaning forward just in the nick of time, he deliberately shared the half-match with his blustering companion. In that instant the blue eyes above the pipe looked straight into the black eyes above the cigarette, and a faint twinkle of approval met a serious glance of understanding.

Gathering up his reins and sorting them carefully, the driver spoke to his team: "You, Buck! Molly! Jack! Pete!" The mules heaved ahead. Again the silence of the world-old hills was shattered by the rattling rumble of the heavy-tired wagon and the ring and clatter of iron-shod hoofs.

Stolidly the Irishman pulled at the short-stemmed pipe, the wagon seat sagging heavily with his weight at every jolt of the wheels, while from under his tattered hat rim his fierce eyes looked out upon the wild landscape with occasional side glances at his silent, indifferent companion.

Again the team was halted for a rest on the heavy grade. Long and carefully the Irishman looked about him and then, turning suddenly upon the still silent driver, he gazed at him for a full minute before saying, with el iborate mock formality: "It may be, Sorr, that bein' ye are sich a hell av a conversationalist, ut wouldn't tax yer vocal powers beyand their shtrength av I should be so baould as to ax ye fwhat the divil place is this?"

The soft, slow drawl of the other answered: "Sure. That there is No Man's Mountains ahead."

"No Man's, is ut; an' ut looks that same. Where did ye say ye was thryin' to go?"

"We're headed for Rubio City. This here is the old San Felipe trail."

"Uh-huh! So *we're* goin' to Rubio City, are we? For all I know that may as well be nowhere at all. Well, well, ut's news av intherest to me. *We* are goin' to Rubio City. Ut may be that ye would exshplain, Sorr, how I come to be here at all."

"Sure Mike! You come in this here wagon from San Felipe."

At the drawling answer the hot blood flamed in the face of the short-tempered Irishman and the veins in his thick neck stood out as if they would burst. "Me name's not Mike at all, but Patrick Mooney!" he roared. "I've two good eyes in me head that can see yer danged old wagon for meself, an' fwhat's more I've two good hands that can break ye in bits for the impedent dried herrin' that ye are, a-thinkin' ye can take me anywhere at all be abductin' me widout me consent. For a sup o' wather I'd go to ye——" He turned quickly to look behind him for the driver was calmly pointing toward the end of the seat. "Fwhat is ut? Fwhat's there?" he demanded.

18

"The water," drawled the dark-faced man. "I don't reckon you drunk it all the other time."

Again the big man lifted the canteen and drank long and deep. When he had wiped his mouth with the back of his hairy hand and had returned the canteen to its place, he faced his companion—his blue eyes twinkling with positive approval. Scratching his head meditatively, he said: "An' all because av me wantin' to enjoy the blessin's an' advantages av civilization agin afther three long months in that danged gradin' camp, as is the right av ivery healthy man wid his pay in his pocket."

The teamster laughed softly. "You was sure enjoyin' of it a-plenty."

The other looked at him with quickened interest. "Ye was there?" he asked.

"Some," was the laconic reply.

The Irishman scratched his head again with a puzzled air. "I disremimber entire. Was there some throuble maybe?"

The other grinned. "Things was movin' a few."

Patrick Mooney nodded his head. "Uh-huh: mostly they do under thim circumstances. Av course there'd be a policeman, or maybe two?"

"Five," said the man with the lines, gently.

"Five! Howly Mither! I did mesilf proud. An' did they have the wagon? Sure they wud—five policemen niver walked. Wan av thim might, av ut was handy-like, but five—niver! Tell me, man, who else was at the party? No—howld on a minut!" He interrupted himself, "Thim cops stimulate me mimory a bit. Was there not a bunch av sailor-men from wan av thim big ships ?"

The driver nodded.

The other, pleased with the success of his mental effort, continued: "Uh-huh—an' I was havin' a peaceful dhrink wid thim all whin somewan made impedent remarks touchin' me appearance, or ancestors, I disremimber which. But where was you?"

"Well, you see," explained the driver in his slow way, "hit was like this. That there saloon were plumb full of sailor-men all exceptin' you an' me. I was a heap admirin' of the way you handled that big hombre what opened the meetin' and also his two pardners, who aimed to back his play. Hit was sure pretty work. The rest of the crowd sort o' bunched in one end of the room an' when you began addressin' the congregation, so to speak, on the habits, character, customs and breedin' of sailor-men in general an' the present company in particular, I see right there that you was a-bitin' off more 'n you could chaw. It wasn't no way reasonable that any human could handle that whole outfit with only just his bare hands, so I edged over your way, plumb edified by your remarks, and when the rush for the mourners' bench come I unlimbered an' headed the stampede pronto. Then I made my little proposition. I told 'em that, bein' the only individual on the premises not a sailor-man nor an Irishman, I felt it my duty to referee the obsequies, so to speak, and that odds of twenty to one, not to mention knives, was strictly agin my convictions. Moreover, bein' the sole an' only uninterested audience, I had rights. Then I offers to bet

20

my pile, even money, that you could handle the whole bunch, takin' 'em two at a throw. I knowed it were some odds, but I noticed that them three what opened the meetin' was still under the influence. Also I undertook to see that specifications was faithfully fulfilled."

"Mither av Gawd, fwhat a sociable!" broke in the Irishman. "An' me too dhrunk to remimber rightly! Did they take yer bet? Ye sun-burned limb av the divil—did they take ut?"

"They sure did," drawled the driver. "I had my gun on them all the time."

"Hurroo! An' did I do ut? Tell me quick—did I do ut? Sure I could aisy av nothin' happened."

"You laid your first pair on top of the three, then the police called the game and the bets were off."

"They pinched the house?"

"They took you an' me."

"Sure! av course they would take us two. 'Tis thim San Felipe police knows their duty. But how could they do ut?"

"I forget details right here, bein' temporarily incapacitated by one o' them hittin' me with a club from behind. I woke up in a cell with you."

The Irishman rubbed the back of his head. "Come to think av ut, I have a bit av a bump on me own noodle that 'tis like helps to exshplain the cell. But fwhat in the divil's name brung us here in this Gawd-forsaken Nobody's Place? Pass me another pipeful an' tell me that av ye can."

The driver passed over the tobacco sack and, stopping his team for another rest, rolled a cigarette for himself. "That's easy," he said. "This here is Jefferson Worth's outfit. He wanted me to start home this morning, so he got me off. I don't know how he done it; mostly nobody knows how Jefferson Worth does things. There was a man with him who knowed you and, as I was some disinclined to leave you under the circumstances, Mr. Worth fixed it up for you, too, then we all jest throwed you in and fetched you along. Mr. Worth with the other man and his kid are comin' on in a buckboard. They'll catch up with us where we camp to-night. I don't mind sayin' that I plumb admired your spirit and action and—sizin' up that police bunch—I could see your talents would sure be wasted in that San Felipe country for some time to come. There'll be plenty of room in Rubio City for you, leastwise 'till you draw your pay again. If you don't like the accommodations you're gettin' I reckon you'd better make good your talk back there and we'll see whether you takes this outfit back to San Felipe or I takes her on to Rubio City."

The Irishman spat emphatically over the wheel. "An' 'tis a gintleman wid proper instincts ye are, though, as a rule, I howld ut impolite to carry a gun. But afther all, 'tis a matter av opinion an' I'm free to admit that there are occasions. Anyhow ye handle ut wid grace an' intilligence. An', fists er shticks, er knives, er guns, that's the thing that marks the man. 'Tis not Patrick Mooney that'll fault a gintleman for ways that he can't help owin' to his improper bringin' up. Av ye don't mind, will ye tell me fwhat they call ye? I'll not be so indelicate as to ax yer name. Fwhat they call ye will be enough."

The other laughed. "My name is Joe Brannin. They call me Texas Joe—Tex, for short."

"Good bhoy, Tex! Ye look the divil av a lot like a red herrin', but that's not sich a bad fish, an' ye have the right flavor. How could ye help ut? Brannin an' Texas is handles to pull a man through hell wid. But tell me this—who is this man that says he knows me?"

Texas Joe shook his head and, picking out his lines, called to his team. When they were under way again he said: "I didn't hear his name but I judge from the talk that he is one o' them there civil engineers, an' that he's headin' for Rubio City to build the railroad that's goin' through to the coast. Mr. Worth told me that there would be another man and a kid to go back with us, but I know that Mr. Worth hadn't never seen them before himself."

Pat shifted his heavy bulk to face the driver and, removing his pipe from his mouth, asked with deliberation: "An' do ye mane to tell me that this place we're goin' to is on the new line av the Southwestern an' Continental?"

"Sure. They're buildin' into Rubio City from the East now."

The Irishman became excited. "An' this man that knows me—this engineer—is he a fine, big, upstandin' man wid brown eyes an' the look av a king?"

"I ain't never seen no kings," drawled Tex, "but the rest of it sure fits him."

"Well, fwhat do ye think av that? 'Tis the Seer

23

THE WINNING OF BARBARA WORTH

himsilf, or I'm not the son av me own mither. I was
hearin' in Frisco, where I went the last time I
drawed me pay, that he was like to be on the S. an'
C. extension. 'Twas that that took me to San Felipe,
bein' wishful to get a job wid him again. Well, well,
an' to think ut's the Seer himsilf!"

"What's that you call him?"

"The Seer. I disremimber his other name but he's
got wan all shtraight an' proper. He's that kind.
They call him the Seer because av his talk av the
great things that will be doin' in this country av no
rain at all whin ignorant savages like yersilf learn
how to use the wather that's in the rivers for irrigation. I've heard him say mesilf that hundreds av
thousands av acres av these big deserts will be turned
into farms, an' all that be what he calls 'Reclamation.' 'Twas for that some danged yellow-legged surveyor give him the name, an' ut shtuck. But most
av the engineers—the rale engineers do ye mind—
is wid him, though they do be jokin' him the divil av
a lot about what they calls his visions."

"He didn't *look* like he was locoed," said Texas
Joe thoughtfully, "but he's sure some off on that
there desert proposition as you'll see before we lands
in Rubio."

"I dunno—I've seen some quare things in me time
in the way av big jobs that nobody thought could be
done at all. But lave ut go. 'Tis not the likes av
me an' you that's qualified to give judgment on sich
janiuses as the Seer, who, I heard tell, has the right
to put more big-manin' letters afther his name than
ye have teeth in yer head."

24

"All the same it ain't the brand on a horse that makes him travel. A man'll sure need somethin' more hefty than letters after his name when he goes up against the desert."

"Well, lave ut go at that. Wait 'til ye know him. But fwhat's this yer tellin' me about a kid? The Seer has no family at all but himsilf an' his job."

Texas grinned. "Maybe not, pard; but he's sure got together part of a family this trip."

"Is ut a gurl, or a bhoy?"

"Boy—'bout a ten-year-old, I'd say."

The Irishman shook his head doubtfully. "I dunno. 'Tis a quare thing for the Seer. Av it was me, or you, now—but the Seer! It's danged quare! But tell me, fwhat's this man, yer boss? 'Tis a good healthy pull he must have to be separatin' us from thim San Felipe police."

Texas Joe deliberated so long before answering this that Pat glanced at him uneasily several times. At last the driver drawled: "You're right there; Jefferson Worth sure has some pull."

Pat grunted. "But fwhat does he do?"

"Do?" Tex swung his team around a spur of the mountain where the trail leads along the side of a canyon to its head. Far below they heard the tumbling roar of a stream in its rocky course.

"Sure the man must do something?"

"As near as I can make out Jefferson Worth does everybody."

"Oh ho! So that's ut? I've no care for the cards mesilf, but av a man's a professional an'—"

"You're off there, pardner. Jefferson Worth ain't

that kind. He's one o' these here financierin' sports, an' so far as anybody that I ever seen goes, he's got a dead cinch."

"Ye mane he's a banker?"

"Sure. The Pioneer in Rubio City. He started the game in the early days an' he's been a-rollin' it up ever since. Hit's plumb curious about this here financierin' business," continued Tex, in his slow, meditative way. "Looks to me mostly jest plain, common hold-up, only they do it with money 'stead of a gun. In the old days you used to get the drop on your man with your six, all regular, an' take what he happened to have in his clothes. Then the posse'd get after you an' mebbe string you up, which was all right, bein' part of the game. Now these fellows like Jefferson Worth, they get's your name on some writin's an' when you ain't lookin' they slips up an' gets away with all your worldly possessions, an' the sheriff he jest laughs an' says hits good business. This here Worth man is jest about the coolest, smoothest, hardest proposition in the game. He fair makes my back hair raise. The common run o' people ain't got no more show stackin' up agin Jefferson Worth than two-bits worth o' ice has in hell. Accordin' to my notion hit's this here same financierin' game that's a-ruinin' the West. The cattle range is about all gone now. If they keeps it up we won't be no better out here than some o' them places I've heard about back East."

" 'Tis a danged ignorant savage ye are, like the rest av yer thribe, wid yer talk av ruinin' the West. Fwhat wud this counthry be without money? 'Tis thim same financiers that have brung ye the railroads, an' the cities, an' the schools, an' the churches, an' all the other blessin's an' joys of civilization that ye've got to take whither ye likes ut or not. Look at the Seer, now. Fwhat could a man like him—an engineer, mind ye—fwhat could the Seer do widout the men wid money to back him?"

The Irishman's words were answered by a cheerful "Whoa!" and a crash of the brakes as Texas Joe brought his team to a stand near the spring at the head of the canyon. "We camp here," he announced. "This is the last water we strike until we make it over the Pass to Mountain Springs on the desert side. Jefferson Worth will be along with the Seer and his kid most any time now."

A little before dusk the banker, with his two companions, arrived.

"Hello, Pat!" The man who leaped from the buckboard and strode toward the waiting Irishman was tall and broad, with the head and chin of a soldier, and the brown eyes of a dreamer. He was dressed in rough corduroys, blue flannel shirt, laced boots, and Stetson, and he greeted the burly Irishman as a fellow-laborer.

A joyful grin spread over the battered features of the gladiator as he grasped the Seer's outstretched hand. "Well, dang me but ut's glad I am to see ye, Sorr, in this divil's own land. I had me natural doubts, av course, whin I woke up in the wagon, but ut's all right. 'Tis proud I am to be abducted by ye, Sorr."

"Abducted!" The engineer's laugh awoke the echoes in the canyon. "It was a rescue, man!"

"Well, well, let ut go at that! But tell me, Sorr"—he lowered his voice to a confidential rumble—"fwhat's this I hear that ye have yer bhoy wid ye? Sure I niver knew that ye was a man av family." He looked toward the slender lad who, with the readiness of a grown man, was helping the driver of the buckboard to unhitch his team of four broncos. " 'Tis a good lad he is, or I'm a Dutchman."

"You're right, Pat, Abe is a good boy," the Seer answered gravely. "I picked him up in a mining camp on the edge of the Mojave Desert when I was running a line of preliminary surveys through that country for the S. and C. last year. He was born in the camp and his mother died when he was a baby. God knows how he pulled through! You know what those mining places are. His father, Frank Lee, was killed in a drunken row while I was there, and Abe showed so much cool nerve and downright manliness that I offered him a place with my party. He has been with me ever since."

Pat's voice was husky as he said: "I ax yer pardon, Sorr, for me blunderin' impedence about yer bein' a man av family. I'm a danged old rough-neck, wid no education but me two fists, an' no manners at all."

The engineer's reply was prevented by the approach of Jefferson Worth who had been talking with Texas Joe. The banker's head came but little above the Seer's shoulders and in comparison with the Irishman's heavy bulk he appeared almost insignificant, while his plain business suit of gray seemed altogether out of place in the wild surroundings. His smooth-shaven face was an expressionless gray mask and his deep-set gray eyes turned from the Irishman to the engineer without a hint of emotion. The two men felt that somewhere behind that gray mask they were being carefully estimated—measured—valued —as possible factors in some far-reaching plan. He spoke to the Seer, and his voice was without a suggestion of color: "I see that your friend has recovered." It was as though he stated a fact that he had just verified.

Laughing at the memory of the Irishman's San Felipe experience, the engineer said: "Mr. Worth, permit me to introduce Mr. Patrick Mooney whom I have known for years as the best boss of a grading gang in the West. Pat, this is Mr. Jefferson Worth, president of the Pioneer Bank in Rubio City."

The Irishman clutched at his tattered hat-brim in embarrassed acknowledgment of the Seer's formality. Jefferson Worth, from behind his gray mask, said in his exact, colorless voice: "He looks as though he ought to handle men."

As the banker passed on toward the big wagon the Irishman drew close to the Seer and whispered hoarsely: "Now fwhat the hell kind av a man is that? 'Tis the truth, Sorr, that whin he looked at me out av that grave-yard face I could bare kape from crossin' mesilf!"

CHAPTER II.

JEFFERSON WORTH'S OFFERING.

WHEN day broke over the topmost ridges of No Man's Mountains, Jefferson Worth's outfit was ready to move. The driver of the lighter rig with its four broncos set out for San Felipe. On the front seat of the big wagon Texas Joe picked up his reins, sorted them carefully, and glanced over his shoulder at his employer. "All set?"

"Go ahead."

"You, Buck! Molly!" The lead mules straightened their traces. "Jack! Pete!" As the brake was released with a clash and rattle of iron rods, the wheelers threw their weight into their collars and the wagon moved ahead.

Grim, tireless, world-old sentinels, No Man's Mountains stood guard between the fertile land on their seaward side and the desolate forgotten wastes of the East. They said to the country of green life, of progress and growth and civilization, that marched to their line on the West, "Halt!" and it stopped. To the land of lean want, of gray death, of gaunt hunger, and torturing thirst, that crept to their feet on the other side, "Stop!" and it came no farther. With no land to till, no mineral to dig, their very poverty was their protection. With an air of grim finality, they declared strongly that as they had always been they would always remain; and, at the beginning of my story, save for that one, slender, man-made trail, their hoary boast had remained unchallenged.

Steadily, but with frequent rests on the grades, Jefferson Worth's outfit climbed toward the summit and a little before noon gained the Pass. The loud, rattling rumble of the wagon as the tires bumped and ground over the stony, rock-floored way, with the sharp ring and clatter of the iron-shod hoofs of the team, echoed, echoed, and echoed again. Loudly, wildly, the rude sounds assaulted the stillness until the quiet seemed hopelessly shattered by the din. Softly, tamely, the sounds drifted away in the clear distance; through groves of live oak, thickets of greasewood, juniper, manzanita and sage; into canyon and wash; from bluff and ledge; along slope and spur and shoulder; over ridge and saddle and peak; fainting, dying—the impotent sounds of man's passing sank into the stillness and were lost. When the team halted for a brief rest it was in a moment as if the silence had never been broken. Grim, awful, the hills gave no signs of man's presence, gave that creeping bit of life no heed.

At Mountain Spring—a lonely little pool on the desert side of the huge wall—they stopped for dinner. When the meal was over, Texas Joe, with the assistance of Pat, filled the water barrels, while the boy busied himself with the canteen and the Seer and Jefferson Worth looked on.

" 'Tis a dhry counthry ahead, I'm thinkin',"

remarked the Irishman inquiringly as he lifted another dripping bucket.

"Some," returned Tex. "There are three water holes between here and the river where there's water sometimes. Mostly, though, when you need it worst, there ain't none there, an' I reckon a dry water hole is about the most discouragin' proposition there is. They'll all be dry this trip. There wasn't nothin' but mud at Wolf Wells when we come through last week."

Again the barren rocks and the grim, forbidding hills echoed the loud sound of wheel and hoof. Down the steep flank of the mountain, with screaming, grinding brakes, they thundered and clattered into the narrow hall-way of Devil's Canyon with its sheer walls and shadowy gloom. The little stream that trickled down from the tiny spot of green at the spring tried bravely to follow but soon sank exhausted into the dry waste. A cool wind, like a draft through a tunnel, was in their faces. After perhaps two hours of this the way widened out, the sides of the canyon grew lower with now and then gaps and breaks. Then the walls gave way to low, rounded hills, through which the winding trail lay— a bed of sand and gravel—and here and there appeared clumps of greasewood and cacti of several varieties.

At length they passed out from between the last of the foot-hills and suddenly—as though a mighty curtain were lifted—they faced the desert. At their feet the Mesa lay in a blaze of white sunlight, and beyond and below the edge of the bench the vast King's Basin country.

At the edge of the Mesa Texas halted his team and the little party looked out and away over those awful reaches of desolate solitude. The Seer and Pat uttered involuntary exclamations. Jefferson Worth, Texas, and Abe were silent, but the boy's thin features were aglow with eager enthusiasm, and the face of the driver revealed an interest in the scene that years of familiarity could not entirely deaden, but the gray mask of the banker betrayed no emotion.

In that view, of such magnitude that miles meant nothing, there was not a sign of man save the one slender thread of road that was so soon lost in the distance. From horizon to horizon, so far that the eye ached in the effort to comprehend it, there was no cloud to cast a shadow, and the deep sky poured its resistless flood of light upon the vast dun plain with savage fury, as if to beat into helplessness any living creature that might chance to be caught thereon. And the desert, receiving that flood from the wide, hot sky, mysteriously wove with it soft scarfs of lilac, misty veils of purple and filmy curtains of rose and pearl and gold; strangely formed with it wide lakes of blue rimmed with phantom hills of red and violet —constantly changing, shifting, scene on scene, as dream pictures shift and change.

Only the strange, silent life that, through long years, the desert had taught to endure its hardships was there—the lizard, horned-toad, lean jack-rabbit, gaunt coyote, and their kind. Only the hard growth that the ages had evolved dotted the floor of the Basin in the near distance—the salt-bush and greasewood, with here and there clumps of mesquite.

And over it all—over the strange hard life, the weird, constantly shifting scenes, the wondrous, ever-changing colors—was the dominant, insistent, compelling spirit of the land; a brooding, dreadful silence; a waiting—waiting—waiting; a mystic call that was at once a threat and a promise; a still drawing of the line across which no man might go and live, save those master men who should win the right.

After a while the engineer, pointing, said: "The line of the Southwestern and Continental must follow the base of those hills away over there—is that right, Texas?"

"That'll be about it," the driver answered. "I hear you're goin' through San Antonio Pass, an' that's to the north. Rubio City lies about here—" he pointed a little south of east. "Our road runs through them sand hills that you can see shinin' like gold a-way over there. Dry River Crossin' is jest beyond. You can see Lone Mountain off here to the south. Hit'll sure be some warm down there. Look at them dust-devil's dancin'. An' over there, where you see that yellow mist like, is a big sand storm. We ain't likely to get a long one this time o' the year. But you can't tell what this old desert 'll do; she's sure some uncertain. La Palma de la Mano de Dios, the Injuns call it, and I always thought that —all things considerin'—the name fits mighty close. You can see hit's jest a great big basin."

"The Hollow of God's Hand." repeated the Seer

in a low tone. He lifted his hat with an unconscious gesture of reverence.

The Irishman, as the engineer translated, crossed himself. "Howly Mither, fwhat a name!"

Jefferson Worth spoke. "Drive on, Texas."

And so, with the yellow dust-devils dancing along their road and that yellow cloud in the distance, they moved down the slope—down into The King's Basin —into La Palma de la Mano de Dios, The Hollow of God's Hand.

"Is that trúe, sir?" asked Abe of the Seer.

"Is what true, son?"

"What Texas said about the ocean."

"Yes it's true. The lowest point of this Basin is nearly three hundred feet below sea level. The railroad we are going to build follows right around the rim on the other side over there. This slope that we are going down now is the ancient beach." Then, while they pushed on into the silence and the heat of that dreadful land, the engineer told the boy and his companions how the ages had wrought with river and wave and sun and wind to make The King's Basin Desert.

Wolf Wells they found dry as Texas had anticipated. Phantom Lake also was dry. Occasionally they crossed dry, ancient water courses made by the river when the land was being formed; sometimes there were glassy, hard, bare alkali flats; again the trail led through jungle-like patches of desert growth or twisted and wound between high hummocks. Always there was the wide, hot sky, the glaring flood of light unbroken by shadow masses to relieve the

35

eye and reflected hotly from the sandy floor of the old sea-bed.

That evening, when they made camp, a heavy mass of clouds hung over the top of No Man's Mountains and the long Coast Range that walled in the Basin. Texas Joe, watching these clouds, said nothing; but when Pat threw on the ground the water left in his cup after drinking, the plainsman opened upon him with language that startled them all.

The next day, noon found them in the first of the sand hills. There was no sign of vegetation here, for the huge mounds and ridges of white sand, piled like drifts of snow, were never quite still. Always they move eastward before the prevailing winds from the west. Through the greater part of the year they advance very slowly, but when the fierce gales sweep down from the mountains they roll forward so swiftly that any object in their path is quickly buried in their smothering depths.

In the middle of the afternoon Texas climbed to the top of a huge drift to look over the land. The others saw him stand a moment against the sky, gazing to the northwest, then he turned and slid down the steep side of the mound to the waiting wagon.

"She's comin'!" he remarked, laconically, "an' she's a big one. I reckon we may as well get as far as we can."

A few minutes later they saw the sky behind them filling as with a golden mist. The atmosphere, dry and hot, seemed charged with mysterious, terrible power. The very mules tossed their heads uneasily

36

and tugged at the reins as if they felt themselves pursued by some fearful thing. Straight and hard, with terrific velocity, the wind was coming down through the mountain passes and sweeping across the wide miles of desert, gathering the sand as it came. Swiftly the golden mist extended over their heads, a thick, yellow fog, through which the sun shone dully with a weird, unnatural light. Then the stinging, blinding, choking blast was upon them with pitiless, savage fury. In a moment all signs of the trail were obliterated. Over the high edges of the drift the sand curled and streamed like blizzard snow. About the outfit it whirled and eddied, cutting the faces of the men and forcing them, with closed eyes, to gasp for breath.

Of their own accord the mules stopped and Texas shouted to Mr. Worth: "It ain't no use for us to try to go on, sir. There ain't no trail now, and we'd jest drift around."

As far from the lee of a drift as possible, all hands —under the desert man's direction—worked to rig a tarpaulin on the windward side of the wagon. Then, with the mules unhitched and securely tied to the vehicle, the men crouched under their rude shelter. The Irishman was choking, coughing, sputtering and cursing, the engineer laughed good-naturedly at their predicament, and Abe Lee grinned in sympathy, while Texas Joe accepted the situation grimly with the forbearance of long experience. But Jefferson Worth's face was the same expressionless gray mask. He gave no hint of impatience at the delay; no uneasiness at the situation; no annoyance at the discomfort. It was as though he had foreseen the situation and had prepared himself to meet it. "How long do you figure this will last, Tex?" he asked in his colorless voice.

"Not more than three days," returned the driver. "It may be over in three hours."

The morning of the second day they crawled from their blankets beneath the wagon to find the sky clear and the air free from dust. Eagerly they prepared to move. Against their shelter the sand had drifted nearly to the top of the wheels, and the wagon-box itself was more than half filled. The hair, eye-brows, beard and clothing of the men were thickly coated with powdery dust, while every sign of the trail was gone and the wheels sank heavily into the soft sand.

Three times Texas halted the laboring team and, climbing to the summit of a drift, determined his course by marks unknown to those who waited below. Again they stopped for the plainsman to take an observation, and this time the four in the wagon, watching the figure of the driver against the sky, saw him turn abruptly and come down to them with long plunging strides. Instinctively they knew that something unusual had come under his eye.

The Seer and Jefferson Worth spoke together. "What is it, Tex?"

"A stray horse about a mile ahead."

For the first time Texas Joe uncoiled the long lash of his whip and his call "You, Buck! Molly!" was punctuated by pistol-like cracks that sounded strangely in the death-like silence of the sandy waste.

As they came within sight of the strange horse the poor beast staggered wearily to meet the wagon—the broken strap of his halter swinging loosely from his low-hanging head.

"Look at the poor baste," said Pat. " 'Tis near dead he is wid thirst." He leaped to the ground and started toward the water barrel in the rear of the wagon.

"Hold on, Pat," said the colorless voice of Jefferson Worth. And his words were followed by the report of Texas Joe's forty-five.

The Irishman turned to see the strange horse lying dead on the sand. "Fwhat the hell—" he demanded hotly, but Texas was eyeing him coolly, and something checked the anger of the Irishman.

"You don't seem to sabe," drawled the man of the desert, replacing the empty shell in his gun. "There ain't hardly enough water to carry us through now, an' we may have to pick up this other outfit."

No one spoke as Pat climbed heavily back to his seat.

For two miles the tracks of the strange horse were visible, then they were blotted out by the sand that had filled them. "He made that much since the blow," was Texas' slow comment. "How far we are from where he started is all guess."

As they pushed on, all eyes searched the country eagerly and before long they found the spot for which they looked. A light spring wagon with a piece of a halter strap tied to one of the wheels was more than half-buried by the sand in the lee of a high drift. There was a small water keg, empty, with its seams already beginning to open in the fierce heat of the sun, a "grub-box," some bedding and part of a bale of hay—nothing more.

Jefferson Worth, Pat and the boy attempted to dig in the steep side of the drift that rose above the half-buried outfit, but at their every movement tons of the dry sand came sliding down upon them. "It ain't no use, Mr. Worth," said Texas, as the banker straightened up, baffled in his effort. "You will never know what's buried in there until God Almighty uncovers it."

Then the man of the desert and plains read the story of the tragedy as though he had been an eye witness. "They was travelin' light an' counted on makin' good time. They must have counted, too, on, findin' water in the hole." He kicked the empty keg. "Their supply give out an' then that sand-storm caught 'em and the horses broke loose. Of course they would go to hunt their stock, not darin' to be left afoot and without water, an' hits a thousand to one they never got back to the outfit. We're takin' too many chances ourselves to lose much time and I don't reckon there's any use, but we'd better look around maybe."

He directed the little party to scatter and to keep on the high ground so that they would not lose sight of each other. Until well on in the afternoon they searched the vicinity, but with no reward, while the hot sun, the dry burning waste and the glaring sands of the desert warned them that every hour's delay might mean their own death. When they returned at last to the wagon, called in by Texas, no

40

one spoke. As they went on their way each was busy with his own thoughts of the grim evidence of the desert's power.

Another hour passed. Suddenly Texas halted the mules and, with an exclamation, leaped to the ground. The others saw that he was bending over a dim track in the sand.

"My God! men," he shouted, "hit's a woman."

For a short way he followed the foot-prints, then, running back to the wagon and springing to his seat, swung his long whip and urged the team ahead.

"Hit's a woman," he repeated. "When the others went away and didn't come back she started ahead in the storm alone. She had got this far when the blow quit, leavin' her tracks to show. We may—" He urged his mules to greater effort.

The prints of the woman's shoe could be plainly seen now. "Look!" said Tex, pointing, "she's staggerin'—— Now she's stopped! Whoa!" Throwing his weight on the lines he leaned over from his seat. "Look, men! Look there!" he cried, as he pointed. "She's carryin' a kid. See, there's where she set it down for a rest." It was all too clear. Beside the woman's track were the prints of two baby shoes.

The Seer, with a long breath, drew his hand across his sand-begrimed face. "Hurry, Tex. For God's sake, hurry!"

The Irishman was cursing fiercely in impotent rage, clenching and unclenching his huge, hairy fists. The boy cowered in his seat. But not a change came over the mask-like features of Jefferson Worth.

41

Only the delicate, pointed fingers of his nervous hands caressed constantly his unshaven chin, fingered his clothing, or gripped the edge of the wagon seat as he leaned forward in his place. Texas—grim, cool, alert, his lean figure instinct now with action and his dark eyes alight—swung his long whip and handled his reins with a master's skill, calling upon every atom of his team's strength, while reading those tracks in the sand as one would scan a printed page.

It was all written there—that story of mother love; where she staggered with fatigue; where she was forced to rest; where the baby walked a little way; and once or twice where the little one stumbled and fell as the sand proved too heavy for the little feet. And all the while the desert, dragging with dead weight at the wheels, seemed to fight against them. It was as though the dreadful land knew that only time was needed to complete its work. Then the hot sun dropped beyond the purple wall of mountain and the mystery of the long twilight began.

"Dry River Crossing is just ahead," said Tex, and soon the outfit pitched down the steep bank of a deep wash that had been made in some forgotten age by an overflow of the great river. Occasionally, after the infrequent rains of winter, some water was to be found here in a hole under the high bank a short way from the trail.

With a crash of brakes the team stopped at the bottom. The men, springing from the wagon and leaving the panting mules to stand with drooping heads, started to search the wash. But in a moment

He had lifted the canteen and was holding it upside down

Texas shouted and the others quickly joined him. Near the dry water hole lay the body of a woman. By her side was a small canteen.

The engineer bent to examine the still form for some sign of life.

"It ain't no use, sir," said Texas. "She's gone." He had lifted the canteen and was holding it upside down. With his finger he touched the mouth of the vessel and held out his hand. The finger was wet. "You see," he said, "when her men-folks didn't come back she started with the kid an' what water she had. But she wouldn't drink none herself, an' the hard trip in the heat and sand carryin' the baby, an' findin' the water hole dry was too much for her. If only we had known an' come on, instead of huntin' back there where it wasn't no use, we'd a-been in time."

As the little party—speechless at the words of Texas—stood in the twilight, looking down upon the lifeless form, a chorus of wild, snarling, barking yowls, with long-drawn, shrill howls, broke on the still air. It was the coyotes' evening call. To the silent men the weird sound seemed the triumphant cry of the Desert itself and they started in horror.

Then from the dusky shadow of the high bank farther up the wash came another cry that broke the spell that was upon them and drew an answering shout from their lips as they ran forward.

"Mamma! Mamma! Barba wants drink. Please bring drink, mamma. Barba's 'fraid!"

Jefferson Worth reached her first. Close under the bank, where she had wandered after "mamma" lay down to sleep, and evidently just awakened from a tired nap by the coyotes' cry, sat a little girl of not more than four years. Her brown hair was all tumbled and tossed, and her big brown eyes were wide with wondering fear at the four strange men and the boy who stood over her.

"Mamma! Mamma!" she whimpered, "Barba wants mamma."

Jefferson Worth knelt before her, holding out his hands, and his voice, as he spoke to the baby, made his companions look at him in wonder, it was so full of tenderness.

The little girl fixed her big eyes questioningly upon the kneeling man. The others waited, breathless. Then suddenly, as if at something she saw in the gray face of the financier, the little one drew back with fear upon her baby features and in her baby voice. "Go 'way! Go 'way!" she cried. Then again, "Mamma! Barba wants mamma." Jefferson Worth turned sadly away, his head bowed as though with disappointment or shame.

The others, now, in turn tried to win her confidence. The plainsman and the Irishman she regarded gravely, as she had looked at the banker, but without fear. The boy won a little smile, but she still held back—hesitating—reluctant. Then with a pitiful little gesture of confidence and trust, she stretched forth her arms to the big brown-eyed engineer. "Barba wants drink," she said, and the Seer took her in his arms.

At the wagon it was Jefferson Worth who offered her a tin cup of water, but again she shrank from him, throwing her arms about the neck of the Seer.

The engineer, taking the cup from the banker's hands, gave her a drink.

While Mr. Worth and the boy prepared a hasty meal, Texas fed his team and the Irishman, going back a short distance, made still another grave beside the road already marked by so many. The child—still in the engineer's arms—ate hungrily, and when the meal was over he took her to the wagon, while the others, with a lantern, returned to the still form by the dry water hole. At the banker's suggestion, a thorough examination of the woman's clothing was made for some clue to her identity, but no mark was found. With careful hands they reverently wrapped the body in a blanket and laid it away in its rude, sandy bed.

When the grave was filled and protected as best it could be, a short consultation was held. Mr. Worth wished to return to the half buried outfit to make another effort to learn the identity of the Desert's victim, but Texas refused. " 'Tain't that I ain't willin' to do what's right," he said, "but you see how that sand acted. Why, Mr. Worth, you couldn't move that there drift in a year, an' you know it. I jest gave the mules the last water they'll get an' we're goin' to have all we can do to make it through as it is. If we wait to go back there ain't one chance in a hundred that we-all 'll ever see Rubio City again. It ain't sense to risk killin' the kid when we've got a chance to save her—jest on a slim chance o' findin' out who she is."

Returning to the outfit they very quietly—so as not to awaken the sleeping child—hitched the team to the wagon and took their places. As the mules started the baby stirred uneasily in the Seer's arms and murmured sleepily: "Mamma." But the low, soothing tones of the big man calmed her and she slept.

Hour after hour of the long night dragged by. They had left the sand hills behind three miles before they reached Dry River and now the wide, level reaches of the thinly covered plain, forbidding and ghostly under the stars, seemed to stretch away on every side into infinite space. Involuntarily all the members of the little party, except Texas Joe, strained their eyes looking into the blank, silent distance for lights, and, as they looked, they turned their heads constantly to listen for some sound of human life. But in all that vast expanse there was no light save the light of the stars; in all that silent waste there was no sound save the occasional call of the coyote, the plaintive, quivering note of the ground-owls, the muffled fall of the mules' feet in the soft earth, and the dull chuck, creak, and rumble of the wagon with the clink of trace chains and the squeak of straining harness leather. And always it was as though that dreadful land clung to them with heavy hands, matching its strength against the strength of these who braved its silent threat, seeking to hold them as it held so many others. The men spoke rarely and then in low tones. The baby in the Seer's arms slept. Only Texas, and perhaps his team, knew how they kept the dimly marked trail that led to life. Perhaps Texas himself did not know.

At daybreak they halted for a brief rest and for breakfast. The child ate with the others, but still clung to the engineer, and while asking often for "mamma," seemed to trust her big protector fully. From the shelter of his arms she even smiled at the efforts of Texas, Pat and the boy to amuse and keep her attention from her loss. From Jefferson Worth she still shrank in fear and the others wondered at the pain in that gray face as all his efforts to win a smile or a kind look from the baby were steadily repulsed.

It was Texas who, when they halted, poured the last of the water from the barrel into the canteen and carefully measured out to each a small portion. It was Texas now who gave the word to start again on their journey. And when the desert man placed the canteen with their meager supply of water in the corner of the wagon-box under his own feet the others understood and made no comment.

At noon, when each was given his carefully measured portion from the canteen, Jefferson Worth, before they could check him, wet his handkerchief with his share of the water and gave it to the Seer to wipe the dust from the hot little face of the child. The eyes of the big engineer filled and Texas, with an oath that was more reverent than profane, poured another measure and forced the banker to drink.

As the long, hot, thirsty hours of that afternoon dragged slowly past, the faces of the men grew worn and haggard. The two days and nights in the trying storm, the exertion of their search among the sand hills, the excitement of finding the woman's body and the discovery of the child, followed by the long sleepless night, and now the hard, hot, dreary hours of the struggle with the Desert that seemed to gather all its dreadful strength against them, were beginning to tell. Texas Joe, forced to give constant attention to his team and hardened by years of experience, showed the strain least, while Pat, unfitted for such a trial by his protracted spree in San Felipe, un-doubtedly suffered most.

After dinner the Irishman sat motionless in his place with downcast face, lifting his head only at long intervals to gaze with fierce hot eyes upon the barren landscape, while muttering to himself in a growling undertone. Later he seemed to sink into a stupor and appeared to be scarcely conscious of his companions. Suddenly he roused himself and, bend-ing forward with a quick motion, reached the canteen from under the driver's seat. In the act of unscrewing the cap he was halted by the calm voice of Texas: "Put that back."

"Go to hell wid ye! I'm no sun-dried herrin'."

The cap came loose, but as he raised the canteen and lifted his face with open parched lips he looked straight into the muzzle of the big forty-five and back of the gun into the steady eyes of the plains-man. "I'm sorry, pard, but you can't do it."

For an instant the Irishman sat as if suddenly turned to stone. The water was within reach of his lips, but over the canteen certain death looked at him, for there was no mistaking the expression on the face of that man with the gun. Beside himself with thirst, forgetting everything but the water, and

48

utterly reckless he growled: "Shoot an' be domned, ye murderin' savage!" and again started to lift the cloth-covered vessel.

At that instant the baby, catching sight of the canteen, called from the rear seat: "Barba wants drink. Barba thirsty, too."

As though Texas had pulled the trigger the Irishman dropped his hand. Slowly he looked from face to face of his companions—a dazed expression on his own countenance, as though he were awakening from a dream. The child, clinging to the Seer with one hand and pointing with the other, said again: "Barba thirsty; please give Barba drink."

A look of horror and shame went over the face of the Irishman, his form shook like a leaf and his trembling hands could scarcely hold the canteen. "My Gawd! bhoys," he cried, "fwhat's this I was doin'?" Then he burst suddenly upon Tex with: "Why the hell don't ye shoot, domn ye? A baste like me is fit for nothin' but to rot in this Gawd-forsaken land!"

The fierce rage of the man at his own act was pitiful. Texas dropped his gun into the holster and turned his face away. Jefferson Worth held out a cup. "Give the little one some water, Pat," he said, in his cold, exact way.

With shaking hands the Irishman poured a little into the cup and, screwing the cap back on the canteen, he returned it to its place. Then with a groan he bowed his face in his great, hairy hands.

Just before sun-down they climbed up the ancient beach line to the rim of the Basin and the Mesa on the east. Halting here for a brief rest and for supper, they looked back over the low, wide land through which they had come. All along the western sky and far to the southward, the wall-like mountains lifted their purple heights from the dun plain, a seemingly impassable barrier, shutting in the land of death; shutting out the life that came to their feet on the other side. To the north the hills that rim the Basin caught the slanting rays of the setting sun and glowed rose-color, and pink, and salmon, with deep purple shadows where canyons opened, all rising out of drifts of silvery light. To the northwest two distant, gleaming, snow-capped peaks of the Coast Range marked San Antonio Pass. To the west Lone Mountain showed dark blue against the purple of the hills beyond. Down in the desert basin, drifting above and woven through the ever-shifting masses of color, shimmering phantom lakes, and dull, dusky patches of green and brown, long streamers, bars and threads of dust shone like gleaming gold.

Texas Joe, when he had poured for each his portion of water, shook the canteen carefully, and a smile spread slowly over his sun-blackened features. "What's left belongs to the kid," he said. "But we'll make it. We'll jest about make it."

The Irishman lifted his cup toward the Desert, saying solemnly: "Here's to ye, domn ye! Ye ain't got us yet. May ye burn an' blishther an' scorch an' bake 'til yer danged heart shrivels up an' blows away."

Then he fell to amusing the child with loving fun-talk and queer antics, until she laughed aloud and permitted him to catch her up in his big hairy hands and to toss her high in the air. Texas and Abe, joining in the frolic, shared with Pat the little lady's favor, while the Seer looked smilingly on. But when Jefferson Worth approached, with an offering of pretty stones and shells which he had gathered on the old beach, she ran up to the engineer's arms. Still coaxing, the banker held out his offering. The others were silent, watching. Timidly at last, the child put forth her little hands and accepted the gift, shrinking back quickly with her treasures to the shelter of the big man's arms.

It was just after noon the next day when the men at the wagon yard on the edge of Rubio City looked up to see Jefferson Worth's outfit approaching. The dust-covered, nearly-exhausted team staggered weakly through the gate. On the driver's seat sat a haggard, begrimed figure holding the reins in his right hand; and in his lap, supported by his free arm, a little girl lay fast asleep. Then as one of the mules lay down, the men went forward on the run.

Texas stared at them dully for a moment. Then, as he dropped the reins, his parched, cracked lips parted in what was meant for a smile and he said, in a thick, choking whisper: "We made it, boys: we jest made it. Somebody take the kid."

Eager hands relieved him of his burden and he slid heavily to the ground to stand dizzily holding on to a wheel for support.

One of the men said sharply: "But where's Mr.

Worth, Tex? What have you done with Jefferson Worth an' what you doin' with a kid?"

Texas Joe gazed at the questioner steadily as if summoning all his strength of will in an effort to think. "Hello, Jack! Why—damned if I know— he was with me a little while ago."

The engineer, the banker, the Irishman and the boy were lying unconscious on the bottom of the wagon.

CHAPTER III.

MISS BARBARA WORTH.

MRS. WORTH, sitting on the wide veranda of her home after a lonely supper, lifted her eyes frequently from the work in her lap to look down the street. Perhaps it was unusual for a banker's wife to be darning her husband's socks; it may be, even, that bankers do not usually wear socks that have been darned. But Mrs. Worth was not sensible that her task was at all strange.

A group of dust-covered cow-boys, coming into town for an evening's pleasure, jogged past with loud laughter and soft-clinking spurs and bridle-chains. "There's Jefferson Worth's place," said one. "D'ye reckon he'll make good corralin' all the money there is in the world?"

Now and then a carriage, filled with well-to-do citizens out for an evening ride, drove slowly by. The people in the carriages always saluted Mrs. Worth and she returned their salutations with a prim little bow. But no one stopped to chat or to offer her a seat. In this, also, there was nothing strange to the woman on the porch of the big, empty house. Sometimes the people in the carriages, entertaining visiting friends, pointed to Jefferson Worth's house, with proper explanations, as they also called attention to the Pioneer Bank—Jefferson Worth's bank.

When dusk came and she could no longer see, Mrs. Worth laid aside her work and sat with folded hands, her face turned down the street. Inside the house the lights were not yet on; there was no need for them and she liked to sit in the dark.

The Indian servant woman came softly to the door. "Does the Senora wish anything?"

"No, thank you, Ynez; come and sit down."

Noiselessly the woman seated herself on the top step.

"It has been warm to-day, Ynez."

"Si, Senora."

"It is nearly three weeks since Mr. Worth left with Texas Joe for San Felipe, Ynez."

"Si, Senora."

"Do you know how far it is across the Desert to San Felipe?"

"Si. I think three—four day, maybe five, Senora."

"It will be very hot."

"Si, Senora. Las' year my sister's man—Jose—go for San Felipe. No much water. He no come back."

"Yes, I remember. What is it your people call The King's Basin Desert? The Hollow of God's Hand, isn't it?"

"Si, Senora. La Palma de la Mano de Dios."

"I wish they would come."

"He come pretty quick, I think. Mebbe so he not start when he think. Mebbe so what you call 'beesness' not let him come," said the Indian woman, soothingly.

"But Mr. Worth expected to be back two days ago and he is always on time, you know, Ynez."

"Si, Senora. But mebbe so this one time different."

"I do wish they would—— Look, Ynez, look! There's some one stopping!"

A carriage was turning in toward the house.

"It is Senor Worth," said the Indian woman.

"Someone is with him, Ynez. They have a child."

As Jefferson Worth and the Seer came up the walk—the engineer carrying the little girl—Mrs. Worth rose unsteadily to her feet. "Run, quick, Ynez—quick! The lights!"

That night when the Seer, with everything possible done for his comfort, had retired, and the baby—bathed and fed—was sound asleep in a child's bed that Ynez had brought from an unused room in the banker's big house and placed in Mrs. Worth's own chamber, Jefferson Worth and his wife crept softly to the little girl's bedside. Silently they looked at the baby form under the snow-white coverlet and at the round, baby face, with the tumbled brown hair, on the pillow.

Mrs. Worth clasped her hands in eager longing as she whispered: "Oh, Jeff, can we keep her? Can we?"

Jefferson Worth answered in his careful manner: "Did you look for marks on her clothing?"

"There was nothing—not a letter even. And all that she can tell of her name is Barba. I'm sure she means Barbara." As she answered, Mrs. Worth searched her husband's face anxiously. Then she exclaimed: "Oh you do want her; you do!" and added wistfully: "Of course we must try to find her folks, but do you think it very wrong, Jeff, to wish—to wish that we never do? I feel as though she were sent to take the place of our own little girl. We need her so, Jeff. I need her so—and you—you will need her, when—" There was a day coming that the banker and his wife did not talk about. Since the birth and death of their one child, Mrs. Worth had been a hopeless invalid.

Several weeks passed and every effort to find little Barbara's people was fruitless. Inquiry in Rubio City and San Felipe and through the newspapers on the Coast brought no returns. The land in those days was a land of strangers where people came and went with little notice and were lost quickly in the ever-restless tide. It was not at all strange that no one could identify an outfit of which it was possible to tell only of a woman and child and one bay horse. There were many outfits with a woman and child in the party and many that had among the two, four, six, or more animals one bay horse.

In the meantime, little Barbara, in her new home, was growing gradually away from all that had gone before her long ride in the big wagon with the men. Already she was beginning to talk of her "other mamma and papa." Mrs. Worth slipped into the other woman's place in the childish heart, even as little Barbara filled the empty mother-heart of the woman.

Toward Mr. Worth, though she no longer shrank from him in fear, the little girl maintained an attitude of questioning regard. With Texas or Pat or the boy Abe, who often went together to see her, she laughed and chattered like a good little comrade and play-fellow. But when the Seer came, as he did whenever his duties and his presence in town would permit, she flew to him with eager love, climbing on his knee or snuggling under his arm with entire confidence and understanding.

Public interest in Rubio City, keen at first, died out quickly. Rubio City, in those days of railroad building, had too many things of interest to retain any one thing long. Still, because it was Jefferson Worth, Rubio City could not altogether drop the matter. So it was one evening in the Gold Bar saloon, where Pat, coming into town for a quiet evening from the grading camp on the new road, and Texas Joe, who was just back from another trip across the Desert, were having a friendly glass in a quiet corner.

"Is there anythin' doin' in that San Felipe I don't know?" was Pat's natural question. "Things is that slow in this danged town I'm gettin' all dead on me insides."

Texas grinned in his slow way. "There'll be another pay day before long."

"Yes, an' 'tis ye that'll be 'round agin to kape me from proper enjoyment av the blissin's av civilization wid yer talk av the gold that's to be found in thim mountains that nobody but ye knows where they are. 'Tis a fool I am to be listenin' to yer crazy drames."

"Just keep your shirt on a little longer, pard,"

returned the other soothingly. "We've most enough for a grub-stake now. When we're a little mite better fixed we'll pull out of this sinful land o' temptation an' when we come back"—he drew a long breath— "we'll do the thing up proper."

Pat dropped his glass with a thump. "We will," he said. "We will that. An' it's to San Felipe we'll go. Tell me, did you see no wan there inquirin' afther me good health this last thrip?"

"I kept away from Sailor Mike's place, not wishin' to deprive you of your share o' the sport. But I met a big policeman who said: 'Tell that red-headed Irish bum that it'll be better for his health to stay away from San Felipe.'"

"He did, did he? He towld ye that? The big slob! He knows ut will be better for him. Fwhat did ye tell him?"

"I said you'd decided to locate here permanent."

Pat gasped for breath. "Ye towld him that! Ye did! Yer a danged sun-baked herrin' av a man wid no proper spirit at all. Fwhat the hell do ye mane to be so slanderin' me reputation an' two or three hundred miles av disert between me an' him? For a sup av wather I'd go to ye wid me two hands."

Texas Joe laughed outright. "Let's have another drink instead," he said.

In the silence occasioned by the re-filling of their glasses the two friends caught the name of Jefferson Worth. Instantly their attention was attracted to a well-dressed, smart-looking stranger, who stood at the bar talking loudly to a man known to Rubio City as a promoter of somewhat doubtful mining schemes.

58

Pat and Texas listened with amused interest while the two in concert cursed Jefferson Worth with careful and exhaustive attention to details.

"Go to it, gentlemen!" put in the bar-keeper, as he returned to his place from the table in the corner. "We-all sure endorses your opinions. Have one on the house." He graciously helped them to more liquor.

"Brother Worth sure stands high with this here congregation," drawled Texas Joe to his companion.

"Hst!" whispered Pat. "They're askin' afther the kid." The casual, amused interest of the two friends became intense.

"They sure tried everything to find her folks," the saloon man was saying, "but there ain't nothin' doin' so far. They say if nobody shows up with a claim Jefferson Worth is goin' to adopt her an' bring her up like his own."

This statement of Jefferson Worth's intentions called forth from the stranger an exhaustive opinion as to the banker's fitness to have the child and her probable chances for right training and happiness in the financier's hands. His remarks being cordially commended by the promoter and the man in the white apron, the speaker was encouraged to strengthen his position in reference to the future of this poor, helpless orphan and to point out freely the duties of Rubio City in the matter. He was interrupted by a light hand on his shoulder. Turning with a start that spilled the liquor in his glass, he looked into the lean face of Texas Joe. Behind the plainsman stood the heavy form of the Irishman, a look of pleased anticipation on his battle-scarred features. There was a sudden sympathetic hush in the room. Every face was turned toward the group.

"Excuse me, stranger," said Texas, in his softest tones; "but I sure am moved to testify in this here meetin'."

The man would have made some angry, blustering reply, but a warning look from the promoter and a slight cough from the bar-tender checked him.

Tex proceeded. "That you-all has rights to your opinion regardin' Mr. Jefferson Worth's character I ain't denyin', an' there's plenty in Rubio City that'll agree with you. Mebbe you has reasons for feelin' grieved. I don't sabe this here business game nohow. Mebbe you stacked the deck an' he caught you at it. You sure impresses me that a-way, for I've noticed that it ain't the sport who plays fair or loses fair that squeals loudest when the cards are agin him. But when you touches on said Jefferson Worth an' the future of that little kid, with free remarks on the duties of Rubio City regardin' the same, you're sure gettin' around where I live. Me an' this gent here"—he waved his hand toward Pat with elaborate formality, to the huge delight of his audience—"me an' this here gent is first uncles to that kid, an' any pop-eyed, lop-eared, greasy-fingered cross between a coyot' an' a jack-rabbit that comes a-pouncin' out o' the wilds o' civilization to jump our claim by makin' insinuations that we ain't competent to see that the aforementioned kid has proper bringin' up an' that Brother Worth ain't a proper daddy for her, had best come loaded for trouble.

For trouble'll sure camp on his trail 'til he's reformed
or been safely planted."

In the significant pause that followed no one
moved. Texas stood easily, looking into the eyes of
the stranger. Pat shot fierce, watchful glances
around the room, from face to face.

"I trust you get's the force o' my remarks," concluded Texas suggestively.

The stranger moved uneasily and looked hurriedly
about for signs of sympathy or assistance. Every
face was a blank. Texas waited.

"I suppose I was hasty," said the stranger, sul-
lenly. "I beg your pardon, gentlemen."

"Consider the meetin' dismissed, gentlemen," said
Texas, easily. "Me an' my pardner trusts that the
congregation will treasure our remarks in the future.
Now, you bar-tender, everybody drinks on us to the
health and happiness of our respected niece—Miss
Barbara Worth."

On the street a few minutes later Pat growled his
disappointment. "The divil take a man wid no
bowels."

Ignoring his friend's complaint, Texas returned
meditatively: "Do you think, Pat, that there might
be anything in what that there gent said? In spite
o' what we seen of him on that trip, Jefferson Worth
is sure a cold proposition. Give it to me straight.
What will he do for the little one?"

"An' it's just fwhat we see'd on that thrip that
makes me think ut's a question av fwhat the little
girl will do to him," answered Pat, thereby sustain-
ing the reputation of his race.

CHAPTER IV.

YOU'D BETTER MAKE IT NINETY.

IFTEEN years of a changing age left few marks on Rubio City. Luxurious overland trains, filled with tourists, now stopped at the depot where, under the pepper trees, sadly civilized Indians sold Kansas City and New Jersey-made curios—stopped and went on again along the rim of The King's Basin, through San Antonio Pass to the great cities on the western edge of the continent. But the town on the banks of the Colorado, in an almost rainless land, had little to build upon. Still on the street mingled the old-timers from desert, mountain and plain; from prospecting trip, mine or ranch; the adventurer, the promoter, the Indian, the Mexican, the frontier business man and the tourist.

But there were few of the citizens of Rubio City now who knew the story of the baby girl whom Jefferson Worth and his party had found in La Palma de la Mano de Dios. For, though Rubio City was changed but little since that day when Texas Joe brought the outfit with the child safely out of the Desert, the people came and went always as is the manner of their moving kind. The few "old-timers" who remained had long ceased to tell the story. No one thought of the young woman, who

rode down the street that afternoon, save only as the
daughter of Jefferson Worth.

As she passed, the people turned to follow her with
their eyes—the "old-timers" with smiles of recognition and picturesque words of admiring comment;
the townspeople with cheerful greetings—a wave of
the hand or a nod when they caught her eye; the
strangers from the East with curious interest and
ready kodaks. Here, the visitors told themselves,
was the *real* West.

"How interesting!" gasped a tailor-made woman
tourist to her escort. "Look, George, she is wearing
a divided skirt and riding a man's saddle! And
look! quick! where's your camera? She has a
revolver!"

That revolver, a dainty but effective pearl-handled
weapon, was a gift to Barbara from her "uncles,"
Texas and Pat; and though ornamental was not for
ornament. The girl often went alone, as she was
going to-day, for a long ride out on the Mesa, and
the country still harbored many wild and lawless
characters.

But the tailored woman tourist did not need to
urge George to look. There was something about the
girl on the quick-stepping, spirited horse that challenged attention. The khaki-clad figure was so richly
alive—there was such a wealth of vitality; such an
abundance of young woman's strength; such a glow
of red blood expressed in every curved line and
revealed in every graceful movement—that the
attraction was irresistible. To look at Barbara
Worth was a pleasure; to be near her was a delight.

63

At the Pioneer Bank the girl checked her horse and, swinging lightly to the ground, threw the reins over the animal's head, thus tying him in western fashion. As she stood now on the sidewalk laughing and chatting with a group of friends, who had paused in passing to greet her, her beautiful figure lost none of the compelling charm that made her, on horseback, so good to look at. Every movement and gesture expressed perfect health. The firm flesh of her rounded cheeks and full throat was warmly browned and glowing with the abundance of red blood in her veins. Though framed in a mass of waving brown hair under a wide sombrero, her features were not pretty. The mouth was perhaps a bit too large, though it was a good mouth, and, as she laughed with her companions, revealed teeth that were faultless. But something looked out of her brown eyes and made itself felt in every poise and movement that forced one to forget to be critical. It was the wholesome, challenging lure of an unmarred womanhood.

"Oh, Barbara, how could you—how *could* you miss last Thursday afternoon at Miss Colson's? We had a perfectly lovely time!" cried a vivacious member of the little group.

"Yes indeed, young lady; explanations are in order," added another. "Miss Colson didn't like it a bit. She had an exquisite luncheon, and you know how people depend upon your appreciation of good things to eat!"

"Well, you see," answered Barbara, turning to pat her horse's neck as the animal, edging closer to her side, rubbed his soft muzzle coaxingly against her shoulder, "Pilot and I were out on the Mesa and he said he didn't want to come back. Pilot doesn't care at all for afternoon parties, do you old boy?"—with another pat—"so what could I do? I didn't like to hurt Miss Colson's feelings, of course, but I didn't like to hurt Pilot's feelings either; and the day was so perfect and Pilot was feeling so good and we were having such fun together! I guess it was a case of 'a bird in the hand,' or 'possession being nine points,' you know; or something like that. Only for pity's sake, girls, don't tell Miss Colson I said that."

They all laughed understandingly and the vivacious one said: "I guess it was possession all right. Could anything on earth induce you to give up your horse and your desert, Barbara?"

Inside the bank Jefferson Worth, with his customary careful, exact manner, was explaining to a small rancher that it was impossible to extend the loan secured by a mortgage on the farmer's property. Personally Mr. Worth would be glad to accommodate him. But the loan had already been extended three times and there were good reasons why the bank must call it in. The farmer must remember that a bank's duty to its stockholders and depositors was sacred. It was not a question of the farmer's honesty; it was altogether a question of Good Business.

The farmer was agitated and presented his case desperately. Mr. Worth knew the situation—the unforeseen circumstances that made it impossible for him to pay then. Only two months more were needed —until his new crop matured. He could not blame

Mr. Worth, of course. He understood that it was business, but still—— The farmer searched that cold, mask-like face for a ray of hope as a man might hold out his hands for pity to a machine. He was made to feel somehow that the banker was not a man with human blood, but a mechanical something, governed and run by a mighty irresistible power with which it had nothing to do save to obey as a locomotive obeys its steam.

Jefferson Worth began explaining again in exact, precise tones that the loan, wholly for business reasons, was impossible, when Barbara entered the bank. As the girl greeted the teller in front, her voice, full and rich, with the same unconscious power that looked out of her eyes and spoke in every movement of her body, came through the bronze grating at the window and carried down the room. Jefferson Worth paused. With the farmer he faced the open door of his apartment. Every man in the place looked up. The desk-weary clerks smilingly answered her greeting and turned back to their books with renewed energy. The cashier straightened up from his papers and—leaning back in his chair—exchanged a jest with her as she passed.

"Oh, excuse me, father, I thought you were alone. How do you do, Mr. Wheeler? And how is Mrs. Wheeler and that dear little baby?"

The man's face lighted, his form straightened, his voice rang out heartily. "Fine, Miss Barbara, fine, thank you. All we need in the world now is for your father to give me time enough on that blamed note to make a crop."

66

Barbara Worth was just tall enough to look straight into her father's eyes. As she looked at him now the banker felt a little as he had felt that night in the Desert, when the baby, whose dead mother lay beside the dry water hole, shrank back from him in fear.

"Oh, I'm sure father will be glad to do that," the girl said eagerly. "Won't you fatl.er? You know how hard Mr. Wheeler works and what trouble he has had. And I want some money, too," she added; "that's what I came in for."

The farmer laughed loudly. Jefferson Worth smiled.

"But I don't want it for myself," Barbara went on quickly, smiling at them both. "I want it for that poor Mex'can family down by the wagon yard —the Garcias. Pable's leg was broken in the mines, you know, ar d there is no one to look after his mother and the children. Someone must care for them."

They were interrupted by a clerk who handed a paper to the banker. "This is ready for your signature, sir."

Jefferson Worth's face was again a cold, gray mask. Methodically he affixed his name to the document. Then to the clerk: "You may give Miss Worth whatever money she wants."

The employe smiled as he answered: "Yes, sir," and withdrew.

Barbara turned to follow. "Good-by, Mr. Wheeler. Tell Mrs. Wheeler I'm going to ride out to see her soon. I haven't forgotten that good buttermilk you see."

"Good-by, Miss Barbara, good-by! I'll tell the wife. We're always glad to see you."

The farmer could not have said that Jefferson Worth's face changed or that his voice altered a shade in tone as they turned again to the business in hand "I guess we can fix you out this time, Wheeler Sixty days, you say? You'd better make it ninety so you will not be crowded in marketing your crop.'

Quickly the black horse carrying Barbara passed through the streets to the outskirts of the city, where the adobe houses of the earlier days, with tents and shacks of every description, were scattered in careless disorder to the very edge of the barren Mesa. Beyond the wagon yard Barbara turned Pilot toward a white washed house that stood by itself on the extreme outskirts. Her approach was announced by the loud barking of a lean dog and the joyful shouts of three half-naked Mexican children; and as the horse stopped a woman appeared in the low doorway.

"Buenas dias, Senorita," she called; then, still in her native tongue: "Manuel, take the lady's horse You Juanita, drive that dog away. This is not the manner to receive a lady. Come in, come in, Senorita May God bless you for a good friend to the poor Come in."

Everything about the place, although showing un mistakable signs of poverty, was clean and orderly, while the manner of the woman, though quietly respectful and warmly grateful, showed a dignified self-respect. In one corner of the room, on a rude bed, lay a young man.

The girl returned the woman's greeting kindly in

68

Spanish and, going to the bedside, spoke, still in the soft, musical tongue of the South, to the man. "How are you to-day, Pablo? Is the leg getting better all right?"

"Si, Senorita, thank you," he replied, his dark face beaming with gladness and gratitude and his eyes looking up at her with an expression of dumb devotion. "Yes, I think it gets better right along. But it is slow and it is hard to lie here doing nothing for the mother and the children. God knows what would become of us if it were not for your goodness. La Senorita is an angel of mercy. We can never repay."

The people were of the better class of industrious poor Mexicans. The father was dead, and Pablo, the eldest son, who was the little family's sole support, had been hurt in the mine some two weeks before. Barbara visited them every few days, caring for their wants as indeed she helped many of Rubio City's worthy poor. For this work Jefferson Worth gave her without question all the money that she asked and often expressed his interest in his own cold way, even telling her of certain cases that came to his notice from time to time. So the banker's daughter was hailed as an angel of mercy and greatly loved by the same class that feared and cursed her father.

For a little while the girl talked to Pablo and his mother cheerfully and encouragingly, with understanding asking after their needs. Then, placing a gold piece in the woman's hand and promising to come again, she bade them—"Adios."

For a short distance Barbara now followed the old San Felipe trail along which, as a baby, she had been brought by her friends to Jefferson Worth's home. But where the old road crosses the railroad tracks, and leads northwest into The King's Basin, the girl turned to the right toward the end of that range of low hills that rims the Desert.

As her horse traveled up the long gradual slope in the easy swinging lope of western saddle stock, the view grew wider and wider. The sun poured its flood of white light down upon the broad Mesa, and away in the distance the ever-widening King's Basin lay, a magic, constantly changing ocean of soft colors. Nearer ahead were the hills, brown and tawny, with blue shadows in the canyons shading to rose and lilac and purple as they stretched their long lengths away toward the lofty, snow-capped sentinels of the Pass. Free from the city with its many odors, the dry air was invigorating like wine and came to her rich with the smell of the sun-burned, wind-swept plains. The girl breathed deeply. Her cheeks glowed—her eyes shone. Even her horse, seeming to catch her spirit, arched his neck and, in sheer joy of living, pretended to be frightened now and then at something that was really nothing at all.

At the foot of the first low, rounded hill Barbara faced Pilot to the northwest and bade him stand still. Motionless now the girl sat in her saddle, looking away over La Palma de la Mano de Dios. It was to this point that Barbara so often came, and as she looked now over the miles and miles of that silent, dreadful land her face grew sad and wistful

70

and in her eyes there was an expression that the Seer sometimes said made him think of the desert.

Gentle Mrs. Worth had lived just long enough to leave an indelible impression of her simple genuineness upon the life of the child, who had come to take in her heart the place left vacant by the death of her own baby girl. Since the loss of her second mother the girl had lived with no woman companion save the Indian woman Ynez, and it was the Seer rather than Jefferson Worth to whom she turned in fullest confidence and trust. The childish instinct that had led the baby to the big engineer's arms that night on the Desert had never wavered through the years when she was growing into womanhood, and the Seer, whose work after the completion of the S. and C. called him to many parts of the West, managed every few months a visit to the girl he loved as his own. To Mr. Worth who, as far as it was possible for him to be, was in all things a father to her, Barbara gave in return a daughter's love, but she had never been able to enter into the life of the banker as she entered into the life of the engineer. So it was the Seer who became, after Mrs. Worth, the dominant influence in forming the character of the motherless girl. His dreams of Reclamation, his plans and efforts to lead the world to recognize the value of that great work, with his failures and disappointments, she shared at an early age with peculiar sympathy, for she had not been kept in ignorance of the tragic part the desert had played in her own life. Particularly did The King's Basin Desert interest her. She felt that, in a way, it belonged to her; that she belonged to it. It was *her* Desert. Its desolation she shared; its waiting she understood; something of its mystery colored her life; something within her answered to its call. It was her Desert; she feared it; hated it; loved it.

Often as Barbara sat looking over that great basin her heart cried out to know the secret it held. Who was she? Who were her people? What was the name to which she had been born? What was the life from which the desert had taken her? But no answer to her cry had ever come from the awful "Hollow of God's Hand."

Before Barbara had left her home that afternoon a man, walking with long, easy stride, followed the San Felipe trail out from the city on to the Mesa. He was a tall man and of so angular and lean a figure that his body seemed made up mostly of bone somewhat loosely fastened together with sinews almost as hard as the frame-work. His face, thin and rugged, was burned to the color of saddle leather. He was dressed in corduroy trousers, belted and tucked in high-laced boots, a soft gray shirt and slouch hat, and over his square shoulders was the strap of a small canteen. His long legs carried him over the ground at an astonishing rate, so that before Barbara had left the Mexicans the pedestrian had gained the foot of the low hill at the mouth of the canyon.

With remarkable ease the man ascended the rough, steep side of the hill, where, selecting a convenient rock, he seated himself and gave his attention to the wonderful scene that, from his feet, stretched away miles and miles to the purple mountain wall on the west. So still was he and so intent in his study of the landscape, that a horned-toad, which had dodged under the edge of the rock at his approach, crept forth again, venturing quite to the edge of his boot heel; and a lizard, scaling the rock at his back, almost touched his shoulder.

When Barbara had left the San Felipe trail and was riding toward the hills, the man's eyes were attracted by the moving spot on the Mesa and he stirred to take from the pocket of his coat a field glass, while at his movement the horned-toad and the lizard scurried to cover. Adjusting his glass he easily made out the figure of the girl on horseback, who was coming in his direction. He turned again to his study of the landscape, but later, when the horse and rider had drawn nearer, lifted his glass for another look. This time he did not turn away.

Rapidly, as Barbara drew nearer and nearer, the details of her dress and equipment became more distinct until the man with the glass could even make out the fringe on her gauntlets, the contour of her face and the color of her hair. When she stopped and turned to look over the desert below he forgot the scene that had so interested him and continued to gaze at her, until, as the girl turned her face in his direction and apparently looked straight at him, he dropped the glass in embarrassed confusion, forgetting for the instant that at that distance, with his gray and yellow clothing so matching the ground and rock, he would not be noticed. With a low chuckle at his absurd situation he recovered himself and again lifting the glass turned it upon Barbara, who was now riding swiftly toward the mouth of a little canyon that opened behind the hill where he sat.

Suddenly with an exclamation the young man sprang to his feet. The running horse had stumbled and fallen. After a few struggling efforts to rise the animal lay still. The girl did not move. With long, leaping strides the man plunged down the rough, steep side of the hill.

When Barbara slowly opened her eyes she was lying in the shadow of the canyon wall some distance from the spot where her horse had stumbled. Still dazed with the shock of her fall she looked slowly around, striving to collect her scattered senses. She knew the place but could not remember how she came there. And where was her horse—Pilot? And how came that canteen on the ground by her side? At this she sat up and looked around just in time to see a tall, gaunt, roughly-dressed figure coming toward her from the direction of the canyon mouth.

Instantly the girl reached for her gun. The holster was empty.

The man, quite close now, seeing the suggestive gesture, halted; then, coming nearer, silently held out her own pearl-handled revolver.

Still confused and acting upon the impulse of the moment before, Barbara caught the weapon from the out-stretched hand and in a flash covered the silent stranger.

Very deliberately the fellow drew back a few paces and stretched both hands high above his head.

"Who are you?" asked the girl sharply.

"A white man," he answered whimsically, adding as if it were an afterthought, "and a gentleman."

"But why—— What—— How did I get here? Where did you come from?"

'I was up on the hill back there. I saw your horse fall and went to you the quickest way. You were unconscious and I carried you here out of the sun.'

"I remember now," said Barbara. "We were running and Pilot fell. He must have stepped into a hole." She put up her free hand to her forehead and found it wet. Her eyes fell on the canteen and the color came back into her face with a rush. "But you haven't told me who you are," she said sternly to the man who still stood with hands uplifted.

"I'm a surveyor going south with a party on some preliminary work. We arrived in Rubio City this morning expecting to find the Chief, who wrote me from New York to meet him here with an outfit. He has not arrived and there was nothing to do so I walked out on the Mesa to have another look at this King's Basin country."

Barbara knew that the Seer had been called to New York by some capitalists who had become interested in the financial possibilities of the reclamation work. At the stranger's explanation of his presence she regarded him with excited interest. "Do you mean —— Is it the Seer whom you expected to meet? Are you—with him?"

The young man smiled gravely. "I was sure that it was you," he answered. "You are the little girl whom we found in the desert."

75

"And you"—burst forth Barbara, eagerly—"you must be Abe Lee!"

The surveyor answered whimsically: "Don't you think I might take my hands down now? I'm unarmed you know and you could still shoot me if you thought I needed it."

In her excitement Barbara had forgotten that she still held her weapon pointed straight at him. She dropped the gun with a confused laugh. "I beg your pardon, A— Mr. Lee. I did not realize that I was holding up my"—she hesitated, then finished gravely —"my only brother."

A quick glad light flashed into the sharp blue eyes of the surveyor. "You have not forgotten me then?"

"Forgotten! When father and the Seer and Texas and Pat and you are all the—the family I have in the world." Her lips quivered, but she went on bravely: "The Seer has told me so many things about you and I have thought about you so much. But I did not realize, though, that you were a big, grown-up man. The Seer always speaks of you as a boy and so I have always called you my brother Abe as I call Texas and Pat my uncles. But I think you might have come to see me sometimes. Why didn't you come straight to me this morning instead of tramping 'way out here alone?"

Abe Lee was silent. How could he explain the place in his life that was filled by the little girl whom he had known for the two years that the building of the railroad had kept him with the Seer in Rubio City? How could she understand the poverty and grinding hardship of his boyhood struggle when the

only time he could snatch from his work he must
spend on his books, while she was growing up in the
banker's home? He was more alone in the world
than Barbara. Save for the Seer he had no one.
Texas and Pat he had met at intervals when they
came together on some construction work, and always
they had talked about her; while the engineer had
often told him of Barbara's interest in her "brother";
and sometimes the Seer even shared with him her
letters. But all this had only served to emphasize the
distance that lay between them. It was not a distance
of miles but of position—of circumstances. The
nameless little waif of the desert had become the
daughter of Jefferson Worth. The child of the
mining camp was—Abe Lee. So when, at last, his
work had brought him to Rubio City again he shrank
from meeting her and had gone out on to the Mesa
to look away over La Palma de la Mano de Dios—
to be alone.

Barbara, seeing his embarrassment at her question,
guessed a part of the reason and gently sought to
relieve the situation. "I think we had better find
my horse and start for home now," she said.

The thin, sun-tanned face of the surveyor was
filled with sympathy as he replied: "I'm sorry, but
your pony is down and out."

"Down and out! Pilot? Oh! you don't mean—
You don't ——"

Abe explained simply. "His leg was broken and
he couldn't get up. There was nothing that could
possibly be done for him. He was suffering so that
I—— It was for that I borrowed your gun."

For a long time she sat very still, and the man understanding that she wished to be alone, quietly went a little way up the canyon around the jutting edge of the rocky wall. Deliberately he seated himself on a boulder and taking from the pocket of his flannel shirt tobacco and papers, rolled a cigarette. A deep inhalation and the gray cloud rose slowly from his lips and nostrils. Stooping he carefully gathered a handful of sharp pebbles and—one by one —flipped them idly toward the opposite side of the canyon. Another generous puff of smoke and a second handful of pebbles followed the first. Then rising he dropped the cigarette and went back to her

"I think we should be going now"—he hesitated—"sister."

She looked up with a smile of understanding. "Thank you—Abe. Can we go back over the hill there, do you think? I—I don't want to see him again."

Together they climbed the low hill at the mouth of the canyon from which he had seen the accident, the girl resolutely keeping her eyes fixed ahead so as not to see the dead horse on the plain below. When the top of the hill was between them and the canyon she made him stop and together they stood looking down and far away over the wide reaches of The King's Basin.

"Isn't it grand? Isn't it awful?" she said in a low, reverent tone. "It fairly hurts. It seems to be calling—calling; waiting—waiting for some one. Sometimes I think it must be for me. I fear it—hate it—love it so." Her voice vibrated with strong passion and the surveyor, looking up, saw her wide-eyed, intense expression and felt as did the Seer that somehow she was like the desert.

"Do you come out here often?" he asked curiously.

"Yes, often," she answered. "I could not get along without my Desert and this is the finest place to see it. The Seer always comes out here with me when he can. Do you think that land will ever be reclaimed?" She faced him with the question.

"Why, no one can say about that, you know," he answered slowly. "There has never been a survey."

"Well," she declared emphatically, "I know. It will be. Listen! Don't you hear it calling? I think it's for that it has been waiting all these ages."

The surveyor smiled as one would humor a child. "Perhaps you are right," he said.

"Now you are laughing at me," she returned quickly. "They all do; father and the Seer and Texas and Pat. But you shall see! I believe, though, that the Seer thinks that I am right, only he always says as you do that there has never been a survey; and sometimes I think that even father— away down in his heart—believes it too."

All the long walk to Barbara's home they talked of the Desert and the Seer's dreams of Reclamation; and Abe told her how at last those "stupid capitalists," as Barbara called them, had opened their eyes. The great James Greenfield himself had read an article of the Seer's on "Reclamation from the Investor's Point of View" and had written him. As a result of their correspondence the engineer had gone to New York; and now a company organized by Greenfield was sending him south to look over a big territory and to report on the possibilities of its development.

When they arrived at Barbara's home they found the Seer himself. The fifteen years had made no perceptible change in the general appearance of the engineer. His form was still strongly erect and vigorous, but his hair was a little gray, and to a close observer, his face in repose revealed a touch of sadness—that indescribable look of one who is beginning to feel less sure of himself, or rather who, from many disappointments, is beginning to question whether he will live to see his most cherished plans carried to completion—not because he has less faith in his visions, but because he has less hope that he will be able to make them clear to others.

When the evening meal was over the surveyor said good-by, for the expedition was to start in the morning and he had some work to do. When he was gone Barbara joined her father and the engineer on the porch. "Here they are," she said. "Haven't I kept them nicely for you?" She was holding toward the Seer a box of cigars.

"Indeed you have," returned the engineer in a pleased tone, helping himself to a cool, moist Havana. "You are a dear, good girl."

Jefferson Worth did not use tobacco, but it was an unwritten law of the household that the Seer, when he came, should always have his evening smoke on the porch and that Barbara should be the keeper of supplies. She liked to see her friend's strong face brought suddenly out of the dusk by the flare of the match and to watch the glow of the cigar end in the dark while they talked.

"And what do you think of your brother Abe, Barbara?" the big engineer asked when his cigar was going nicely. "Didn't he talk you nearly to death?"

The girl laughed. "I guess he didn't have a chance. I always do most of the talking, you know."

The Seer chuckled. "Abe told me once that most of the time he felt like an oyster and the rest of the time he was so mad at himself for being an oyster that he couldn't find words to do the subject justice."

"I think he is splendid!" retorted Barbara, enthusiastically.

"He is," returned the engineer earnestly. "I don't know of a man in the profession whom I would rely upon so wholly in work of a certain kind. You see Abe was born and raised in the wild, uncivilized parts of the country and he has a natural ability for his work that amourts almost to genius. With a knowledge of nature gained through his remarkable powers of observation and deduction, I doubt if Abe Lee to-day has an equal as what might be called a 'surveyor scout.' I believe he is made of iron. Hunger, cold, thirst, heat, wet, seem to make no impression on him. He can out-walk, out-work, out-last and out-guess any man I ever met. He has the instinct of a wild animal for finding his way and the coldest nerve I ever saw. His honesty and loy-alty amount almost to fanaticism. But he is diffi-dent and shy as a school girl and as sensitive as a bashful boy. I verily believe he knows more to-day about the great engineering projects in the West than nine-tenths of the school men but I've seen him sit for an hour absolutely dumb, half scared to death, listening to the cheap twaddle of some smart 'yellow legs' with the ink not dry yet on their diplomas. Put him in the field in charge of a party of that same bunch, though, and he would be boss to the last stake on the line or the last bite of grub in the outfit if he had to kill half of them to do it. I guess you'll think I'm a bit enthusiastic about my right hand man," he finished, with a short, apologetic laugh, "and I am. It's because I know him."

He struck another match and Barbara saw his face for an instant. As the match went out she drew a long breath. "I'm glad you said that," she said softly. "I wanted you to. I'm sure he has earned it."

Then they talked of the Seer's new expedition that would start south at daybreak, and it seemed to Barbara that the very air was electric with the coming of a mighty age when the race would direct its strength to the turning of millions of acres of desolate, barren waste into productive farms and beautiful homes for the people.

At daybreak the girl was up to tell the Seer good-by. "I wish," she said wistfully, as she stood with him a moment at the gate, "I wish it was *my* Desert that you and Abe were going to survey."

The engineer smilingly answered: "Some day, perhaps, that, too, will come."

"I know it will," she said simply.

And as she stood before him in all the beautiful strength of her young womanhood, the Seer felt that sweet, mysterious power of her personality—felt it with a father's loving pride. "I believe you do know, Barbara," he said; "I believe you do."

CHAPTER V.

WHAT THE INDIAN TOLD THE SEER.

IN the making of Barbara's Desert the canyon carving, delta-building river did not count the centuries of its labor; the rock-hewing beach-forming waves did not number the ages of their toil; the burning, constant sun and the drying, drift-ing winds were not careful for the years. Therefore is the time of the real beginning of what happened in this, the land of my story, unknown.

Somewhere in the eternity that lies back of all the yesterdays, the great river found the salt waves of the ocean fathoms deep in what is now The King's Basin and extending a hundred and seventy miles north of the shore that takes their wash to-day. Slowly, through the centuries of that age of all beginnings, the river, cutting canyons and valleys in the north and carrying southward its load of silt, built from the east across the gulf to Lone Mountain a mighty delta dam.

South of this new land the ocean still received the river; to the north the gulf became an inland sea. The upper edge of this new-born sea beat helpless against a line of low, barren hills beyond which lay many miles of a rainless land. Eastward lay yet more miles of desolate waste. And between this sea and the parent ocean on the west, extending south-

ward past the delta dam, the mountains of the Coast
Range shut out every moisture-laden cloud and turned
back every life-bearing stream. Thus trapped and
helpless, the bright waters, with all their life, fell
under the constant, fierce, beating rays of the semi-
tropical sun and shrank from the wearing sweep of
the dry, tireless winds. Uncounted still, the centuries of that age also passed and the bottom of that
sea lay bare, dry and lifeless under the burning
sky, still beaten by the pitiless sun, still swept by the
scorching winds. The place that had held the glad
waters with their teeming life came to be an empty
basin of blinding sand, of quivering heat, of dreadful
death. Unheeding the ruin it had wrought, the river
swept on its way.

And so—hemmed in by mountain wall, barren
hills and rainless plains; forgotten by the ocean;
deserted by the river, that thirsty land lay, the lone-
liest, most desolate bit of this great Western Continent.

But the river could not work this ruin without
contributing to the desert the rich strength it had
gathered from its tributary lands. Mingled with the
sand of the ancient sea-bed was the silt from far-
away mountain and hill and plain. That basin of
Death was more than a dusty tomb of a life that had
been; it was a sepulchre that held the vast treasure
of a life that would be—would be when the ages
should have made also the master men, who would
dare say to the river: "Make restitution!"—men
who could, with power, command the rich life within
the tomb to come forth.

But master men are not the product of years—
scarcely, indeed, of centuries. The people of my
story have also their true beginnings in ages too
remote to be reckoned. The master passions, the
governing instincts, the leading desires and the driving fears that hew and carve and form and fashion
the race are as reckless of the years as are wave and
river and sun and wind. Therefore the forgotten
land held its wealth until Time should make the
giants that could take it.

In the centuries of those forgotten ages that went
into the making of The King's Basin Desert, the
families of men grew slowly into tribes, the tribes
grew slowly into nations and the nations grew slowly
into worlds. New worlds became old; and other new
worlds were discovered, explored, developed and
made old; war and famine and pestilence and prosperity hewed and formed, carved and built and fashioned, even as wave and river and sun and wind.
The kingdoms of earth, air and water yielded up
their wealth as men grew strong to take it; the
elements bowed their necks to his yoke, to fetch and
carry for him as he grew wise to order; the wilderness fled, the mountains lay bare their hearts, the
waste places paid tribute as he grew brave to
command.

Across the wide continent the tracks of its wild
life were trodden out by the broad cattle trails, the
paths of the herds were marked by the wheels of
immigrant wagons and the roads of the slow-moving
teams became swift highways of steel. In the East
the great cities that received the hordes from every

land were growing ever greater. On the far west coast the crowded multitude was building even as it was building in the East. In the Southwest savage race succeeded savage race, until at last the slow-footed padres overtook the swift-footed Indian and the rude civilization made possible by the priests in turn ran down the priest.

About the land of my story, forgotten under the dry sky, this ever-restless, ever-swelling tide of life swirled and eddied—swirled and eddied, but touched it not. On the west it swept even to the foot of the grim mountain wall. On the east one far-flung ripple reached even to the river—when Rubio City was born. But the Desert waited, silent and hot and fierce in its desolation, holding its treasures under the seal of death against the coming of the strong ones; waited until the man-making forces that wrought through those long ages should have done also their work; waited for this age—for your age and mine—for the age of the Seer and his companions—for the days of my story, the days of Barbara and her friends.

The Seer's expedition, returning from the south, made camp on the bank of the Rio Colorado twenty miles below Rubio City. It was the last night out. Supper was over and the men, with their pipes and cigarettes, settled themselves in various careless attitudes of repose after the long day. Their sun-burned faces, toughened figures and worn, desert-stained clothing testified to their weeks of toil in the open air under the dry sky of an almost rainless land. Some were old-timers—veterans of many a similar

campaign. Two were new recruits on their first trip.
All were strong, clean-cut, vigorous specimens of
intelligent, healthy manhood, for in all the profes-
sions, not excepting the army and navy, there can
be found no finer body of men than our civil engineers.

Easily they fell to talking of to-morrow night in
Rubio City, of baths and barbers and good beds and
clean clothes and dinners and the pleasures of civilization and prospective future jobs. Much good
natured chaff was passed with hearty give and take.
Jokes that had become time-worn in the many days
and nights that the party had been cut off from all
other society were revived with fresh interest. Incidents and accidents of the trip were related and
reviewed with zest, with here and there a comment
on the work itself that was still fresh in their minds.

Abe Lee, sitting with his back against a wagon
wheel and his long legs stretched straight out in
front, listened, enjoying it all in his own way, taking
his share of the chaff with a slow smile, exhaling
great clouds of cigarette smoke and only at rare
intervals contributing a word or a short sentence to
the talk. Abe was at home with these men out there
in the desert night. Under the Chief he was their
master—respected, admired and loved. But the old-
timers knew that to-morrow, in town with these same
men, dressed in conventional garb, on the street or
in the hotel, the surveyor would be as bashful and
awkward as a country boy. So they joked him
about his numerous sweethearts in Rubio City and
related many entirely fictitious love adventures and

romantic experiences that he was said to have passed through in different parts of the country during the years they had known him. Not one of them but would have been astonished beyond words had he known of Abe's adventure the afternoon before they left Rubio City, and how, through every day of the hard, grilling labor with the expedition, the image of the girl he had watched through his field glass was before him.

When the fire of the wits was turned on another mark Abe slowly arose to his feet and slipped out of the circle. Going quietly to the cook-wagon where the Chinaman sat smoking in solitary grandeur, he asked: "Wing, where is the Chief? I saw him talking to you a little while ago."

"Me no sabe, Boss Abe. Chief, him go off that way." He pointed toward the river with his long bamboo pipe. "Wing sabe Chief feel velly bad, Boss Abe; damn."

The white man regarded the Chinaman silently for a moment, then: "You're a good boy, Wing. Good night."

"Night, Boss Abe," came the plaintive answer and the surveyor went on to where a group of Cocopah Indian laborers made their rude camp. These he greeted in Spanish and asked: "Has the Chief been with you since supper?"

"No, Senor. He by river there little time past," said one, pointing to a clump of cottonwood trees that rose above a fringe of willows.

"Buenos noches, hombres," said Abe.

88

"Buenos noches, Senor," came the chorus of soft voices in the dusk.

On the high bank under the cottonwoods the Seer sat with bowed head. He did not heed the broad yellow tide of silt-laden water that swept by him so silently; he did not see the myriad stars in the velvet sky, nor notice the golden moon climbing slowly up from the dark level of the land. The jovial voices and merry laughter of his men came to him from the camp, but he did not hear. To-morrow the expedition would be over, the party disbanded. He would make his report to the capitalists who had sent him forth. His report!—the Seer groaned. Few words would be needed to sum up the work of the last two months but it would not be easy to frame them.

His ear caught the snap of a twig and a whiff of cigarette smoke floated to him. He turned his head quickly. "That you, Abe?"

The long figure of the surveyor settled on the bank by his side. For a little neither spoke, while the Seer, with slow care, filled and lighted his pipe.

"Well, lad," he said at last, "we have about reached the end of another failure."

"Will you go to New York, sir?"

"No, it will not be necessary. I can write in fifty words all there is to say."

"Perhaps they will send you out again," offered the surveyor.

"Their interest is not strong enough. They only tackled this because some other fellows were considering the proposition. That made them think there might be something in it. If I had the capital to

make surveys and could go to them with data for
some other project they might consider it, but—"

Abe rolled another cigarette and with the first
cloud of smoke came the slow words: "Well, then.
let's get the data."

Even at what seemed a hopeless suggestion the dis
couraged heart of the old engineer beat more quickly.
He turned his face toward the younger man.
"Where?"

Abe stretched forth a long arm toward the broad
Colorado at their feet and toward the desert beyond.
'The King's Basin. You've often told me about that
country. If I sabe the lay of the land we're somewhere at the southern end of it, at the beginning of
the high ground of the delta that shuts out the ocean
There's water enough here for five times that territory."

"Do you mean—" the Seer began quickly and
stopped

"I mean this: you already know the north and
northeastern part of the Basin from the railroad.
You have been through it from the west on the San
Felipe trail. Send the outfit in to-morrow with the
boys. Give them orders on the bank for their pay
and let them go. You and I can scout around the
delta end of that country over there for a week or
two and if it looks good, with what you have already
seen, you have enough to talk on. Then go on to New
York and when you report on the southern project
turn loose on 'em with this."

"Abe," said the engineer thoughtfully, "if anyone
but you were to propose that I go before these capi-

talists to interest them in a project without ever having put an instrument on it I would knock him
down. Such recklessness would ruin any civil engineer in the world, if—"

"If he guessed wrong," finished Abe dryly.

"If he guessed wrong," admitted the Seer reluctantly.

"If it looked good enough for you to risk an opinion you would have some strong talking points," ventured Abe. "There must be five hundred thousand
acres in that old sea-bed. The Colorado carries
water enough for five times that area. There's the
railroad already built along one side; there's San
Felipe and the whole Coast country within easy
reach. It beats the other proposition a hundred to
one, if it can be done at all."

The Seer rose and paced up and down in the
bright moonlight. Presently he said: "If you
accept the position with Hunt up north you
should go on at once. That job would be the best
thing you ever had. Don't you want to take it?"

"You know what I want, if you can use me."

"I could manage your present salary for this trip
but beyond that you know how uncertain it all is.
Hunt can't wait any longer."

"Look here," said Abe, angrily, "I understood
when I made my proposition that our salaries would
stop when we cut the outfit. Do you think I meant
for you to take all the risk? I'm only a surveyor
and you an educated engineer but this thing means
as much to me as it does to you. Let me share the
expense and I'm with you but not on any other terms.

Hunt and his job can go hang. I don't see why you should assume that it's only my pay that I work for."
It was a long speech for Abe.

The engineer put his big hand on the young man's shoulder. "Thank you, Abe," he said. "That does me good. I've always known that it was there. But it's a hard road, lad, a mighty hard road!" Then. "I wonder if we have an Indian in the outfit who knows this country."

"Yes, sir," Abe answered promptly. "Jose knows it well. I've been pumping him for a month. I'll get him."

As the tall figure of the surveyor disappeared in the direction of the Cocopah camp the Seer smiled to himself. "Been pumping him for a month," he repeated. "That means that he saw almost before I did that the other proposition was no good. Humph!"

He faced toward the river and looked away into the night where The King's Basin lay—a weird dream-country under the light of the moon. And because it was impossible to think of Barbara's Desert without thinking of Barbara he smiled again musing that there would be little sleep that night for the girl in Rubio City if she knew what he and Abe were considering. From across the river came the shrill, snarling, yelping coyote chorus and the engineer saw again the body of a dead woman at the dry water hole, an empty canteen, and a big-eyed, brown-haired baby stretching out her arms to him.

While the Seer was too careful an engineer to take quickly the suggestion of Abe, he had seen too many tests of the desert-bred surveyor's genius not to con sider his proposition seriously. He was also too much of a dreamer not to be influenced by thoughts of Barbara and her association in his mind with this particular project. Could it be that the land which had so tragically given the child into his life was now to realize his dreams of Reclamation.

He was interrupted by the return of Abe, who was followed by an old, grizzly-haired Cocopah.

"Tell the Chief what you have told me, Jose," said the surveyor and, stepping aside, he rolled the inevitable cigarette with an air of taking himself wholly out of the matter under consideration.

"You sabe that country over there, Jose?" asked the Chief.

"Si, Senor," came the soft answer, and reaching out, the Indian gently turned the engineer so that the latter stood with his back squarely to the river. Taking the Seer's right hand and holding it outstretched with open palm upward in one of his own and tracing with the other dark-skinned finger, as one might trace on a relief map, he continued in Spanish, as he drew his finger carefully along the white man's thumb from the wrist: "Here are the mountains that shut out the country by the Big Sea where is San Felipe. I go there once, long time ago. My people live there." He indicated the space between the first and second joints of the thumb. Next he touched the base of the Seer's little finger. "Here is Rubio City." Then tracing the outer rim of the palm toward the wrist: "Here are the hills, and the railroad that the Senor made." His finger paused in the depression between the base of the thumb and the outer edge of the palm at the wrist. "The Senor's railroad goes through the Pass in the high mountains here." Next, from the outer edge of the hand he traced across the palm at the base of the fingers. "The river goes this way to the big water that comes in from the sea here." He indicated the open space between the extended thumb and the inner edge of the palm.

"We stand now here." He touched the base of the Seer's index finger. "It is The Hollow of God's Hand, Senor—La Palma de la Mano de Dios," he repeated reverently. He dropped the engineer's hand and stood quietly waiting to be questioned.

Again the Seer put forth his hand and pointing with his own finger to the inner edge of the palm between the base of the index finger and the thumb, he asked: "The land is high here?"

"Si, Senor, a little. Just like the hand. It is much low here." He touched the deepest part of the palm. "And a little high here where we stand. Sometimes when much water comes the river goes all over here." He indicated the extreme inner edge of the palm. "Most always this water go all this way"—toward the open space between the thumb and palm. "Sometimes a little goes here." He traced the lines that cross the palm towards the wrist.

"You can show us this country?"

"Si, Senor."

"How long will it take?"

"What you like. From here to Lone Mountain straight—maybe one day go, maybe two day go."

"There is water?"

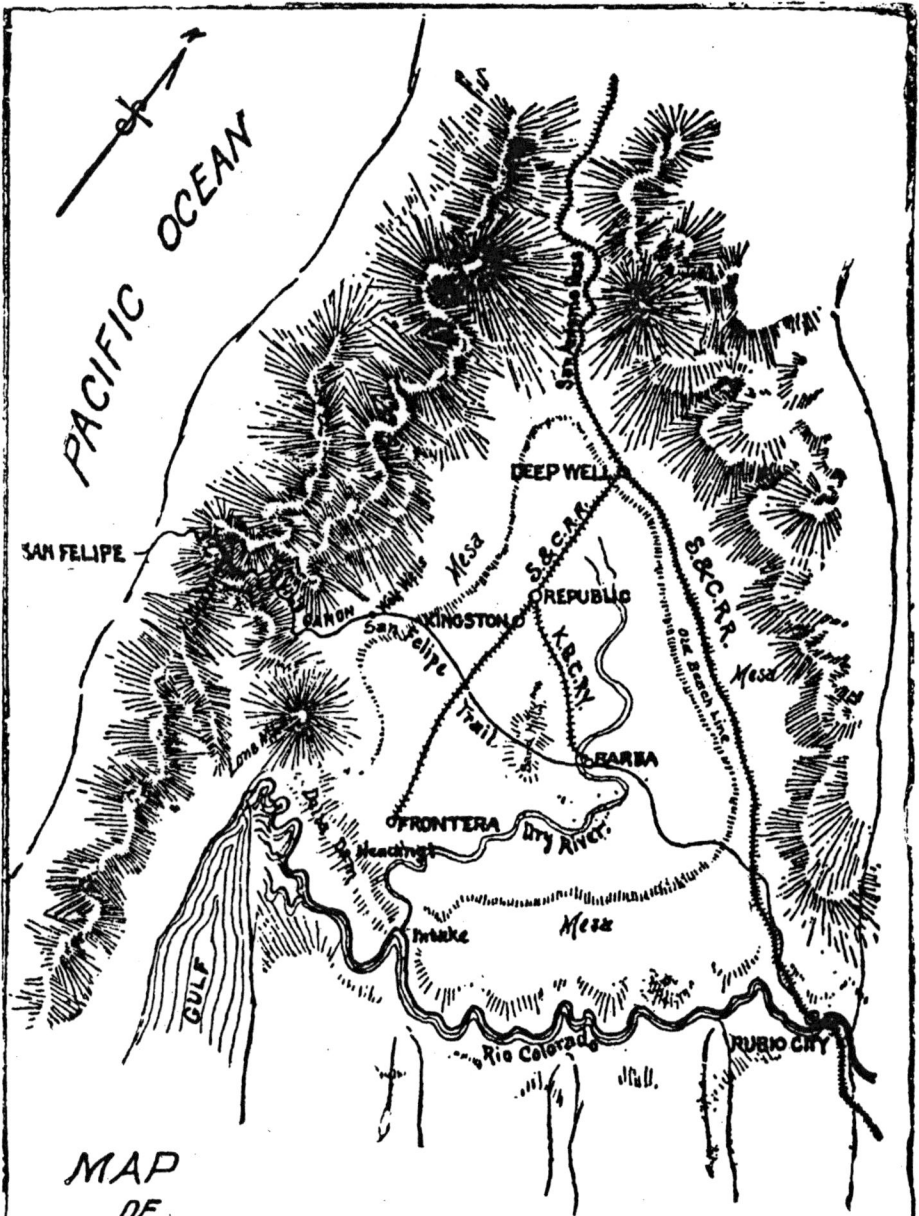

PACIFIC OCEAN

SAN FELIPE

DEEP WELL

Mesa

S.&C.R.R.

S.&C.R.R.

REPUBLIC

KINGSTON

San Felipe

KRCN

Oak Beach Line

Mesa

CANON

San Felipe Trail

Lone M.

BARBA

FRONTERA

Dry Arroyo

Heading

Intake

Mesa

GULF

Rio Colorado

Hill

RUBIO CITY

MAP
OF
LA PALMA DE LA MANO DE DIOS
(THE HOLLOW OF GOD'S HAND)

DRAWN BY
ALLEN KELLY

TECOLOTE RANCHO
1911

"Si. Much water left from the river last time big water come."

The Chief looked at the silent Abe, then back to the old Indian. "All right, Jose; we go in the morning—you, Senor Lee and I. Be ready."

"Si, Senor. Buenos noches, Senores."

"Good night! Good night!" returned the two white men.

There was much conjecturing among the surprised surveyors next morning, when the Chief gave to each man his pay check and placed an old-timer in charge with instructions as to the disposition of the outfit when they should arrive in Rubio City.

Two loaded pack-mules and three saddle ponies were ready when the Seer had finished his business with the men. Good-bys were spoken all around and the Seer and Abe, with Jose in the lead, turned back toward the south.

"Looks like they had forgotten something," said one of the recruits as the group stood watching the little party jog steadily into the distance, apparently retracing the tracks the expedition had made the day before.

"Sonny," remarked the veteran left in charge, "what one of that pair forgets the other is dead sure to remember. All the signs say that they're makin' big medicine. All we have to do with it is to push for Rubio City pronto and cash our pay checks. Lord! but wouldn't I like to be in it," he added regretfully as he turned away.

With provisions for three weeks on the pack-animals and the assurance of Jose that there was

feed and water in the overflow lands for the horses,
the Seer and Abe proposed to cover most of the territory lying between the Rio Colorado and Lone Mountain. It was here that the great river, in the ages
long past, had built the delta dam, thus cutting off
the northern end of the gulf that was now The King's
Basin Desert. It was their plan to follow this high
land that separated the ocean from the Basin to the
mountains, then to work back as far out in the Basin
from water and feed as they could. They would then
follow the river on the Basin side to Rubio City.

They had barely passed beyond sight of the main
party when Jose turned directly toward the river.
At that stage of water a long bar put out into the
stream and from its point the current set strongly
toward the opposite bank.

"Here we cross," said the Indian briefly.

Constructing a rude raft for their supplies and
swimming the animals, they reached the other shore
some distance below the point of launching with no
accident, and that night camped well back from the
river on the delta land.

Day after day they rode from sunrise until dark;
studying the land, estimating distances and grades,
observing the courses of the channels cut by the
overflow and the marks of high water, noting the
character of the soil and the vegetation; sometimes
together, sometimes separated; with Jose to select
their camping places and to help them with his
Indian knowledge of the country.

And always at night, after the long hard day, when
supper—cooked by their own hands—was over, with

pipe and cigarettes they reviewed their observations and compared notes, summing up the results before rolling in their blankets to sleep under the stars.

Some day, perhaps, when the world is much older and very much wiser, Civilization will erect a proper monument to the memory of such men as these. But just now Civilization is too greedily quarreling over its newly acquired wealth to acknowledge its debt of honor to those who made this wealth possible.

But the Seer and his companion concerned themselves with no such thoughts as these. They thought only of the possibility of converting the thousands of acres of The King's Basin Desert into productive farms. For this they conceived to be their work.

They had worked across the Basin to Lone Mountain and back to the river to a point nearly opposite the clump of cottonwoods where they had left the expedition. To-morrow night they would be in Rubio City.

"Abe," said the Seer, "our intake would go in right here. We could follow the old channel of Dry River with our canal about twenty miles out, put in a heading and lead off our mains and laterals."

For two or three hours they discussed plans and estimates, then the engineer shut his note-book with a snap. "If those New Yorkers don't listen to what I can tell them of this country now they're a whole lot slower than I take them to be."

"Then you think you will make a guess on the proposition," asked Abe slyly.

The Seer laughed like a boy. "I start for New York to-morrow night," he answered.

In the afternoon of the next day they struck the

98

San Felipe trail a few miles from Rubio City.
Perhaps it was the sight of that old road, with its
memories for the Seer and his companion, that led
the engineer to say: "It's curious, Abe, but I can't
shake off the odd feeling that Barbara's life is somehow wrapped up in that country out there." As he
spoke he turned in his saddle to look back toward the
Basin. "She seems to belong to it somehow as, in a
way, it belongs to her. There is a look in her eyes
sometimes that makes me think of the desert and the
desert always reminds me of her. I know one thing,"
he finished with a short laugh, "if I was to let out
some of the fancies that have come to me in this
connection it would ruin me forever so far as my
profession goes."

Abe made no reply, possibly because he also had fancies—fancies that he could not tell even to the Seer.

It is astonishing what a great cloud of dust five
animals can stir up on a desert trail. As the little
outfit jogged slowly along, the great yellow mass
rolled up into the air high above their heads and
hung—a long, slow-drifting streamer—above the trail
until it vanished in the distance.

Barbara, who was riding out from town on the
Mesa, saw that cloud and stopped to study it intently
for a few moments as if debating some question.
Then touching her animal with the spur, she set off
rapidly in the direction of the approaching horsemen; while the two men watched the dust that arose
from the single horse's feet with the interest that
travelers in lonely lands always feel in any life that
chances to come their way.

"Abe, that's a woman," exclaimed the Seer after a time.

Abe said nothing. He had discovered that interesting fact some moments before.

The engineer rose in his stirrups. "Abe, I'll bet a month's salary it's Barbara."

"I'm not gambling," returned the other, smiling at his companion's excitement. "I know it is."

The big engineer dropped into his saddle with a grunt of disgust. "Young man, you've got eyes like a buzzard," he said, twisting about to face his companion. "By all traditions I suppose I should say 'eagle,' but you certainly don't look much like that noble king of birds. You're carrying dirt enough to bury a horse."

The Seer took off his sombrero and began beating the dust from his shoulders, while the surveyor looked on in silent amusement.

"She'll think by the dust you're a-raisin' that there's some kind of a scrap goin' on and that she'd better head the other way."

"Not much she wouldn't head the other way from a scrap. She would come on all the faster. I thought you knew Barbara better than that." He replaced his hat. "Why Abe, one time when she was—"

The surveyor interrupted his Chief by standing up in his stirrups in turn and swinging his hat in greeting, while the Seer, in waving his own sombrero and whooping like a wild man, forgot what he was about to relate.

The girl came on at a run and—guiding her horse between the two dust-covered men—held out a hand to each.

CHAPTER VI.

HREE days after the Seer's letters to Abe and Barbara telling them that James Greenfield and his associates would finance an expedition to make the preliminary surveys in The King's Basin Desert, the west-bound overland dropped a passenger in Rubio City from New York.

The stranger was really a fine looking young man with the appearance of being exceptionally well-bred and well-kept. Indeed the most casual of observers would not have hesitated to pronounce him a thoroughbred and a good individual of the best type that the race has produced.

A company of men and women—traveling acquaintances evidently—followed him from the Pullman to bid him good-by and to look at the Indians, who with their wealth of curios spread before them, squatted in a long row beside the track—objects of never failing interest to travelers from the East.

"Ugh!" said a tall blonde, who displayed more bracelets, bangles, chains and charms—both natural and manufactured—than any blanketed squaw in the party of natives, "I suppose if we ever see you again you'll be the color of that thing there." She pointed to a smoky, copper-colored Papago in a green headcloth and decorated shirt, who posed in a watchful attitude near his thrifty help-meet.

101

"How perfectly romantic!" gushed a billowy divorcee, clinging to the young fellow's athletic arm with little shivers of delight. "To think of you in this great, savage, wild land, among these strange people. Aren't you just a little bit frightened?"

"By George, I half wish I was going to stop with you. You'll get some great shooting, don't you know!" exclaimed one of the men, while the chorus joined in: "You'll die of loneliness!" "You'll find nothing fit to eat!" "And do take care of yourself!"

Then as the warning, "All aboard!" and the clang of the engine bell came down the platform, there were quick good-bys and a rush for the car. The colored porters tossed their steps aboard and followed. Smoothly the long, dust-covered coaches slid past. There was a waving of handkerchiefs and caps from the rear of the observation car, and the young man turned to look curiously about.

"Hotel?"

The stranger glanced doubtfully at the tough-looking citizen who reached for his suit case, and without replying stepped into the questionable looking hack standing nearby. The driver threw the suit-case into the vehicle after his passenger and climbing to his seat, yelled to the team.

There was no rush of brass-buttoned bell-boys to meet the guest at the door of the hotel, and the room was well-filled with a group strange to the eyes of the young man from New York. Bronzed-faced men in flannel shirts and belted trousers talked to men well-dressed in more conventional business clothes; others in their shirt sleeves sat smoking with companions in blue overalls; two or three wore guns loosely belted at their hips. Here and there was the pale-faced, white-collared, tied and tailored tourist. In the corner near the big window a group of women, some in white duck, some in khaki or corduroy, sat chatting and enjoying the scene. No one paid the least attention to the newcomer. The tough-looking driver of the hack dropped the suit case near the desk with a bang and turned to reply to a good natured remark addressed to him by a jovial, well dressed man standing near. Only the clerk regarded the stranger.

"Have you a room with bath?"

The clerk smiled. "Certainly, sir." Then to a young fellow talking over the cigar counter to a man in high-heeled boots and spurs: "Jack, show this gentleman to forty-five."

In the well-furnished room the guide threw open long French windows and pointed to a cot on the screened-porch outside. "Better sleep on the porch," he volunteered.

"Sleep on the porch?"

"Suit yourself," came the answer as the independent one turned away.

"Look here!" The employe of the house paused. "I want my trunk sent up immediately."

"Sure Mike! Let's have your checks. So-long!"

The stranger stood staring at the door, which the breezy young man, as he disappeared with a cheery whistle, had shut behind him with a vigorous bang.

In the dining room the man from New York found the same easy freedom in the manner of dress, the

same lack of conventionalities and the same atmos
phere of general good-fellowship; yet he could not
say that there was any lack of real courtesy and
certainly there was no rude and boisterous talk. It
was, to say the least, unsettling to the exceptionally
well-bred and well-kept stranger, accustomed to the
hotels and restaurants in the East frequented by his
class.

Early that evening the Easterner sallied forth,
clearly bent on sight-seeing. He had dressed for the
occasion. The gray traveling suit had been put aside
for a tailor-made outfit of corduroy. The coat—worn
without a vest over a fine negligee shirt of silk—
was Norfolk; the trousers were riding trousers and
above the tan shoes were pig-skin puttees. All this,
with the light, soft hat, neat tie and the undeniably
fine figure and handsome face, would have made him
attractive on any stage. The tourists turned to look
after him with expressions of admiring envy; the
natives—white, red, black, yellow and brown—
accepted him with no more than a passing glance as
a part of the strange new life that the railroad was
constantly bringing to Rubio City.

Calmly conscious of himself and openly interested,
in a mildly condescending way, the young man
strolled down one side of the main street to the end
of the business section, then back on the other. Twice
he made the round, then, seeking scenes of further
interest, pushed open the swinging doors of Rubio
City's most popular place of amusement—the Gold
Bar saloon.

At a table in one corner two men—one tall, dark-faced, coatless, with unbuttoned vest, leather wrist-guards, and a heavy gun loosely buckled about his slim waist; the other thick-set, heavy, red-faced— were holding animated conversation over their glasses. That is to say: the thick, red-faced man was animated. Glaring at his companion he banged his huge, hairy fist on the table until the glasses jumped.

"Ye're a domned owld savage wid yer talk. Fwhat the hell is yer counthry good for as ut is? A thousan' square miles av ut wouldn't feed a jack-rabbit. 'Tis a blistherin', sizzlin', roastin', wilderness av sand an' cactus, fit for nothin' but thim side-winders, horn'-toads, heely-monsters an' all their poisonous relations, includin' yersilf."

The New Yorker, standing at the end of the bar nearest the table occupied by Barbara's "uncles," who had just arrived from the Gold Center mines, heard the words of Pat and turned toward the two friends with amused interest.

Texas Joe silently lifted his glass and with a look of undisguised admiration for his belligerent part-ner, waited for more. More came with another thump of the huge fist.

" 'Tis civilization that ye need, an' 'tis civilization that we're bringin' to ye, an' 'tis civilization that ye've got to take whether ye like ut or not. Look at the Seer, now! Wan gintleman wid brains an' educa-tion like him is wort' more to this counthry than all the hell-roarin' savages like yersilf between the Coast an' Oklahoma, which is not so much better than it was. We've brung ye money; we've brung ye schools; we've brung ye railroads; an' we'll kape on bringin' ye the blissin's an' joys av civilization 'til ye mend yer ways an' live like Christians."

He paused. Texas was staring with child-like simplicity at the immaculate figure of the stranger in puttees. Pat turned to follow the gaze of his companion just as the plainsman drawled softly "And you've brought us that."

The Irishman's heavy jaw dropped. He gasped and gulped like an uncouth monster. Then—speechless—he drained his glass.

The stranger's face flushed but he did not move.

"Pardner," drawled Texas, "your remarks is sure edifyin' a heap an' some convincin'. But I'm still constrained to testify that the real cause an' reason for the declinin' glory of this yere great western country is poor shootin'. That same, in turn, bein' caused by the incomin' herds from the effete East bein' so numerous as to hinder gun practice."

"Guns is ut?" interrupted the other with a roar. "A man—mind ye: a man—should be ashamed to go about all the time wid a cannon tied to his middle. 'Tis the mark av a child. Look at ye, now, wid all yer artillery an' me wid fingers that niver pushed a thrigger." He held out his great paws and studied them admiringly. "Why, ye herrin', wid thim two hands I could break ye, gun an' all, like I've ——"

He was interrupted by a wild-eyed individual who rushed into the room from the street and, springing toward them, burst forth with: "Give me your gun, Texas, quick! I ain't got mine on and that damned Red Hoyt is a layin' for me at the corner!"

Texas Joe dropped his slim hand caressingly on the big forty-five at his side, leaned easily back in his chair and eyed the excited citizen in a manner calmly judicial. "Bill, you're comin' is some opportune. You're sure Johnny-on-the-spot."

"Le' me have yer gun, Tex. Jes' loan her to me! I'll be back in a minute."

"Oh, I ain't doubtin' that you'd be back all right, Bill. That's jest the p'int. When you blew in so promisc'us an' interrupted the meetin', me an' my friend here was jest resolvin' that there's too much bad shootin' bein' done in this here Rubio town. It's a spoilin' the fair name an' a ruinin' the reputation of this country. For which said reason us two undertakes to regulate an' reform some." He turned with elaborate politeness to Pat. "I voices yer sentiments correct, pard?"

The Irishman's fist struck the table and his eyes flashed. "To the thrim av a gnat's heel," he roared.

Texas bowed and continued: "Therefore, Bill, this here's our verdict. You camp right here peaceable while I go out an' fetch this Red Hoyt person what's been annoyin' you. We'll stand you up at fifteen steps, with nothing between to obstruct ceremonies, an' drop the hat. Me an' my friend referees the job an' undertakes to see that the remains is duly and properly planted with all regular honors. Sabe?"

The blood-thirsty one, growling something about attending to his own funeral and finding a gun somewhere else, went quietly and quickly out.

Before the pugnacious Pat could voice his disgust and disappointment at the disappearance of the trouble-hunting citizen, a low, contemptuous laugh from the well-built stranger at the bar drew the attention of the two friends. The young man was watching them with an amused smile.

Texas Joe and the Irishman regarded each other thoughtfully. "Pard," said Tex in a low, earnest tone, "do you reckon that there hilarity was in any ways directed toward this corner of the room?"

The stranger, receiving his change from the bartender, was moving leisurely toward the door when his way was barred by the heavy bulk of Pat. There was no misunderstanding the expression on the battle scarred features of the Irish gladiator. Eyeing the athletic Easterner fiercely, he growled with deliberate meaning: "Ye same to be findin' plenty av amusement in the private affairs av me friend an' mesilf. D'ye think that we are a coople av hoochy-koochy girls to be makin' sphort for all the domned dudes that runs to look at us whin their mammas don't know they're out?"

The other regarded him with well-bred surprise "Stand aside," he said curtly.

"Oh, ho! ye will lave widout properly apologizin' for yer outrageous conduc' will ye? 'Tis an ambulance that ye'll nade to take ye home whin I've taught ye manners, ye danged yellow-legged cock-a-doodle!"

He lifted his fists and the stranger, without giving back an inch or exhibiting the slightest suggestion of fear, but rather with the calm self-confidence of a trained athlete, squared himself for the encounter.

Eagerly the patrons of the place—miners. cowboys,

ranchers, adventurers, Mexicans, Indians—had gathered around the two men, delighted with the prospect of what promised to be no tame exhibition. Already several bets had been placed and critical estimates and comments on the comparative merits of the two were being made freely when a hand fell on Pat's uplifted arm. Turning with an oath of rage at the interruption, the Irishman faced Abe Lee.

"Hello, Pat! Amusing yourself as usual?" To the angry protests from the crowd the tall surveyor gave not the slightest heed.

For a moment the Irishman, looking up into that thin, sun-tanned face, was speechless as though he faced some apparition. Then with a yell of delight he caught the lank form of the Seer's assistant in a bear-like hug. "For the love av Gawd is ut ye, ye owld sand-rat? Where the hell did ye drop from, an' fwhat are ye doin' in this dishreputable company! Look at Uncle Tex, there! The sentimental owld savage is fair slobberin' wid delight an' eagerness to git at ye. Come, come; we must have a dhrink."

As quickly as it had risen the storm had passed. The crowd, as if moved by a single impulse, separated and the room was filled with loud talk and laughter. Glancing around, Pat's eye met the still defiant look of the stranger who had not moved from his place but stood calmly watching the Irishman and Abe as if waiting the pleasure of the man who had challenged him.

The Irishman grinned in appreciation. "Howld on a minut," he said to Abe who was moving away with Texas Joe toward a vacant table. Then to the

109

stranger: "I axe yer pardon, Sorr, for goin' off me head that way. 'Tis a habit I have, worse luck to me—bein' sensitive, do ye see, about me personal appearance an' some wishful for a bit av honest enjoyment. Av ye'll have a dhrink wid me an' my friends here I'll take ut kindly until we can find some betther cause for grievance."

The young man's tense figure relaxed. A smile broke over his face. "And I beg your pardon," he said heartily. "The fact is I was not laughing at you at all but at the way you two men called the bluff of that fellow who wanted the gun. I should have said so and apologized but I, too, was a little upset and thrown off my guard."

"Faith, ut looked to me that ye were thrown on your guard. 'Tis the science ye have or I'm a Dutchman." He eyed the athletic limbs, deep chest, broad shoulders and well-set head, with eyes that twinkled his approval. "Some day— But niver mind now! Come." He led the way to the table.

As they seated themselves Pat regarded the surveyor with pleased interest. "Well, well! 'tis a most unexpected worrld. Av 'twas the owld divil himsilf that clapped his hand on me arm I'd be no more surprised than I was to see the lad here. Tell us, me bhoy, fwhat 'tis that's brung ye here."

"Haven't you two been to see Barbara yet?" the surveyor demanded as though charging them with some neglected duty.

"We have not; an' by that ye will know that we've been in this town less than an hour by Tex's watch that Barbara give him an' that he lost down the shaft at Gold Center."

When the surveyor had explained his presence in Rubio City and Texas and Pat had agreed to join the King's Basin party, the stranger said: "I think it is quite time now that I introduce myself. You are Mr. Lee, I believe."

Abe assented and with his two companions regarded him with interest.

Taking a letter from his pocket and handing it to the surveyor, the young man continued: "I am a civil engineer. I have instructions from the Chief to report to you. My name is Willard Holmes."

The next morning the young engineer from the East presented his card at the Pioneer Bank and asked for Mr. Worth. The man who received the correctly engraved bit of pasteboard merely nodded toward the other end of the long partition of polished wood, plate glass and bronze bars. "You'll find him back there, Mr. Holmes."

The New Yorker smiled at the provincialism but sought the banker without further ceremony.

Closing the door with one hand Jefferson Worth with the other indicated the chair at the end of his desk. "Sit down."

"You have a letter from Mr. Greenfield relative to my coming?" asked Willard Holmes.

The banker lifted a typewritten sheet from his desk, glanced at it and turned back to his visitor. "Yes," he said.

The involuntary movement was the instinctive act

of one who habitually verifies every statement.
Then, as those expressionless blue eyes were fixed
on the stranger's face, the engineer's sensation was
as though from behind that gray mask something
reached out to grasp his innermost thoughts and
emotions. He felt strangely transparent and ex-
posed as one, alone in his lighted chamber at night,
might feel someone in the dark without, watching
through the window. Presently the colorless, exact
voice of Jefferson Worth asked: "This is your first
visit West?"

"Yes sir. My work has been altogether in New
York and the New England states."

"Five years with the New York Contracting and
Construction Company?" said Jefferson Worth
exactly, laying his hand again on the letter on his
desk.

"Yes. For the past two years I have had charge of
their more important operations." The engineer's
tone was a shade impressive.

But there was not the faintest shadow of a hint in
the face or manner of that man in the revolving
chair to intimate that he was impressed. The visitor
might as well have spoken to the steel door of the big
safe in the other room. "You are well acquainted
with Mr. Greenfield and his associates?"

"My father and Mr. Greenfield were boyhood
friends and college classmates," the engineer explained. "Since the death of my father when I was
a little chap, I have lived with Uncle Jim. He was
my guardian until I became of age."

The young man did not think it necessary to add

112

that the death of his father had left him penniless and that his father's friend, who had never married, had reared and educated the child of his old classmate as his own son. Neither did he explain that his rapid advancement in his profession was due largely to the powerful influence of the capitalist and those closely associated with him, together with the strength of the proud social position to which he was born, rather than to hard work and experience Probably Willard Holmes himself did not realize how much these things had added to his own native ability and technical training. He had never known anything else but these things and he accepted them as unconsciously as his voice was colored with the, accent of the cultured East.

"How do you size up this King's Basin proposition?" questioned the banker.

Again Willard Holmes smiled at the western man's words. "Sizing up" and "proposition" were pleasingly novel forms of expression to him. "Really," he answered, "I haven't gone into it very thoroughly as yet. Mr. Greenfield asked me to come out because he and his associates felt"—he paused; perhaps it would be just as well not to say what Mr. Greenfield and his associates felt—"that with my experience in connection with large corporations I could be of value to them in certain phases of the work," he finished. He wondered if the man, who listened with such an air of carefully considering e ery word and mentally reaching out for whatever lay back of the verbal expression, had grasped what he had been about to say.

Jefferson Worth waited and Holmes continued:
"Mr. Greenfield and his friends are very anxious
that you should come in with them on the organization of this company, Mr. Worth; that is, of course,
providing the scheme proves to be practicable. They
instructed me to urge you personally to consider their
proposal favorably and to ask you, by all means, to
represent them on this expedition if possible. They
realize that a man of your recognized ability and
standing in the financial world, particularly in the
West, in close touch as you are with Capital and
conditions in this part of the country and no doubt
familiar with the Reclamation work, would be a
valuable addition to their strength. In fact I may
say they would depend largely upon your judgment
as to whether the scheme was practicable from a
business standpoint. On your side I am sure you
recognize the advantage of allying yourself with such
a group of capitalists, who are strong enough to
finance any undertaking, no matter how great. Their
interests are already enormous. As you know, they
operate only on the largest scale and, if this survey
justifies the report already made, they will make a
big thing out of this for everyone interested."

The cold, exact voice of Jefferson Worth came as
if from a machine incapable of inflection. "I have
written Mr. Greenfield that I would look into the
proposition for him. I will go out with the outfit.
Have you seen Abe Lee?"

"I met him last night and we had a little talk
over things. I confess I was a little surprised."

"Why?"

114

"Well—that he is in charge. I was instructed to report to him. I find that he has had no schooling whatever; that, in fact, he is nothing but a kind of a self-educated surveyor. I have no doubt that he is a good, practical fellow, but it seems to me somewhat reckless to put him in such a responsible position."

Jefferson Worth did not say that he himself had had no more schooling than the Seer's lieutenant. Perhaps that, also, was not necessary to explain. He did say: "We have only one standard in the West, Mr. Holmes."

"And that?"

"What can you do?" came the words as if spoken by cold iron.

CHAPTER VII.

DON'T YOU LIKE MY DESERT, MR. HOLMES?

AFTER his noon-day meal, Willard Holmes, following the example of others, sought the shade of the arcade in front of the hotel. Helping himself to a chair and moving a little away from the general company, he sat enjoying his cigar, musing on the novelty of his surroundings and reviewing his impressions of the last few hours.

It was natural that he should make comparisons—that he should see men and things in the light of the only men and things he had ever known. Abe Lee he measured by the standing of his own school-trained engineering friends, demanding that the desert-born and desert-trained surveyor exhibit all the hall-marks of Boston. He might as consistently have demanded that the flood of sunlight that fell in such blinding glory upon the new world before him should shine as through the smoke-grimed city atmosphere of New York. One was no more impossible than the other. Jefferson Worth he compared with the college and university friends of his father—with Mr. Greenfield and the New York-bred business men of his class, demanding that the western pioneer banker show the same characteristics that distinguished the cultured capitalists whose great-great-grandfathers were pioneers. Rubio City he saw in the light of those eastern cities that were founded in the days when men knew not that there was any world west of the Alleghanies.

Turning his head now and then to look over the typical groups that sat in the shade of the arcade, dressed—or undressed—with all the easy freedom of a land too young as yet to have conventions, he recalled his favorite hotels in his home cities and smiled to think what would happen if some of these roughly clad individuals were to appear there among the guests. He did not know yet that some of these roughly clad individuals were as much at home in those same favorite hotels as was he himself. Likewise as he watched the passing citizens in the street he recalled the scene from the windows of his club at home—a famous club on a famous avenue.

That young woman, for instance, with her khaki divided skirt, wide sombrero, fringed gauntlets and the big western saddle coming there on a horse whose feet seemed scarcely to touch the ground as he plunged and pranced impatiently along, springing side-wise, with arched neck and pointed ears, at every object that could possibly be made into something frightful by his playful fancy! What a sensation she would create at home! By Jove! but she could ride, though. He watched with admiring eyes the strong, graceful figure that sat the high-strung, uncertain horse as easily and unconsciously as any one of his women friends at home would rest in a comfortable chair.

As the horsewoman drew nearer he fell to wondering what she was like. Could she talk, for instance, of

117

anything but the homely details of her own rough
life? He shrugged his shoulders as he fancied her
rude attempts at conversation, her uncouth language and raw expressions. The girl turned her
horse toward the hotel entrance. As she drew still
nearer he saw that she was not pretty. Her mouth
was too large, her face too strong, her skin too tanned
by the sun and wind.

At the sidewalk the girl swung from the saddle
lightly, and throwing the bridle reins over the horse's
head with a movement that brought out the beautiful
lines of her figure, she turned her back upon the
pawing, restless animal with as little concern as
though she had delivered him to a correctly uni-
formed groom. No she was not pretty; she was—
magnificent. The adjective forced itself upon him.

All along the arcade people were smiling in greeting, the men lifting their hats. Two cowboys in
high-heeled boots and "chaps" paused in passing.
"That new hawss of yours is sure some hawss, Miss
Barbara," said one admiringly, sombrero in hand.

The girl smiled and Holmes saw the flash of her
perfect teeth. "Oh, he'll do, Bob, when I've worked
him down a little."

She passed into the hotel, followed by the eyes
of every man in sight including the engineer, who
had noted with surprise the purity and richness of
her voice.

The New York man had turned and was watching
a company of Indians farther down the street when
that voice close beside him said: "I beg your pardon. Is this Mr. Holmes?"

He turned quickly, rising to his feet.

She smiled at his astonished look. "The clerk pointed you out to me. I am Barbara Worth. You met father at the bank this morning. Texas Joe and Pat told me about your being here and I could scarcely wait to see you. I'm afraid you must have thought them a little rough last night but really it's only their fun. They're as good as gold."

As she stood now close to him—the red blood glowing under the soft brown of her cheeks—Willard Holmes felt her rich personality as distinctly as one senses the presence of the ocean, the atmosphere of the woods or the air of meadows and fields. But by all his conventional gods, this was the unconventional limit! that this girl, the daughter of a banker, should openly seek out a total stranger to introduce herself to him on the public street before a crowd of hotel loungers! And the way she spoke of those rough men in the saloon, one would think they were her intimate friends.

He managed to say: "Really, I am delighted, Miss Worth. May I escort you to the hotel parlor?"

She looked at him curiously. "Oh, no indeed! It is much nicer out here in the arcade, don't you think? But you may bring another chair."

Dumbly he obeyed, feeling that every eye was on him and flushing with embarrassment for her.

"When Texas and Pat told me that you were one of the engineers going out with The King's Basin party I could scarcely wait to see you. It makes it all seem so real, you know—your coming all the way out here from New York. I have dreamed so much about the reclamation of The King's Basin Desert, and you see I consider all civil engineers my personal friends."

"Indeed," he said. It is always safely correct to say "indeed" as he said it, particularly when you have nothing else to say.

She regarded him doubtfully with an open, straight-forward look which was somewhat disconcerting. She was so unconscious of the strength of her splendid womanhood and he felt her presence so vividly.

"I suppose you must find everything out here very strange," she said slowly. "Father says this is your first visit to the West and of course it *can't* be like your part of the country."

"It is all very interesting," he murmured. This also was sane and safe.

"I know that Abe is very busy and father never leaves the bank except on business, so there is no one but me to look after you"—she smiled—"that is— no one of our King's Basin people."

Willard Holmes was of that type of corporation servant who recognizes no interests but the financial interests of the capital employing him. His services as a civil engineer belonged wholly to those who bought them for their own profit. Barbara's innocent words aroused him. What the deuce did she mean by "our King's Basin people"? Greenfield and his friends thought that *they* were The King's Basin people. In the interests of his employers he must look into this.

120

"It is very kind of you, I am sure," he said with a little more warmth. "To tell the truth I *was* feeling a bit strange, you know."

"I'm sure you must be nearly dead with lonesomeness. Wouldn't you like to go for a ride? I would so like to show you my Desert."

"*Her* Desert!" he mentally observed. Indeed he must look into this. Fully alert now he answered heartily: "I should be delighted, I'm sure. You are more than kind. When could we go?"

"Right now," she said quickly. "Here comes Pablo Garcia. I'll send him for another horse." She called to the passing Mexican: "Here Pablo."

The young fellow came to her quickly and stood, sombrero in hand, his dark eyes shining with pride at the recognition. In Spanish she directed him to fetch a horse for the Senor.

"Si, Senorita." With a low bow the Mexican turned to obey.

The eastern man, not understanding the words, but awakening suddenly to the meaning of the action, broke forth with—"Here, wait a minute."

"Wait," repeated Barbara in Spanish. Pablo paused.

"You are sending him for a horse and saddle?" asked Holmes.

"Yes; it will take only a few minutes."

"But I don't ride, you know."

"You don't ride?" The girl looked at him in blank amazement. "I don't think I ever saw a man before who didn't ride."

He laughed indulgently. Something in her voice and manner touched his sense of humor. "I'm very sorry. I know I ought to," he said in mock humility.

"Oh, well; we can drive. I'll have Pablo bring a rig." She explained what she wanted to the Mexican in his native tongue, and this time he mounted her horse and rode away.

When the man returned a little later with a span of restless, half-wild broncos hitched to a light buggy, the girl stepped into the vehicle and took the reins is a matter of course. With a low chuckle of amusement the engineer took his place at her left. He was beginning really to enjoy the situation. Shying anc plunging the team demanded all of Barbara's attention but she managed to steal a look at her silent companion now and then, as if expecting him to show signs of nervousness. Willard Holmes, on his part, was wrapped in silent admiration of her strength and skill.

"They'll cool down in a little while," the girl volunteered, as if to reassure her guest, after a particularly wild break on the part of the horses. But on the extreme edge of town, where the wagon road runs closest to the railroad track, a passing switch engine proved too much for the excited team. In a moment the frightened animals were running toward the Mesa at full speed. With all her strength Barbara struggled to regain control, but her arms were a woman's arms and the horses, quick to recognize their advantage, put back their ears and ran the faster in mad defiance.

The girl was not frightened; she was annoyed.

"But I don't ride, you know"

"I—I'm afraid they are running away," she gasped at last.

To her surprise a hearty laugh was the only answer to her confession. She shot a quick glance over her left shoulder. Her companion was leaning back in his seat, his merry face expressing the keenest enjoyment.

Then the girl felt a big hard shoulder pressing against her; long powerful arms stretched over hers; and two masterful hands closed on the reins above her cramped fingers. She relinquished her hold and shrank back out of the way with a sigh of relief and —yes, a look of admiration as the horses, with a few wild leaps and ineffectual attempts to run again, settled down to a more rational gait.

"My!" she gasped, at the exhibition of the engineer's strength, "I believe you could pull their front feet off the ground."

Her companion was still smiling.

"Why didn't you tell me you could drive?" she demanded.

He chuckled maliciously, for he had understood her reason for taking the reins at the start and he had not been insensible of the meaning of her glances at the beginning of the ride. "You didn't ask me, and besides I enjoyed seeing you handle them."

"But you told me you couldn't *ride*," she said reproachfully.

"I can't," he returned. "That is I never did; not as you people in this country ride." Then he laughed again. "Confess now. Didn't you expect me to jump, back there?"

"I shall confess nothing," she retorted, sharply. "And hereafter I shall take nothing for granted."

On the high ground near the foot of the hill at the canyon's mouth she asked him to turn around and stop. Willard Holmes had been too much occupied with the team and the girl to notice the landscape; and now that wonderful view of the Mesa, The King's Basin and the mountains burst upon him without warning. No sane man could be insensible of the grandeur of that scene. The man, whose eyes had looked only upon eastern landscapes that bore in every square foot of their limited range the evidence of man's presence, was silent—awe-stricken before the mighty expanse of desert that lay as it was fashioned by the creative forces that formed the world. Turning at last from the glorious, ever-changing scenes, wrought in colors of gold and rose and lilac and purple and blue, to the girl whose eyes were fixed questioningly upon him, he said in a low voice: "Is it always like this?"

Barbara nodded. "Always like that, but always changing. It is never the same, but always the same. Like—like life itself. Do you understand?"

He turned again to the scene in silent wonder.

"Do you like my Desert?" she asked, after a little time had passed.

His mind caught at the expression. "Do you mean to say that that is The King's Basin—that we are going *there* to work?"

"Why, of course." She laughed uneasily. "Don't you like it?"

124

"Like it?" he repeated. "But is there anyone living out there?"

She was amazed at his words. "Living there? Of course not. But you are going to make it so that thousands and thousands can live there—you and the others. Don't you understand?" Her voice expressed a shade of impatience.

"I'm afraid I did not realize," he answered slowly.

"That's just it!" she cried, thoroughly aroused now and speaking passionately. "That's just the trouble with you eastern men; you don't realize. For years the dear old Seer and a few others have been trying to make you see what a work there is to do out here, and you won't even look up from your little old truck patches to give them intelligent attention. You think this King's Basin is big? Why, the Seer says that if every foot of that land was under cultivation it wouldn't be a posy bed beside what there is to do in the West. I suppose you must have done some great things in your profession, Mr. Holmes, or those capitalists wouldn't have sent you out here; but you can't have done anything that will mean to the world what the reclamation of The King's Basin Desert will mean one hundred years from now, because this work is going to *make* the people realize, don't you see?"

The young engineer's face flushed under her words, and as he watched her strong face glowing with enthusiasm for the Seer's dream, he felt the sweet power of her personality sweep over him as he felt the breeze from off the desert. He was held as

125

though by some magic spell—not by the lure of her splendid womanhood, but by that and something else —something that was like the country of which she spoke so passionately. And he remembered wonder ing if this girl could talk!

He relieved the tense strain of the situation by holding out the reins and saying, with a whimsica' smile:

"Here, you can drive."

She caught his meaning and smiled in acknowl edgment. "Thank you, but I don't want to drive That's really the man's part, you know. I suppose,' she added, "that you think me bold and mannish and coarse and everything else that a girl ought not to be, but I"—she turned away her face and her voice trembled—"but you can't understand, Mr. Holmes, what this desert means to me."

"Perhaps I don't understand," he said seriously. "But I am sure of this: somewhere back of every really great work that has ever been accomplished in any age there has been a woman like you."

Then they drove back to the hotel where she left him and drove to the barn herself. A few minutes later he saw her pass again, riding her own quick- stepping horse.

During the two weeks that followed before the Seer's return, while Abe Lee was busy getting ready for the work in Barbara's Desert, Willard Holmes and the girl were often together. The man from New York admitted somewhat proudly, Barbara thought—as if the very confession somehow estab- lished the superiority of the East—that he was shockingly ignorant of all things Western. But apparently overlooking the subtle assumption in the manner of his confession, she laughingly undertook his education. For one thing he must learn to ride.

"Really," he demurred, "I don't think I care for that particular amusement. I have never taken it up at home, you know, but of course if it is the thing to do, why—"

"Amusement!" she laughed. "Riding isn't an amusement; it's a necessity. The horse is our street car and railroad and steamboat. Where you think city blocks and squares we think miles; and where you think miles we think hundreds of miles. Two legs are not enough in this country, so we double the number and go on four. You'll find yourself wishing for eight before you get back from The King's Basin."

So, at her bidding, Texas Joe secured a horse for him and almost every afternoon the two were in their saddles. And every night over his evening cigar at the hotel the engineer found himself reviewing the incidents and conversations of the ride; forced to wonder at some new and unexpected revelation of the mind and character of this western girl who was so interested in the reclamation work and so unconscious of her womanly power. He came quickly to look forward to their hours together and to plan and carry out many conversational experiments. Invariably he had his reward.

One afternoon he tried skillfully to shape the conversation to the end that he might tell her—quite without ostentation—of the proud history and social position of his family and of his own rank in the upper eastern world.

She humored him patiently, helping him out with questions and artless, admiring exclamations and comments, until he was quite sure that she was properly impressed. Then she said, in a tone of honest sympathy: "But you musn't let all this worry you, you know."

"Worry me?" he echoed in amazement.

She nodded seriously, but with a glint of mischief in her eyes. "Yes, I can understand that it must be hard for a man to do his work handicapped as you are but no one away out here will count it against you. Every man here has a chance no matter what his past has been. You see, we don't care what a man has been or what his fathers were; we accept him for what he is and value him for what he can do. So all you need to do is to forget and go straight ahead with your work and you'll easily live it down. Only, of course," she added gently, "I wouldn't advise you to tell *everybody* what you have told me. Some might not understand."

He retorted warmly: "Of course you cannot understand our point of view. Everything is so new and raw out here that you have no social standards."

"New and raw?" She laughed again. "Why, Mr. Holmes, you are the only new thing in this country. Do you see that man over there?"

They were riding south on the road that follows the river and she pointed to an Indian who sat idly in the shade of his pole and mud hut.

"What's the matter with him?" asked the engineer.

"Nothing. Only he, too, has ancestors. Ages and ages before your forefathers knew that this continent existed, that man's people lived in a city not far from here—a city with laws, customs, religions, social standards—yes, and civil engineers, for you can easily trace the lines of their canals, in which they brought water from the river and carried it through a tunnel in the mountains to irrigate their land, just as you modern engineers are planning to do. The Seer and I rode over there once and he told me about it. I'll show you, if you like. *New!* Why the West was ages old before the East was discovered! The Seer says that if Columbus had come first to the western coast New England to-day would still be an uninhabitable, howling wilderness."

"But I don't see what all this has to do with social standards," he said, nettled at her reply.

"Simply this. If a man's position in life is to be fixed by the age of his family or the number of years that they have occupied a certain section of the country, then that Indian is your superior. His ancestors lived here long before yours settled in New England."

"But we are proud of our ancestors because of what they were and what they accomplished. We have a right to be. Think of what the world owes them!"

"Oh, I must have misunderstood you. You seemed to place so much emphasis on their having come over in the Mayflower. They *were* grand—those brave old pioneers. I am proud of them too for what they were. And did they have social positions by which they fixed a man's place in life, I wonder?"

"Of course they could not have had a society with the wealth and culture that we have now. The country was all new—something like the West is to-day, I suppose."

She laughed aloud. "And you are proud of them! How fine! Isn't it splendid to think that in two or three hundred years, when the West has been civilized and the Desert reclaimed as your pioneer forefathers civilized and reclaimed the East, when wealth and culture have come, a man's social standing will be determined by his relation to *us* and people will be proud of what *we* are doing? After all, Mr. Holmes, the only difference between the East and the West esems to be that you *have* ancestors and that we are *going to be* ancestors. You look back to what has been; we look forward to what will be. You are proud and take rank because of what your forefahers did; we are proud and take rank because of what we are doing. And we are doing exactly what they did! Honestly now, which would you rather—worship an ancestor or be an ancestor worshipped?"

When they had laughed together over this he said: "I am beginning to understand, Miss Worth, that the ideal American, whom we are always hearing about but never meet, must be a Westerner; he couldn't possibly be of the East, could he?" His words were almost a sneer.

"The ideal American is neither Eastern nor

Western in the way you mean, Mr. Holmes. He is both."

"Indeed? You admit that we of the East could give him something, then?"

"You could give him all that your forefathers have given you."

"And what could the West give him?"

She looked at him steadily a moment before answering slowly: "I think you will have to find that out for yourself."

He was taken a little aback by her answer. It sounded as though she wished to end the conversation. But her talk had stirred him strongly, though he tried to hide this under cover of a cynical tone. He said triumphantly: "But you see, after all, you admit that one is not altogether hopeless because he happens to come of a good family!"

"Certainly I admit it!" she cried, "but don't you see what I mean? Ancestors are to be counted as a valuable asset, but not as working capital."

As she spoke she turned toward him again with that steady look, and the man felt the strange, mysterious power of her personality, the challenging lure of her young womanhood—that and more. What was it back of those steady eyes that called to him, inspired him, that almost frightened him; that made him feel as Barbara herself felt in the presence of the Desert.

There was no trace of cynicism in his voice now, nor any hint of a sneer on his face, as Willard Holmes straightened unconsciously in his saddle.

"By George!" he said, "it's good to hear you say

131

those things. Nobody talks that way nowadays. I
suppose our great-great-grandmothers did, though."

She colored with pleasure, but answered lightly :
"That puts me a long ways behind the times, doesn't
it ?"

"Or a long way ahead," he offered.

In the meantime, while the education of Willard
Holmes progressed, the party that was to make the
first survey in Barbara's Desert was being formed
and equipped under the direction of Abe Lee
Horses, mules, wagons, camp outfits and supplies
with Indian and Mexican laborers, teamsters of sev
eral nationalities and here and there a Chinese cook
were assembled. Toward the last from every part
of the great West country came the surveyors and
engineers—sunburned, khaki-clad men most i them,
toughened by their out-of-doors life, overflowing with
health and good spirits. They hailed one another
joyously and greeted Abe with extravagant delight,
overwhelming him with questions. For the word had
gone out that the Seer, beloved by all the tribe, and
his lieutenant, almost equally beloved, were making
"big medicine" in The King's Basin Desert. Not a
man of them would have exchanged his chance to go
for a crown and scepter.

The eastern engineer met these hardened professional brothers cordially He listened to their rem-
iniscences of life and work in mountain, plain and
desert with interest, discovering to his surprise that
most of them were eastern born and bred, with
technical training in the schools with which he was
familiar. But their almost boyish enthusiasm over

132

the work ahead, their admiration for the Chief and for Abe Lee he viewed with cold indifference.

With all his duties Abe found frequent opportunity to report to Barbara, for the girl's interest in every detail of the preparations was never failing. Her friends protested that they never saw her now at their little social affairs, for she was always off somewhere with some engineer, and that when they did chance to catch her alone she would talk of nothing but that horrid King's Basin country.

Every evening, early after supper, the surveyor would slip away from his companions at the hotel to spend an hour on the veranda at the banker's home talking in his straightforward way with Barbara and her father, of the work that was so dear to the heart of the girl. And because it was his work and in the nature of a report to one who, he felt, had in some subtle way authority to hear, Abe talked with a freedom that would have astonished many of his friends who thought they knew him best.

Three times while Abe was there Willard Holmes appeared, and each time, at the engineer's presence, the surveyor's painful diffidence became apparent and he soon—with some stammering excuse—left.

The last time this happened Barbara walked down to the gate with the painfully embarrassed surveyor. Everything was in readiness for the coming of the Chief, who would arrive the next day, and the following morning the expedition would start for the field.

"Buenos noches, hermano—Good night, brother," called Barbara, as the tall surveyor walked away down the street.

"Buenos noches," came the answer.

Willard Holmes heard and frowned. "You seem to be very fond of Spanish, Miss Worth," he said, when the girl came back to the porch. "I notice you use it so often with our long friend there."

Barbara laughed at his evident displeasure. "The language seems to belong so to this country. To me its colors are all soft and warm like the colors of the Desert. I never thought of it before, but I suppose I use it so often with Abe because he, too, seems to belong to this country."

The engineer looked at her curiously. "I don't think I quite see the connection. You mean that he has Spanish blood?"

"Not at all," said Barbara quickly. "But he is desert-born and desert-trained. He has the same patient stillness, the same natural bigness and the same unconquerable hardness."

"Oh, but you say the desert is not unconquerable; that it will be subdued. Your analogy is at fault."

"No, Mr. Holmes, it is you who do not understand. There is something about this country that will always remain as it is now. Abe Lee is like that. Whatever changes may come, he will always be Abe Lee of the Desert."

"Your views are really poetical and your character analyses very clever, Miss Worth, but after all men are men wherever you find them. Human nature is the same the world over."

"Oh, I'm sure that is so, Mr. Holmes. I know there must be many western men in the east, only they haven't found themselves yet"

He laughed heartily as he rose to go. "Will you ever bid me good night in your language of the desert?" he asked.

"Perhaps, when you have learned that language," she said with an answering smile.

"By George, I shall try to learn it," he answered.

"Oh, I wish you would," came the earnest answer. "I know you could."

And again the engineer felt strongly, back of her words, that unvoiced appeal. As he went down the street he knew that she did not refer to the Spanish tongue when she wished him to learn the language of her Desert.

Alone in her room that night Barbara's mind was too active for sleep and she sat for a long time by the open window, looking out into the vast silent world under the still stars.

Until she introduced herself to Willard Holmes, Barbara had never known eastern people. Tourists she had seen and, at rare intervals, met in a casual way. But they had always examined her with such frankly curious eyes that she had felt like some strange animal on exhibition and had repaid their interest with all the indifference she could command. Occasionally also she had been introduced to eastern business men, whom she chanced upon talking with her father in the bank, but they had turned quickly away to the matters of their world after the usual polite nothings demanded by the introduction. The home-land and life of Willard Holmes were as foreign to her as her land and life were strange to him.

So it happened in this instance also that in the

education of the eastern engineer the teacher learned quite as much as the pupil.

The traits that stood out so prominently in the western men whom Barbara knew and so much admired were, in Willard Holmes, buried deeply under the habits and customs of the life and thought of the world to which he belonged—buried so deeply that the man himself scarcely realized that they were there and so was led to wonder at himself when his blood tingled with some strong presentation of this western girl's views.

But Barbara knew. Beneath the conventionalities of his class the girl felt the man a powerful character, with all the latent strength of his nation-building ancestors. She wanted him—as she put it to herself—to wake up. Would he? Would he learn the language of her Desert? She believed that he would, even as she believed in the reclamation of The King's Basin lands.

And she was glad—glad that the Seer and Abe and Tex and Pat and her father—the men who had brought her out of the Desert—were going now back into that land of death to save that land itself from itself. And—she whispered it softly under the stars —she was glad—glad that Willard Holmes had come to go with them—to learn the language of her land.

CHAPTER VIII.

WHY WILLARD HOLMES STAYED.

SLOWLY, day by day, the surveying party under the Seer pushed deeper and deeper into the awful desolation of The King's Basin Desert. They were the advance force of a mighty army ordered ahead by Good Business—the master passion of the race. Their duty was to learn the strength of the enemy, to measure its resources, to spy out its weaknesses and to gather data upon which a campaign would be planned.

Under the Seer the expedition was divided into several smaller parties, each of which was assigned to certain defined districts. Here and there, at seemingly careless intervals in the wide expanse, the white tents of the division camps shone through the many colored veils of the desert. Tall, thin columns of dust lifted into the sky from the water wagons that crawled ceaselessly from water hole to camp and from camp to water hole—hung in long clouds above the supply train laboring heavily across the dun plain to and from Rubio City—or rose in quick puffs and twisting spirals from the feet of some saddle horse bearing a messenger from the Chief to some distant lieutenant.

Every morning, from each of the camps, squads of khaki-clad men bearing transit and level, stake and pole and flag—the weapons of their warfare—put out in different directions into the vast silence that seemed to engulf them. Every evening the squads returned, desert-stained and weary, to their rest under the lonesome stars. Every morning the sun broke fiercely up from the long level of the eastward plain to pour its hot strength down upon these pigmy creatures, who dared to invade the territory over which he had, for so many ages, held undisputed dominion. Every evening the sun plunged fiercely down behind the purple wall of mountains that shut in the Basin on the west, as if to gather strength in some nether world for to-morrow's fight.

Always there was the same flood of white light from the deep, dry sky that was uncrossed by shred of cloud; always the same wide, tawny waste, harshly glaring near at hand—filled with awful mysteries under the many colored mists of the distance; until the eyes ached and the soul cried out in wonder at it all. Always there were the same deep nights, with the lonely stars so far away in the velvet purple darkness; the soft breathing of the desert; the pungent smell of greasewood and salt-bush; the weird, quavering call of the ground owl; or the wild coyote chorus, as if the long lost spirits of long ago savage races cried out a dreadful warning to these invaders.

And in all of this the land made itself felt against these men in the silent menace, the still waiting, the subtle call, the promise, the threat and the challenge of La Palma de la Mano de Dios.

To Barbara, who rode often in those days to the

very rim of the Basin, there to search the wild, wide land with straining eyes for signs of her friends, the white glare of the camps was lost in the bewildering maze of color. The columns, clouds and spirals of dust—save perhaps from a near supply wagon coming in or passing out—could not be distinguished from the whirling dust-devils that danced always over the hot plains. The toiling pigmy dots of the little army were far beyond her vision's range. It was as though the fierce land had swallowed up horses, wagons and men. Only through the frequent letters brought by the freighters did she know that all was going well.

Perhaps the gray lizard that climbed to the top of a line stake wondered at the strange new growth that had sprung so suddenly from the familiar soil; or perhaps the horned-toad, scuttling to cover, marveled at the strange sounds as the stakes were driven and man called to man figures and directions. Perhaps the scaly side-winder, springing his warning rattle at the approaching step, questioned what new enemy this was; or the lone buzzard, wheeling high over head, watched the tiny moving figures with wondering hopefulness, and the coyote, that hushed for a little his wild music to follow up the wind this strange new scent, laughed at the Seer's dream.

These lines of stakes that every day stretched farther and farther into and across the waste seemed, in the wideness of the land, pitifully foolish. Looking back over the lines, the men who set them could scarcely distinguish the way they had come. But they knew that the stakes were there. They knew that some day that other, mightier company, the main

army, would move along the way they had marked
to meet the strength of the barren waste with the
strength of the great river and take for the race the
wealth of the land. The sound of human voices was
flat and ineffectual in that age-old solitude, but the
speakers knew that following their feeble voices
would come the shouting, ringing, thundering chorus
of the life that was to follow them into that silent
land of death.

With the slow passing of the weeks came the trying
out and testing of character inevitable to such a
work. The concealing habits of civilization were
dropped. Kindly, useful conventionalities were lost.
Face to face with the unconquered forces of nature,
nothing remained but the real strength or weakness
of the individual himself. In some there were
developed unguessed powers of endurance that bore
the hard days without flinching; cheerful optimism
that laughed at the appalling immensity of the task;
strength of spirit that made a jest of galling discomforts; courage that smiled in the face of dangers.
These were the strength of the party. Some there
were who grew sullen, quarrelsome, and vicious in a
kind of mad rebellion. These must be held in check,
controlled and governed by the Seer with the assistance of Abe Lee and his helpers. Some became silent
and moody, faint hearted and afraid. These were
strengthened and guarded and given fresh courage.
Some grew peevish and fretful, whining and complaining. These were disciplined wisely, forced
gently into line. Some staggered and fell by the

way. These were sent back and the ranks closed up. But the work—always the work went on.

To Willard Holmes the life was a slow torture, a revelation and an education. He found himself stripped of everything upon which he was accustomed to rely—family traditions, social position, influential friends, scholarship, experience in the world to which he was born—all these were nothing in The Hollow of God's Hand. Slowly he learned that the power of such wealth is limited to certain fields. New York was very far away. He felt that he had been hope-lessly banished to a strange world. Many times he would have thrown it all up and turned back with other deserters, but there was red blood in his veins. Stubborn pride and the thought of the girl who had hoped that he would "learn the language of her country" enabled him to hold on.

Once he ventured to speak to the Chief in a hope-less voice of the evident impossibility of ever con-verting that terrible land into a habitable country, and the Seer, strong in the strength of his dream, had looked at him from the still depth of his brown eyes without a word—looked until the younger man had turned away, his cheeks flushed with shame and his spirit doing homage to the strength of the master spirit of the work. And the eastern engineer remem-bered with new understanding his talks with Barbara Worth.

When they pulled the dead coyote from the only water hole within two days' travel and Holmes nearly fainted at the sickening sight, it was Texas Joe who saved the day for him by remarking, with an air of philosophical musing, after a deep draught of the tepid, tainted water: "Hit ain't so bad as you might think, Mr. Holmes, onct your oilfactory nerves has become somewhat regulated to the aroma and your palate has been eddicated to the point of appreciatin' the deliciously foreign flavor. In the judgment of some connysoors, it has several points the lead of them imported fancy drinks you get in Frisco."

When a Mexican died horribly from the bite of a rattlesnake, and Holmes himself was barely saved from a like fate by the prompt action and ready knowledge of Abe Lee, it was the slow smile of the desert-bred surveyor that stiffened him to go on.

And when he was nearly beaten by a three days' sand-storm so searching that even the flap-jacks and bacon gritted in his teeth and his blood-shot eyes smarted in his head like coals of fire and his skin felt as though it had been sand-papered, when he would have sold his soul for a bath and actually began to get his things together in readiness for the next wagon out, it was Pat, who, with the devilish ingenuity of an Irish imp, mocked and jeered at him for a quitter, "fit to act only as lady's maid or to serve soft dhrinks in a corner drug-sthore," until his fainting heart took fire and, cursing his tormentor with all the oaths he could muster, he offered to whip, single-handed, the whole grinning camp and stayed.

Thus he was advanced to the second degree, when he began to sense the spirit of the untamed land and of the men who went to meet it with sheer joy of the conquest; when he began to glory in the very greatness of the task; and the long dormant spirit of his ancestors stirred within him as he caught glimpses of the vision that inspired the Seer or, perhaps it should be written, the vision that tempted his employers, James Greenfield and his fellow capitalists.

He was still far from ready for the final degree; but even that might come.

Through all those hard days Jefferson Worth moved with the same careful, precise, certain manner that distinguished him in his work at home. Even the desert sun that so tanned, blistered and blackened the faces of his companions could not mark the gray pallor of that mask-like face. No disturbing incident or unforeseen difficulty could wring from him an exclamation or change the measured tones of his colorless voice. He seemed to accept everything as though he had foreseen, carefully considered and dismissed it from his mind before it came to pass. Day after day he rode in every direction over the land within easy reach of the many camps; familiarizing himself with every detail of the work, observing soil, studying conditions, poring over maps and figures with the Seer, verifying estimates, listening to and taking part in the many councils of the leaders. But not once did anyone catch a hint of what was going on behind those expressionless blue eyes that seemed to see everything without effort and to be incapable of expressing the emotions of the soul within.

To the men he was the visible representative of that invisible power that willed their going forth,

He was Capital—Money—Business incarnate. They set him apart as one not of their world. In his presence laughter was hushed, jests were unspoken. Silently they waited for him to speak first. When he conversed with them they answered thoughtfully in subdued tones, seeming to feel that their words were received by one who placed upon them undreamed-of values. Filled as these men were with the enthusiasm of their work, they were never unconscious of the knowledge that but for the power represented by Jefferson Worth their work would be impossible.

Small wonder, then, that there was consternation in the headquarters camp that night when Pat appeared, hat in hand, before the company of leaders in the Seer's office tent. "I beg yer pardon, Sorr."

"What is it, Pat?" asked the Seer, and all eyes were turned upon the burly Irishman, whose face and voice as well as his presence at that hour betrayed some unusual incident. " 'Tis this, Sorr. Has anywan seen Mr. Worth this avenin'?"

Every head was shaken negatively.

"Was he not at supper wid you gintlemen?"

"Why no, he was not," returned the Seer. "But it is nothing unusual for him to be late. Have you asked the cook?"

"We have, Sorr. Ye see, whin ut come time to turn in an' he hadn't shown up an' Tex seen that his horse wasn't wid the bunch, we got a bit unaisy like. We axed the cook, an' we've been to his tent, an' we've axed the men."

"Perhaps he has put up at one of the other camps," suggested a surveyor.

"That's not like, Sorr, for he rode northeast this mornin'. Me an' Tex watched him go; an' there's divil a camp in that direction as we all know."

"He surely intended to return here or he would have told us," said the Seer. "You know how careful he is. What do you think, Abe?"

Before Abe could answer a Mexican ran up, and Pat, turning, hauled him into the tent by the neck. "Fwhat the hell is ut, ye greaser?"

"Senor Texas send me quick," the little brown man panted, bowing low to the company, sombrero in hand. "Senor Worth's horse, he just come. In the saddle is no one. Senor Worth he is not come. I think he is gone."

Before the Mexican finished speaking there was a rush of feet and he was alone. With a shrug of his shoulders and a flash of his white teeth, he turned leisurely to follow, saying half aloud: "It is all in La Palma de la Mano de Dios, Senor Worth. Maybe so you come back, maybe this time not." He stood for a moment looking into the black vault of the night; then, with another shrug, retired to his blanket to sleep.

Abe Lee was first to reach the corral where Texas Joe, by the light of a lantern, was examining Mr. Worth's horse. No word was exchanged between them while the surveyor in turn looked carefully over the animal. The others, coming up, stood silent a little apart, waiting for the word of these two.

145

"What do you make of it, Abe?" asked the Seer when the long surveyor turned toward him.

Deliberately rolling a cigarette, Abe answered from a cloud of smoke: "He is left afoot too far out to walk in, likely. We'll go for him in the morning."

A startled exclamation came from Willard Holmes, but no one heeded as the surveyor turned to Texas Joe. "How do you figure it, Tex?"

"The same," came the laconic answer. "This here cayuse wasn't broke to stand. He must have been tied somewheres, 'cause the reins are busted." He pointed to the pieces of leather hanging from the bit. "The canteen is gone. Jefferson Worth is too old a hand on the desert to leave it on the horse. He likely tied the pony to a bush and went to climb a hill or something. Mr. Hawss breaks loose and pulls for home. It happened a good way out, 'cause the pony's pretty well tired, which he wouldn't a-been travelin' light, if Mr. Worth hadn't ridden some distance before it happened. An' if he was nearer the pony would have been in earlier. He'll likely show us a smoke in the morning and even if he don't it'll be easy to trail him, 'cause there ain't no wind. Will I go, sir?" He looked at the Chief.

"Yes; you and Abe, don't you think?"

Abe assented and the men turned toward the tents while Texas led the tired horse away.

The New York engineer approached the Chief. "Do I understand, sir, that you propose to do nothing until morning?"

The Seer faced him. "There is nothing to do, Mr. Holmes," he said simply.

146

Willard Holmes was amazed at the man's apparent unconcern. "Nothing to do?" he exclaimed. "Why don't you arouse the men and send them in every direction to search? Why man, don't you realize the situation? Mr. Worth may be hurt. He may even be dying alone out there! I protest! It's monstrous! It's cowardly, inhuman, to do nothing!"

The company, attracted by the loud words, paused. Abe Lee, standing beside his Chief, rolled another cigarette while the engineer was speaking.

The Seer answered patiently: "But Mr. Holmes, we could accomplish nothing by such a search as you suggest. The territory is too large to cover with a hundred times the number of men we have in camp. At daylight, when they can follow his trail, Abe and Tex will ride to him as fast as their horses can go. Granting that the worst you suggest may be true, our plan is the only sane way."

"But I protest, sir. You should make the attempt. I will not submit to idly doing nothing while a life is in danger—particularly that of a man like Mr. Worth. I shall go alone if no one will help me, and"—he straightened himself haughtily—"I shall report this to Mr. Greenfield and the men interested with him in this work."

At the last words one of those rare changes swept over the big engineer, and the witnesses saw a side of the Chief's nature that was seldom revealed. His eyes flashed and his face hardened as he burst forth in tones that startled his hearers: "Report me? You! Report and be damned, sir. I was old at this work when you were a sucking babe. These men

147

were learning the desert when you were attending a fashionable dancing school. Why, you damned lily-fingered tenderfoot, you couldn't find your way five hundred yards in this country without a guide or a compass. Now, sir, I'm running this outfit and if you have any protests against my cowardly inhumanity I advise you to smother them in your manly breast, or, by hell! I'll ship you out on the first wagon to-morrow morning and let you report to Greenfield that you were fired because you didn't know your work yourself and hadn't intelligence enough to listen to those who did!"

The Chief paused for breath, and Willard Holmes, whose experience with large corporations was expected to make him peculiarly valuable to the capitalists who sent him out, turned away with what dignity he could command.

"Howly Mither!" came a hoarse whisper from Pat to Abe; "I made sure the poor bhoy wud shrivel up. Sich a witherin', blistherin' tongue lashin' wud scorch the hide av the owld divil himsilf." He looked admiringly after the Seer. "D'ye think, now, that the poor lad will be afther tacklin' the job alone, like he said? Sure, ut's nerve he has all right but he lacks judgment."

"Yes, he has the nerve all right," returned Abe slowly, "and we'd better keep an eye on him. Tell Tex."

Willard Holmes knew that he owed his Chief an apology and he promised himself to make it in the morning. But neither the explanation of the Seer nor the bitter humiliation that he had brought upon himself could turn his thoughts from Mr. Worth alone on the desert. To sleep was impossible. The banker might be—— As he tossed in his blankets the engineer pictured to himself a hundred things that might have happened to Barbara's father.

It was some two hours later when Pat touched Abe Lee on the shoulder.

"All right, Pat," said the surveyor, fully awake and in possession of all his senses in an instant.

"There's a light bobbin' off into nowhere an' the lad's blankets are impty."

Fifteen minutes later a quiet voice within three feet of Willard Holmes asked: "Shall I go with you, sir?"

The eastern man jumped like a nervous woman. He had not heard the approach of the surveyor, who walked with the step of an Indian. "I couldn't sleep," he explained. "I thought I would follow the tracks a little way out at least. He may not be so far away as you think."

After Abe had taken time to make his cigarette he spoke meditatively. "Mr. Worth rode a horse."

"I understand that," returned the man with the lantern tartly. "I saw him go this morning and I saw the horse to-night. This is the track."

From another cloud of smoke came the quiet, respectful answer: "But this is a mule's track, Mr. Holmes. It is Manuel Ramirez's mule. See, he has a broken shoe on the off fore-foot. I noticed it yesterday when I sent Manuel to hunt a water hole. Besides, Mr. Worth rode northeast; not in this direction."

CHAPTER IX.

THE MASTER PASSION—"GOOD BUSINESS."

WHEN Jefferson Worth left headquarters camp that morning, his purpose was to ride over a part of the territory lying southeast of the old San Felipe trail between the sand hills and the old beach-line. He had covered practically all of the land on the western side of the ancient sea-bed, from the delta dam at the southern end north to the lowest point in the Basin, and southward again on the eastern side as far as the old trail. There remained for him to see only this section in the southeast.

It was nearly noon when the banker, from a slight elevation that afforded him a view of the surrounding country, recognized the group of sand hills and, by the general course of Dry River, distinguished the spot where the San Felipe trail crosses the deep arroyo. Occupied with his thoughts, he had ridden farther from camp than he had realized. He should turn back. But the distant scene of the desert tragedy called him. He became possessed of a desire to visit once more the spot that was so closely associated with the child, who had so strangely come into his life and whom he loved as his own daughter.

An hour later he dismounted to stand beside the water hole where, with his companions, he had found the dead woman with the empty canteen by her side.

The incidents of that hour were as vivid in the banker's memory as if it had all happened only the day before. He remembered how Texas Joe had lifted the canteen and, inverting it, had held out to them his finger moistened with the last drop of water in the cloth-covered vessel; and how he and his companions, standing by the dead body of the woman, had turned to each other in startled awe at the coyotes' ghostly call in the dusk. He heard again with thrilling clearness the baby's plaintive voice: "Mamma, mamma! Barba wants drink. Please bring drink, mamma. Barba's 'fraid!"

Going a short way up the wash, he stood with uncovered head on the very spot where he had knelt with out-stretched hands before the big-eyed, brown-haired baby girl, who, crouching under the high bank, shrank back from him in fear. He saw the frightened look in her eyes and heard the sweet voice cry: "Go 'way! Go 'way! Go 'way!" Then he saw the expression on the little face change as Pat and Tex and the boy tried to reassure her; saw her hold up her baby hands in full confidence to the big engineer; and felt again the pain and humiliation in his heart.

Why had the baby instinctively feared him? Why had she turned from him to the Seer? Why, he asked himself bitterly, had she always feared him? Why did she still shrink from him? For Barbara did shrink from him, unconsciously—unintentionally —but, to Jefferson Worth, none the less plainly now than when he knelt before her that night in the desert. And it hurt him now as it had hurt him then; hurt the more, perhaps, because Barbara did not know—because her attitude was instinctive.

Still living over again the incidents and emotions of that hour in the desert night, he walked back to the crossing and, leading his horse, climbed the little hill out of the wash to the spot where, with Texas and Pat, he had rendered the last possible service to the unknown woman, who had given her life for the life of the child—the child that was his but not his. Long ago he had marked the grave with a simple headstone bearing the only name possible—the one word: "Mother"—and the date of her death.

Then mounting again, he rode swiftly along the old trail toward the sand hills in the near distance. The great drifts, in the years that had passed, had been moved on by the wind until the wagon and all that remained of the half-buried outfit were now hidden somewhere deep in its heart. But the general form of the sand hill was still the same.

Dismounting, Mr. Worth tied his horse to a scraggly, half-buried mesquite and, taking his canteen from the saddle, climbed laboriously up the steep, sandy slope. He would look over the country from that point and then make straight for camp, for it was getting well on in the afternoon. From the top of the hill he could see the wide reaches of The King's Basin Desert sweeping away on every side. At his feet the bare sand hills themselves lay like huge, rolling, wind-piled drifts of tawny snow glistening in the sunlight with a blinding glare. Beyond these were the gray and green of salt-bush, mesquite and greasewood, with the dun earth showing here

152

and there in ragged patches. Still farther away the detail of hill and hummock and bush and patch was lost in the immensity of the scene, while the dull tones of gray and green and brown were over-laid with the ever-changing tints of the distance, until, to the eyes, the nearer plain became an island surrounded on every side by a mighty, many-colored sea that broke only at the foot of the purple mountain wall.

The work of the expedition was nearly finished. The banker knew now from the results of the survey and from his own careful observations and estimates that the Seer's dream was not only possible from an engineering point of view, but from the careful capitalist's standpoint, would justify a large investment. Lying within the lines of the ancient beach and thus below the level of the great river, were hundreds of thousands of acres equal in richness of the soil to the famous delta lands of the Nile. The bringing of the water from the river and its distribution through a system of canals and ditches, while a work of great magnitude requiring the expenditure of large sums of money, was, as an engineering problem, comparatively simple.

As Jefferson Worth gazed at the wonderful scene, a vision of the changes that were to come to that land passed before him. He saw first, following the nearly finished work of the engineers, an army of men beginning at the river and pushing out into the desert with their canals, bringing with them the life-giving water. Soon, with the coming of the water, would begin the coming of the settlers. Hummocks would

be leveled, washes and arroyos filled, ditches would
be made to the company canals, and in place of the
thin growth of gray-green desert vegetation with the
ragged patches of dun earth would come great fields
of luxuriant alfalfa, billowing acres of grain, with
miles upon miles of orchards, vineyards and groves.
The fierce desert life would give way to the herds
and flocks and the home life of the farmer. The
railroad would stretch its steel strength into this new
world; towns and cities would come to be where now
was only solitude and desolation; and out from this
world-old treasure house vast wealth would pour to
enrich the peoples of the earth. The wealth of an
empire lay in that land under the banker's eye, and
Capital held the key.

But while the work of the engineers was simple,
it would be a great work; and it was the magnitude
of the enterprise and the consequent requirement of
large sums of money that gave Capital its opportunity. Without water the desert was worthless.
With water the productive possibilities of that great
territory were enormous. Without Capital the water
could not be had. Therefore Capital was master of
the situation and, by controlling the water, could
exact royal tribute from the wealth of the land.

Knowing James Greenfield and his business
associates as he knew them, familiar with their
operations as he was and knowing that they represented the power of almost unlimited capital, Jefferson Worth realized that they would plan to share in
every dollar of wealth that The King's Basin lands
could be made to produce. Already his trained mind

saw how easily, with the vast power in their hands, this could be brought about. And these men, recognizing his peculiar value in such an enterprise as this, wanted him to join them.

It was a triumphant moment in the life and business career of the western banker, the culmination of long, hard years of unceasing toil, of unfaltering devotion to business, of struggle and disappointments, of small victories and steady advance gained at the cost of sacrifice and hard fighting. This proposed alliance with the great eastern capitalists opened the door and invited him into the company of the real leaders of the financial world. As one of the powerful corporation that would literally hold the life of the future King's Basin in its hand, the multitudes of toilers who would come to reclaim the desert would be forced to toil not only for themselves but for him. A part of every dollar of the millions that would be taken from that treasury by the labor of the people would go to enrich him.

The financier's thoughts were interrupted by a sound. He turned to see his horse tugging at the bridle reins, snorting in fear. The man started quickly down the hill, but before he could cover half the distance that separated him from his mount the frightened animal broke the reins and, wheeling about, disappeared down the trail on a wild run. At the same instant a coyote trotted leisurely out from under the lee of the sand drift and, with a side glance over his shoulder at the banker, slipped around the point of the next low ridge.

The man knew that to catch his horse would be

impossible. The animal would not stop until he reached his companions at the feed-rack in camp. He knew also that to attempt to find his way to headquarters such a distance and on foot, with night so near at hand, would be worse than folly. He would only exhaust his strength and make it harder for his friends to find him before his water, which could not last another day, should give out. Some-one, he knew, would take his trail in the morning. The only thing he could do was to wait—to wait alone in the heart of this silent, age-old, waiting land.

Somewhere in those forgotten ages that went into the making of The King's Basin Desert, a company of free-born citizens of the land, moved by that master passion—Good Business, found their way to the banks of the Colorado. In time Good Business led them to build their pueblos and to cultivate their fields by irrigation with water from the river and erect their rude altars to their now long-forgotten gods. Driven by the same passion that drove the Indians, the emigrant wagons moved toward the new gold country, and some financial genius saw Good Business at the river-crossing near the site of the ancient city. At first it was no more than a ferry, but soon others with eyes for profit established a trading point where the overland voyagers could replenish their stock of supplies, sure to be low after the hundreds of miles across the wide plains. Then also, in obedience to Good Business, pleasures heard the call, saloons, gambling houses and dance halls appeared, and for profit the joys of civilization arrived in the savage land. Good Business sent the prospectors who found the mines, the capital that developed them and the laborers who dug the ore. Good Business sent the cattle barons and their cowboys, sent the speculators and the pioneer merchants. Good Business sent also, in the fulness of time, Jefferson Worth.

Of old New England Puritan stock, Worth had come through the hard life of a poor farm boy with two dominant elements in his character: an almost super-human instinct for Good Business, inherited no doubt, and an instinct, also inherited, for religion. The instinct for trade, from much cultivation, had waxed strong and stronger with the years. The religion that he had from his forefathers was become little more than a superstition. It was his genius for business that led him, in his young manhood, to leave the farm, and it was inevitable that from making money he should come to making money make more money. It was the other dominant element in his character that kept him scrupulously honest, scrupulously moral. Besides this, honesty and morality were also "good business."

Seeking always larger opportunities for the employment of his small, steadily-increasing financial strength, Mr. Worth established the Pioneer Bank. Later, as he had foreseen, the same master passion brought the great railroad with still larger opportunities for his money to make more money. And now the same master passion that had driven the Indian, the emigrant, the miner, the cowman, the banker and the railroad was driving the eastern capitalists to spend their moneyed strength in the reclamation of The King's Basin Desert. It was Good Business that led Greenfield and his friends to seek the co-operation of the western financier. It was Good Business that called to Jefferson Worth now as he saw the immense possibilities of the land.

As truly as the ages had made the barren desert with its hard, thirsty life, the ages had produced Jefferson Worth, a carefully perfected, money making machine, as silent, hard and lonely as the desert itself. With apparently no vices, no passions, no mistakes, no failures, his only relation to his fellow-men was a business relation. With his almost supernatural ability to foresee, to measure, to weigh and judge, with his cold, mask-like face and his manner of considering carefully every word and of placing a value upon every trivial incident, he was respected, feared, trusted, even admired—and that was all. No; not all. By those who were forced, through circumstances—business circumstances—to contribute to his prosperity and financial success, he was hated. Such is the unreasonableness of human kind.

Business, to this man as to many of his kind, was not the mean, sordid grasping and hoarding of money. It was his profession, but it was even more than a profession; it was the expression of his genius. Still more it was, through him, the expression of the age in which he lived, the expression of the master passion that in all ages had wrought in the making of the race. He looked upon a successful deal as a good surgeon looks upon a successful operation, as an architect upon the completion of a building or an artist upon his finished picture. But to a greater degree than to artist or surgeon, the success of his work was measured by the accumulation of dollars. Apart from his work he valued the money received from his operations no more than the surgeon his fee, the artist his price. The work itself was his passion. Because dollars were the tools of his craft he was careful of them. The more he succeeded, the more power he gained for greater success.

But extremely simple in his tastes, lacking, with his lack of education, knowledge of the more costly luxuries of life, with the habits of an ascetic, Jefferson Worth could not evidence his success; and success hidden and unknown loses its power to reward. It is not enough for the engineer to run his locomotive; he must have train loads of goods and passengers to carry to some objective point. It is not enough for the captain to have command of his ship; he must have a port Self to Jefferson Worth meant little; his nature demanded so little. Nor could Mrs. Worth in this fill the need in her husband's life, for her nature was as simple as his own. But a child, whose life could be part of his life, filling out, supplementing and complementing his own nature; a child who, dependent upon him, should have all the training that he lacked, who should share his success and for whom he could plan to succeed—a child, an heir, would fill the blank in his empty career. For a brief time he had looked forward to a child of his own blood. Then the death of the baby and the ill health of his wife had left him hopeless. He con-

tinued his work because he knew no life apart from
his work.

Then came the little girl so strangely the gift of
the desert. The banker's mind, trained to act quickly,
had grasped the possibilities of the situation instantly as he ran with his companions to answer the
call of that childish voice. From the moment when
he knelt with outstretched hands and pleading words
before little Barbara, he had never ceased trying to
win her. Mrs. Worth, knowing that she could not
be with him many years, had said: "You need her,
Jeff," and he did need her.

But Jefferson Worth knew that Barbara was not
his. She shrank from him as instinctively and
unconsciously as she had drawn back that night of
her mother's death when he knelt before her in the
desert. As she had turned to the Seer then, she
turned from the banker now. And now, far more
than then, his lonely heart hungered for her; for
with the years his need of her had grown. Envied
of foolish men as men so foolishly envy his class, the
banker knew himself to be destitute, an object of
their pity. The poorest Mexican in his adobe hut,
with his half-naked, laughing children, was more
wealthy than he.

Jefferson Worth, that afternoon on the very scene
of the tragedy that had given Barbara to him,
realized that in the land before him he faced the
greatest opportunity of his business career. He
realized also that he was as much alone in his life
as he was alone in the silent, barren waste that surrounded him. Would La Palma de la Mano de Dios,

which had given him the child that was not his child, give him wealth that still never could be his?

At last, from his place on the sand drift that held the secret of Barbara's life, he saw the sun as it appeared to rest for a moment on the western wall before plunging down into the world on the other side. Watching, he saw the purple of the hills deepen and deepen and the wondrous light on the wide sea of colors fade slowly out as the colors themselves paled and grew dim in the misty dusk of the coming night. Slowly the twilight sky grew dark, and into the velvet plain above came the heavenly flocks until their number was past counting save by Him who leadeth them in their fields. Against the last lingering light in the west that marked where the day had gone, the mountains lifted their vast bulk in solemn grandeur as if to bar forever the coming of another day. Closing about him on every hand, coming dreadfully nearer and nearer, the black walls of darkness shut him in. In the cool, mysterious breath of the desert, in the grotesque, fantastic, nearby shapes and monstrous forms of the sand dunes, in the mysterious phantom voices that whispered in the dark, Jefferson Worth felt the close approach of the spirit of the land; the calling of the age-old, waiting land—the silent menace, the voiceless threat, the whispered promise.

And there, alone—held close in The Hollow of God's Hand as the long hours of the night passed— the spirit of the man's Puritan fathers stirred within him. In the silent, naked heart of the Desert that, knowing no hand but the hand of its Creator, seemed

to hold in its hushed mysteriousness the ages of a
past eternity, he felt his life to be but a little thing.
Beside the awful forces that made themselves felt
in the spirit of Barbara's Desert, the might of
Capital became small and trivial. Sensing the dreadful power that had wrought to make that land, he
shrank within himself—he was afraid. He marveled
that he had dared dream of forcing La Palma de la
Mano de Dios to contribute to his gains. And so at
last it was given him to know why Barbara instinctively shrank from him in fear.

With the coming of the day the banker went a
little way back on the trail where the vegetation was
not entirely covered by the drifting sand, and there
gathered materials for a fire. Later, when he judged
his friends would be in sight, he fired the pile and,
watching the tall, thick column of smoke ascend,
awaited the answer. In a little while it came, faint
and far away, the report of Texas Joe's forty-five.
Soon he heard the sound of voices calling loudly and,
following his answer, the swift hoof-beats of galloping horses; and Tex and Abe, leading another horse,
appeared.

But the Jefferson Worth who rode back to camp
with his friends, there to be greeted and congratulated by the party, was not the same Jefferson Worth
who had left camp the morning before, though no
one congratulated him because of that.

It was three weeks later when a portly, well-fed
gentleman entered the Pioneer Bank in Rubio City
and asked of the teller: "Is Mr. Worth in?"

The man on the other side of the counter looked through his grated window at the speaker with unusual interest. And in the teller's voice there was a shade of unusual deference as he replied, "Yes, sir."

"Tell him that Mr. Greenfield is here."

At the magic of that name every man in the bank within sound of the speaker's voice lifted his head and turned toward the face at the window.

"Yes, sir. Come this way, sir."

A door in the partition opened and the visitor was admitted to the sacred precincts behind the gratings, the bars and the plate glass. As he moved down the room past counters and desks, every eye followed him and there was an electrical hush in the atmosphere like the hush that marks the massing of the forces in Nature before a conflict of the elements.

Jefferson Worth looked up as the imposing figure of the great financier appeared on the threshold of his room, and at the name of James Greenfield carefully pushed back the papers he had been considering and rose. The movement, slight as it was, was as though he cleared his decks for action. The clerk, withdrawing, carefully, closed the door.

The two men shook hands with much the air of two wrestlers meeting for a bout. For a moment neither spoke. Each knew that in the silence he was being measured, estimated, searched for his weakness and his strength, and each gave to the other this opportunity as his right. No time was wasted in idle preliminaries. These men knew the value of time. No formal words expressing pleasure at the meeting were spoken. They tacitly accepted the fact that pleasure had not called them together.

James Greenfield was a fair representative of his class. His full, well-colored face with carefully clipped gray mustache, bright blue eyes and gray hair, was the calmly alert, well-controlled, thoughtful face of power: not the face of one who does things, but of one who causes things to be done; not the face of one who is himself powerful, but of one who controls and directs power; such a face as you may see leaning from the cab of a great locomotive that pulls the overland limited, or looking down at you from the bridge of the ocean liner. It was courageous, but with a courage not personal—a courage born rather of an exact knowledge of the strength and duty of every bolt, rivet and lever of the machine under his hand. It was confident, not in its own strength, but in the strength that it ruled and directed.

Jefferson Worth motioned toward a chair at the end of his desk and seated himself. The man from the East found himself forced to make the opening.

"Mr. Worth," he said, "we find it very difficult to understand your attitude toward our company. We do not see why you decline our proposition. Your own report gives every reason in the world why you should accept and you suggest no reason at all for declining. Frankly, it looks strange to us and I have come out to have a little talk with you over the matter and to see if we could not persuade you to reconsider your decision, or at least to learn your

THE WINNING OF BARBARA WORTH

reasons for refusing to go in with us. Your report and your answer to our proposition are so conflicting that we feel we have a right to some definite reason for your unexpected decision."

As he spoke, the president of The King's Basin Land and Irrigation Company tried in vain to see behind the mask-like face of the man in the revolving chair. His failure only excited his admiration and respect. Instinctively he recognized the genius before him, and his desire to add this strength to his forces increased.

"My report was satisfactory?" The words were absolutely colorless.

"Very. It was exactly what we wanted. With your opinion, confirming our engineer's statements, we felt safe to go ahead with the organization of the Company and have already set the wheels moving toward actual work. It is because you so unhesitatingly and so strongly commend the project as warranting our investment that we cannot understand your refusal to share the profits of our enterprise."

He paused for an answer, but was forced to continue. "Let me explain more fully than I could outline in my letter just what we propose doing. The King's Basin Land and Irrigation Company, Mr. Worth, will not confine its operations simply to furnishing water for the reclamation and development of these lands. That is no more than the beginning—the basis of our operations. With the settlement and improvement of the country will come many other openings for profitable investments—townsites, transportation lines, telephones, electric power, banking and all that, you understand. Our connections and resources make it possible for us to finance any industry or operation that promises attractive returns, while our position as the originators of the whole King's Basin movement and the owners of the irrigation system will give us tremendous advantage over any outside capital that may attempt to come in later, and will make competition practically impossible."

"I figured that was the way you would do it," was the unemotional reply.

More than ever James Greenfield wanted this man. He considered carefully a few minutes, with no help from Jefferson Worth, then tried again. "If you feel that our proposition to you is not liberal enough, Mr. Worth, I am prepared to double our offer."

If the financier from New York thought to startle this little western banker with a proposal that was more than princely he failed. His words seemed to have no effect. It was as though he talked to a marble figure of a man.

"I appreciate your proposition, but must decline it."

"May I ask your reason, sir?"

"I must decline to give any."

The other arose, the light of battle in his eyes, for to James Greenfield's mind there could be only one possible meaning in the answer. "That is, of course, your privilege, Mr. Worth," he said coldly. And then with the weight of conscious power he added: "But I'll tell you this, sir: if you think you can enter The King's Basin in opposition to our Company you're making the mistake of your life. We'll smash you, with your limited resources, so flat that you'll be glad for a chance to make the price of a meal. Good day, sir!"

"Good day."

Before the great capitalist was out of the building, Jefferson Worth was bending over the papers on his desk again as though declining to accept flattering offers from gigantic corporations was an hourly occurrence.

CHAPTER X.

BARBARA'S LOVE FOR THE SEER.

JEFFERSON WORTH had not proceeded far with the work before him after James Greenfield left when he was again interrupted This time it was the voice of Barbara in the other room.

The banker lifted his head quickly. Again he pushed his papers from him, but now the movement seemed to indicate weariness and uncertainty rather than readiness for action. His head dropped forward, his thin fingers nervously tapped the arms of his chair. When the girl's step sounded at the door he looked up the fraction of a second before she appeared.

"I don't want to disturb you, father, but they told me that that big, fine-looking man just going out was Mr. Greenfield. Is he—did he come all the way from New York to see you?"

"He came in here to see me," said Jefferson Worth exactly.

"And the work?"

"He says they have already started the wheels to moving."

"And you, daddy; you?"

Jefferson Worth arose and carefully closed the door. Then silently indicating the chair at the end of his desk he resumed his seat.

As Barbara looked into that mask-like face, the eager expectant light in her brown eyes died out and a look of questioning doubt came. She seemed to shrink back from him almost as she had turned away that first time in the desert.

If Jefferson Worth felt that look his face gave no sign; only those thin, nervous fingers were lifted to caress his chin.

"Are you—are you going to help, daddy? Will you join Mr. Greenfield's company?"

Still the man was silent, and the girl, watching, wondered what was going on behind that gray mask, what questions were being weighed and considered.

At last he spoke one cold word: "Why?"

Barbara flushed. "Because," she answered, carefully, "because it is such a great work. You could do so much more than simply make money."

"That is as you and the Seer see it."

"But, father; it *is* a great work, isn't it, to change the desert into a land of farms and homes for thousands and thousands of people?"

"Do you think that Greenfield and his crowd are going into this scheme because it is a great thing for the people?"

"But don't even capitalists sometimes undertake a great work just because it is great and because thousands upon thousands of people, through years and years to come, will be benefited even though the men themselves do not make so awfully much money?"

If Jefferson Worth felt her unconscious insinuation his face gave no sign. Carefully he listened with his manner of considering and weighing every word, while to Barbara his mind seemed to be reaching out on every side or running far into the future. When he answered his words were carefully exact "Capitalists, as individuals might and do, spend millions in projects from which they, personally, expect no returns. But *Capital* doesn't do such things. Anything that Capital, *as Capital,* goes into must be purely a business proposition. If anything like sentiment entered into it that would be the end of the whole matter."

Barbara moved uneasily. "I don't think I quite understand why," she said.

There was a shade of color now in the banker's voice as he explained by asking: "How long do you think this bank could exist if we made loans to Tom, Dick and Harry because they needed help, or put money into this and that scheme simply because it was a beneficial thing? How long would it be before we went to smash?"

"But don't business men ever do anything except to make money? Doesn't Capital, as you say, ever consider the people?"

"This bank is a very substantial benefit to the people. But it can only benefit them by doing business on strictly business principles. As an individual any officer or stock holder can do what he pleases for whatever reason moves him. He can burn his money if he wants to. But as officers and directors of this corporation we can't burn the capital of the institution."

"But Mr. Greenfield and these New York men,

who have organized the company—are they not careful financiers?"

"Very."

"It seems to me that they must believe in the Seer and his work or they wouldn't furnish him the money, would they?"

"They believe in the Seer and his work from their standpoint. Their capital is invested for just one purpose—dividends."

Barbara sighed and moved impatiently. "You always make it so hard to believe in men, father. I can't think that all business men—all financiers, I mean,—are so cold and heartless."

Again if Jefferson Worth felt the unconscious implication in her words he gave no sign. The banker was not ignorant of the public sentiment toward himself and the men of his class in his profession. He had come to accept it with the indifference of his exact, machine-like habit.

Barbara continued: "I feel sure that Mr. Greenfield and the men with him are going to furnish the money for the Seer to do this work for more than just what they will make out of it. I know that Mr. Holmes does, and I had hoped that you"—her voice broke—"that you would——"

If only Jefferson Worth could have broken the habit of a lifetime. If he could have laid aside that gray mask and permitted the girl to look into his hidden life, perhaps——

His colorless voice broke the silence, coldly exact: "What do you figure Willard Holmes is in this thing for?"

171

Barbara's face lighted up proudly. "He is in the work for the same reason that the Seer and Abe are —because it is such a great work and means so much to the world. I know, because since he returned he has talked to me so much about it. When he first came out—just at first—he didn't understand what the work really was. But now he understands it as the Seer sees it."

"Did the Seer send him out here?"

"No, I believe Mr. Greenfield sent him."

"Why?"

"I suppose they wanted an eastern man, whom they knew better than they knew the Seer, to represent them? It would be very natural, wouldn't it?"

"Very natural," agreed Jefferson Worth.

"Have you given the Company your final answer, father?"

"Yes."

"And you—you won't have anything to do with the reclamation of my Desert?"

"I declined to join the Company."

Blindly Barbara made her way out of the building. The place, with its air of business and suggestions of wealth, was unbearably hateful to her. At home she ordered her horse and started for the open country. But she did not ride toward the Desert. She felt that she could not bear the sight of The King's Basin that day.

In her father's attitude toward the Company Barbara saw only his seeming desire for selfish gain. He had told her so often that only one thing could justify an investment of capital. Evidently he did not think

The King's Basin project would pay. She felt ashamed for him; he seemed so incapable of consid ering anything but profit. Nothing but profit, the sure promise of gain, could move him. He believed in the work; he had reported in favor of it to the Company. He knew that the Company was going ahead. He was willing enough that others should do the work, she thought bitterly. They might take the risk. It was even likely that he had some way planned by which, without risking anything himself, he would reap large returns through their efforts. She thought proudly of the Seer, who had given so many unpaid years to the Reclamation work; of Abe and his loyalty to the Seer; and of Willard Holmes, who was going to give himself to the work.

Utterly sick at heart the girl did not meet her father at their evening meal. She could not. Jefferson Worth ate alone and alone spent the evening on the porch. On the way to his room he paused a moment at her door. He knocked softly so as not to waken her if she was asleep. When there was no answer he stole quietly away. But Barbara was not asleep.

For three days Mr. Greenfield remained in Rubio City, "on the business of The King's Basin Land and Irrigation Company," the papers said in a long article setting forth the greatness of the work that was to be undertaken in the desert through the magnificent enterprise of these mighty eastern capitalists.

During that time Barbara had not seen either the Seer, Holmes or Abe Lee. She understood that they were engaged with Mr. Greenfield. She read the glowing articles in the paper, the afternoon of Mr. Greenfield's departure, with a thrill of pride. At last it had come—the day for which the Seer had hoped all these years. The dear old Seer! She was a little disappointed that the papers did not give his name more prominence. It seemed to be all Greenfield and the Company. But after all that did not matter. It was the Seer's work; the Seer had brought it about.

The front gate clicked and Barbara looked up from her paper to see her old friend coming up the walk. She saw at a glance that something was wrong. She thought he was ill. The big form of the engineer drooped with weakness, his head dropped forward, his eyes were fixed on the ground and he walked slowly, dragging his feet as with great weariness. With a startled cry she ran to meet him, and as he caught her hands in both his own she saw his face drawn and haggard and his brown eyes filled with hopeless pain. He did not speak.

Leading him to the shade of the porch she brought forward his favorite chair. He sank into it as if overcome with exhaustion, but attempted to smile his thanks.

"What is it? Are you ill? Let me call a doctor?"

"No, no, dear, I'm not sick. It's not that. I'm—I'm upset a bit, that's all. I'll be all right in a little while. Only it was rather unexpected." He turned his face away as though to hide something from her.

"What is it? Can't you tell me? What is the matter?" Barbara had never seen the Seer so hopeless.

"They have let me out "

She did not understand. "Let you out?"

He bowed his head slowly. "Yes; the Company, you know. They have appointed Mr. Holmes chief engineer in my place."

She cried out in indignant dismay. "But how could they? It is your work—all your work! You have given years to bring it before the world. They never would have known of The King's Basin at all but for you. How dare they? They have no right!"

The engineer smiled. "I was only an employe of Greenfield and the men who organized the Company, you know. In their eyes my relation to the work was the same as that of a Cocopah Indian laborer. Of course it was understood in a general way that I was to have some stock in the Company when it was organized, with the chief engineer's position at least, but there was nothing settled. Nothing could be settled until the actual completion of the survey, you know. I never dreamed of this. I can see now that it was planned from the first and that this is what Holmes came out here for. He is a great favorite of Greenfield's, and I suppose they wanted a man of their own kind to look after their interests. But it hurts, Barbara; it hurts."

For an hour he stayed with her and she helped him as such a woman always helps. But when she would have kept him for supper he said: "No, I must find Abe. I want to tell the boy and have it over. You can tell your father."

When Jefferson Worth learned from his indignant daughter of the Company's action he only said, in

175

his precise way: "I figured that would be their first move." There was no feeling in his voice or manner. It was the simple verification of conclusions already reached and considered.

"Father!" cried Barbara. "Do you mean that you expected the Company to put that man Holmes in the Seer's place?"

"What reason was there to expect anything else?"

"But you never said anything all the time the Seer was——" She could not continue. It was maddening to think that while she had been dreaming and planning with the Seer, her father had foreseen that their dreams would come to nought.

"If I had you would not have believed me." The words were merely a calm, emotionless statement of fact. "I told you that the Company would act only from a business standpoint."

Suddenly a new phase of the situation flashed upon Barbara. Controlling her emotions and searching her father's face she asked: "Daddy, tell me please: was it because you saw this that you refused to join the Company?"

Jefferson Worth considered; then with marked caution answered: "That was part of the reason."

"I think I begin to understand a little. I'm glad —glad that you would have nothing to do with those men. It would have killed me if you had had any part in this now."

Presently the banker asked: "Have you seen Abe Lee?"

"No, why? Do you think—have they discharged

him, too? He wouldn't stay anyway after their treatment of the Seer. I wouldn't want him to."

"They won't let him out if they can keep him. Holmes will need him," said Worth. Then he added: "You'd better tell Abe to stay."

Barbara gasped. "What do you mean?"

"Tell him to stay," repeated Worth slowly.

CHAPTER XI.

IN obedience to its master passion—Good Business—the race now began pouring its life into the barren wastes of The King's Basin Desert.

In the city by the sea at the end of the Southwestern and Continental there was a suite of offices with real gold letters on the ground-glass doors richly spelling "The King's Basin Land and Irrigation Company." Behind these doors there was real mahogany furniture, solid, substantial and rich; a high safe; many attractive maps; and a gentleman who—never having traveled west of Buffalo before—could answer with authority every conceivable question relating to the reclamation of the arid lands of the great West. When there were no more questions to ask he could still tell you many things of the wonderland of wealth that was being opened to the public by the Company, demonstrating thus beyond the possibility of a doubt how many times a dollar could be multiplied.

From this office went forth to the advertising departments of the magazines and papers, skillfully prepared copy, which in turn was followed by pamphlets, circulars and letters innumerable. In one room a company of clerks and book-keepers and

178

accountants pored over their tasks at desks and counters. In another a squad of stenographers filled the air with the sound of their type-writers. Through the doors of the different rooms passed an endless procession; men from the front with the marks of the desert sun on their faces—engineers, superintendents, bosses, messengers, agents—servants of the Company; laborers of every sort and nationality came in answer to the cry: "Men wanted!"; special salesmen from foundry, factory and shop drawn by prospective large sales of machinery, implements and supplies; land-hungry men from everywhere seeking information and opportunity for investment.

At Deep Well (which is no well at all) on the rim of the Basin, trainloads of supplies, implements, machinery, lumber and construction material, horses, mules and men were daily side-tracked and unloaded on the desert sands. Overland travelers gazed in startled wonder at the scene of stirring activity that burst so suddenly upon them in the midst of the barren land through which they had ridden for hours without sight of a human habitation or sign of man. The great mountain of goods, piled on the dun plain; the bands of horses and mules; the camp-fires; the blankets spread on the bare ground; the men moving here and there in seemingly hopeless confusion; all looked so ridiculously out of place and so pitifully helpless.

Every hour companies of men with teams and vehicles set out from the camp to be swallowed up in the silent distance. Night and day the huge mountain of goods was attacked by the freighters who, with their big wagons drawn by six, eight, twelve, or more, mules, appeared mysteriously out of the weird landscape as if they were spirits materialized by some mighty unknown genii of the desert. Their heavy wagons loaded, their water barrels filled, they turned again to the unseen realm from which they had been summoned. The sound of the loud voices of the drivers, the creaking of the wagons, the jingle of harness, the shot-like reports of long whips died quickly away; while, to the vision, the outfits passed slowly—fading, dissolving in their great clouds of dust, into the land of mystery.

In Rubio City Jefferson Worth continued on his machine-like way at the Pioneer Bank, apparently paying no heed to the movement that offered such opportunities for profitable investment. Barbara rarely spoke now of the work that had been so dear to her, nor did she ever ride to the foot of the hill on the Mesa to look over the Desert. The Seer was in the northern railroad work again, but Abe Lee, with Tex and Pat and Pablo Garcia, had gone with the beginning of the stream of life that was pouring into the new country.

True to the far-reaching plans of the Company, at the largest and most central of the supply camps, located in the very heart of The King's Basin, the townsite of Kingston was laid out, and even in the days when every drop of water was hauled from three to ten miles town lots were offered for sale and sold to eager speculators.

A year from the beginning of the work at the intake at the river, water was turned into the canals.

With the coming of the water, Kingston changed, almost between suns, from a rude supply camp to an established town with post-office, stores, hotel, blacksmith shop, livery stables, all in buildings more or less substantial. Most substantial of all was the building owned and occupied by the offices of the Company.

With the coming of the water also, the stream of human life that flowed into the Basin was swollen by hundreds of settlers driven by the master passion —Good Business—to toil and traffic, to build the city, to subdue and cultivate the land and thus to realize the Seer's dream, while the engineer himself was banished from the work to which he had given his life. Every sunrise saw new tent-houses springing up on the claims of the settlers around the Company town and new buildings beginning in the center of it all—Kingston. Every sunset saw miles of new ditches ready to receive the water from the canal and acres of new land cleared and graded for irrigation.

Thus it was that afternoon when, from his office window, Mr. Burk, the General Manager of The King's Basin Land and Irrigation Company, watched a freighter with a twelve-mule load of goods stop his team directly across the street in front of the largest and most important general store in the Basin.

Deck Jordan, the merchant, came out and the Manager easily heard the driver's loud voice: "Jim'll be along in 'bout another hour, I reckon. We aim to get the rest in two more trips."

"Six twelve-mule loads in that shipment," thought

the Company's manager; "and that fellow set up business with a two-horse load of stuff!"

An empty wagon was driven up to the store and the General Manager recognized in the driver one of the Company's men from a grading camp six miles away; while another wagon—a Company wagon also —nearly filled with supplies moved away toward the open desert.

Deck's business was assuming quite respectable proportions thought Mr. Burk. And Deck's business was mostly with employes of the Company. Taking a cigar from a box on his desk, Mr. Burk scratched a match on the heel of his shoe and, leaning back in his office chair, continued thinking. The Manager of The King's Basin Land and Irrigation Company was paid to think. The Company hired Mr. Burk's peculiar talent even as they hired the physical strength of their laborers or the professional skill of their engineers.

As he meditated, the Manager still watched from the window the activities of the street. Soon from the open desert, beyond the last new building down the street, he saw a horseman approaching. At an easy swinging lope the rider came straight toward the Company's headquarters and, as he drew near, the Manager recognized the chief engineer. Greeting the man at the open window as he passed, Willard Holmes dismounted at the entrance of the building and, going first to the water tank, soon appeared in the doorway of the Manager's room. The engineer's clothes from boots to Stetson were covered with dust and his face was deeply bronzed by the months in the open air.

Turning from the window Mr. Burk held out the box of cigars.

"No thanks," said the Chief with a smile. "I'm hot as a lime kiln now. Wait until after supper."

Throwing his hat and gloves on the floor, he dropped into a chair with a sigh of relief at the grateful coolness of the room after hours of riding in the dazzling light of the desert sun.

The other, returning the box to its place, tipped back in his chair and elevated his well-dressed feet to his desk and, with his cigar in one corner of his mouth and his head cocked suggestively to one side, looked his companion over with a critical smile. "I say, Holmes, how would you like to be in little old New York this evening?"

At the question and the manner of the speaker the engineer held up his hands with a motion of protest as he commanded, in tragic voice: "Get thee behind me, Satan!" Then, at the Manager's laugh, he added seriously: "New York is all right, Burk, but I guess I can manage to stick it out here a while longer."

Burk looked at the engineer with the same thoughtful expression that had marked his face when he watched the wagon-load of supplies before the store across the street. "I have noticed that you show symptoms of slowly developing an interest in your job," he murmured. "You were at the river yesterday."

"No; I was at Number Five Heading. Abe Lee will be in from the intake this afternoon. I was there day before yesterday."

"How is the little old Colorado behaving herself?"

"All right so far. Our work is all a guess though. There is not a scrap of data to go on, you know." There was a hint of anxiety in the chief engineer's answer.

"I suppose you find the talkative Abe cheerfully optimistic about the future of our structures as usual?"

Holmes did not smile at the jesting tone of the Manager. "Lee is certainly doing all he can to make things safe. He is a fiend for thoroughness, and between you and me, Burk, the Company *ought* to spend more money on that intake at least. A few more thousands would make it what it should be."

The man who was paid to think held out a hand protestingly. "My dear boy, how many times have we gone over that? The Company will spend just what they must spend to get this scheme going and not a cent more. Later, when the business justifies, they will improve the system. Don't get yourself sidetracked by the notion that this whole project is for the benefit of the dear people and that the Company is made up of benevolent old gentlemen, who have nothing to do with their wealth but promote philanthropic enterprises. You should know your Uncle Jim better. Dividends, my boy, dividends; that's what we're all here for, and you can't afford to forget it. By the way, did you have any dinner to-day?"

"I struck Camp Seven on the Alamitos at noon."

"Hum-m. Sour bread, sow-belly, frijoles? Or was it canned corn? I say, old man, do you remember some of the places where we used to dine at home —flowers and music, and table linen, and real dishes, and waiters with real food, and women—God bless 'em!—real women? What would you give to-night, Holmes, for something to eat that had never been preserved, embalmed, cured, dried or tinned? It's not a dream of fairyland, my boy; there are such places in the world and there are such things to eat. Come, what do you say? Where shall we dine to-night and what will you have?"

"You fiend!" growled Holmes. "You know I'd sell my soul this minute for one good red apple."

Lowering his feet to the floor and rising, the Manager of The King's Basin Land and Irrigation Company crossed the room stealthily and carefully closed the door. Then taking a bunch of keys from his pocket, with an air of great secrecy he unlocked a drawer in his desk, pulled it open and took out—*an apple.*

The Company's chief engineer fell on the Manager with an exclamation of amazement and delight.

"Really," said Burk as he watched the fruit disappear, "your child-like pleasure almost justifies my crime. I even feel repaid for my self-denial. There were only three in the basket."

"How did you do it?" asked Holmes between bites, gazing at the apple in his hand as though to devour the treat with his eyes also, thereby doubling the pleasure.

"It was one of our dearly beloved prospective settlers," the thoughtful Manager explained with an air of conscious merit. "He came in from somewhere yesterday to spy out the land and, being a prudent and thrifty farmer, he possesses, or is possessed by, a prudent and thrifty wife. Said wife fitted out said farmer for his journey into this far country with a market basket of provisions. Home-made provisions, Willard, my son; *home made!* A whole basket full! He had one feed left and was finishing it out there on the sidewalk when I returned from what we of this benighted land call dinner. How could I help looking. I watched him devour the leg of a chicken. I watched him eat real bread with jelly on it. Then I caught sight of three apples—*three!* Holmes, such wealth is criminal. I considered—I became an anarchist. He was a big husky and I dared not assault him, so I talked—Lord forgive me!—how I talked. I offered confidential advice, I conjured up visions of wealth untold. I laid him under a spell and gently led him and his basket into the office even as he finished the pie. I showed him maps; I gave him a cigar; I urged him to leave his basket and satchel here in my private office for safe-keeping while he looked around. Gladly he accepted my invitation. His confidence was pathetic. How could the poor, trusting farmer know that I was ready, if necessary, to murder him for his fortune? When he had gone I locked the door and I—I—I only took two, Holmes; I dared not take them all, for he was big and rough, as I say. But I could not believe that a man with such wealth could miss a part of it."

"But you said you ate two," said the engineer severely, taking another long, lingering bite.

"I did," returned the Manager, with awful solemnity. "When that trusting but husky farmer returned later for his possessions he thanked me many times for my kindness while I trembled with the consciousness of my guilt, assuring him that it was no trouble at all—no trouble at all. And then—just as I felt sure that he was going and was beginning to breathe easier—he stopped and fumbled around in his basket. My heart stood still. 'Hannah put some fine apples in my dinner,' he muttered. 'I thought maybe you might like some. Reckon I must a-et 'em after all. I thought there was—no, by jocks! here she is.' Holmes, as I live he handed me that other apple. It was positively uncanny. I was speechless. Not until he was gone did I realize that it was prophetic. In like manner shall the settlers, the farmers, save this land and us from destruction."

"It's Good Business," returned Holmes. "It exactly illustrates your methods of dealing with the confiding public."

"Humph!" grunted the other. "I observe that you do not hesitate to enjoy the fruits of my financiering."

A knock at the door prevented the engineer's reply.

"Come in!" called Burk.

The door opened and Abe Lee stood on the threshold. The two men greeted the surveyor cordially but with that subtle touch in their voices that hinted at consciousness of superior position and authority.

Abe addressed himself directly to his Chief, saying: "We finished at the intake last night, sir, and moved to Dry River Heading this morning as you directed."

"You left everything at the river in good shape, of course?"

The surveyor did not answer. The tobacco and paper that, in his long fingers, were assuming the form of a cigarette seemed to demand his undivided attention. Burk was thoughtfully watching the two men. At the critical moment he handed Abe a match. From the cloud of smoke Abe spoke again. "The outfit will be ready to begin work at the Heading to-morrow morning."

Before Holmes could speak the Manager said: "You evidently still think, Lee, that the work at the river is not satisfactory. Are you still predicting that our intake will go out with the next high water?"

"I don't know whether the next high water will do it or not. The Rio Colorado alone won't hurt us, but when the Gila and the Little Colorado go on the war-path and come down on top of a high Colorado flood you'll catch hell. It may be this season; it may be next. It depends on the snowfall in the upper countries and the weather in the spring, but it *has* come and it will come again."

"How do you know? There have been no records kept and no surveys. We have no data."

"There's data enough. The Colorado leaves her own record. I know the country; I know what the river has done and I know what the Indians have told me." ·

At the surveyor's words his Chief stirred impatiently and the Manager answered: "But we can't spend twenty or thirty thousand dollars on a mere guess at what *may* happen, Lee. When the country is fairly well settled and business justifies, we will put in a new intake. In the meantime those structures will have to do. The K. B. L. and I. is not in business for glory, you know."

Abe spoke softly from a cloud of smoke. "And are you explaining this situation to the people who are coming here by the hundreds to settle? Do they understand the chances they are taking when they buy water rights and go ahead to develop their ranches?"

"Certainly not. If we talked risks no one would come in. The Company must protect its interests."

"Who protects the settlers' interests?"

The Manager stiffened. "I don't recognize your right to criticise the Company's policy, Lee. Mr. Holmes is our chief engineer and he assures me that our structures are as good as they can be made with the money at our disposal. We can only carry out. the policies of the Company and we are responsible to them for the money we spend. You have no responsibility in the matter whatever."

"Oh, hell, Burk," drawled Abe, though his eyes contradicted flatly his soft tone. "There's no occasion for you to climb so high up that ladder. You've been a corporation mouthpiece so long you have no more soul than the Company." He turned to his

189

Chief. "I left Andy in charge at camp. He understands that I will not be back. I dropped my resignation in your box in the office as I came in. Adios."

Leaving the office, Abe walked slowly down the street through the heart of the Company's little town. On every hand he saw the work that was being wrought in the Desert. There were business blocks and houses in every stage of building from the new-laid foundation to the moving-in of the tenants. The air rang with sound of hammer and saw. Teams and wagons from the ranches lined the street. The very faces of the people he met glowed with enthusiasm, while determination and purpose were expressed in their very movements as they hurried by.

A mile west of town the surveyor stopped on the bridge that spanned the main canal. He paused to look around. He saw the country already dotted with the white tent-houses of the settlers, and even as he looked three new wagons, loaded with supplies and implements, passed, bound for the claims of the owners. Under his feet the water from the distant river ran strongly. To the west was a grading camp on the line of a Company ditch; to the south was another. Far to the north and east, along the rim of the Basin, he knew the railroad was bringing other pioneers by the hundreds. He drew a deep breath and, taking off his sombrero, drank in the scene. How he loved it all! It was the Seer's dream, but the Seer could have no part in it. It was Barbara's Desert, but Barbara was shut out—exiled. It was his work, but he was powerless to do it. The Seer

190

had told him to stay for his work's sake. He smiled grimly, remembering the Manager's words. Barbara had told him to stay, but the girl knew nothing of conditions—how could she know? Jefferson Worth had told him to stay. Why? Barbara, in her letters, never spoke of the work. The Seer seldom wrote; Jefferson Worth, never. Every month the situation had grown more unbearable. Burk might insist that he had no responsibility and Holmes might argue that they could only do their best with what funds the Company would supply. Abe was not of their school. Well, he was out of it now for good. He was not the kind of a man the Company wanted.

Returning to town he had supper at the little shack restaurant and, going to the tent house owned by himself and two brother-surveyors that they might have a place to sleep when in town, he gathered his few possessions together in readiness for departure in the morning.

When the brief task was finished and he had written a note to his two friends, who were away, he went out again on the main street, because there was nothing else to do. It was evening now and the usual crowd was gathered in front of the post-office to watch the arrival of the stage, the one event of never-failing interest to these hardy pioneers. In the throng there were teamsters, laborers, ranchers, mechanics, real-estate agents, speculators, surveyors—gathered from camp and field and town. Some were expecting letters from the home folks in the world outside; a few were looking for friends among the passengers.

191

Many were there, as was Abe, because it was the point of interest. All were roughly clad, marked by the semi-tropical desert wind and sun.

It was among such men as these that Abe Lee's life had been spent. Such scenes as these were home scenes to him. In a peculiar way, through the Seer and Barbara, the work that these men were doing was dear to him. He felt that he was being cast out of his own place. As he passed through the throng Abe heard always the same topic of conversation: the work—the work—the work. News to these men meant more miles of canal finished, new ditches dug, more land leveled and graded, new settlers located. The surveyor thought of the future of these people, given wholly into the hands of the Company; of the men in the East, who knew nothing of their hardships but who would force them to pay royal tribute out of the fruits of their toil; of how, even then, they were increasing the value of the Company property.

"Here she comes!" cried someone, and all eyes were turned to see the stage swinging down the street. Abe drew back a little—to the thin edge of the crowd; he was expecting neither letters nor friends. The six broncos were brought to a stand in the midst of the crowd, the mail bag was tossed to the post-master and the passengers began climbing down from their seats.

As the last man rose from his place he stood for a moment in a stooped position, gripping with each hand one of the standards that supported the canvas top of the vehicle. Looking out thus over the crowd he seemed to be gathering data for an estimate of the population before he felt cautiously with his foot for the step.

Abe Lee started forward with an exclamation.

It was Jefferson Worth!

CHAPTER XII.

SIGNS OF CONFLICT.

NOT a line of Jefferson Worth's countenance changed as the tall surveyor, pushing his way through the crowd about the new arrivals, greeted him. But Abe Lee felt the man from behind his gray mask reaching out to grasp his innermost thoughts and emotions.

"Where is the hotel?"

Abe explained that the rough board shelter that bore that name was full to the door. People were even sleeping on the floor. "But there is room in our tent, Mr. Worth," he finished and led the way out of the crowd.

To the surveyor's eager questions the banker answered that Barbara was visiting friends in the Coast city.

When they had reached the tent and Abe had found and lighted a lantern, Mr. Worth said—and his manner was as though he were continuing a conversation that had been interrupted only for a moment—"well, I see you stayed."

At his words the surveyor, who was filling a tin wash-basin with fresh water that his guest might wash away the dust of his journey, felt the hot blood in his cheeks. Before answering he pulled an old cracker-box from under a cot in one corner of the canvas room and, rummaging therein, brought to light a clean towel. When he had placed this evidence of civilization beside the basin on the box that did duty as a wash-stand, he answered: "I quit the Company this afternoon."

"Why?"

"Because I won't do the kind of work the Company wants." The surveyor spoke hotly now. The man busy with the basin of water made no comment, and Abe continued: "Mr. Worth, they are putting in the cheapest possible kind of wooden structures all through the system, even at points where the safety of the whole project depends on the control of the water. The intake itself is nothing but the flimsiest sort of a makeshift. One good flood, such as we have every few years, and there wouldn't be a damned stick of it left in twelve hours. You remember what the grade is from the river at the point of the intake this way into the Basin and you know how water cuts this soil. If that gate goes out the whole river will come through; and these settlers, who are tumbling over each other to put into this country every cent they have in the world, will lose everything."

"The Company takes its chances with the settlers, doesn't it?"

"The Company takes mighty small chances compared to the risk the settlers are carrying. As a matter of fact, Mr. Worth, it is the people who are building this system; not the Company at all. To prove up on these desert claims the government compels them to have the water. They can't use the

water without paying the Company for the right.
After they have bought the water rights then they
must pay for every acre-foot they use. All Greenfield and his bunch did was to put up enough to start
the thing going and the people are doing the rest.
The Company knows the risk and stakes a com-
partively small amount of capital. The settlers
know nothing of the real conditions and stake everything they have in the world. If the Company would
tell the people the situation it would be square, but
you know what would happen if they did that. No
one would come in. As it is, the Company, by risking the smallest amount possible, leads the people to
risk everything they have and yet the Greenfield crowd
stands to win big on the whole stake."

Mr. Worth was drying his slim fingers with careful
precision. "I figured that was the way it would be
done. That's the way all these big enterprises are
launched. The first work is always done on a promoter's estimate. Later, when the business justifies,
the system will be strengthened and improved."

"Which means," retorted the surveyor, "that when
the Company has taken enough money from the settlers, whom they have induced to stake everything
they have on the gamble by letting them think it is
a sure thing, they will use *a part of it* to give the
people what they *think* they are getting now."

The banker laid the towel carefully aside and dis-
posed of the water in the wash-basin by the primitive
method of throwing it from the tent door. Then he
spoke again: "The people themselves could never
start a work like this, and if there wasn't a chance

to make a big thing Capital wouldn't. It's the size
of the profit compared with the amount invested that
draws Capital into this kind of a thing. If the Company had to take all the chance in this project they
would simply stay out and the work would never be
done. This feature of unequal risk is the very thing,
and the only thing, that could attract the money to
start this proposition going; and that's what people
like you and the Seer and Barbara can't see. Holmes
and Burk can't help themselves. It's Greenfield and
the Company, and they are just as honest as other
men. They are simply promoting this scheme in the
only way possible to start it and the people will share
the results."

"Holmes and Burk are all right, except that
they're owned body and soul by the Company," said
Abe quickly. "But Greenfield and the men who
engineered this thing look to me like a bunch of
green-goods men who live on the confidence of the
people."

"The people will gain their farms just the same,"
returned the financier. "They wouldn't have anything without the Company."

The surveyor shrugged his shoulders. "Well, you
may be right, Mr. Worth; but I've had all I can
stand of it."

Again Jefferson Worth looked full into the
younger man's eyes and Abe felt that Something
behind the mask reaching out to seize the thoughts
and motives that lay back of his words: "What are
you going to do?"

"I don't know. Punch steers or get a job in a

mine somewhere, I reckon. I'm going somewhere out of this. I've had enough of promoter's estimates."

"Suppose you stay and work for me."

Abe Lee sprang to his feet. "Work for you? Here? I thought you had refused to go into this deal?"

"I declined to join Greenfield's Company," said the banker exactly.

"Do you mean, Mr. Worth, that you are going to operate in the Basin independently, knowing the Company's strength and the whole situation as you do?"

"I have decided to take a chance with the rest," was the unemotional answer. "I sold out of the bank and cleaned up everything in Rubio City last week."

"But what are you going into here?"

"I can use you if you want to stay," came the cautious answer.

"Stay? Of course I'll stay!"

It was characteristic of these men that nothing was said of salary on either side. Extinguishing the lantern, Abe led the way out into the night. The darkness was intense and unrelieved save by the thin broken line of twinkling lights from the windows of the buildings, which gave them the direction of the main street, and the few dull glowing tent houses, whose tenants were at home. Overhead the desert stars shone with a brilliance that put to shame the feeble efforts of the earth-men, while about the little pioneer town the desert night drew close with its circling wall of mystery.

Did Jefferson Worth think, as he stumbled along by the surveyor's side, of that other night in The Hollow of God's Hand, when he had faced, alone, the spirit of the land?

"This town needs an electric lighting system," he said in his colorless voice.

When Jefferson Worth had finished supper in the shack restaurant he proposed cautiously that they look around a little. The street was lined with teams and saddle horses, their forms shadowy and indistinct in the dark places of vacant lots or where buildings were under construction, but standing forth with startling clearness where the light from a store streamed forth. The sidewalk was filled with men from the ranches and grading camps, who had come to town after sunset for their mail or supplies so that no hour of the day should be lost to the work that had called them into the desert; and these ever-shifting figures passed to and fro through the bands of light and darkness, gathered in groups in front of the stores and dissolved again, to form other groups or to lose themselves in the general throng. Every moment a wagon-load of men, a party of horsemen, or a single rider would appear suddenly and mysteriously out of the night, while others, leaving the throng to depart in like manner, would be swallowed up as mysteriously by the blackness. In the center of the picture and the very heart of the activity was the general store opposite the office of The King's Basin Land and Irrigation Company.

Deck Jordan had opened his store in the days when Kingston was still a supply camp. No one knew much about Deck or how he had guessed that the camp would become the chief town in the new country. He was a pleasing, capable, but close-mouthed man, who knew what to buy, paid his bills promptly and—with one exception—conducted his business on a cash basis.

The exception to the cash rule was in favor of the Company's employes. It was on Deck's initiative that an arrangement was made with Mr. Burk by which the Company men received credit at the store, the amount of their bills being deducted from their wages each month by the Company paymaster. It was this plan that, by giving Deck practically all of the trade from the hundreds of Company employes, had increased his business so rapidly. To the thoughtful Manager, also, the plan seemed good. He foresaw how, with the Company thus controlling the bulk of the merchant's business, he could, when the proper time came, "persuade" Deck to enter into a still "closer" arrangement—thus carrying out the Good Business policy of the Company. That very afternoon Mr. Burk had decided the time had come and had so written Mr. Greenfield.

Leisurely Jefferson Worth and his companion worked their way through the crowd and into the store where Deck and his helpers were toiling to supply the various needs of a small army of customers. From the open doors and from the big implement shed in the rear of the building, a steady stream of provisions, clothing, dry goods, hardware, blankets, harness and tools flowed forth.

In the midst of the confusion Deck himself was

holding an animated conversation with a would-be purchaser. "I'd be mighty glad to accommodate you, Sam, if I could, but you know we're running this store on a cash basis and I can't break my rules. If I begin with you I'll have to do it for everybody and I can't."

"You don't make these Company men pay cash. Anybody—Injuns, greasers or anything else—gets what he wants and no questions asked if he works for the Company."

"But that's different, you see," explained Deck. "We have an arrangement with the Company by which they hold out from each man's pay the amount of my bills against him."

"I understand that, but you'll find out that it's the rancher's trade that'll keep you going. We'll be here long after these ditchers an' mule skinners have left the country and we'll have money to spend. You'll find, too, that when things *do* begin to come our way we'll stand by the store that'll stand by us now when we've got everything goin' out an' nothin' comin' in."

Deck, over the shoulder of the rancher, saw Jefferson Worth and the surveyor, who with several others had drawn near, attracted by the loud tones of the farmer. Abe thought that he caught a look of recognition as Deck's eyes fell on his companion but the banker gave no sign.

The merchant, answering his customer, said: "I know you are right about that part of it, Sam, and I'd like to back every rancher in this Basin if I could. But I can't."

"Why not? Ain't you runnin' this store?"

Before Deck could reply, to Abe's astonishment the quiet voice of Jefferson Worth broke in. "You are improving a ranch of your own near here?"

The settler turned sharply. "You bet I am, Mister; leastwise, I'm tryin' to, and if workin' from sun-up 'til dark an' livin' on nothin' 'til I can make a crop will pull me through I'll make it."

"I suppose the heaviest expense is all in getting started?" asked Mr. Worth, as if seeking to verify an observation.

"It sure is," replied the pioneer. "There's the outfit you've got to have—work-stock an' tools; you've got to build your ditches and grade your land; and you've got to buy water rights and pay for your water; and you've got to make your payments to the government. Then there's feed for your work-stock and yourself, an' there ain't nothin' to bring in a cent 'til you can make a crop. The farmers that are comin' into this country ain't got a great big pile of ready money stacked away, Mister, an' they're mighty apt to run a little short the first year. When our home merchants, who expect to make their money off from us, won't even trust us for a few dollars' worth of provisions 'til we can get a start, I'm damned if it ain't tough."

"But everyone is a stranger in this new country," said Mr. Worth. "How can a merchant know whether a man will pay or not? I suppose there are ranchers coming in here who would beat a bill if they could. The merchants have to pay for their goods or close up."

"I reckon that's all so," returned the other. "And of course everybody knows that there never was such a thing as dishonest store-keepers. Merchants don't never beat anybody with short weight and all that?"

This raised a laugh in which Deck joined as heartily as anyone. Even the banker smiled coldly as he asked: "What did you say your name was?"

"Didn't say; but it's Sam Warren."

"Where is your ranch?"

"Six miles north on the Number One main."

"Well, Mr. Warren, I've been considering this proposition and I've got it figured out like this. We all want to make what we can in this new country; that's what we came in for. This store can't get along without the ranchers' support and you ranchers can't get along without the store. We've all got to pull together and help each other. I don't believe that many of the men who come into this Desert to actually settle on and improve the land are the kind of men who beat their bills. I figured to run on a cash basis only until things got started and sort of settled down, you see. I know that you people need credit until you get on your feet. From now on you come here—for whatever you actually need, you understand—and we'll carry you for any reasonable amount until you get something coming in. All we ask in return is that you ranchers do as you say and stand by us when you do get on top."

At Jefferson Worth's simple and quietly spoken words a hush fell over the group of men. Abe Lee looked at his companion in amazement. Sam Warren turned from the stranger to the store-keeper and back to the stranger. The man behind the counter was smiling broadly as if enjoying the situation.

When no one could find a word with which to break the silence, Deck Jordan said: "Gentlemen, this is Mr. Jefferson Worth, the owner of this store. George!" he called to a passing clerk, "give Sam whatever he wants as soon as you can get around to it, and charge it."

At this such a yell went up from the bystanders that a crowd from the outside rushed in, and as the word passed and others voiced their approval as loudly, the Manager of The King's Basin Land and Irrigation Company in his rooms across the street thought that another fight was on.

The Manager was not far wrong in his conclusion.

CHAPTER XIII.

BARBARA'S CALL TO HER FRIENDS.

THAT night, long after Kingston was still and the Manager of The King's Basin Land and Irrigation Company was fast asleep, Jefferson Worth and Abe Lee talked in the little tent that, from the lantern within, glowed in the darkness, seemingly the one spot of light under the desert stars.

The next morning the surveyor left town on the stage, but not as he had planned. Abe knew now where he was going and what he was going to do. He was bound for the city by the sea and he carried in his pocket several letters of introduction, written by his employer and addressed to different firms engaged in manufacturing and selling things electrical. And more than this, Abe would see Barbara.

Jefferson Worth did not breakfast with Abe that morning nor did he see him off on the stage, but a few minutes after the surveyor had left town his employer passed down the street in the direction of the store.

As Mr. Worth drew near his place of business he saw, posed just without the door, one whom the most casual of observing strangers would have supposed instantly to be the proprietor of the store, the owner of the building—if not, indeed, the proprietor and owner of all Kingston and many miles of country round about.

The portly figure, clad in a business suit of gray, with a vast, full-rounded expanse of white vest, expressed in every curve opulent wealth and lordly generosity. The clean-shaven face, fat and florid, beamed upon the world from above the clerical severity of a black tie with truly paternal benevolence; while the massive head was not in reality crowned but was covered by a hat such as commanding generals always wear in pictures. The pose of the figure, the lift of the countenance, the kingly mien of eye and brow made it impossible to mistake his majesty. In comparison with this august personage, the figure and air of Jefferson Worth were pitifully inadequate.

The great one welcomed the financier at the latter's own door with an air of royal hospitality. Extending his hand as if he stepped down only one step from his throne and speaking in a tone that was meant to confer marked distinction upon the humble recipient of his favor, he said: "Mr. Worth, I am delighted, more delighted than I can express, to welcome you to our city. It is a great day for this country—a great day!" He wrung the financier's timid hand with two hundred and fifty pounds of emotional energy. "Mr. Greenfield and I, with our friends and associates in the East, and Mr. Burk and Holmes here in the field, are doing what we can for these people, but there is a great work here yet for men like you—men of some means and financial ability, who will get behind the smaller business interests and build them up on a solid foundation. My heart rejoiced for the country, sir, when I heard this morning that you had purchased this establishment. Deck is a good honest fellow, you know, but——" An expansive smile of confidential understanding finished this sentence, and the words—"My name is Blanton, Mr. Worth—Horace P. Blanton"— seemed to settle at once any doubt as to the position and authority of the speaker.

Jefferson Worth did not explain that he had owned the store from the beginning and that Deck Jordan was no more than his very capable agent. Indeed Mr. Worth said nothing at al   He even appeared to shrink with becoming modesty though there was the faintest hint of a twinkle in the corners of his eyes—a hint so faint that Horace P. Blanton, from his great height, overlooked it.

The big man, in a lower tone of confidential familiarity, asked: "H ve you heard from Greenfield lately?"

"No."

"I wrote Jim some time ago that he would have to come out here himself. There are some conditions developing here that should have his personal attention, and I'll be blessed if I'll stand seeing him neglect them! I'm a western man myself, Worth; and you know we do things in this country."

"You are interested in The King's Basin Company?"

The answer was given in a tone of tolerant surprise that any one should think he would toy with a thing of such trifling importance. "Me? Oh no!—that is, not directly you understand. But I am deeply interested in the development of the country. Let me

207

show you a little of what we are doing here. It's amazing how the world outside fails utterly to grasp the magnitude of the enterprise. Even the news papers are criminally negligent. Quite recently I had occasion to tell my good friend, the editor of the Times, that if he didn't give us something like a fair showing I would see to it personally that the bulk of our business went to San Felipe. It's a burning shame the way they have persistentl ignored us."

Mr. Worth made an ineffectual attempt to escape but the white vest blocked his move. Pointing to a half-finished building on the nearest corner, the great one explained in the tone of a personal conductor: "That is our new hotel—one of the finest buildings in the southwest. The young man who will run it for us is personally superintending the construction. Bright boy, too. You must let me introduce you to him."

Jefferson Worth, gazing at the modest building under construction, murmured: "You are interested, you say?"

"Oh no; that is—only in a way, you understand. I have a hand in most of these enterprises."

"This town needs a good hotel," said Mr. Worth, mildly.

"That building farther down—the one where the foundation is just completed—is our Opera House. It is being erected by one of the big Coast syndicates and will be a magnificent hall of amusement and entertainment as well as a place for public gatherings of all kinds. I have been in close personal touch with the men in charge of the enterprise and they understand that we will tolerate nothing that is not first class."

"The people need such a building," was the quiet comment.

"In the block opposite our bank will be located. They will be working on the vault in another two weeks. While the building is well under way, as you see, the organization of the institution is not yet made public. Only a few of us on the inside, you understand, know who is back of the enterprise."

"I see," said Jefferson Worth. "A bank is a good thing for the country."

Pointing up the street, the great one in the white vest continued: "There you see the office of our paper—The King's Basin Messenger. The machinery is being installed now. I'm mighty proud of the young man who is starting that work. He will be a credit to us I promise you. Directly opposite is The King's Basin Land and Irrigation Company building with the offices of the Company. You must let me introduce you to the manager, Mr. Burk, and to Holmes, the engineer. Come, we will go over there now." He started forward with perspiring energy, but Jefferson Worth, seizing the opportunity, gained the doorway of the store and vanished.

For two weeks Mr. Worth seemed to devote his time wholly to his store. Though Deck Jordan still continued the active management, it was generally understood that Mr. Worth, having but recently purchased the establishment, retained Deck until, as it was generally expressed, he got the run of the business. At an old desk in a cubby-hole of an office roughly partitioned off in one corner of the room, the financier spent nearly every hour of the day apparently poring over his accounts.

Here the Manager from across the street found him when he called to explain to Mr. Worth the advantage of an alliance between the store and the Company. Mr. Burk did not stay long, but upon his return to his office wrote a long, confidential letter to his superiors. The thoughtful Manager's letters to his superiors were always confidential.

Willard Holmes also called to pay his respects; to inquire whether Miss Worth was well; and—as Holmes put it to himself when he was again safely outside the building—to turn himself inside out for the critical inspection of the man who hid behind that gray mask.

So far as the Manager of The King's Basin Land and Irrigation Company observed, Jefferson Worth, beside buying the store, made only one small investment. He purchased from the Company a small tract of land just inside the limits of the townsite. Then almost before Mr. Burk knew that it was before them, the town council passed an ordinance granting permission to the Worth Electric Company to place their poles and to stretch wires on the streets of the town, and the first issue of The King's Basin Messenger announced with a great flourish of trumpets that Kingston was to have lights.

The article explained that Mr. Abe Lee, the well known engineer, formerly with the K. B. L. and I. Company, would have charge of the construction work and would push it with his usual energy. For some time Mr. Lee had been in the city arranging for material, which would be shipped immediately. Mr. Worth had stated to the Messenger that Mr. Lee would return to Kingston in a day or two and would break ground for the power plant at once. The Messenger also gave an interesting history of Jefferson Worth's successful career from farm-boy to financier with an appreciation of his character and congratulated the citizens that a man of such financial strength and genius had come to invest the fruit of his toil in the new country.

Mr. Burk read the Messenger's article thoughtfully. Then Mr. Burk wrote another confidential letter to his superiors.

Over this enterprise of Jefferson Worth, as set forth in the Messenger, the citizens were enthusiastic. Horace P. Blanton was more than enthusiastic. Meeting Mr. Burk as the latter was returning to his office after dinner he blocked the Manager's way with his white vest and, wiping the sweat of honest endeavor from his brow, delivered himself. "Well, sir; we landed it. Biggest thing that ever happened to Kingston. Double our population in three months. I told my friend Worth that they would have to come through with that franchise whether they wanted to or not, and by George! we landed it. There was nothing else to do."

The Manager thoughtfully flicked the ashes from his cigar. "And what is this that you have landed?"

"What! haven't you heard? Have you seen the Messenger?" He drew a paper from his pocket and placed a finger on the headlines: "Electric Lights for Kingston."

The Manager shifted his cigar to the corner of his mouth and, casting his head in the opposite direction, surveyed the excited Horace P. as an artist might view an interesting picture. "So you are interested in the Worth Electric Company?"

"Oh no; that is, not exactly, you know. My name will not appear in the company. But Jeff and I are very warm friends, you understand, and for the sake of Kingston I am bound to take an interest in his enterprise."

At this the thoughtful Mr. Burk became suddenly confidential. Tapping his companion impressively on the arm and speaking in a low tone of vast import, he said: "Blanton, be careful; be careful. Don't get into Worth's schemes too deeply. A man of your standing and influence, you know, can't afford to play into the hands of a four-flusher."

Then the Manager of The King's Basin Land and Irrigation Company slipped easily away before the other could reply.

Three minutes later the man in the big white vest overtook the Company's chief engineer in the doorway of the restaurant. "Good morning, Holmes; good morning." The simple greeting seemed to come from a great heart that was fairly staggering under a burden of other people's woes.

As the boy placed their dinners before them, Horace P. Blanton, shaking his massive head, murmured sadly: "It's a burning shame, Holmes; a burning shame."

"The coffee, you mean?" queried the engineer, digging up a spoonful of sediment from the bottom of his heavy cup and inspecting it critically. "It looks shameful, all right; and it may have been over-heated some time in past ages, but the temperature doesn't appear to be above normal to-day."

The big man did not smile; his burden was too heavy. "I mean," he explained, "the way these four-flushers come in here and attempt to work their graft right under our eyes. Did you hear about this man Worth getting that franchise out of the council? I did my level best, but what's the use. It's all as plain as day but you can't hammer an idea into the boneheads that run this town. I had a little talk with Burk over the matter this morning. He agrees with me perfectly. We've got to take hold of this thing, Mr. Holmes, or the town will go to the dogs. I wish Greenfield would come on."

The engineer agreed heartily that it might be well to take hold of something. But what? That was the rub—what? He gently intimated that if Horace P. Blanton could not find a way to avert the awful calamity that threatened the public, the public was in a bad way. Clearly it was up to Horace P. to save Kingston.

The dinner over the men separated quickly: the man in the white vest to carry the burden of Kingston's future on his fat shoulders, and the engineer to inspect the work at Dry River Heading.

The evening of the third day after Abe Lee's return to Kingston the surveyor and his employer were in Mr. Worth's office. The work of excavation

for the foundation of the power plant would begin
in the morning, and Mr. Worth had planned to leave
town the following morning for a week's business
trip to the city.

The two men were interrupted in their conversation by a loud familiar voice on the store side of the
board partition.

"Busy, be they? Well, fwhat the divil should they
be but busy? Do ye suppose I thought they was
a-playin' dominoes?"

Abe grinned at his employer. They both listened.

Deck Jordan's voice said: "But you better not
go in now, boys. They will be through in a little
while."

"Go in? Who the hell's talkin' av goin' in? Do
ye think, ye danged counter-hopper, that we've no
manners at all? For a sup o' wather I'd go over to
ye wid me two hands!"

And another softer voice drawled: "Run along
Deck. Me an' my pardner promises not to turn
violent or break into the sanctuary. We'll just camp
here peaceful 'til the meetin's over."

Abe chuckled. "I knew they would be along as
soon as they heard the news." He lifted his voice.
"Come in, boys."

Instantly Barbara's "uncles" appeared. "We axes
yer pardon, Sorr, for not comin' before to pay our
respects, but we only heard yestherday that ye was
in the counthry. Ye see, afther we finished at the
river we was transferred over on Number Three at
the tail end av nowhere an' knew nothin' at all 'til

someone brung into camp the paper that towld about yer doin's. An' how is our little girl?"

"Very well," said Mr. Worth. "She told me to be sure and remember her to you."

"I saw her the other day," said Abe. "She sent you both her love."

"Well, now, fwhat do ye think av that? Tex, ye danged owld sand rat, ut's proud av yersilf ye should be to be the uncle av sich a darlin'. An' tell us now, Sorr, fwhat's this I hear about yer buildin' a power plant for electric lights, or street cars, or somethin'? We thought that the lad here left the danged counthry for good, an' sarves thim danged yellow-legs that boss the Company right for not knowin' a man whin they see wan."

"We begin work in the morning. Abe is in charge."

"Hurroo!" exclaimed the delighted Irishman. "An' ut's men ye'll be wantin' av course; wan to handle the greasers, which is cake to me, an' wan to boss the mule skinners, which is pie for Tex. I'm thinkin' the Company will be short handed at Number Three in the mornin'."

"I have been holding these places open for you," Abe laughed. "If I could get hold of Pablo, now, I would be all right. Barbara said to be sure and get him too. He's still at Dry River Heading, I hear."

As the two were leaving Texas Joe said to Abe: "Are you plumb certain Pablo is at the Heading?"

"That's what one of the crew told me to-day."

"Well, then I reckon he'll be along pronto."

The next morning when Abe went to the site of the work the first man he saw was Barbara's friend, Pablo. The Mexican greeted the surveyor with a show of white teeth.

"Did you come to work?" asked Abe.

"Si, Senor. Senor Texas he come las' night with two horses. He say Senor Abe want you quick, Pablo. La Senorita say you come. So I am come pronto, like he say."

"Texas Joe went for you last night?" repeated Abe.

"Si, Senor. If you want me come—if La Senorita want me come—Senor Tex he go tell me come. I come. It is no much ride for vaqueros like Senor Tex and me."

"But you have your job with the Company?"

The Mexican shrugged his shoulders and his teeth showed. "Senor Worth and Senores Lee and Tex and Pat good company for Pablo. Beside, is there not La Senorita? She was good to me when I was sick with no one to help. Do not we all—Senores Lee and Tex and Pat, and Senor Worth and me— do not we all work for La Senorita in La Palma de la Mano de Dios? Is it not so? Beside I think sometime La Senorita come—then I would be near. In the Company there is no Senorita."

CHAPTER XIV.

MUCH CONFUSION AND HAPPY EXCITEMENT.

S the trying months of the semi-tropical summer approached, the great Desert, so awful
in its fierce desolation, so pregnant with the
life it was still so reluctant to yield, gathered all its
dreadful forces to withstand the inflowing streams
of human energy. In the fierce winds that rushed
through the mountain passes and swept across the
hot plains like a torrid furnace blast; in the blinding,
stinging, choking, smothering dust that moved in
golden clouds from rim to rim of the Basin; in the
blazing, scorching strength of the sun; in the hard,
hot sky, without shred or raveling of cloud; in the
creeping, silent, poison life of insect and reptile; in
the maddening dryness of the thirsty vegetation; in
the weird, beautiful falseness of the ever-changing
mirage, the spirit of the Desert issued its silent
challenge.

It was not the majestic challenge of the mountains
with their unscaled heights of peak and dome and
impassable barriers of rugged crag and sheer cliff.
It was not the glad challenge of the untamed wilderness with its myriad formed life of tree and plant
and glen and stream. It was not the noble challenge
of the wide-sweeping, pathless plains; nor the wild
challenge of the restless, storm-driven sea. It was

the silent, sinister, menacing threat of a desolation that had conquered by cruel waiting and that lay in wait still to conquer.

With grim determination, nervous energy, enduring strength and a dogged tenacity of purpose, the invading flood of humanity, irresistibly driven by that master passion, Good Business, matched its strength against that of the Desert in the season of its greatest power.

Steadily mile by mile, acre by acre, and at times almost foot by foot, the pioneers wrested their future farms and homes from the dreadful forces that had held them for ages. Steadily, with the inflowing stream of life from the world beyond the Basin's rim, the area of improved lands about Kingston extended and the work in the Company's town went on. By midsummer many acres of alfalfa, with Egyptian corn and other grains, showed broad fields of living green cut into the dull, dun plain of the Desert and laced with silver threads of water shining in the sun.

Save for occasional brief business trips to the city, Jefferson Worth did not leave Kingston. In the most trying of those grilling days of heat and dust, when a man's skin felt like cracking parchment and his eyes burned in their sockets and it seemed as though every particle of moisture in his body was sucked up by the dry, scorching air, Barbara's father gave no sign of discomfort. He accepted the most nerve-racking situation with the even-tempered calmness of one who had foreseen it and to whom it was but a trivial incident, inevitable to his far-reaching plans.

When others—their tempers tried to the breaking point—cursed with dry, high-pitched, querulous curses the heat, the land, the sun, the dust, the Company and their fellow-sufferers, Jefferson Worth's cool, even tones and unruffled spirit helped them to a needed self-control and gave them a new and stronger grip on things. And many a baffled, discouraged and well-nigh beaten settler, ready to give up, found in the man whose gray, mask-like face seemed so incapable of expression, fresh inspiration and new courage; while the store continued its policy of helping the worthy, hard-pressed ranchers with necessary material assistance.

And so it was that while James Greenfield and his fellow-capitalists of The King's Basin Land and Irrigation Company were taking their much needed vacations and seeking relaxation and rest from business cares at their seaside and mountain retreats, the desert pioneers were coming more and more to Jefferson Worth for advice and counsel, for strength and courage and help to go on with the work. By fall the financier's position in the life of the new country seemed to be securely won. Perhaps only Jefferson Worth himself, alone behind his gray mask, knew the real value of his apparent victory.

The Company's thoughtful Manager went out— as the pioneers had come to say of those who left the Basin—for over a month, and for the rest of the summer spent only a part of his time in Kingston. But the Company's chief engineer refused to leave even for a week. To a pressing invitation from Greenfield to join him on his vacation, Holmes answered that he could not get away. All through the June rise of the river, while the settlers, ignorant of the danger that threatened them through the Good Business policy of the Company, were risking everything that Capital might gain its greater profits, the engineer lived in his camp at the intake. Day and night, as he watched the swelling yellow torrent that threw its weight against his work, he remembered the words of the desert-bred surveyor: "When the Gila and the Little Colorado go on the warpath and come down on top of a high Colorado flood, you'll catch hell." It had come in the past, Abe had declared, and it would come again.

But the flood waters of the Gila and the Little Colorado did not come down on top of the larger river that year and the promoter's estimate work stood. When the danger was past and the engineer was free again to make Kingston his headquarters, his acquaintance with Jefferson Worth grew into something like friendship. It became, indeed, an established custom for Mr. Worth, Abe Lee and the chief engineer of the Company to sit at the same table in the shack restaurant and, during their meals of canned stuff, to talk over the work that held them from the comforts and pleasures of civilization.

But little work toward extending the Company system could be undertaken during the hot summer months. It was difficult for Holmes to hold even enough men to maintain that which was already in operation. But Jefferson Worth did not fare so badly. Abe Lee was steadfast, of course, while Texas, Pat and Pablo would, as the Irishman said, "have fried thimsilves on the coals av hell" before they would quit their job. Were there not letters every week from Barbara with messages to the surveyor and his three helpers? Pablo said truly that "there was no Senorita in the Company." So through Abe's leadership, Texas Joe's diplomacy, Pat's wisdom and Pablo's influence with his countrymen, the Worth enterprises did not suffer for lack of laborers but went steadily ahead.

In Kingston the different buildings for the power plant and lighting system were nearly completed and several cottages were under construction on lots owned by Jefferson Worth, while men and teams were busy excavating and hauling materials for a large ice plant. In Frontera, a little town that "just happened" to grow from a supply camp in the southern end of the Basin, a hotel and a bank building were being erected, while between the two communities poles for a telephone system were being placed.

Thus far very few women had come into the desert. When the torrid summer was past, the first crops on the new ranches harvested and more comfortable homes prepared, they would come with the children to join the men-folks. Until then the new country would continue a man's country—the poorest possible kind of a country, the men themselves declared.

Therefore when, late in September, The King's Basin Messenger, with an extraordinary blare of trumpets, announced the birth of a child and that the first-born of the new country was a boy, the news was received with the greatest excitement. In Kingston, in Frontera, at grading camps and ranches, as the word was passed, there were wild and joyous celebrations. Such a crowd of male visitors closed in on the humble tent home to beg for a look at the little pink stranger that the matter-of-fact pioneer parents were heard to express the wish that they themselves had never been born. Had the baby been forced to carry through life all the names that were suggested he would undoubtedly have echoed the parents' wish at an early age.

Then came the terrible word to Kingston, brought by Texas Joe, that the baby was ill. Tex, returning to town from a trip to Frontera, had turned a mile aside to bring the latest news of the baby. It was early evening and the light yet lingered in the sky back of No Man's Mountains, when the citizens, relaxing after the heat of the day and the evening meal, looked up to see him coming, riding like a mad man, his horse white with foam.

Jefferson Worth, with Abe and Holmes coming from the restaurant, had paused a moment in front of the store before separating when Texas leaped from his staggering mount. One thought flashed into the mind of each: "The intake! The river!" Holmes went white under his tan; Abe's jaws came together with a click; Jefferson Worth's slim fingers caressed his chin.

As the word passed quickly through the town, the crowd that followed Mr. Worth and Texas Joe into the store grew until it over-flowed the building and filled the street. Over all there was a solemn hush, save for low-spoken words of inquiry, or explanation, and of advice. What to do was the question. What could they do? There was no doctor nearer than Rubio City and men who pioneer in a desert land are not men experienced with sickness.

On a high shelf in one back corner of the store there was a small dust-covered stock of assorted patent medicines. Desperately they pulled the bottles down and studied the labels and directions, but only to their further confusion and doubt. At last, his pockets laden with everything that seemed to promise a possible relief, Texas Joe set out on a fresh horse, the first one handy, to be followed later by a spring wagon drawn by four fast broncos and carrying four women. The entire female population of Kingston had been mustered by Abe Lee, whom the ladies declared then and there to be the only man of sense in all The King's Basin.

For the first evening since his arrival Jefferson Worth left his office in the store to mingle with the restless crowds on the street that, in ever-changing knots and groups, discussed in fearful voice this public calamity. No one dreamed of retiring. No one had thoughts for sleep, nor indeed for anything save the little sufferer in the tent house ten miles out on the Desert. They smoked and talked and swore softly in hushed tones and waited the return of Texas Joe.

It was after midnight when he came again. Before he could dismount, the crowd of silent men hemmed him in. From the saddle the old plainsman looked down into their eager solemn faces and that slow smile broke over his sun-blackened features.

"Boys," he drawled, "I'm sure proud to bring you-all the unanimous verdict of the female relief expedition sent out by our illustrious fellow-citizen, Abe Lee. The kid's better and is headed straight for good health and six or eight square meals a day."

When the joyous chorus of yells that would have startled a coyote two miles away subsided, Tex dismounted and approached Jefferson Worth. "Mr. Worth, them women commanded me also to return to you with their compliments and gratitude the various and sundry bottles with which same my clothes is full. One of them angels of mercy, it seems, went to the scene of action loaded with a flask of castor oil."

Just before retiring that night Mr. Worth said to his superintendent: "Abe, I'm going out in the morning. You had better push the work on that largest cottage as fast as possible. I'll ship in an outfit of furniture and things as soon as I get to the city. Let me know when the house is finished and the goods arrive. You can stack the furniture up on the porches or anywhere until I get back. The hot weather is about over and the hotel will open up next week."

"All right, sir," the surveyor answered quietly and made no comment on this unexpected move of his employer, though his nerves tingled at the evident purpose of his instructions. Abe Lee could not know how the events of the evening had awakened in Jefferson Worth memories of another baby in the desert—memories that stirred the child-hungry heart of the lonely man and drove him to his daughter without an hour's delay.

Did Abe Lee push the work on the house? Did he? Every man in Jefferson Worth's employ, who could find a place to lay his hand on the building, was put on the job. By the time the house was finished the furniture had arrived.

It was quitting time and Pablo, who with four Mexican laborers had been at work grading the yard and removing the rubbish that had accumulated incident to building, dismissed his helpers. The surveyor was gloomily contemplating the pile of boxes, bales and crates on the front porch. Evidently there was something not to the surveyor's liking.

"Senor Lee."

The surveyor turned sharply to face the Mexican, whose dark features were glowing with pleasure. "Well?"

"Pardon, but Senor Lee seems not pleased. Is not the work well done?"

"The work is all right, Pablo. You have done well. It is not that. I was wishing I had nerve enough to tackle another job."

The Mexican smiled. "Oh, Senor, you make fun. What can not El Senor do? He can do everything."

"There is a job here all right I don't sabe, Pablo." Abe turned again to the pile of household goods.

"Si Senor, me sabe. It is that La Senorita come pronto an' Senor Lee would have the house what you call ready."

225

Abe started at the tone of quiet conviction. "How the devil do you know that La Senorita is coming?" he asked sharply.

The answer came with a flash of white teeth: "For what else does El Senor hurry so the house? For what else does he all time cry—'Pronto! pronto!' and go not much to the other work but stay all time here? And is there not all this—" He waved his hand gracefully to indicate the household goods. "For who should it be that Senor Lee is hurry so? When Texas Joe come say—'Senor Worth is here,' I think quick some time La Senorita come. I work for Senor Worth, as La Senorita send word, that I may be near. All time I work I say—'It is for La Senorita.' Pretty quick now she come and with Senor Lee will be happy to live in the house he make."

A deeper red than the desert color stained the surveyor's thin cheeks as he said: "You're a good hombre, Pablo, but you're away off on part of what you say. I reckon you're right enough that Miss Worth is coming, but she will live here with her father just as they did in Rubio City. And listen, Pablo. You must never say to anyone what you have said to me. You sabe, Pablo? I am with La Senorita as you are, and Tex and Pat; sabe?"

"Si, Senor; forgive me; I am sorry. But sometime it will be if El Senor is patient."

The surveyor, annoyed at the Mexican's talk, but unwilling, because of the spirit that prompted the words, to speak sharply, sought to dismiss the matter by changing the subject. He explained to Pablo how he was wishing that he could unpack the furniture and have the house all ready when Mr. Worth and Barbara arrived.

"Why not ?" asked the Mexican.

Abe shook his head. "It's out of my line. I don't sabe the job, Pablo."

"Maybe so Tex and Pat, they would sabe."

"By George, I believe Pat would. Texas wouldn't be any better than I, but Pat ought to know something about such things. You go tell them I want them at the office to-night. Pat was at the power house to-day and Texas will be coming in from the line early."

"Si, Senor. And Senor Lee! La Senorita will want a horse."

"Hell, I forgot that!"

Pablo smiled. "I know where is good one—a beautiful horse, Senor. Long time I watch him and think some day he be for La Senorita when she come. The man will sell for enough. Shall I go to-morrow ?"

"Yes, get him. Tell the man it is for me and that I will pay. No"—he corrected himself—"tell him it is for Senor Worth and that he will pay. Sabe ? You must not speak of me."

"Si, Senor; it shall be as you say. To-morrow night I return."

That evening at the office in the rear of the store Abe laid the situation before Pat and Texas Joe. Could the three undertake to have the furniture unpacked and the house properly settled ? The hotel had been opened to receive guests, of course, but——

Texas Joe shook his head solemnly. "I pass, Abe.

"There air't no use in my affirmin' that I knows any thing about such undertakin's. Household furnishin' such as is proper in a case like this is a long way off my range."

But the Irishman waxed indignant. "Sich ignorance as ye two do be showin' is heathenish," he declared. "I suppose now ye wud be for puttin' the cook stove in the parlor an' settin' up the piany in the young lady's budwar."

The strange word caught the attention of Texas instantly. "An' what might that be, pard?" he drawled. "What's a budwar?"

Pat snorted. "Budwar, ye ignorant owld limb, is polite for the girl's bedroom, which in civilization is not discussed by thim as has manners."

Such overwhelming evidence of the Irishman's familiarity with the best social customs was not to be rejected. The morning stage carried a telegram to be sent from Deep Well to Jefferson Worth, and all that day the three toiled under command of Pat. When the evening stage brought a message from Mr. Worth saying that he and Barbara would arrive the following evening, they decided that a night shift was necessary and worked until nearly morning, redoubling their efforts the following day.

When the dusty old stage with its four half-broken horses pulled into Kingston that night, three tired and anxious, but joyful, desert men occupied the front rank of the waiting crowd before the new hotel.

With all the grace of generous curves and ponderous dignity, Horace P. Blanton was first to alight. When he turned his broad back to the "common

herd" and, with an indescribable air of proprietor-
ship, assisted Miss Worth to the ground, three dark-
ened faces scowled with disapproval and three smothered oaths expressed deep disgust.

The excited citizens behind the three crowded
closer. Even Ynez, climbing down from the stage,
was received with another cheer by the delighted
men. The irrepressible Horace P., quick to recognize the spirit of the company and ever ready to do
more than his part, burst into an eloquent address
of welcome in behalf of the entire population of
The King's Basin. But the ceremony was interrupted
and the imposing personage in the white vest was
thrust roughly aside while Barbara, with glad eyes
and hands outstretched, greeted the rude disturbers
of the great man's dignity.

"Texas! Pat! Mr. Lee! Oh, I'm glad! I have
been hoping all day that you would be here to meet
me. It seemed to me that I would never get here.
It has been the longest day of my life." Which, considering that the impressive attentions of Horace P.
Blanton had been continuous since the moment when
he had forced an introduction from Mr. Worth on
the train that morning, was rather hard on his
majesty.

But much experience in similar situations had
made Horace P. Blanton immune to such thrusts.
Even while Barbara was speaking he regained his
place at her side. With his voice and manner of a
"personal conductor"—before either of the three
could speak—he followed her words with: "Ah,
Miss Worth, I see you already know some of our

men. Texas, Pat and Abe here are three of the best
fellows we have. They—"

Again he was interrupted. The young woman
turned easily aside to Abe, and Horace P. found
himself very close to and facing the tall plainsman
and the heavy shouldered Irish boss.

"Excuse me, Colonel," drawled Texas in tones so
soft that no one in the noisy crowd could hear; "but
the welfare of the citizens of this here community,
as well as the safety of the country, demands your
immediate presence up the street."

Without hesitation the lordly one exclaimed: "Ah,
thank you, Tex. Miss Worth will excuse me I'm
sure. Please explain my absence to her." Then
before their startled eyes he faded away—if the
vanishing of such a bulk can be so described.

A few minutes after the passing of Horace P.
Blanton, Tex and Pat also disappeared, for it was
part of the carefully arranged plot that Barbara's
"uncles" were to see to the disposal of the girl's
trunks while she was at supper at the hotel with her
father and Abe.

At the table Barbara was all eagerness in her
desire to know everything about the work; and the
surveyor, in answering her questions, found himself
drawn out of the dumbness that usually beset him
in such situations.

"And our house?" asked the girl. "When can I
begin settling? You see I brought Ynez with me.
Can we begin in the morning, Abe? And could you
spare Pat and Tex to help us?"

Abe glanced at his employer. "If you would like

to see the house we can look at it this evening after supper."

"Can we? Can we go, daddy?"

Jefferson Worth met Abe's look with a twinkle in the corner of his eye, but he only answered his eager daughter with a calm, "If you like."

They found the house with every window brilliantly lighted, and on the front porch, on opposite sides of the wide-open door, Texas and Pat standing to welcome them. From one room to another Barbara ran in laughing delight, followed by the three, who were perspiring in an agony of suspense while Jefferson Worth looked on. The cook stove was not in the parlor, nor was the piano—out of place. In the proper room Barbara even found her trunks. There was a supply of provisions in the pantry and kindlings even ready by the kitchen stove for the morning fire. If there were little irregularities here and there, Barbara, with graceful tact, did not see them but, to the delight of the three men, declared again and again that no woman could have done it better.

The climax came when she said that unless her father insisted she would not even return to the hotel that evening. Could not someone go for the hand luggage and Ynez? Breathless the three waited, and when Mr. Worth said he saw no reason why they should leave their own home for a hotel Tex and Pat could hold themselves no longer but made a wild run for the door.

When Barbara's "uncles" had returned with the Indian woman and the grips, Pat stood in the center of the living room and looked curiously about—an expression of wonder upon his battle-scarred Irish countenance. "Now don't that bate the divil! Tell me"—he faced the girl with mock severity—"fwhat's this ye've been doin' already?"

"Doing?" exclaimed Barbara, "I haven't been doing anything, Uncle Pat."

"Aw, go on, don't be tellin' me that. Aven Uncle Tex here can see that ye've changed ivery blissid thing in the place. 'Tis not the same, at all, an' afther us a-workin' our fingers to the bone to fix ut up. 'Tis quare. I know now that Tex hung that curtain there. Ye could have heard him swearin' a mile away, but ut's not that same curtain at all, at all. 'Tis mighty quare."

For an hour or more Barbara, at the piano, sang for them the simple songs they loved, while many a tired horseman, riding past on his way to his lonely desert shack or to some rough camp on the works, paused to listen to the sweet voice and to dream perhaps of the time that was to come when such sounds would no longer seem strange on the Desert.

When the hour came for Texas and Pat and Abe to go, and Barbara with shining eyes tried again to express her gratitude while insisting that they must always come to her home as to their own, the three felt that indeed they had their reward. And when later the girl kissed her father good night Jefferson Worth also knew in his lonely heart that he had done well.

CHAPTER XV.

BARBARA COMES INTO HER OWN.

EFFERSON WORTH and his daughter had just finished their first breakfast in the new home when their Indian servant woman entered the room.

"What is it, Ynez?" asked Barbara, seeing that the woman wished to speak.

Ynez's black eyes were shining and her voice was eager as she answered: "There is someone without waiting for La Senorita."

"Someone waiting outside for me, Ynez?"

"Who is it?" asked Mr. Worth.

"It is Pablo Garcia, Senor, and he say please ask La Senorita to come. If La Senorita will go only to the door she can see."

With an expression of excited interest Barbara, followed by her father, went out on the porch. In front of the house stood Pablo holding a beautiful saddle horse fully equipped and ready for a rider. The Mexican's dark face shone with the pride and triumph of the moment toward which he had looked forward for months. The horse, too, as if sensing the importance of the occasion, pawed the earth with his dainty hoofs, arched his neck and tossed his head—proudly impatient.

Uttering low exclamations and little cries of

delight the girl left the porch and ran forward, greeting Pablo and moving about the horse, admiring the animal from every point of view. "What a beauty! He is perfect, Pablo; perfect! Where did you find him? Is he yours? What's his name?" Her questions came tumbling from her lips in such eager bursts that Pablo answered only the last.

"He is yours, Senorita. His name El Capitan."

"Mine?" Barbara turned to her father, who explained, Abe having told him the night before of the purchase.

When her father finished, the delighted girl announced that she "simply couldn't wait" but must go for a ride immediately. Running into the house she returned a few minutes later in her riding dress and, mounting with—"I'll be back for dinner, daddy," and "Adios, Pablo!"—rode away toward the open country, while the Mexican and the banker watched her out of sight.

By the time they had passed the last of the tent houses in the town Barbara and El Capitan were friends. There is no doubt whatever that a worthy horse appreciates a worthy rider and the girl, accustomed to riding since childhood, certainly appreciated her mount.

"Oh, you beauty!" she cried, leaning forward in the saddle to pat the shining neck. "Oh, you beauty!"

As though to return the compliment and express his pleasure at finding such an agreeable companion, El Capitan turned his delicate pointed ears forward, arched his neck, and, stepping as on a velvet carpet, sprang lightly to the other side of the road in sheer overflow of good spirits and confidence in his rider, while the girl, at his play, laughed aloud.

But Barbara had eyes and thoughts for more than her horse that morning. It was her first day in "her Desert" and there was much for her to see. Through her father she had kept in close touch with every phase of the work of reclaiming The King's Basin and had often begged him to take her with him into the new country. Now at last her wish was realized. She was where she could see with her own eyes the Seer's dream—the Seer's and her own— coming true.

On either hand as she rode, stretching away until all fixed lines and objects were lost in the shifting mirage and many-colored lights of the desert, the dun plain with its thin growth of thirsty vegetation was broken by the green cultivated fields, newly leveled acres, buildings and stacks of the ranches, with canals, ditches and ponds filled with water that reflected the colors of the morning. Everywhere, in what had been a land of death, life was stirring. In one field beside the road a herd of soft-eyed cattle, knee-deep in rich alfalfa, lifted their heads to greet her. In another a band of horses and colts scampered along with her as far as their fence would permit, as if good-naturedly seeking her further acquaintance. Everywhere men with their teams were at work in the fields newly won from the desert. At one house a woman was hanging her weekly wash on the line, while a group of children played in the yard. As the girl passed the woman waved her hand

235

and the children shouted a greeting. And a littl:
farther on a meadow-lark, perched on a fence-post
filled the world with liquid music.

The wine-like atmosphere, the glorious light, the
odor of the fields and the strength and beauty of the
life new-born in the desert, with the spirit and freedom of the animal she rode, all appealed with almost
painful intensity to the girl who was herself so richly
alive. She felt her close kinship with it all and
answered to it all out of the fullness of her own
young woman's strength. She wanted to cry aloud
with the joy and gladness of the victory over barrenness and desolation. It was her Desert that was
yielding itself to the strong ones; for them it had
waited—waited through the ages, and at last they
had come.

Busy with her thoughts, Barbara rode on until she
had passed out of the settled district of which Kingston was the center and found herself in the desert.
Save for the lightly marked trail she was following
and the thin line of her father's telephone poles that
led southward to Frontera, she saw no sign of a
human being. Checking her horse and turning, she
looked back. A tiny spot of thin color—the red of
brick, the yellow of new lumber and the white of
tents—marked Kingston. The ranches about the
desert town were scattered spots of green scarcely
seen at that distance. All the rest, from the distant
snow-capped sentinels of the Pass in the north to
Lone Mountain in the south and from the purple
mountain wall on the west to the sky-line of the Mesa

on the east, was the same dun plain as she had always known it.

Barbara caught her breath. Seen near at hand the work accomplished had seemed so great, so brave; seen from even so short a distance as she had come, it looked so pitifully small, so helpless. The desert was so huge, so masterful, so dominating in its silent grandeur, in its awful loneliness. All her life Barbara had seen the desert from her home in Rubio City. Many, many times she had ridden into it and back a day's ride. But never had she felt the dreadful spirit of the land as she felt it now, alone in the still, lonely heart of it. She was afraid with an unreasoning fear.

El Capitan, too, seemed to share her uneasiness. Tossing his head, tugging at the bridle reins and pawing the ground and starting nervously, he turned this way and that, signifying his desire to be away. But just as Barbara, on the point of yielding to his impatience and her own feeling of fear, lifted the reins to turn toward Kingston again, he threw up his head with a loud neigh and with ears pointed looked away toward the south, standing rigid and motionless as a horse of stone. A cloud of dust rising from the trail told her that someone was approaching. Instantly the girl's feeling of fear vanished. She laughed aloud.

"Company is coming, Capitan," she said. "Shall we wait until we see who it is? We can easily run away if we don't like his looks."

As she finished speaking, the light wind that was just strong enough to carry the dust with the coming

rider shifted for a moment and revealed the horseman clearly. Barbara, not wishing to appear as
though waiting, started ahead toward Kingston,
while the stranger, evidently catching sight of a
horse and rider on the road ahead and desiring company, quickened his pace.

Barbara glanced over her shoulder. "Shall we
run, Capitan? No, we'll not run yet. But be
ready." Again she glanced quickly back. "It's no
one we know, Capitan. Be ready."

Nearer and nearer came the stranger.

When she heard the sound of his horse's feet on
the sand Barbara turned again, this time openly.
Then she laughed. "I don't think we'll run this
time, Capitan."

A moment later the horseman had overtaken her.

"Good morning, Mr. Holmes. How do you do?"

"Miss Worth!"

Had the engineer checked his horse so suddenly a
few months before he would undoubtedly have gone
over the animal's head. El Capitan also stopped,
while the man and the girl sat looking at each other,
Barbara smiling at the man's surprise.

"Is it really you?" asked Holmes at last, "or is it
some new trick of this confounded desert?" He
rubbed his eyes. "I never saw a mirage like this
before and I don't think the heat has affected my
brain." He moved his horse closer. "Could you
shake hands?"

Barbara held out her hand. "I assure you that I
am very substantial," she laughed, "and I am here to
stay, too."

238

"That's great! By George! it's good to see you," cried Holmes so heartily that the girl turned away her face and caused her horse to move ahead.

The engineer's horse, with a word from his rider, kept his place by El Capitan's side.

"It's very nice of you to say that but I didn't see you anywhere around last night when the stage arrived. Abe and Pat and Texas were there and this morning even Pablo came the first thing after breakfast."

Willard Holmes could not altogether hide his pleasure at her hinted rebuke. So she had thought of him—had looked for him—had missed him. "Indeed, you must forgive me. I did not know you were coming," he said and explained how his work took him away from Kingston much of the time.

"Of course, under those circumstances, I must forgive you," agreed Barbara, then added seriously: "I think I could forgive anyone who belonged to this desert work, anything, except one."

"And that?" He was watching her face. "What is it that you could not forgive?"

She returned his look steadily. "Don't you know?"

He drew a little back and she wondered at something in his voice and manner as he answered: "Yes, I know. You could never forgive one for being untrue to his work—for putting anything before the work itself."

"Yes," she returned, "that is it. I could never forgive one who did that."

"But how would you know? How could you

judge?" he asked almost roughly. "Perhaps the very one whom you would call false to the work would, in reality, be doing the best thing for the work. I have noticed that, after all, those who have the loftiest ideals and the highest visions of man's duty to man and all that are seldom the ones who accomplish much of the actual work of the world. Look here, honestly now: how many of the people who are reclaiming this desert—I mean all of us—laborers, business men, ranchers, everybody who has come in here to do this work—how many of them do you think see a single thing beyond the dollars they have hoped to make on the venture? Whether it's the high wage paid by the Company, the big profits of the business man or the heavier crop of the rancher, it amounts to the same. And yet you would insist that they must not be governed by this desire for gain. So far as I can see, it is this same desire for gain that has driven men into doing every really great thing that has ever been done. Look carefully into every great enterprise that is of value to the world and you will find at the beginning of it some-one reaching for a dollar or its equivalent. Your father, for instance—"

Barbara threw out her hand protestingly. "Please don't, Mr. Holmes. I know that what you say is every bit true. Father and I have gone over it so many times. And yet I know, I *know* that what I feel is true also. Oh, dear! what a muddle it is, isn't it? It seems so wrong to spend one's life work-ing for nothing but money. And yet all the really good work in the world is done by those who don't

work to do good at all but for what they get out of it.
I suppose now that you stayed in the Desert all this
past summer and worked so hard without any vacation at all just for your salary."

"How did you know that I took no vacation?"

"Father told me. You seem to have made quite
an impression on my father. He has told me a great
deal about you. But I want to know—did you stay
in the desert for money?"

Holmes wondered if she knew the danger that
threatened the settlers because of the unsubstantial
character of the Company's structures. "Perhaps,"
he said, "it was to save my professional reputation.
That would amount to the same thing, wouldn't it?"

Barbara laughed. "I don't think that your taking
a vacation would have lost you your reputation.
That won't do, Mr. Chief Engineer." For some
reason Barbara seemed highly pleased at the turn the
conversation had taken.

The man thought of those anxious days and nights
at the intake, when the safety of the success of the
whole King's Basin project hung on the whim of an
uncertain river, but he did not explain to Barbara
nor did he tell her that a vacation would have made
no difference in his salary.

"I'll tell you why you stayed with the work in the
Desert this summer, Mr. Holmes," she said, and in
her voice was a note of pleased triumph.

"Why?" he asked.

"Because you are learning the language of the
country."

For an instant he was puzzled. Then he remem-

bered the evening he had said good-by. "Si, Senorita
I suppose one could not help learning a little in La
Palma de la Mano de Dios, could he?"

"Not if he had ancestors," came the answer.

Holmes flushed. "What a snob I must have
seemed to you that day," he said in deep disgust at
the recollection of his first attempt to impress the
western girl with the importance of his place in life.

"I don't think snob is just the word," she answered. "I didn't mind that ancestor business and
all that one bit. In fact I think I rather enjoyed it.
You were *such* a tenderfoot! But there was something else I did mind. Did you know that there was
a time when I hated you with my whole heart?"

"Miss Worth!"

"It's so. I even promised myself that I would
never speak to you again—never! Then I came
after awhile to understand how foolish it was of me
to blame you and father told me so much of your
work here this summer that I became heartily
ashamed of myself. I'm telling you now because,
you see, I have come here to stay and to be, in a
way, a tiny little part in this great work you are
doing, and I feel that I ought to tell you so that we
can start square again."

"But, Miss Worth, what in the world are you
talking about?"

"I know it was foolish of me for you were not at
all to blame. But I couldn't help it. It is all over
though and we are square now—or will be when you
have said that you forgive me."

"But I don't know what you mean. What on earth did I do?"

She looked straight at him. "Can't you even guess?"

"I haven't the ghost of an idea."

"Well, I'm glad you haven't," she declared, "even if it does make me appear so foolish. It was because the Seer was discharged and you were put in his place."

"But I—"

"Oh, I know all about it," she interrupted. "You didn't do it. You were not to blame. The Company did it because it was Good Business. I told you it was all over now. But please, I don't think we'd better talk about it only just for you to say that you forgive me. I had to tell you for that, you see."

Then the once carefully proper Willard Holmes did a thing that would have astonished his most intimate eastern friends beyond expression. Reining his horse close to El Capitan he held out his hand to Barbara.

"Shake, pard! You're the squarest girl I ever knew."

It was no flimsy, two-fingered ceremony, but a whole-hearted, whole-handed grip that made the man's blood move more quickly. Unconsciously, as he felt the warm strength in the touch of the girl's hand, he leaned toward her with quick eagerness. And Barbara, who was looking straight into his face with the open frankness of one man to another, started and drew back a little, turning her head aside.

For some distance they rode in silence, then she began questioning him about his life in the desert and all the rest of the way home made him talk of the work so dear to her heart. As he talked and the girl watched his strong bronzed face and listened to his words, she found something in his voice and manner that was not there that day when she introduced him to "her Desert." There was a self-reliance, an enthusiasm, a purpose that was good to hear.

At the door of her new home when he, pleading his work, would not stay for lunch but promised to call in the evening, she bade him "Adios" in the soft tongue of the Southland and when he had wheeled his horse and was riding away, Barbara turned on the porch to look after him. Watching the khaki clad figure that was so easily at home in the saddle and that, with the loping horse, seemed so much a part of the country, the girl wondered at the change that was being wrought by the wild land upon the man from the eastern city.

"Indeed," she thought, "he *is* learning the language of the desert!" And she, too, was glad.

When Holmes arrived at the Company headquarters the General Manager shifted his cigar to the corner of his mouth and cocked his head to one side, looking him over critically.

"Buenas dias, Senor," cried the engineer gaily, throwing his sombrero, quirt and gloves on the floor and helping himself from the box of cigars on the desk. Holmes was still thinking in the language of Barbara's land.

"Humph!" grunted the slender man at the desk,

"I said 'hello' to you when you passed the office, also I bowed my best New York bow, but you were too engaged to see. Were you practicing your greaser lingo on her? I suppose she talks it like a native."

"She talks a language you would not understand, my friend," said Holmes coolly, lighting a cigar.

"Probably not," agreed the other. "Who am I that I should understand the words of a being of such exalted rank? The whole fool town is crazy over her already. I've heard nothing but Miss Worth, Miss Worth, all morning. You would think the hotel was a ladies' sewing circle. Every man on the street is wearing his Sunday clothes and walks with his head twisted over his shoulder for fear he will miss a glimpse of her. Horace P. Blanton is the man of the hour. He came in with her last night and is arranging a public reception, talking like the business manager of a Greek goddess. And now here you go riding down the street with her, so interested that you can't even see me. Permit me to congratulate you. You certainly have lost no time."

Holmes scowled. "That fellow Blanton is an officious ass," he growled, "and you"—he checked himself.

"Go on; go on!" cried the delighted Burk. "Don't spare me. In the name of the goddess, smite!"

The engineer laughed in spite of himself, though he spoke sharply. "Cut it out, Burk. I met Miss Worth in Rubio City when I landed fresh from New York. She's a mighty charming girl, whom you'll be as glad as anybody to know. She was riding over in the West District this morning and I overtook

THE WINNING OF BARBARA WORTH

her on my way in. Of course we came on together.
Have you heard from Uncle Jim?"

The Manager dropped his bantering tone instantly
and taking an open letter from his desk, scanned it
thoughtfully as he answered: "He'll be here Saturday. He's not at all pleased, Holmes, with my report
on the Worth operations. Our friend Jeff's getting
altogether too strong a grip on things. It beats all
the way he hops into a game and draws all the high
cards before you know he is on the other side of the
table."

The thoughtful Manager of The King's Basin
Land and Irrigation Company was evidently wor-
ried. Holmes made no reply.

With his eyes still on the letter in his hand Burk
asked: "How are you getting on with the survey of
the South Central District?"

"Black finished yesterday. I brought in the data."

"What do you think of it?"

"It's no good, Burk. The land is a rough jumble
of small hummocks, covered with a heavy growth
of greasewood and mesquite, and practically all of it
lies so high that we could never get the water on it
at all."

Burk considered. "Do you know whether Abe
Lee ever went over that district?"

Holmes stiffened. "No, he never worked in that
part of the Basin at all, but what the deuce has Lee
to do with it? Black is a graduate engineer and as
good a man as ever looked over a transit. If you
can't trust the men I send out, why"—

"Wow, wow!" cried Burk, "keep your shirt on,

old man! I'm not making insinuations against your pet surveyor. I merely asked for information. Now if you please, turn your South Central data over to your office force and tell them to get it in shape by Saturday without fail. It's an order, my son. Selah!"

CHAPTER XVI.

JEFFERSON WORTH'S OPERATIONS.

HE crowd that waited in front of the new hotel for the arrival of the stage, the evening James Greenfield came to Kingston, was unusually large. The King's Basin Messenger had announced the coming of the promoter and president of The King's Basin Land and Irrigation Company and the pioneers had assembled to see the famous capitalist whose power in the money world was making possible the reclamation of the desert.

Mr. Greenfield's greeting in the lobby, under the perspiring efforts of Horace P. Blanton, soon assumed the proportions of a public reception. With his Manager to introduce the prominent citizens, and Horace P., who was never farther than a yard from the capitalist's elbow to assist in receiving them, the man from New York entered graciously into the spirit of the occasion. And when the man in the white vest, intoxicated by the atmosphere of greatness, burst forth in a speech of welcome, setting forth the wonders of The King's Basin, the marvelous growth and future of Kingston, the greatness of Greenfield and—quite incidentally—the greatness of Horace P. Blanton, all in behalf of the people, the Easterner replied with a few modest remarks, in which he hinted at even greater things to come, promising by subtle suggestion unlimited wealth for all who would invest their money and their lives in The King's Basin project.

Then Mr. Greenfield slipped away with Willard Holmes to his room. The friendship between the engineer's own parents and his benefactor had been lifelong and very close. It was a story, years ago forgotten by the world, of how Grace Winton had chosen one of the two college chums and why the other had never married. In the repeated business failures of his old schoolmate and the consequent loss of his fortune the successful financier had proven himself many times a friend in need, and through the long illness of the man who had been successful in winning the woman they both loved, Greenfield, with his wealth, had been steadfast in his thoughtful care. When baby Willard's mother died soon after the death of his father, she—knowing the heart of the man whose love for her had kept him childless—committed to him her only child, and Greenfield, accepting the trust, had taken the boy into his life and heart as his own son.

After the loss of William Greenfield, his only brother, James Greenfield—whose power in the financial world was steadily increasing—had no one to intimately share his success but young Holmes, and when Willard had finished his school and chosen his profession the older man used the influence of his own position to give the young engineer every advantage.

As the two men faced each other now after the longest separation they had ever known, the Company's president studied his chief engineer with interest.

"Well, Willard, my boy," he said at last; "how do you like it? Say, but you are looking fine. You always were a handsome youngster but you're— you're improving, young man. I'm blessed if you don't look like a work of art done in bronze." He laughed with the pleasure of his own conceit and the other laughed with him.

"Wait until this sun gets a shot at you, Uncle Jim."

"Humph! I suppose you think it will make me into some sort of an hideous old idol. I don't propose to stay long enough to give it a chance," he added grimly, and as he finished a shadow fell over his face and the laughter died out of his voice.

"What's the matter; don't you like the West, Uncle Jim?"

"I hate it, and with good reason. Don't you get too interested out here, Willard. We'll clean up a nice little pile out of this scheme and get back home where we belong. I miss you like the deuce, boy!"

The engineer started to say something about the work, but Greenfield held up his hand. "Not a word about business to-night, Willard. We'll take that up to-morrow. Tell me where I can get a shave and then we'll have dinner and after that a quiet evening together."

Holmes laughed. "We have a barber, all right, Uncle Jim. He landed with his outfit this afternoon. There was no place for him, and the freighter unloaded him on a vacant lot about a block west of the hotel. It's been a long time since most of us have seen a real barber and the boys couldn't wait. Trade came with such a rush that he set up his chair in the street and has been doing a land-office business ever since. They say he's all right, too, but it looks funny."

Mr. Greenfield, his curiosity aroused and being really in need of a shave, sought out the shopless barber. He was easily found, for the crowd that had gathered to witness the arrival of the great financier, James Greenfield, had already drifted to the scene of Kingston's other chief attraction. Piled in a vacant lot was the necessary furniture for a well-equipped shop, but only the chair was in use. A goods-box nearby held the instruments of the craft while a bucket of water, a tin basin, and a supply of towels completed the arrangements. The delighted crowd filled the air with good natured chaff and laughter as the customers compared notes and attempted to express their emotion at finding them-selves properly groomed.

Mr. Greenfield, highly amused at the novel sight, pushed his way well into the circle.

"Next!" shouted the man with the brush and razors in a voice that was heard a block away.

Some joker shouted: "Your turn, Mr. Greenfield," and "Greenfield! Greenfield!" chimed the crowd.

Amid yells of delight the president of The King's Basin Land and Irrigation Company took his place in the chair.

As the barber worked he talked. Never before in all his professional career had he been so prominently in the public eye. "Yes sir, gents, I'm here to tell you that that there man, Jefferson Worth, is a prince —a prince. Let me tell you what he done for me. You see things was gone all to the bad. Looked like every way I turned I went up against it proper, and first thing I knowed my furniture was piled out on the sidewalk and Mr. Sheriff he was a-sellin' it. Well, sir, Mr. Worth he happened to come along just as they begun to ask for bids and I'm darned if he didn't take the whole works just as if he had done nothin' but buy barber shops all his life. I was layin' low in the crowd, watchin', you see; and there was somethin' about him—the way he stopped and bid the stuff in, or somethin', I dunno what—that struck me, so I edged alongside and says, says I: 'Are you a barber?' Whew! the minute he looked at me I seen my mistake, but he never batted a eye. 'Not yet,' he says. 'This is a pretty good outfit, ain't it?' 'You bet it is,' says I. 'It was mine a few minutes ago.' An' then I tells him how I was up against it an' asks what he was goin' to do with the stuff. 'I'm goin' to ship it to Kingston in The King's Basin country,' says he. 'We need a good barber down there and I figured that if I got the shop ready I could find the man to run it. How would you like to tackle the job? I'll send you and your outfit to Kingston and sell you your shop on good time, too, for just what it cost me.' An' here I am—— Next!"

Mr. Greenfield slipped from the chair and silently tendered the talkative barber a five dollar bill. As the barber was counting out the change the eastern financier heard behind him murmurs of hearty approval and admiration of Jefferson Worth. The barber's story had made a deep impression and certainly no one in the crowd was more deeply impressed than was the president of The King's Basin Land and Irrigation Company.

At dinner that evening the boy with the weekly edition of the Messenger came into the dining room. Mr. Burk, taking his copy, glanced once at the first page, folded it carefully and laid the sheet before his employer with the headlines of a leading article uppermost.

Mr. Greenfield read: "The Citizens Bank of Kingston—Jefferson Worth owns the building opposite the opera house and has organized a bank."

Mr. Greenfield did not need to read further.

"Who did you say was building the opera house block?" he asked the Manager.

"It is owned by a syndicate. The local man in charge sits at that table in the corner"—he nodded toward a clean, solid-looking young fellow, who was enjoying his dinner and chatting with Abe Lee.

In the lobby, a few minutes later, Greenfield whispered to Holmes: "Introduce me to that young man, Willard."

His order was easily obeyed and soon, in a corner, the president and his new acquaintance were chatting pleasantly over cigars furnished by the New Yorker.

"That building of yours seems to be a very creditable piece of work," offered Greenfield. "The investment ought to pay big later on. But isn't it rather heavy for the present size of the town?"

The other smiled pleasantly. "True; but you see

253

we are not building it for a town of this size, Mr.
Greenfield. We expect Kingston to grow rapidly and
we realize the importance of being on the ground
first."

"That's right, too," returned Greenfield. "With
the capital to do it that is undoubtedly the right plan.
I understand you represent a Coast syndicate."

Again the young man smiled. "That is the general
understanding, Mr. Greenfield, and until to-night I
have not been at liberty to contradict it. I can tell
you now, however, that the syndicate which is putting up that building is Mr. Jefferson Worth."

Greenfield was too well-schooled to give vent to the
slightest expression of surprise. His tone was courtesy
itself as he replied: "Indeed? Mr. Worth seems to
be doing a great deal for Kingston."

Then the talk shifted easily into other channels
until the president found opportunity to leave his
companion. Rejoining his Manager and Holmes,
Greenfield requested Burk's presence in his room
and, once there, threw aside the mask of politeness,
making it clearly evident, in words chosen for forcefulness rather than politeness, that he did not approve
of the situation that had developed under the
thoughtful Manager's eye.

"And now," he finished, "send the proprietor of
this hotel up here."

The uncomfortable Burk obeyed. When the landlord arrived with an anxious face, Greenfield was
his courteous, affable self again.

"Mr. Wheeler," he said, "there is a little business
proposition I wish to lay before you while I am here

and I thought it better to mention it this evening so that you can have time to think it over and give me your answer before I leave. I can see, of course, that this hotel, building and all, represents quite an investment and that, for a time, the returns will not be large. I don't know, of course, how much capital you have to swing it, but I can see that without good, substantial backing the enterprise might not hold up, which would be very bad for the reputation of the town in which, as you know, our Company is so heavily interested. Now if we could bring about some alliance between you and the Company it would be a good thing all around, do you see?"

"Yes sir, I see. This is a big undertaking for Kingston as conditions are now, but later it is bound to be a good paying investment and we realize the importance of getting in on the ground floor. But I am not at liberty to consider or make any proposition whatever until I have consulted the owner—"

"The owner?"

"Yes, sir."

"I was told that you were the proprietor. Your name is on the hotel stationery."

"I have only a very small interest. My associate would not permit his name to be used at all. I may tell you, however, confidentially, that Mr. Worth owns the building and practically all the hotel equipment. You can easily place your proposition before him. Whatever he does I am bound to accept."

James Greenfield chewed his cigar in savage silence. Clearly it was time that he visited his town.

"Do you know where Mr. Worth is this evening?"
he asked as mildly as he could speak.

"In his office, I think."

"Would you be good enough to send him a message
that I would like to see him on a matter of importance? I will wait in my room."

"Certainly, sir."

When the landlord was gone the president of The
King's Basin Land and Irrigation Company walked
the floor, carefully reviewing his dealings with Jefferson Worth from the beginning. So this was what the
banker had "up his sleeve" when he declined to join
the Company!

He was interrupted by the boy with Mr. Worth's
answer. Mr. Worth would be in his office at the
store until ten o'clock.

The eastern capitalist made his way to the little
room in the store where Jefferson Worth sat at his
battered old desk. "How do you do?"

"Sit down," came the colorless greeting as the
western man with one hand closed the door and with
the other motioned toward the chair at the end of
the desk. Then seating himself again in his own
chair he waited behind his mask.

"Well, Mr. Worth, I see you decided to come into
the Basin after all."

"I concluded to make a few small investments,"
came the exact reply.

Greenfield laughed shortly. "Yes—this store, the
electric power plant and system, the bank building
and bank, the opera house block, the hotel, the telephone system——" The Company president's tone

and manner were intended to imply that he understood clearly the other's attitude and that he recognized a fellow-craftsman. "Come now, Worth; let's
get down to good business. It's poor policy for you
and me to go against each other. You know what
there is in it for all of us if we hang together and
you know as well as I that we can't afford, and that
we don't want, to fight each other. What sort of a
deal will it take to get you into the Company? I tell
you squarely, we are going to make it almighty hot
for any independent operator who tries to start in
here."

"I must decline to consider any proposition at all
from the Company, Mr. Greenfield."

In the silence that followed Greenfield sought in
vain to look back of that gray mask. He felt for the
first time in his business career powerless to make
the next move in the game and somewhere back in
his active brain a warning signal flashed: "Go slow!"

"Very well, Mr. Worth," he said at last, rising to
go. "When you are ready to consider the matter let
me know. In the meantime"—he shrugged his
shoulders and smiled—"good night."

Outside the store Greenfield paused irresolutely as
one hesitates whose mind is too preoccupied to direct
his steps. Then his eye caught the gleam of light
from the printing office across the street next to the
Company building.

A moment later he greeted the young man who
edited and published the Messenger. "You seem to
be pretty well fixed here," offered Greenfield after
the usual greetings. "Seems to me your prospects

257

are mighty good for a young man. Your profits ought to be big if you can hold on and grow with the development of the country."

"Yes sir, I feel that our chances are good. Kingston is growing rapidly and we are in on the ground floor."

Greenfield looked at him sharply as he uttered the now familiar expression. "You have all the capital you need?"

"We are doing very well so far."

"I have been looking your paper over with some care," the president went on, "and I believe you have the right idea. A newspaper is a powerful factor in a great enterprise like this and of course I am anxious that everything that makes for the advancement of our project should succeed. I would be sorry to see you crippled in any way for lack of funds. If you are open to consider the matter I should be glad to take a good big interest with you and to undertake to back you handsomely."

"I don't think my partner, who really furnished all the capital, would sell, sir."

"Ah! Then you are not alone?"

"No sir. Mr. Jefferson Worth practically owns the plant."

The first thing that met Mr. Greenfield's eye as he stepped through the doorway on his return to the hotel was the broad back of Horace P. Blanton, who —carried away as usual by the importance of the occasion—was "orating" to a group of strangers. It should be said that, save when the Kingston citizens were in a certain mood, Horace "orated" usually to strangers. In this case so convincing was his logic, so eloquent his flights of rhetoric, so irresistible his appeals, that Greenfield saw the fat neck of him, where it showed between the fat shoulder and the picture-general hat, grow red with the fierceness of his eloquence.

"There is no question in the world, gentlemen, that by long odds the most able financier in the West to-day is my friend, Mr. Jefferson Worth. His startling genius as a captain of industry is equaled only by his splendid public spirit and his magnificent generosity to everyone who needs a helping hand. Look what he has accomplished for Kingston, while only a few of us who were on the inside knew what he was doing—our opera house, our bank, our newspaper, our telephone lines, our ice plant, and our power plant—which to-morrow night for the first time will illuminate the heavens. Think of it! electric lights in the midst of a desert that, since God made it, has known only the light of the stars. I maintain, gentlemen, that it is the duty of every soul in The King's Basin to be present at the celebration of the splendid accomplishment and in honor to my friend, Worth. Not only has this wizard given us in Kingston the blessings of modern civilization, but there is scarcely a rancher for miles around whom he has not aided materially by furnishing him with needed supplies from the big department store, or by advancing him necessary capital. I am proud, gentlemen—proud, to call such a public benefactor my friend. Kingston is proud of her most distinguished citizen; the whole King's Basin country is proud of him. I—Oh, excuse me a minute, gentle men; as I see my friend, Mr. Greenfield, the presi dent of The King's Basin Land and Irrigation Com pany, has just arrived."

Greenfield made an effort to escape. He had heard quite enough. But it was useless. The white-vested bulk of the orator barred the way; the kingly coun tenance of Horace P. Blanton compelled recognition. "My dear Greenfield, how are you?" The voice was the anxious voice of unmistakable disinterested affec tion. "You have arrived at a most auspicious moment. I have promised our people that you would address them at the public meeting to-morrow even ing in the opera house."

"It is impossible, Mr.—Ah! Mr. Blanton; I never make public speeches."

Before Greenfield had finished his curt reply the perspiring one had him by the arm in friendly familiarity, and with the president's last word the answer came in a low, confidential tone of complete understanding. "Of course you understand that I have arranged this little affair simply to encourage every one to do his part to boom Kingston. It is to our interest, you know, to keep things going."

Until a late hour the president of The King's Basin Land and Irrigation Company, with his Gen eral Manager and chief engineer, in the Manager's private office, discussed Jefferson Worth's operations and his growing influence in The King's Basin country. James Greenfield had evidently forgotten his determination to spend the evening with Willard Holmes.

It was notable that the president and his Manager did most of the talking. The engineer was, for the most part, a silent listener. When appealed to directly he answered briefly, giving such information as he had at his command, and several times his answers caused Greenfield to look at him with questioning sharpness.

Once the older man remarked: "I believe you wrote me, Burk, that Worth's daughter had arrived and that they are to make their home in Kingston. Is she likely to prove a factor in the matter of her father's popularity and influence? Sometimes a woman, you know——"

Burk's cigar shifted to the corner of his mouth and his head was cocked to one side. "Ask Holmes," he muttered with a grin.

"I think you'd better leave Miss Worth out of this, Uncle Jim," said Holmes so sharply that Barbara's name was not mentioned again. Which does not mean at all that Greenfield had dismissed the matter from his mind.

"You have that South Central District survey ready?" he asked.

"I believe the boys have it in shape," answered Burk. The engineer laid a map before them, explained the boundaries of the proposed district, the line of the proposed canal, and on another sheet pointed out the character of the land with the elevations that made irrigation of the larger part of the tract impossible.

"You can vouch for the correctness of these figures, Willard?" asked Greenfield at last.

"Certainly, sir. Black is one of the best men we have."

"And it is your opinion that it would be a heavy loss to the Company to build this canal and attempt to develop this section?"

"I am sure that it would, sir. The district is prac tically worthless."

"All right, boys; that will be all for this evening We will start on that inspection tour day after to-morrow instead of in the morning as I had planned. I have a little business with our friend Worth to-morrow morning."

CHAPTER XVII.

HE next morning Jefferson Worth, in his office in the store building, again received the president of The King's Basin Land and Irrigation Company. James Greenfield, with outstretched hand, was quite cordial in his greeting.

"I owe you an apology, sir. I did not know until my return to the hotel last night of the demonstration to be held this evening in your honor and in celebration f the turning on of our new lights, or I should have congratulated you sooner. I am glad the people of Kingston are recognizing you in this public manner. Permit me to express my personal appreciation also."

"Thank you," said Worth from behind his mask. "I figure that my interests in Kingston will pan out all right some day."

Greenfield dropped his complimentary manner and came at once to business. "Look here, Mr. Worth, I have been thinking over the matter I mentioned last night. I can see the strength of your position here and I appreciate the value of your operations in the development of this country, which mean, of course, an added value to the Company's property and interests. We don't want to fight you; such things are bad for all concerned. We would all lose money and it would have a bad effect on the whole project.

263

If you won't come in with us, will you conside:
proposition that you can handle independently ?"

"What is your proposition ?"

"It is this. In forming our plans for extending
the Company's system we have laid out a new district
—the South Central. Before placing the water rights
on the open market, it occurred to me that we might
make a deal whereby the development of the district
would be assured and at the same time we would be
free to use our forces in still further extensions. As
you know, the settlers are coming in so rapidly now
that we need all our equipment to get the water to
them as fast as they are located. My proposition is
this: We will sell you the entire amount of water
rights covering this South Central District—sixty
thousand hares—at the lowest figure we can make;
you to build your own canals and structures. The
entire district will thus be altogether in your hands
to handle as you see fit, we, of course, being bound
only to deliver into your canals the amount of water
called for by the regular contract under which the
rights are sold."

"You have already completed the survey and
formed the district ?"

"We have. The surveys have just been completed.
We are all ready to go ahead with our work and to
sell the water." Greenfield did not say that the Company was ready to go to work on this particular
district, nor did he say that the stock would be offered
for sale save to Mr. Worth. The president of course
expected Worth to apply his statement to the particular tract of land under consideration and to

accept it as establishing beyond question the value of the South Central District. If Jefferson Worth noted the general character of Greenfield's answer he gave no sign.

"Where is the land located?"

"If you will step over to our office I can show you the maps."

When Jefferson Worth saw the boundaries of the South Central District showing the course of Dry River and the San Felipe trail, for the first time his long, tapering fingers, tapping softly the arm of his chair, smoothing his gray cheek and caressing his chin betrayed emotion. The spot where the San Felipe trail crossed Dry River and where the banker and his party had found the baby girl was just within the boundary of the district.

Apparently studying the map before him, Barbara's father sat motionless save for those nervous fingers; and Greenfield, thinking that the man's mind was intent upon the business under consideration, spoke no word. But Jefferson Worth was not thinking of business. He was seeing again a brown-eyed, brown-haired baby girl, who shrank back from his outstretched arms as though in fear.

But that mask-like face betrayed no hint of emotion, and when the banker spoke again it was to ask mechanically: "Where is your engineer?"

Greenfield looked inquiringly at Burk. The Manager touched a button on his desk. To the young man who answered the signal the Manager said: "Charlie, if Mr. Holmes is in the building please ask him to step in here a moment."

Presently the chief engineer stood before them. An expression of surprise flashed over his bronzed face as he saw Mr. Worth. From the banker his glance moved swiftly to Burk and Greenfield, then fell on the map before the three men.

Instantly he saw Greenfield's purpose. But what did they want of him? Surely they would not dare ask him to make a false statement regarding the surveys! He could not interfere; it was not his business. It was the creed of his type that in business transactions every man must take care of himself; but the Company must not ask him to lie for them. As these thoughts went through his mind his form straightened and his eyes shot a warning—almost a defiant—look at his two superiors.

Greenfield saw and signaled caution. Burk saw and smiled. But none of the three Company men could have told whether Jefferson Worth, who was bending over the map, saw or not.

Before the others could speak the banker, without looking up, said: "I just wanted to ask, Mr. Holmes, whether you can tell me about the character of the soil in this new district?"

"The soil, Mr. Worth, is, I believe, as good as there is in the Basin."

The three men awaited the next question with breathless interest.

"Thank you, Mr. Holmes. Mr. Greenfield, I will consider the proposition."

The president and manager could scarcely believe their ears. The engineer vanished.

Jefferson Worth continued: "How long have

you planned to be in the Basin this trip, Mr. Green
field ?"

"This week only, I start on my inspection with
Mr. Burk and Mr. Holmes in the morning."

"I asked because I must go out in the morning for
a few days, and I suppose you wish to close the deal
before you leave."

"You think favorably of the proposition, then ?"

"If we can get together on the terms"—Worth
spoke exactly, as if he wished his words to be remembered—"I will accept it. Suppose you put your
proposition in writing and mail it to me in the city
to-morrow. Then when I get back we will be in shape
to finish the matter one way or the other. If everything is satisfactory and I see I can't get home before
you leave I will wire you."

Thirty minutes after Jefferson Worth had returned
to his office, Abe Lee came in. "You se t for me,
sir ?"

Abe's employer arose and closed the door.

That evening about dusk the surveyor rode out of
Kingston on the road toward Frontera. And that
night, while the celebration was in full swing and
the new electric lights were sputtering and hissing
in honor of Jefferson Worth, a loaded wagon, drawn
by four mules, quietly left the rear of the Worth
store. On the driver's seat sat Pablo. With litt'e
noise the outfit, with its lone driver, left the town
in the midst of its demonstration and was soon in the
open country on the road leading south.

An hour later they had passed the ranches and
were in the Desert. Just beyond where a party of

Jefferson Worth's linemen, who were stringing the telephone wires, was encamped, the Mexican halted his team and the heavy form of Pat came out of the darkness and climbed with smothered grunts and curses to his side.

Another hour and they reached the point where the new road crossed the old San Felipe trail. Again Pablo halted his team. Ten—fifteen—twenty minutes they waited in listening silence, save for an occasional grunt from the Irishman. Then from the south came the sound of wheels and horses' feet.

"Git under way, Pablo," mumbled Pat. "Ut may not be thim, an' Abe will hang yer black hide on the new tiliphone line av anybody goin' to town stops to pass ye the time av night."

Pablo swung his team to the left and drove slowly ahead on the old trail. A hundred yards farther on they were overtaken by Abe Lee and Texas Joe, who were driving a light spring wagon.

"Everything all right, boys?" asked the surveyor sharply.

"Si, Senor," and "Yis, Sorr," came the answers.

"Good. We'll hit the grit good and hard now for we must be in the sand hills by morning."

Twenty-four hours after Jefferson Worth left Kingston, the east bound overland express came to a full stop in the Desert at a point about twenty miles west of Rubio City.

The trainmen and porters ran to the vestibules and, throwing open the doors, looked out. Three or four passengers who had risen early followed the crew, inquiring anxiously the reason for the delay.

The big conductor was standing by the rear steps of the Pullman and a medium sized man swung down to the ground by his side. Back from the track, in the gray of the morning, the watchers saw a tiny fire, over which two roughly dressed figures crouched, evidently preparing breakfast, while a team, with a light spring wagon, stood tied to a nearby mesquite tree. On every hand the great desert stretched its vast dun plain without a sign of life save for the train and the men and horses by the lonely fire.

"Right, sir?" asked the conductor of the man who alighted by his side.

"All right," answered the other in a low tone.

"Good-by, sir."

"Good-by."

The conductor lifted his hand, and, as the train started swung aboard. The watchers saw the man walk, without a glance at the departing train, straight toward the little group at the fire.

"Well, what do you make of that?" cried an excited tourist as the conductor came up the steps into the vestibule and the porter slammed down the platform and closed the door. And—"Who is he?" "Where is he going?" "What is he doing?" came in chorus from the others.

The conductor shook his head with a smile. "Don't ask me. I had orders to stop here to let him off; that's all I know."

Jefferson Worth greeted Abe Lee and Texas Joe as coolly as though it was his daily habit to meet them at that hour and place. "How is everything, Abe?"

"Not a hitch so far," answered the surveyor; and Tex drawled: "Coffee and frijoles ready, Mr. Worth."

"Can we make it to the outfit today?" asked Mr. Worth as they finished their rude meal and prepared to start.

"Easy," answered Abe. "We have plenty of water with us and this team will do it without turning a hair."

Just before sundown at a point on Dry River they found Pat and Pablo with the outfit in a comfortable camp.

While Abe Lee, with his helpers, was running his levels over the proposed line of the canal staked out by the Company surveyors in the South Central District, Willard Holmes was trying to make Mr. Greenfield see the necessity of spending more money on the unsafe structures and at Dry River heading. He explained, argued and pleaded in vain.

"My dear boy," said the Company's president. "You must understand that we are not in this country for sweet charity's sake. Burk, here, can tell you that we have not yet begun to get our investment back. When the returns justify it we will give you the money for your construction work, but we can't do it now. The rights of the men who are putting up the capital for this project must be considered, you know. We can't use a dollar of the Company's money except when it is necessary. If I were to let you spend all the money you want, we never would pay a dividend."

"But, Uncle Jim, you are forcing these settlers to

take terrible chances blindly. Have they not rights also? The interest of the Company is mighty small compared with the interests of the men who are buying the water rights and developing the land."

Greenfield flushed angrily. "Look here, Willard, you have nothing to do with the Company's business policy. As the engineer in charge, your work is to protect both the settlers and us to the best of your ability, but don't get any fool notions into your head. You can't afford to go the way of that dreamer who started this work with the exalted idea of making it a benefit to the whole human race. That line of talk is all right for the boosters like Horace P. Blanton, but we've got to make good in dollars and cents or the whole thing goes to smash."

With the South Central deal still on his mind and the picture of Barbara, as she talked to him of his work the morning he had met her in the desert, in his heart, these business discussions with Greenfield and Burk were almost unbearable to the engineer. After they had inspected the intake, the Dry River heading and the levees of the main canal he pleaded an urgent need of his presence at the office and left the party, to reach Kingston two days in advance of their return.

Barbara was on the porch when he stopped at the gate, tired, hot and dusty from his long trip. The girl, dressed in some cool simple white stuff and seated in her easy wicker chair in the deep shade of the wide porch, made a picture wonderfully attractive to the man who had ridden all day in the scorching heat of the desert sun. Of course he must come in. What nonsense to talk of his appearance. He was not making a fashionable social call. The weary engineer dropped into a chair and gratefully accepted the glass of cool lemonade she brought.

"I made it myself not five minutes ago, just as if I had known you were coming," she said with a laugh that was as refreshing as the drink itself. "Ynez is up town shopping for supper. Father is in the city. Abe has gone away somewhere. Even Pablo has vanished and I haven't seen Texas Joe nor Pat for a week. I was wishing someone would happen along. I suppose that's really why I made the lemonade."

Holmes set his glass carefully on the porch railing near at hand.

"Won't you have some more?"

"Thank you, no. You *are* quite deserted, aren't you? How long has Lee been gone?"

"Oh, he went the evening before father left and Pablo vanished the same night. It was quite tragic, and the next day I was in the office when a man from the line came in asking for Pat. He seems to have disappeared the same way. I think they might at least have left some word or said good-by."

In her innocent talk Barbara had told the whole story. It was easy for the Company engineer to guess where the surveyor and his helpers had gone and what they were doing. "Are you sure that your father is in the city?" he asked jokingly.

Barbara laughed. "Oh, there's no doubt about father. His departure was regular in every way."

On his way to the office a little later Holmes

chuckled to himself, keenly enjoying the situation. He mentally pictured the chagrin of Greenfield and Burk when he should tell them what he had learned. But would he tell them? He had not told Mr. Worth what he knew of the Company's survey in the South Central District. Why should he tell the Company what he knew of Worth's surveyors? Once he would have considered that loyalty to his employers demanded that he tell what he had learned. But now, since he had been assured so very emphatically and very recently that the policy of the Company was none of his business, let the shrewd Manager and the president find out for themselves. Anyway, he told himself, it could make no difference, for he knew what the result of Abe's surveys would be and he was glad indeed that Barbara's father had not walked into the trap set for him. The engineer had concerned himself not a little about the probable view Barbara would take of his attitude in permitting her father to purchase water rights that he knew to be worthless. But now Mr. Worth himself would discover the trick of the Company men and it would not matter.

To his surprise and chagrin Jefferson Worth walked into the Company office a few days later and, in his exact colorless voice, said: "I will accept your proposition Mr. Greenfield. If you wish we can fix up the contract and close the deal to-day."

CHAPTER XVIII.

THE GAME PROGRESSES,

HE purchase of the South Central District water rights by Jefferson Worth was immediately announced by The King's Basin Messenger in a lengthy article which began with the modest statement that this was the largest and most important business transaction that had yet occurred in the new country. The article declared that the name of Jefferson Worth was a guarantee that the new district would be made the richest and most prosperous section of the Basin and that—splendid as the undertaking was—it was only the beginning of far greater things to be wrought by the wizard of the desert whose genius had made him the greatest factor in the reclamation and development of The King's Basin country. The work would be begun at once—as soon as men and teams could be secured.

The thoughtful Manager of The King's Basin Land and Irrigation Company read the article with a grin, shifted his cigar to the corner of his mouth, cocked his head to one side and sent a marked copy of the paper to the Company's president.

James Greenfield read the article with the satisfaction of a good business man who sees his competitor heavily over-stocked with a line of goods for which there is no market. The pioneers in the desert, who were not already located, and the newly arriving prospectors read and called upon Mr. Worth for further information. The article, reprinted in the Rubio City papers, was read by many who, familiar with Jefferson Worth's business record, took the San Felipe trail for the new district.

The main supply camp for the new work was established at Dry River Crossing, the location being ideal, with an abundant supply of running water from the waste gate at the heading coming down the old channel where Barbara's mother had perished of thirst beside a dry water hole. From the camp, the San Felipe trail led in one direction straight to Rubio City and in the other to the main road in the heart of the Basin half way between Kingston and Frontera. At this camp Jefferson Worth made his headquarters. Not a man, whether he presented himself empty-handed or with team and tools, but was forced to talk with Mr. Worth in his tent office before he was set to work under Abe Lee and his three lieutenants—Texas, Pat and Pablo.

It was in those days that Willard Holmes reported to the Manager that many of his men were leaving the Company and were going to work for Jefferson Worth. The news did not appear to alarm Mr. Burk. With a grin he advised the engineer, "Don't worry, old man. They'll be damned glad to come back to us before many weeks."

"I was looking out a route for the new central main yesterday," said Holmes, "and rode over to Worth's camp at the Crossing. Judging from the size and activity of the camp, he is planning to go in good and strong. He must have a big force at work now and he is taking on men all the time."

"Your Uncle Jim will be delighted to hear of Friend Jefferson's enterprise."

The engineer's face did not express appreciation of the Manager's wit. "Have you heard the proposition that Mr. Worth is making to every man on the job?" he asked.

"No, what is he doing? Giving away one hundred and sixty shares of stock with free telephones and electric lights, passes at the opera house, unlimited credit at the store and a deposit at the bank as a bonus to anyone who will locate in his district? He seems to have all kinds of money to throw away."

"It's not quite so bad as that," answered the other with a smile. "But he tells every man, when he hires him, to file on any claim in the district that he wants and he can have the water rights for it without any cash payment and without any interest for five years. In a good many cases he is even advancing money to pay the government entry fee and promising to carry them for their equipment and supplies until they make a crop. But he makes them agree to stay on the land and actually farm the claims. He won't let a speculator even look in."

Mr. Burk expressed his opinion of Jefferson Worth's ability in the strongest terms. The man was insane, childish! Those fellows would leave him high and dry.

"That's what I said at first," agreed Holmes. "I asked Bill Watson, who quit us with his team at Number Five to go to work in the South Central, if he actually thought Worth was going to let his men make all the money."

"What did Bill say ?"

Holmes smiled. "You know how Bill talks ? 'Hell, no,' he said. 'I put it to the old man just that way myself. I says, say I : 'That sounds good all right, Mr. Worth; but it ain't reasonable that you're leavin' yourself out of this deal. Where do you come in ?' says I. 'Who's the joker in this little game ?' "

"And Worth explained ?" put in Burk eagerly, shaken out of his usual thoughtful calm by Holmes's story.

"Bill says that Mr. Worth told him that he owns a big tract of land where the camp is located and that he is going to build a town there and would make his money by the increased value of his property that would result from the development of the district; by business enterprises that would depend on the prosperity of the ranchers; and by the large increase in the value of water rights that he would sell later to those who came in to invest after the district was developed. I suggested to Bill that he could see how Worth was simply using him to gain his own ends."

"And did Bill see the point ?"

"He said: 'You're damned right he is, and so am I usin' Jefferson Worth to gain my ends, ain't I ? I might work for the Company a hundred years and never get a cent more than the wages that you're payin' now. Jefferson Worth, he pays me the same wages and gives me a chance to get my share of all that comes out of what I do. I don't care a damn if he makes ten millions out of the country. I hope he will, because he is giving us poor devils, who ain't got nothin' now, a chance to get a ranch an' do somethin' for ourselves. Of course he uses us to make money for himself. So does the Company use us, don't they? The difference is that Jefferson Worth lets us use *him* and the Company just counts us in with the rest of the live stock.' "

"How did you get around that?" asked Burk, studying his companion's face.

"I didn't get around it," answered the engineer dryly.

Burk leaned back in his chair and spoke with unusual earnestness. "Bill is right, Holmes. We consider the men who work for us as we consider horses and mules. We feed the stock; we pay wages to the men. When an animal is worn out and useless, we kill him and get another. When a man is down and out, we fire him and hire another, and you and I are no better. The Company looks on us exactly the same way. We have no more real interest in this work than the skinniest old plug on the job and the Company won't permit us to have. They think they couldn't afford it—that it wouldn't be Good Business. 'Get up!' 'Whoa!' 'Back!' 'Move, damn you! and here's your corn and hay.' That's all we have to do with it. If you balk and kick, out you go to rustle your own feed. It's a beautiful system—for the Company. I almost wish that Worth had a chance to try out his scheme. It would at least be an interesting experiment to watch."

"Well, why hasn't he a chance to try it out?"

"You know very well why. Because the deal that your talented uncle fixed up for our friend Jeff was loaded for the express purpose of blowing that philanthropic promoter into financial Kingdom-come. Didn't you report that the development of that South Central District was practically impossible because of the elevations?"

"Yes."

"Well, ordinarily the project would have been abandoned then and there. But I suggested to Mr. Greenfield that we go ahead as if everything was all right and then unload it on Worth so that he would smash himself, as he is doing."

"You should be proud of your scheme."

"I am proud of the scheme, but I'm not proud of myself. I'm being a good mule, that's all. Jefferson Worth took our apparent purpose to go ahead with the work as evidence that the proposition was all right and that's why Jefferson Worth will not finish his intended experiment."

"Yes, but the fact is he did *not* accept the proposition without investigation."

"What?"

The engineer told the Manager what he had learned from Barbara. Burk whistled softly. "Then you think the old fox sent Abe Lee out to check our survey and framed up his trip to the city to gain time? Well, I'll be—— But look here, Holmes, Worth didn't accept our proposition until after he had investigated?"

"No."

"Well; who makes the mistake then, your man Black or Abe Lee?"

"That's exactly what I'd like to know," said the Company's chief engineer grimly.

The Manager grinned as he saw the possibilities of the situation, then thoughtfully he selected a cigar. "Pretty game, isn't it, old man," he said and offered the box to Holmes who declined.

When the weed was going well the Manager's head tipped toward his left shoulder and his cigar was in the opposite corner of his mouth. "And you knew what Worth was up to before the deal was closed? Why didn't you report it, Holmes?"

The engineer frowned. "I didn't tell Mr. Worth what Black's survey showed, and you must remember that Uncle Jim rubbed it into me good and hard on the question of the construction work that the policy of the Company was none of my business. This deal was not in my department."

"Dear me," murmured the Manager with another grin. "What a well-broken Company mule it is. And you were so dead sure of your man Black. Which would you rather, my boy, have Black right and Abe wrong—the Company to win; or have Black wrong and Abe right—and Jefferson Worth free to go on with his little experiment?"

"Speak for yourself," growled Holmes.

"I will," returned Burk. "I have been a good mule, so my conscience is clear. If I knew how and thought it would do any good I would pray that Abe Lee made no mistake."

"Well, I won't believe that it's Black's mistake. He comes from too good a school," Holmes replied stubbornly.

"And your confidence in your man is no doubt equaled by Worth's confidence in his. Interesting, isn't it?"

"You go to thunder!" growled the engineer unable to stand more. The Manager's mocking laugh followed him out of the room.

As the engineer passed the open window of the office a moment later Burk called to him softly: "Oh, Holmes; I have an idea that may be helpful to you in the matter."

Against his will the engineer paused and drew close to the window. "Well?"

"Why don't you call on Miss Worth? Perhaps—"

But Willard Holmes fled. And yet that which Burk suggested in jest was exactly what Willard Holmes had already determined in his own mind to do.

The engineer had not seen Barbara since the conclusion of the South Central deal and he was continually asking himself how the girl would look upon his part in that transaction, or rather his failure to take a part in it. Barbara's frank confession, when she had asked him to forgive her for blaming him because of the Seer's dismissal that they might start square, had put their friendship upon such a ground that the man felt guilty in not confessing at once to her how he had aided Greenfield and Burk in their effort to trap her father. He could not shake off the conviction that she would undoubtedly look upon his

281

attitude as being what she had called untrue to the work—the one thing she had declared she could not forgive. Would she forgive him? She had been so interested in his work, and the engineer was beginning to realize how very much this meant to him.

At the Worth home the engineer learned from the Indian woman that Barbara had left Kingston that morning to visit her father in his camp in the South Central District. She had gone with Texas Joe in the buckboard and they had taken her saddle horse, El Capitan.

When would La Senorita return? Ynez did not know.

CHAPTER XIX.

GATHERED AT BARBARA'S COURT.

BARBARA'S trip to the South Central District was full of interest. Riding with Texas Joe in a light buckboard drawn by a span of lively broncos with El Capitan leading behind, she was as merry as a school-girl out for a long-talked-of holiday. The dark-faced old plainsman, whose iron will and marvelous endurance had brought his companions and the baby safely out of that land of death years before, turned often to look at her now while his keen eyes, dark still under their grizzly brows, were soft with fond regard, and his voice, gentle and drawling as ever, was filled with tender affection. Under his drooping gray mustache, black once, his slow smile came in the ready answer of full sympathy with her mood.

Eager as ever to know all about the work of reclaiming her Desert, the young woman plied him with questions and Texas exerted himself to recall scenes and incidents of which he had not told her before. He reviewed the work from that first survey to the present with vivid pictures of life in the camps, in the towns, or on the trail, with construction gangs and grading crews or freighters' outfits, and the glimpses of toil and hardship, discomforts and suffering lost none of their reality in the dry humor of his words. Texas Joe was of that sort who habitually laugh at hardships, who, indeed, could not otherwise live in the wild lands they helped to tame. Nor did the shrewd old frontiersman fail to observe how most of Barbara's questions required in their answers something touching Willard Holmes, or how the incidents that pleased her most were those in which the engineer figured. On her part the young woman was secretly delighted to see how loyally her companion spoke in admiring praise of the desert-bred surveyor, Abe Lee. Whenever the name of Holmes was mentioned, Abe was somehow brought into the story.

"Mr. Holmes is really a fine engineer, don't you think?" asked Barbara mischievously at the conclusion of a story in which both Holmes and Abe figured.

"Sure he is. I don't reckon them eastern schools ever turned out a better. And what counts more, sometimes, he's all man, he is. But you see, honey, he belongs to the Company. Abe now, wal—you see, Abe, he sabeys the country like a burro does the cook shack and he's just as good a man as the Easterner, though not so pretty to look at. And you can bet there don't no Company get a hobble on Abe."

"Do the men who work for the Company like Mr. Holmes?"

"Sure they do. All the men like Holmes fine. But they just naturally love Abe."

But when they had turned into the San Felipe trail and were traveling eastward, Barbara ceased to question Texas about the reclamation work and led him to tell her again the familiar story of his journey from San Felipe with Mr. Worth, the Seer, Pat and the boy Abe, in the days when that old road was the only mark of man in all those miles of desolate waste.

Reaching a point where the sand hills could be distinguished, he pointed them out to her, and the young woman, at sight of the huge rolling drifts that shone all golden in the desert sun, grasped his arm with a low exclamation. In silence, as they drew nearer, they watched the low yellow hills lift their naked bulk up from the gray and green patches of salt-bush and greasewood that so thinly carpeted the plain. When even the desert vegetation could find no life in the ever shifting sands and the first of the great drifts loomed huge and forbidding against the sky, seeming to bar their way, Barbara spoke again. "Now tell me, Uncle Tex; tell me as we go just how it was and show me the places."

The plainsman did not answer and she urged again: "Please, Uncle Tex, tell me. I want to see it all just as it happened. I feel that I must, don't you understand?"

So the old plainsman told her and pointed out the places as nearly as he could, explaining how the drifts moved always eastward under the winds; how at times, most frequently in the spring months, when the fierce gales swept down through the Pass and across the Basin, the huge billows of sand would roll forward so swiftly that tents or wagons in their path would be buried in a few hours, and how, in the calm seasons, with every light breeze they work their silent way inch by inch. Even as he spoke Barbara, looking, saw a thin film of sand, fine as powdered snow, curl like mist over the edge of a drift as a breath of air swept lightly up the western slope and over the summit of the hill.

At the point where Mr. Worth's party had camped to await the passing of the storm, Texas stopped the team and showed her how they had rigged their rude canvas shelter on one side of the wagon to protect themselves from the cutting blast. Farther on he pointed out the spot where they had found the horse with the broken halter strap, and then they came to the great drift where her people had made their last camp and where, later, Jefferson Worth had spent that night alone with the spirit that lives in La Palma de la Mano de Dios.

Again Texas halted his team, and Barbara, leaving her companion in the buckboard, climbed to the top of the hill that held buried deep in its heart— what? Was the body of her true father buried there? Were there brothers, sisters, lying under that huge mound? Could the sands, if they could speak, tell her who she was, her name and people? Could they, if they would, make known to her relatives and friends of her own blood?

Coming slowly down the shoulder of the drift she went around to the foot of the steep eastern side and there, in the lee of the billow that curled high above her, she tried to dig with her hands a tiny hole. At every movement that displaced a handful of sand, a dry golden flood poured down from above, covering instantly the mark she had made. With sudden energy the young woman exerted all her strength digging faster and faster. But still, from above her head, down the steep side of the drift the sand slid without effort, making a faint whispering sound as if to mock her labors. Then Texas called and she went back to him, her brown eyes hard and dry.

The old plainsman, quick to feel her mood, would have driven swiftly on past the remaining scenes of the tragedy and tried to talk of other things. But she would not have it so. She must know all. So he showed her where he had first found the tracks in the sand and then where the baby feet had left their marks when the tired mother had set her down to rest.

Thus they came at last, when the day was almost gone, to the grave beside the trail—the trail that had beside its many miles so many graves. And Barbara stood before the simple headstone that bore only the date and one word "Mother." And the silent man, who had in his wild adventurous life witnessed so many scenes of death, turned away his face that he might not see the girl kneeling beside the mound of earth.

When Barbara, coming back to the buckboard, saw him so, she understood; and when Texas, hearing her light steps, turned quickly toward her he saw the brown eyes filled now with softening tears while her face expressed the gratitude she could not put into words.

Behind them the upper rim of the sun shone blood-red above the top of the purple mountain wall; over their heads in the soft still depths of the velvet sky an early star appeared. Around them on every side the great desert lay under its seas of soft color, its veils of misty light and streaming scarfs of lilac and rose. Even as they looked the dusk of twilight fell upon the great plain. The ground-owl's weird call came from a hummock near the trail, the ghostly form of a coyote slipped stealthily past like a shadow moving from shadow to shadow until he was lost in the deeper shade, out of which, as if in mocking challenge of a spirit band to any mortal who would follow, came the wild, snarling, unearthly cries of his invisible mates. And still to the eastward the higher levels of the Mesa above the rim of the dark Basin, the slow drifting clouds of dust that lifted from the tired feet of the grading teams coming into the camp from the day's work on the canals, or from freighters drawing near their journey's end, caught the last of the light and showed long level bands and bars and threads of gold against the deep purple of the hills beyond, whose peaks and domes and ridges were flaming crimson, burnished copper and gleaming silver on the deep background of the sky. Before them on the other side of the deep Dry River channel, through which now a generous stream of water flowed, they could see the tents of the camp —some glowing brightly from lights within, others showing mere spots of dull white in the gloom, while here and there lanterns, like great fireflies, flitted aimlessly to and fro.

Before two tent houses, some distance apart from the main camp and built under a wide ramada made of willow poles and arrow weed brought from the distant river, Texas stopped his team. From the open door of one of the tents Jefferson Worth came quickly, at the sound of their arrival, to receive his daughter, and from her father's arms Barbara turned to greet Abe Lee who, following his chief from the canvas house, had paused a little back from the group in the shadow of the ramada. Later in the evening, when Barbara had had her supper with her father and Abe in the big camp dining tent and the three were sitting in the dark under the wide brush porch, Pat came with Texas, as the big Irishman said, "to see how the new boss liked her quarters." And then Pablo came softly out of the darkness with his guitar to bid La Senorita welcome and to ask if she would care that night to listen a little to the music that he knew she loved.

So Barbara held her little court before the rude tent house under the arrow weed ramada, in the heart of her Desert, within a stone's throw of the spot where they had gathered once before around a baby girl whose mother lay dead beside a dry water hole. And not one of them thought of the significance of the group or how each, representing a distinct type, stood for a vital element in the combination of human forces that was working out for the race the reclamation of the land. The tall, lean, desert-born surveyor, trained in no school but the school of his work itself, with the dreams of the Seer ruling him in his every professional service; the heavy-fisted, quick-witted, aggressive Irishman, born and trained to handle that class of men that will recognize in their labor no governing force higher than the physical; the dark-faced frontiersman, whom the forces of nature, through the hard years, had fashioned for his peculiar place in this movement of the race as truly as wave and river and wind and sun had made The King's Basin Desert itself; the self-hidden financier who, behind his gray mask, wrought with the mighty force of his age—Capital; and a little to one side, sitting on the ground, reclining against one of the willow posts that upheld the arrow weed shelter, dark Pablo, softly touching his guitar, representing a people still far down on the ladder of the world's upward climb, but still sharing, as all peoples would share, the work of all; and, in the midst of the group, the center of her court—Barbara, true representative of a true womanhood that holds in itself the future of the race, even as the desert held in its earth womb life for the strong ones whom the slow years had fitted to realize it.

"Faith," said Pat, when Pablo's guitar was silent for a little, "av only the Seer was here the family wud be altogether complete."

"Dear old Seer," said Barbara softly. "How he would love to be here; and how we would love to have him!"

But under cover of the darkness a warm blush colored the young woman's cheeks, for when Pat spoke she had not been thinking of the absence of her old friend, but wishing for the presence of another engineer, who also was working for the reclamation of her Desert and who was himself in turn being wrought upon by his work, learning as the girl had hoped he would learn, the language of the land.

Jefferson Worth spoke in his exact way. "Even if he is not here this is all the Seer's work."

And just then from a distance up the old wash came the weird, unnatural cry of a coyote. It was as though the spirit of the desert spoke in answer to the banker's words.

"Yell, ye sneakin', thievin' imp. Yer time in this counthry is about up!" exclaimed the Irishman with a growl of deep satisfaction. And again out of the shadow the soft, plaintively sweet music of Pablo's guitar floated away on the still darkness of the night.

CHAPTER XX.

WHAT THE STAKES REVEALED.

AMES GREENFIELD, returning to Kingston from his tour of inspection, left at once for his own world—a world of offices with mahogany furniture, of men with white collars and pale faces, of banks and trust companies, and Good Business.

The afternoon of the day he left, Willard Holmes rode into the camp at Dry River Crossing. The engineer explained that he was looking over the route of a new main canal that was being surveyed by his men and that, finding himself in the vicinity of Mr. Worth's headquarters, he had taken the opportunity to call.

From Barbara as well as from Jefferson Worth and Abe Lee the Company man received a hearty welcome with a cordial invitation to ride with them the next day over the line of their work. Although Holmes watched with peculiar sensitiveness, there was no sign from either of the three that they had yet discovered the real significance of the South Central deal or that they knew the part he had played in it. His desire to end the whole unpleasant situation by going over the work with Mr. Worth and the surveyor, and by confessing to Barbara how he had permitted her father to walk into the trap, led him to accept the invitation.

The little party left camp early the next morning
and following the line of Black's survey found a
mile or more of the canal already completed, while
a large force of men and teams was at work clearing
the ground and pushing the big ditch still farther in
a general southerly direction toward the Company
canal fifteen miles away.

Abe Lee explained to Barbara that other camps
were located at points farther on, thus dividing the
whole district to be excavated into several sections.
"You see," he said turning to Holmes, "the waste
from Dry River Heading coming down the old channel gives us water at several points so that we can
handle this work to a little better advantage than we
used to do with the first of the Company canals."

"I see," said the Company man. "And how many
head of stock are you working?"

"About fifteen hundred now, but we are increasing
the force right along. We expect to handle about
twice that."

Instantly Willard Holmes saw that he could still
save Jefferson Worth from heavy financial loss. But
it was to the interest of The King's Basin Land and
Irrigation Company for Jefferson Worth to lose
heavily. What should he do?

They had left the first section of the work now
and were following the line of the survey where
the brush had been roughly cleared. The engineer,
preoccupied in his struggle with the question that
confronted him, had dropped behind the others, when
suddenly Barbara, looking back, checked El Capitan.
"What's the matter, Mr. Holmes?" she called.

The others also looked back to see the engineer kneeling on the ground. Jefferson Worth glanced quickly at his superintendent who chuckled outright.

"What is it?" cried Barbara at Abe's unusual laugh. "What's the joke?"

Before either of the men could answer, Holmes sprang to his saddle and, with a quick jab of his spurs in the horse's flanks, rejoined them on the run. In his excitement the mental habits of his life asserted themselves and he was again the typical corporation official dealing with a mere private individual operating on a small scale. "Look here!" he burst forth sharply to Abe; "these are not our Company stakes. You are not following Black's line."

The surveyor grinned. "We followed it for a half mile this side of the cut, then we branched off. You evidently did not notice."

"Where do you strike it again?"

"We don't strike it again."

"Then how do you get to the intake location?"

"We don't get to the intake *you* located at all. We strike your canal three miles farther up."

The Company's chief engineer retorted hotly: "But you can't do that. Our survey shows"—he stopped.

"Your survey shows what?" came Abe Lee's sharp challenge. "You are undoubtedly familiar with the data turned in by your man Black, for you told Mr. Worth the quality of the soil before he closed the deal. What else does your survey show?"

Before the engineer could answer, Jefferson Worth's cool voice broke in. "You understand, Mr.

Holmes, that there is nothing in my contract with your Company that binds me to follow the line of your survey or accept your location of the intake. The Company contracts to deliver the water into my canal, that is all."

The engineer regained control of himself. "I beg your pardon, Mr. Worth; and yours, Lee. I forgot myself. I see that my man Black made a mistake."

Abe laughed dryly. "In checking over Black's work, Holmes, I found his elevations correct at every point."

Holmes himself smiled as he said: "Well, Lee, whether you believe me or not, I am very glad you checked over Black's work, and, Mr. Worth, with all my heart I wish you success in your project."

"Thank you," said Worth, "I am already indebted to you for a valuable piece of information."

"Indebted to me?"

"You remember what I asked you when I was going over this proposition with Greenfield and Burk in the Company office?"

"I remember that you asked me about the soil in the district."

"You answered that the *soil* was all right."

Holmes drew a long breath. "And you let Uncle Jim and Burk think——"

"I let them think what they wanted to think," said Jefferson Worth.

Barbara, who had listened with intense interest to the conversation, at Holmes's unfinished remark and her father's reply moved El Capitan slowly away from his place beside Worth's horse and went close to Abe Lee. All the gladness was gone from the young woman's face now, and while she maintained a show of interest it was plainly forced.

The banker, at his daughter's movement, retreated behind his gray mask and for the rest of the trip spoke only when it was necessary, leaving her entirely to the surveyor and Willard Holmes.

Barbara had understood from the talk of the men that her father, by using the unsuspecting engineer, had in some way shrewdly gained a business advantage over the Company. The incident forced her, as she thought, to see with a cruel clearness that to Jefferson Worth this splendid work of reclaiming the desert was nothing but the opportunity to win larger financial gains; that he was still practicing the tactics for which he was famous. She shrank from him unconsciously but to the man as plainly as she had drawn back in fear that night years before. As the baby had turned from him to the Seer then, the young woman turned from him to Abe Lee now.

During the rest of the day Barbara kept so close to the surveyor's side that Willard Holmes had no opportunity to talk with her alone, and when they arrived again at the headquarters camp the engineer, promising to call upon her soon in Kingston, left for one of his own camps a few miles away.

That evening Jefferson Worth and his daughter sat alone under the arrow weed ramada facing the river. Moving her camp chair closer in the dusk—so close that, reaching out she laid her warm young hand on the hand of her father—Barbara said in a low tone: "Daddy, I wish you would tell me all about this South Central District business."

She felt the slim nervous fingers move uneasily. Never before had Barbara asked him to explain any of his transactions. The man's habit of retiring behind that gray mask whenever the subject of his business was mentioned, together with the girl's instinctive shrinking lest his answers to such a question should drive them farther apart, prevented. But to-night, perhaps because Willard Holmes was concerned, perhaps because of her peculiar interest in the work involved, Barbara forced herself to ask.

"What do you want to know?"

At his expressionless tone it was to Barbara as though she felt the chill of his cold mask coming between them, but she persisted and in her voice was passionate earnestness. "I want to know all about it, father; I must."

"Why?"

"Because"—she hesitated. "Because I understood from the conversation to-day about the surveys that someone had made a mistake. I—I don't want to make a mistake, daddy. Won't you please explain it all to me? What was it that you let Mr. Greenfield and Mr. Burk think?"

Perhaps because of the memories of the place, or because it was the first time Barbara had ever sought an explanation, or again perhaps it was because Willard Holmes was interested, Jefferson Worth answered: "I let them think I was a fool."

"But why was Mr. Holmes so excited to-day when he found out about those stakes?"

"He discovered that I was not such a fool as they thought."

Then Jefferson Worth explained to the girl the whole situation. He made clear Greenfield's reason for offering him the water rights; why he would have taken the stock without investigation but for the hint he received from the Company engineer's manner and the way Holmes had answered that simple question about the soil; how he had made the survey secretly, because Greenfield would have refused to close the deal if he had known that Worth wanted it after he had it investigated, and because if Greenfield believed the district stock to be valueless he would sell at a very low figure rather than not sell at all; and how it was that same low figure that enabled him to give the men who were working on the canal a chance to acquire farms of their own.

When he had made it all plain, the young woman exclaimed: "And this man Greenfield and those with him in the Company are the men who are doing the Seer's work; who are making the reclamation of the desert possible! I don't—I can't understand it."

"It is a very simple business deal," said Worth. "There is nothing unusual about it. Greenfield and his men are good men; they are simply defending their interests from a competitor. This Desert never could be reclaimed at all without them or others like them."

"Tell me again, daddy; was Mr. Holmes *sure* that this land was worthless?"

"Certainly he was sure of it. He had all of Black's data giving the elevations."

"And he knew that they were trying to sell it to you?"

"Yes."

"But did he know *why*? Did he know it was a trap to ruin your work?"

"Certainly, he must have known."

The girl's voice trembled. "Oh, why—why didn't he tell you? Why didn't he warn you?"

"He did."

"Yes, daddy, but he did not *intend* to do it, for to-day he did not know that he had until you explained. And I thought—I thought——" Her voice ended in a sob.

"But Barbara, Holmes did just what he should have done. He is in the employ of the Company. He had no right to interfere with their business."

"Every man has a right to be a man," she answered hotly. "Abe wouldn't have kept still. The Seer would not have helped them in their schemes. I don't wonder that the Company discharged the Seer to give Mr. Holmes his place!"

Jefferson Worth was silent for a little, then he said: "If I had thought that you would blame Holmes I never would have told you."

"But you did right to tell me. I am glad, for I see now that I *was* making a mistake—that I was making two mistakes. I misjudged you, daddy—forgive me; and I—I have been mistaken about Mr. Holmes."

For an hour or more the two sat silent, the mind of each occupied with thoughts that were much the same. Barbara for the first time felt that she could enter fully into her father's life. She had at last seen behind his gray mask and found herself in full sympathy with him. And the lonely man knew that at last he had gained that for which his heart hungered—the fullest companionship of the girl he loved as his only child.

At last Barbara said softly: "Daddy, I am not going back to Kingston to-morrow. I am going to stay here with you. You can have another tent house built and Texas can go for Ynez who will bring what things I need. I am going to make a home for you. You need me, daddy. You are so alone in your work; no one understands you as I do now. Let me come and help you."

Awkwardly Jefferson Worth put out his hand and drawing his daughter closer said in a tone that Barbara had never heard before: "I was wishing that you would want to stay. You—you are not afraid of me now, Barbara?"

"Why, no, of course not; what a strange thing to ask! I have never been afraid of you; why should I be?"

And Barbara thought that she spoke truly—that she had never feared him; though Jefferson Worth knew better.

So another tent house was built and Texas went alone to Kingston, to return with Ynez as Barbara had planned, and the young woman set about making a home for her father in the rude desert camp.

Every day nearly she rode El Capitan out to some part of the work, and the men who were toiling for more than wages learned to know her and to hail her presence as a good omen. Many a rough fellow, dreaming of wife or sweetheart and the home he would make for them in the desert as he drove his team and held the bar of his Fresno, worked the harder for a cheery word from the daughter of his employer.

And every evening under the ramada Barbara sat with her father, often alone, sometimes with one or more of her little court; and always the talk was of the work, save for the times when Pablo would come softly to make music for his Senorita and then they would sit silently, listening to the sweet harmonies that floated away into the night.

Often Barbara would go the short distance from the house to the old wash; there to sit almost on the very spot where her mother had perished beside the dry water hole; and watching the stream that now flowed through the old channel, or looking away across the deep cut to the sand hills that showed clearly in the distance, she would live over the story as she had learned it that day with Texas—asking the old, old question, to which there was still no answer.

One afternoon as she was sitting there, two wagons with a small party of men appeared on the high bank of the stream opposite. As the men climbed down from their seats, someone on horseback rode to the edge of the cut and sat for a moment looking across. Even at that distance she knew him; it was Willard Holmes. Watching she saw him turn and by his motions guessed that he was giving some instructions to the men. Then he rode away toward the Crossing.

Quickly Barbara returned to the rude porch of the tent house and in a few minutes saw the engineer approach. Dismounting and throwing the reins over his horse's head he came to her smiling, sombrero in hand. "Buenas dias, Senorita. Please may I have a drink?"

"Certainly, Mr. Holmes; help yourself." She pointed to the olla hanging in the shade of the ramada.

The engineer started at her cool reply, given as she would have addressed a stranger, and, more to regain his composure than because he was thirsty, helped himself from the earthen water jar. When he could delay no longer he turned again to her, and forcing himself to speak as if he had not noticed the lack of warmth in her greeting said: "I was sorry to miss you in town. I called several times."

"I am keeping house here for father," she answered.

"Then we will be neighbors," he said with assumed lightness; "at least half-way neighbors. A party of my surveyors will be camped over there across the river. I will be with them part of the time."

When she made no reply to this, the man understood. Slowly he drew on his gloves and, laying aside all pretense, said simply: "I have been trying to see you, Miss Worth, because I wanted to tell you myself of the miserable part I took in the shameful trick my uncle attempted to play on your father. I see that you know all about it and I realize that it is quite useless for me to ask you to forgive me."

He paused, but still the young woman was silent.

The man could not know how she was fighting to keep back the tears.

"You told me plainly that you could never forgive one who was untrue to his work," he went on hopelessly, "and you are right. There was a time, before I knew you, when I would have defended my action, when I would have held that it was right; but I cannot now. Perhaps if I had known you longer—— But what's the use. I am a sad bungler in this great work, Miss Worth. I am out of place in the big desert. I should have stayed at home. I wish—I wish you had never wakened me to the possibilities of life—real life. You would not need to feel ashamed for me now."

When she looked up he was mounting his horse. Almost she cried out to him, but he rode quickly out of her sight.

CHAPTER XXI.

PABLO BRINGS NEWS TO BARBARA.

LL through the long hot months of that second summer Barbara stayed in the desert with her father. Many times Mr. Worth insisted that she should go to the coast or the mountains for a few weeks, while Abe, Texas and Pat added their entreaties. But the young woman's answer was always—to her father: "If you must stay, daddy, then I must stay to take care of you;" to Abe it was: "Why don't you take a vacation? This is just as much my work as it is yours;" to Texas it was a laughing question whether he thought she was a "quitter," and to Pat she always declared that the desert could not in the least hurt her complexion.

"And look at the other women," she would argue. There was Jack Hanson's little wife, with their children, in a twelve by fourteen tent out there on their claim alone all day and many nights, while Jack was on the work. And Mrs. White, who stoutly declared that she was "sure going to stand by her Jim if it burned her to a crisp," and that they did not have the money to spend even if they could leave the crops they had managed to plant. And Mrs. Rollins and Mrs. Baird and Mrs. Cole and the others, who were holding down their husbands' claims while the men were earning money on the works to help them in getting their start. Surely if these women

304

could stay with their men-folk Barbara could. So Mr. Worth let her have her way. And the other three strove among themselves, with varied and picturesque figures of speech, and—it must be confessed —some rather strong language, to express their admiration for her courage and endurance, while all four taxed their inventive powers to the limit devising ways to add to her comfort.

The work in the South Central District continued steadily with no delay through lack of help, and when the canal was finished and the water ready, the men who had built it turned to making the ditches on their own claims, leveling their land for irrigation, preparing for the first crops and making what other improvements they could. Meanwhile the new townsite was laid out on the ground already occupied by the headquarters camp and the camp itself became the town of "Barba."

But, perhaps because—as Pablo said—"there was no Senorita in the Company," Greenfield's chief engineer again found it hard to hold his men through the hot months and was obliged to discontinue work on their Central Main. Holmes himself spent the weeks of the flood season at the river, refusing to leave even for a day. Three times, when conditions at the intake and heading were most critical and the danger that threatened the unconscious settlers seemed imminent, the engineer sent for Abe Lee, while Texas, Pat and Pablo were instructed by Mr. Worth to be ready at an hour's notice to move the entire working force of the district to the scene of the expected disaster.

And still, even through those trying times Jefferson Worth continued his operations in all parts of the Basin and started various enterprises in his new town with the conviction of a born fatalist, though he almost constantly now, except when he was with Barbara, wore that expressionless gray mask. Abe Lee's thin face, burned dark by constant exposure to the fierce desert sun, had a look of watchful readiness. And Barbara, seeing, thought that it was all because of the strain of their own work, for even Barbara was not told of the terrible risk that the Company was forcing the pioneers to take.

Meanwhile James Greenfield and the Company officials, from the outside, watched the situation with the calmness of professional gamblers watching the turn of the cards. Though he did not come into the desert during the summer, the Company president spent most of his time in the West now, for the Reclamation project launched by him was assuming such proportions that his personal attention was justified. Only one thing more was needed to bring such a flood of land-seekers, speculators and investors that the Company's immense profits would be assured. The new country must have a railroad.

To this end, in the city by the sea, the eastern financier was bringing every influence he could command to bear upon the officials of the Southwestern and Continental that skirted the rim of the Basin. But the great man who shaped the destinies of the S. & C., secure in the knowledge that his road controlled the only pass through the range of mountains that shut in the new country, for some reason refused

to build a branch line into the territory in which
Mr. Greenfield was so deeply interested.

James Greenfield, himself a power of the first magnitude in the financial world, was always admitted to
the presence of the railroad man without delay and
was always received by the official with every courtesy. His statements as to the extent and value of the
lands that were being developed by his Company,
with his estimates of the volume of business that a
branch line would bring to the Southwestern and
Continental, were received without question. The
railroad man even betrayed unusual interest in the
reclamation of The King's Basin Desert, with a
knowledge of conditions almost as complete as Mr.
Greenfield's. Frequently he asked of Jefferson
Worth's operations and of the development of the
South Central District. But always he shook his
head when Greenfield urged immediate action. There
were certain reasons; he was not at liberty to go into
details. Some day no doubt the branch line would
be built, but he could make no promises.

This was the situation in the fall when, with the
danger from the river past and his canals finished,
Jefferson Worth sought an interview with the president of The King's Basin Land and Irrigation Company at his office in the Coast city.

Mr. Greenfield received the banker cordially, congratulated him upon the success of his South Central
District work and prophesied great things for everybody interested in The King's Basin project.

Jefferson Worth, behind his gray mask, at once
made known the object of his visit. He wished to

secure from the Company the right to take water from their Central Main for a small power house to be located in the Dry River wash. Mr. Worth explained frankly the advantage it would give the new town of Barba, in which he was interested, and stated that he had, some time before, laid his proposition before the Company's manager in order that Mr. Greenfield might be informed of the matter.

Greenfield said that he had heard from Mr. Burk and that he thought it might be arranged. Then, while Jefferson Worth listened with his usual careful attention, the Company man set forth their great need of a railroad. And by the way; was Mr. Worth personally acquainted with the man who controlled the S. & C.?

"I know of him," came the cautious reply.

"Well, Mr. Worth," said the president; "I'll tell you what we'll do. We need that railroad and we need it now. So far I have failed to get any definite promise from the S. & C. that they will give us a branch line. If you can secure a railroad for the Basin this year, we will give you the right of way for your power canal and a contract for the water."

"Is that your only proposition?"

"That is my only proposition."

The president of The King's Basin Land and Irrigation Company would have been astonished if he could have witnessed the meeting of Jefferson Worth and the railroad man an hour later.

"Hello, Jeff!" came in hearty tones from the official as the door of his private office closed behind the banker. "How are you? I hear that Greenfield sold you a gold brick."

Mr. Worth smiled while the other laughed heartily. "I tell you, Jeff, we little Westerners have got to watch out for these big eastern operators or they'll take the whole blamed country away from us."

"The gold brick is panning out pretty well so far," said the banker.

"So I understand. Crawford has been telling me all about it. In fact the whole King's Basin proposition looks mighty good to me, except for that New York bunch. I'm afraid of them, Jeff. Greenfield has been camping on my trail for three months, wanting us to build them a branch line. I told Crawford yesterday that it was about time for you to come around."

"When *are*·you going to build that road?" asked Mr. Worth.

The other shook his head. "Can't do it, Jeff. You know the situation as well as I. If the river comes in the whole country will go to smash; and with the class of structures they have put in to control it and with an eastern engineer in charge, it's too big a chance. The S. & C. is not spending money to help out wild-cat projects promoted by eastern capital."

"But if you give us the branch line it will insure the success of the project, for it will make the Company property so valuable that they will spend more money to protect it."

"Or"—added the other—"*we* would have to spend more money to protect it. I'm sorry Jeff, if that's what you have been figuring on, but we are not an insurance company—we are in the transportation business."

"Then you won't build into the Basin?"

"Not under existing conditions, Jeff."

With as little show of emotion as he would have exhibited had he merely proposed to purchase a morning paper, Jefferson Worth said: "All right, then I'll build it myself."

The railroad man knew that the quietly spoken words meant that the banker had determined to stake everything he had in the world upon a chance that even the S. & C., with its unlimited capital, refused to take. With his already large investments in the new country, the building of the railroad would tax Worth's resources to the very limit and the failure of the Company's project would mean for him financial ruin.

During the flood season just past Jefferson Worth had seen the safety of the Reclamation work hanging on a very slender thread. Every hour he had looked for the disaster that would bring to nothing all that had been accomplished by the desert pioneers, whose ruin he would share, yet he calmly proposed now to throw into the venture everything that years of unceasing toil had brought him—his capital, his credit, his reputation.

"Don't do it, Jeff," said his friend. "You are in deep enough now. Better keep an anchor to windward."

"I figured on taking a chance when I went into that country," said Worth simply. It was as if he had foreseen this situation from the very beginning and had planned how he would meet it. The railroad man's face expressed his admiration for this display of nerve.

"If I can do anything for you let me know, Jeff."

"Thanks. If you would just not mention to anyone that I am connected with this for a little while."

"Oh, I see. Greenfield again, I suppose? What are you up to anyway, Jeff; buying another gold brick?"

Worth explained his plan for a power plant and Greenfield's proposition.

"Hell!" exclaimed the dignified official. "You can't tell me that you are going to build a railroad into Greenfield's town just to get a dinky little power plant in your own district. I'm not from New York, Jeff."

To which Jefferson Worth answered from behind his mask: "The Basin needs a railroad."

The next day Greenfield sought the railroad office in haste. "I understand that you have decided to build that branch road."

The official, who had received his guest with the dignified courtesy befitting one of his position, smiled at the other's manner as a gracious sovereign might smile on granting a subject's petition.

Greenfield accepted the smile as an assent. "May I ask when you will begin the work?"

"I cannot say exactly, Mr. Greenfield. The survey will probably be made at once and the work begun as soon as it is possible to assemble men and material."

When The King's Basin Messenger announced that the survey was being made for a railroad from the main line of the S. & C. at Deep Well to Kingston, it did not mention the fact that Abe Lee was in charge of the work. And James Greenfield, who signed the promised contract following the announcement, did not learn until the next issue of the Messenger that the road was not being built by the S. & C. but by Jefferson Worth himself.

Quickly the news that the railroad was building into The King's Basin was spread by the papers throughout the surrounding country and from every side the swelling flood of life poured in. Every section of the new lands felt the influence of the rush. For miles around the towns, every vacant tract was seized by the incoming settlers. Townsite companies quickly laid out new towns, while in the towns already established new business blocks and dwellings sprang up as if some Aladdin had rubbed his lamp. Real estate values advanced to undreamed figures and the property was sold, re-sold and sold again. And Kingston, the heart and center of it all—Kingston, Texas Joe said, "went plumb locoed."

The name of Jefferson Worth was on every tongue. Was he not the wizard who commanded prosperity and wealth to wait upon The King's Basin? Was he not the Aladdin who rubbed the lamp?

Horace P. Blanton, who seemed to increase magically as if, indeed, he fed on the stuff of which booms are made, did not lack for audience now as he talked in rolling phrases of his friend Worth and what "we" had done, with suggestive hints of still greater things

that "we" again would do. To see the great Horace
P. in all the glory of white vest and picture-hat, as
he escorted parties of awe-stricken newcomers about
the town and pointed out with majestic gestures
"our" opera house, "our" bank, "our" power house,
"our" ice plant, the site of "our" new depot, was
an experience never to be forgotten. To watch him
give orders, when Pat was not near, to some laborer
in the grading gang at work on the roadbed and yards
or to see him instructing a merchant in the finer
points of his business, was a delight. To hear him
speak with authority upon every question relating to
The King's Basin project, from the stage of the
water in the river two years before the first survey,
and the future plans of Jefferson Worth, to the chem-
ical properties of the soil, the proper grade for irri-
gating alfalfa and the kinds and varieties of fruits
and vegetables best adapted to the climate, was as
instructive as it was interesting.

With the beginning of the work on the railroad,
Barbara and her father again made their home in
Kingston, and Horace P. Blanton, whenever he could
escape from his arduous duties, endeavored earnestly
to make himself agreeable to Jefferson Worth's
daughter. There was no mistaking either his purpose or his perfect confidence in his ability to achieve
success. Many and ingenious were the things that
three members of Barbara's court promised each
other should happen to Horace P.

It was on one of those afternoons, when the man
with the white vest was making himself very much at
home on the front porch of the Worth cottage, that

Pablo riding in from the South Central District sought La Senorita. Dismounting from his tired horse the Mexican, his spurs clanking on the walk, approached Barbara, and with his sombrero brushing the ground greeted her in his native tongue, turning an inquiring eye meanwhile upon the portly Horace P.

Barbara returned his greeting in Spanish, following her words in English with: "This is Senor Blanton, Pablo. Mr. Blanton, this is my friend Pablo Garcia."

The white man acknowledged the introduction with a lordly gesture.

The Mexican, with a gleam of his white teeth said: "I have the pleasure to see the Senor sometimes before. He is what they call 'the booster.' I have hear him talk many times on street." Then to Barbara: "I am come quick, Senorita, to find Senor Worth or Senor Lee. You know if it is far to where they are? I ride fast. My horse is tired."

Before the young woman could answer, the big man, with a voice of authority, said: "You will find them out on the line of the railroad somewhere between here and Deep Well. Just follow the grade. You can't miss it."

Pablo should have considered himself dismissed but, ignoring Blanton, he waited for Barbara's answer. "I don't know just where they are, Pablo. You had better wait until they come in. Is there anything wrong?"

The Mexican shrugged his shoulders with another

"Adios. Tell Barbara I'm all right"

glance toward her companion. "I cannot say, Senorita. There is no what you call accident, but I think better I come."

"What is it, my man?" said Horace P., again interrupting. "I will see Mr. Worth about it as soon as he comes in. You have no business troubling Miss Worth."

Barbara's slippered toe tapped the floor nervously although Barbara was not a nervous young woman.

Pablo, with another shrug, said coldly: "It is to tell Senor Worth or Senor Lee that I come. If La Senorita tells me I trouble her that is different."

The young woman spoke. "Put your horse in the barn, Pablo, and then come in. I know you have had nothing to eat since morning and you are all tired out. Ynez is away, but I will find something for you and you can rest here until father comes."

Pablo retreated and Barbara rising, said: "You will excuse me, Mr. Blanton."

"Are you going to let that greaser spoil our afternoon?" he asked in a tone of offended majesty.

The girl laughed outright. "You are so funny when you puff yourself up that way and try to look so kingly. Pray how is this *our* afternoon? What is left of it belongs to Pablo. I am going to find him something to eat and then I mean to talk to him every minute until father comes. You may stay if you like, but we shall talk in Spanish."

The face of Horace P. Blanton expressed fat anguish. Rising, he went closer and stood over her with a look which he imagined to be a look of melting tenderness and, in a voice that fairly dripped with honeyed sweetness, he began: "Miss Worth— Barbara, I—"

"*Sir!*" If Barbara had shot the word at him from Texas Joe's forty-five it could not have been more effective.

"I—I beg your pardon, Miss Worth," he stammered. "Certainly, certainly; by all means, Miss Worth. Good-by."

And that was as near as Horace P. Blanton ever came to achieving the success of which he was so confident.

A few minutes later Pablo, without hesitation, told Barbara what had brought him to Kingston. A Mexican friend, who worked for The King's Basin Land and Irrigation Company, had overheard a conversation between the Company Manager and the chief engineer, who were together inspecting the work on the Central Main Canal. Dropping into his quaint English, Pablo repeated what his friend had told him.

"Senor Holmes he say: 'The canal will go here where the stakes are set.' Senor Burk say: 'No, you shall go that other way.' 'But that will leave the power house away eight miles and the elevation it is not the same,' say Senor Holmes. Senor Burk say: 'Power house is Mr. Worth's not our. This way is good for us.' 'Senor Holmes no like it. He is very mad,' say my friend. He say: 'I will not do it.' Then Senor Burk say: 'All right, you lose your job. Greenfield say it must go there; it is an order.' Then they go 'way and my friend he tell me 'cause he think maybe it is no good for power house. I think maybe so Senor Worth like to know."

The next morning Jefferson Worth called upon the Manager of The King's Basin Land and Irrigation Company.

"Mr. Burk, I understand that you are changing the line of your Central Canal."

"We are."

"But my contract with your Company must be considered."

"We have already considered it, Mr. Worth. It relates only to the delivery of a certain amount of water into your canal. There is nothing in it that binds us to build *our* canal on the line surveyed."

CHAPTER XXII.

GATHERING OF OMINOUS FORCES.

KINGSTON was a boiling, seething, steaming volcano of hot wrath, burning indignation and fiery protest. Kingston cursed, raved, stormed and resoluted, then stormed, raved and resoluted some more. Kingston was tricked, betrayed, cheated, defrauded, insulted and mocked. And the unspeakable villain, the sordid wretch, the miserable gamester who had ruined Kingston was Jefferson Worth.

It is unknown to this day who first brought the news that all work on the railroad for a distance of seven miles out from Kingston was stopped and that the camps with their entire outfits had disappeared, leaving the scenes of their stirring activity as still and lifeless as if they had never existed. Next it was known that from Deep Well southward the construction train was still pushing its way into the Basin and that the work ahead of the train went on.

Then, while Kingston was wondering, questioning, discussing, the word went quickly around that the grading crews were setting up their camps twelve miles east of the Company town and that a line of stakes led one way to the town of Barba and the other way in the direction to meet the construction train working out from the junction with the S. & C. at Deep Well.

Then the startled people grasped the truth of the appalling situation and awoke from their dream. In the line of the railroad survey that had led to Kingston as straight as you could draw a string, there was now a curve seven miles away, the tangent of which would carry it twelve miles east of the Company town and straight into Barba.

Practically all business ceased, while the citizens in knots and groups discussed the situation. Jefferson Worth was in the Coast city and telegrams to him, all save one, received no answer. To a message from Mr. Burk he replied that the line had been changed by his orders. As for Abe Lee, they might as well have questioned one of the surveyor's grade stakes. Even Barbara, besought by the distracted citizens, could tell them nothing except that her father would return Saturday. There was nothing to do save to wait for Mr. Worth and to prepare for his coming.

When the president of The King's Basin Land and Irrigation Company arrived on the scene in answer to an urgent wire from his Manager, he was at once the center of public interest. But Mr. Greenfield escaped quickly from the crowd at the hotel and was very soon closeted with Burk in the office.

Then a boy found Horace P. Blanton. Horace P. was not hard to find. With the word that Mr. Greenfield desired to see him immediately, Horace P. Blanton increased visibly—so visibly that the spectators watched the white vest with no little anxiety.

"Tell Mr. Greenfield that I will see him immediately," he said in a voice that was easily heard across the street. Then Horace P. arrived at the door of the Company office a full length ahead of the messenger.

An hour later, when Blanton reappeared to the public eye, the white vest could no longer be buttoned over his expanding importance and beads of portentous dignity stood on his massive brow.

What did Greenfield want? What was the Company going to do? the crowd demanded eagerly.

From his lofty height the great one answered: "Our Company president simply desired my opinion and advice in this little difficulty. As to what we will do, I am not at liberty to make a public statement, but—" That "but" was filled with tremendous potential power.

"Did Mr. Greenfield know that the change in the railroad line was contemplated?"

"Certainly not. He learned of it first from the telegram that called him to Kingston."

"Why was the change in the road made?"

Horace P. Blanton smiled. It was very easy to understand if they would look over this man Worth's operations since he had been in the Basin. What had he done? First he had quietly invested heavily in Kingston real estate. Next he had as quietly, through his various companies and agents, gained control of all the public utilities in the new country. Then he had so manipulated things that he gained absolute control of the whole South Central District, one of the richest sections of the Basin, and had started the town of Barba on land owned by himself.

His next move was to gain control of the railroad, which, as every one knew, was started as an S. & C. line. "Remember," said the perspiring master of affairs, "that when this man Worth began work on the railroad into Kingston, he still owned a large amount of Kingston real estate with buildings and business establishments. To-day you will find that—save for the newspaper, the telephone line, the power plant, the ice plant, the bank and his home—he does not own a foot of land, a building, or a business establishment in Kingston. What has he done? He used the railroad to start a boom in our beautiful little city, then sold out at an immense profit and now, having no further interest in Kingston, changes the line of his road to Barba—the town that he owns, leaving us to make the most of the situation."

The orator's impressive climax called forth from every hearer furious invectives against the absent financier. Following the announcement of the coming of the road to Kingston, the name of Jefferson Worth had been on every tongue. The same name was on every tongue now, but the man that had been hailed as the good genius of the reclamation was now cursed for a selfish fiend, who would lay waste the whole country for his own greedy ends.

Horace P. Blanton exhausted both himself and the English language in a lurid, picturesque and vigorous delineation of the character of this monstrous enemy of the race. It was such gold-thirsty pirates as Jefferson Worth who, by preying upon legitimate business interests and coining for themselves the heart-blood of the people, made it so hard for such public benefactors as James Greenfield to promote the interests of the country.

It was beautiful to see how the speaker appreciated the splendid character, matchless genius and noble life of his friend Greenfield, the distinguished president of the King's Basin Company and the father of Reclamation. Some day, he declared, the citizens of the reclaimed desert, looking over their magnificent farms and beautiful homes, would appreciate the work of this man and understand then, as they could not now, how he had toiled in their interests. As for this fellow Jefferson Worth, dark and dreadful were the hints that Horace P. dropped as to his future.

It was Horace P. Blanton who arranged for a public indignation meeting in the Worth opera house the afternoon of Jefferson Worth's expected return. When the day arrived Kingston entertained the largest crowd that had ever gathered within the boundaries of the town. For word of the situation had traveled throughout the Basin, and from every corner of the new country men came to the scene of the excitement to attend the mass-meeting and to be present when the man that threatened Kingston with ruin should appear. Teamsters left their teams and Fresnos on the Company works, ranchers left their crops and cattle, newly located settlers forsook their ditching and leveling, zanjeros deserted their water gates and levees. Bold, hardy, venturesome spirits these were, with bodies toughened by hard toil in the open air and faces blackened and bronzed by constant exposure to the semi-tropical sun, for the desert did not yield to weaklings who would submit tamely to being skillfully juggled out of their own by a slim-fingered manipulator of business. Under the natural curiosity and love of entertainment that drew these strong, roughly dressed, roughly speaking pioneers to the point of interest, there was an under-current of grim determination to protect their new country from the schemes of unprincipled corporations. It was an old, old story.

At the mass-meeting there were many vigorous speeches by hot-headed ones, a masterly address by Horace P. Blanton, and—because he could not escape this—a few words by James Greenfield, who was introduced by Blanton as "the father of The King's Basin Reclamation work" and received by the citizens with generous applause. Acting upon Greenfield's suggestion, a committee was appointed to wait upon Mr. Worth immediately upon his arrival and the meeting adjourned until nine o'clock that evening, when the committee would report.

As the eventful day drew near its close, horsemen from the South Central District began to arrive. These were the men who had worked for Jefferson Worth on the canals and who, through him, were now developing ranches of their own. These South Central men scattered quietly through the crowd and soon in every group there was one or more of the new-comers, listening attentively. And it was a significant, though in that country an unnoticed fact, that every man from Jefferson Worth's district wore the familiar side-arms of the West. But these

attentive ones took no part in the discussions, speaking neither in defense nor in condemnation of the
man who had so stirred the public indignation.

As the hour for the arrival of the stage approached,
the crowd massed in front of the hotel, filling the
lobby, the arcade and the street, and still scattered
through the throng were the men from the South
Central District.

When the stage was seen in the distance a low
murmur, like the threatening rumble of a coming
storm, arose from the mass of men and, following
this, a hush like the hush of Nature before the storm
breaks. Into and through the strangely silent crowd
the driver of the six broncos forced his frightened
team. As the stage stopped and the passengers, looking curiously down into the excited faces of the
throng, prepared to alight, a murmur arose. The
murmur swelled into a roar. Jefferson Worth was
not there!

When the main line train discharged its Basin
passengers at the Junction that afternoon, the engine
of the construction train on the new road brought
Mr. Worth as far as the rails were laid. Here Texas
Joe, with a fast team and light buckboard, was waiting. So it happened that while the crowd was massing
in front of the hotel awaiting the arrival of the stage,
Jefferson Worth was at his home quietly eating his
supper and reassuring his frightened daughter.

When the assembled pioneers learned from the
stage driver that the man they waited for had left
the Junction on the engine, they were not long in
arriving at the truth. The excitement, inflamed by

what seemed the fear of Jefferson Worth and increased by the judicious efforts of Horace P. Blanton, was intense. From an orderly company of indignant citizens waiting to interview a public man, the crowd became a mob pursuing an escaping victim. With shouts and yells they started for the Worth home. And with them went the quiet men from the South Central District.

As the sound of the approaching crowd reached the two at the table, Barbara sprang to her feet, her face white with fear. "Daddy, they're coming. They're coming!" she whispered, trembling with anxiety for her father's safety. "Quick! El Capitan is ready. I told Pablo to have him saddled."

But Jefferson Worth, quietly sipping the cup of black coffee with which he always finished his meal, returned calmly: "Sit down, Barbara. I won't need El Capitan to-night."

As he spoke the crowd arrived at the front of the house and, as if to confirm his words, a sudden peaceful silence followed the uproar of their coming.

On the front porch, in the red level light of the sun that across the desert was just touching the topmost ridge of No Man's Mountains, stood the tall, grizzly-haired, dark-faced old-timer, Texas Joe; the heavy-shouldered, bull-necked Irish gladiator, Pat; and the lean, sinewy, iron-nerved man of the desert, Abe Lee; while quietly pushing and elbowing their way to the front were the men from the South Central District.

The quiet was broken by the slow, drawling voice of Texas Joe. "Evenin' boys. What for is the stampede? We-all trusts you ain't aimin' to tromp out the grass none on Mr. Worth's premises."

Within the house Barbara and her father heard the drawling challenge and the color returned to the young woman's cheeks as she smiled and whispered: "Good old Uncle Tex."

There was in that soft, southern voice an undercurrent of such cool readiness, such confident mastery of the situation, that her fears vanished. Nor was the crowd in front slow to recognize that which reassured Barbara.

For a moment following Texas Joe's greeting there was a restless shifting to and fro in the crowd, then the impressive bulk of Horace P. Blanton detached itself from the "common herd." With hands uplifted and a gesture of mingled command and appeal, he called: "No violence, men! No violence! For God's sake don't shoot! Let me talk a minute."

Whether he appealed to the three men on the porch or to the company behind him was not clear, but Texas answered: "You-all has the floor as usual, Senator. I don't reckon anybody here will be so impolite as to interrupt your remarks."

"Is Mr. Worth at home?"

"He sure is; altogether and very much to home."

"Could we—ah—see him to ask about a matter that concerns vitally every gentleman in this company?" Horace P. was regaining his breath and his poise at the same time.

"Mr. Worth, just at this minute, is engaged with his daughter at the supper table. His superintendent, Mr. Lee, is present and will be glad to hear what you have to say." The exact, formal politeness of the old plainsman was delightful. In spite of the gravity of the situation several in the crowd chuckled audibly.

"Mr. Worth will see your committee," said Abe crisply.

The citizens had forgotten their committee. Horace P. Blanton had made it difficult to remember. Three men now came out of the crowd at different points and went forward, James Greenfield's orator following them to the porch. But as the men came up the steps Abe spoke in a low tone to his companions, and Blanton found his way barred by the solid bulk of Pat.

"Were you also appointed to interview Mr. Worth?" asked Abe, dryly. "I understood it was a committee of three."

"I'm not exactly a member of our committee, but I'm always glad to offer my services in the best interests of the people."

"Mr. Worth will see the committee," said Abe.

"But you have no right, sir— This is an outrage, a disgrace! I—"

A growl from the Irishman interrupted him. "That's just fwhat I'm thinkin'. The presence av sich a domned hot air merchant as yersilf is a disgrace to any Gawd-fearin' company av honest workin'men. Av Abe here will only give me lave—"

Horace P. backed away, and from beyond reach of those huge fists said loftily: "My friend Mr. Worth shall hear of this."

" 'Tis likely that he will av ye stand widin rache of me two hands," agreed Pat.

Horace P. backed farther away. "I shall let him know that I offered my services," he declared with all the dignity he could command.

"Do," called the Irishman. "I think that av ye offered yersilf chape enough he might give ye a job wid a shovel on the grade. 'Tis mesilf wud be proud to have ye in me gang av rough-necks. Dom' me but I think I cud rejuce yer waist line to more reshpectable an' presintable deminsions."

At this the crowd laughed outright, for not one of those hardy pioneers but knew the real value of Horace P. Blanton to the reclamation work and therefore the force of the Irish boss's remarks.

While Pat and—against his will—the Company's representative were amusing the crowd, Abe led the committee to Jefferson Worth. One of these men was a prominent merchant who, for the first eight months of his business in Kingston, had occupied a store-room in one of Worth's buildings rent free. Another was a real estate man, whom the banker had supplied with funds that enabled him to make several profitable deals that would otherwise have been lost. The other man was a successful rancher, who owned a half-section of improved land joining the townsite. Deck Jordan had carried him at the store for implements, seed and provisions the first two years.

Jefferson Worth greeted them in his habitually colorless voice, and they—striving to see behind that gray mask—felt that there might be something in the situation that had not appeared on the surface in spite of the fact that the situation had been made so clear by Horace P. Blanton after his interview with the president of the Company. This quiet-voiced, calm-faced man, who had been so ready to help every worthy settler in the new country, did not appear at all the monster in disguise that the chief speaker at the mass-meeting had pictured. The committee, free from the heat of the crowd and the eloquence of Horace P., felt just a little ashamed.

"Mr. Worth," said the spokesman with a smile, "we were appointed to interview you about this railroad business."

"What do you wish to know, Gordon?"

"Well, first, is it true that you have sold out practically all of your property in Kingston?"

"Yes. It was my property." Jefferson Worth did not explain that he had sold because he was forced to turn everything he could into cash in order to build the railroad so badly needed by the new country.

The committee looked serious. "Is it true," continued the spokesman, "that you are changing the line of the railroad so as to take it to Barba and leave Kingston out entirely?"

"The line of the road is changed," came the exact, colorless answer.

"Will it be possible to make some arrangement by which you would carry out your former plan and build the road into Kingston?"

"You mean a bonus?"

"Yes."

"I'm not in the market."

"Is there nothing that we can do to change the situation?"

The answer startled the committee. "Tell Green field that he had better see me himself."

Jefferson Worth's relation to The King's Basin Land and Irrigation Company was always a much discussed question among the pioneers. The new country was settled by working people of limited means, and if there is one belief common to this class it is that all capitalists are members of one great robber band, perfectly organized, firmly united and operating in perfect harmony against their helpless victim—the public. However much they might fight among themselves over the division of the spoils, they were a unit in their common operations against the masses.

From the first Jefferson Worth was held by many to be the secret agent, the silent co-partner, of Greenfield, and the South Central District seemed to justify this opinion, for of course the public knew nothing of the inside of that deal. The people accepted Mr. Worth's personal assistance cheerfully, thankfully, and had come to look upon him as a friend. But this did not in the least alter their belief that he belonged to the band. He was simply a generous, gentlemanly sort of robber, kin to the hold-up man who returns the railroad tickets of the passengers and refuses to rob the ladies. This railroad situation had seemed to deny the relationship between the banker and the Company, and now came Worth's advice: "Tell Greenfield that he had better see me himself." It was no wonder that the members of the committee looked at each other startled and bewildered. Was it, after all, a fight between the members

of the band over the division of the spoils? It was
too deep for the committee. They could feel dimly
that mighty forces were stirring beneath the surface,
but they could not fathom what it was all about.
One thing was clear: the one thing that is always
clear when capital speaks to business men of their
class—they must obey.

"What shall we report to the crowd?" they asked
as they arose to go.

"I figured that you would tell them what I have
told you," came the answer.

The crowd, when the committee briefly reported
their interview, were as puzzled as the members of
the committee, and questioned and discussed, af-
firmed and denied until Pat said to his companions
on the porch that it sounded like "a flock av domned
bumble bees."

When the president of The King's Basin Land and
Irrigation Company, who dared not refuse the request of the committee, stood before Jefferson
Worth, the man behind the gray mask forced him to
speak first.

"I understand you wished to see me about this
railroad matter, Mr. Worth."

"I told the committee that you had better see me,"
came the answer without a trace of emotion in the
colorless voice.

"Well, I am here; what do you want?"

"I want a new contract from your Company bind-
ing you to build your Central Main Canal on the line
of the original survey, bringing it to a point within
four hundred yards of the west line of the South

Central District where the San Felipe trail crosses
Dry River, and agreeing to deliver into my power
canal without charge a flow of three hundred second
feet of water, as in the old contract; and in addition
the exclusive power rights in all of the Company's
canals in the Basin."

"If I give you this contract you will build the
railroad into Kingston?"

"When you change the line of your canal back to
the original route I will change the line of my road."

"Suppose I refuse?"

"My railroad will not come into Kingston and I
will explain to the crowd out there the reason. You
have worked up a pretty strong public feeling against
me, Mr. Greenfield. Now make good or stand in my
place and take the consequences."

James Greenfield was not slow to grasp the point.
A simple explanation of the situation from Jefferson
Worth with the old contract to back it up would turn
the wrath of the people against the Company president. Rising, he said with an oath: "You win, Mr.
Worth. I'll have the contract ready for your signature in the morning. Now what will we do with that
mob out there?"

"It is your mob, Mr. Greenfield," answered Jefferson Worth.

A few minutes later from the front porch of the
Worth cottage, with Texas Joe on his right hand and
Pat on his left, Horace P. Blanton announced: "Our
committee will report at the opera house in half an
hour."

The committee reported that Kingston was saved

and the orator of the day made another speech so far eclipsing all his former efforts that the cheering citizens were evenly divided as to whether it was James Greenfield, Jefferson Worth or Horace P. Blanton who saved it.

"Well, boys," remarked one of the men from the South Central District as the little party of horsemen set out for the long ride home, "one thing is sure. Those Kingston fellows have got the railroad, but we still have Jefferson Worth, an' I reckon that Jeff can build us a railroad any old time he gets ready."

"That's right," returned another, "but what in hell do you suppose it was all about? What's Jeff's game anyhow?"

CHAPTER XXIII.

EXACTING ROYAL TRIBUTE.

N spite of the optimistic view of the man who said that Jefferson Worth could build a railroad for Barba and the South Central District whenever he wished, there was no little disappointment expressed in Worth's town when it became known that the Company town was to have the road.

When the grading camps had returned to their former locations and the construction train drew every day nearer Kingston, with the time approaching when regular trains with passengers and freight would ply to and from the Company town, the feeling of discontent in Barba grew. It even came to be generally understood throughout the Basin that the whole movement had been cleverly planned by Jefferson Worth to force The King's Basin Land and Irrigation Company to make a large contribution to the railroad builder's personal fortune. The people sensed something in the whole transaction that they could not clearly grasp, an intangible, mysterious something, as great as it was indefinite. They felt blindly that they were being used without their consent in a game played by these master financiers, and they resented being sacrificed as dumb pawns in a move, the purpose of which they could not know.

In the meantime, while the people were charging

him with selling them out to gain his own ends, the man whose purpose was known only to himself was putting into his enterprise the last dollar of his resources, and another flood season with its appalling danger was at hand.

Because his laborers on the railroad were not as the men who built the South Central canals, working for more than their day's wage, and because, though no one knew it, Jefferson Worth's finances were so nearly exhausted, work on the road, as on the Company project, was discontinued for the summer months, to be resumed in the fall—perhaps.

Barbara again refused to leave her father and in the close companionship and full understanding of his daughter, the man, who lived so much alone behind his gray mask, found inspiration and strength.

The telephone now connected the heading at the river intake with Kingston, and every hour of these hot days and nights Jefferson Worth listened for a call from Willard Holmes, who also had refused to leave his work, while three of the fastest saddle horses in the Basin were stabled with El Capitan. Texas, Abe and Pablo were ready to ride at an instant's notice to rally the pioneers, who were developing their ranches, building their homes and planning their future unconscious of the real danger that hung over them.

Vague rumors of the dangerous condition of the Company structures floated about and there were not wanting prophecies of disaster. But not one in a hundred of the settlers had even visited the intake at the river, or if they had, what could they judge of conditions there? The settlers were ranchers, not civil engineers. The Company zanjeros turned the water into their ditches when they asked for it; their crops, growing marvelously in the rich soil, demanded constant attention; they had neither time, inclination nor ability to investigate every flying rumor. As for the prophets of evil, only confirmed optimists can reclaim a desert or settle a new country and the croakers received little attention. Besides, the great, all-powerful Company would surely protect its own interests and, in protecting its own, would protect the interests of the settlers. It was the business of the Company engineers to look after the river. The ranchers were looking after the ranches.

Thus another summer went by and the great river, save for the small toll taken by those who were reclaiming the desert it had created in the ages of long ago, continued on its way to the sea. Its time was not yet.

With the return of the cooler weather and the still further increase in the volume of new life that continued to pour into the Basin from the great world outside, work on the railroad was begun again, but Jefferson Worth knew that the first pay day would mark the end. He was as a man with his back to a wall, fighting bravely to the last blow, and he stood alone.

Among the hundreds of pioneers with whom Worth had elected—as he had told Abe Lee the night of his arrival in Kingston—to take a chance, there was not one to take a chance with him now. If he lost he would lose alone, for those who had built upon the work that he had done would not suffer through his defeat. Had any of them known the situation they could have done nothing to help him. But no one knew, and this was the financier's one desperate chance—that no one did know, not even Barbara.

With his capital exhausted and no resources upon which he could realize, he went ahead with the work apparently with the confidence of one with millions behind him. It was, in the language of the West, all a bluff. But it was a magnificent bluff.

Two weeks of the month were gone when a telegram from the high official of the S. & C. summoned him to the city.

The railroad man, in the secrecy of his private office, greeted the promoter with his usual, "Hello, Jeff. I see The King's Basin is still on the map."

Jefferson Worth smiled, then, as the official's eyes were fixed upon his face in a way that he understood, he retreated behind his mask. "Things are going very well," he answered.

"Working full gangs on that railroad of yours?"

"We have taken on all the men we can handle. We will be ready for that last lot of steel in another two weeks."

The other lay back in his chair and laughed with hearty admiration and regard. "Jeff, you are a wonder! How long do you suppose it would take Greenfield to start something with your creditors if he knew what I know?"

Not a line of Jefferson Worth's face changed, only his nervous fingers caressed his chin, and the railroad man, noting the familiar signal, smiled again. Then leaning forward in his chair he said: "Jeff, I have been keeping my eye on you ever since those days when our line was building into Rubio City and you handled the right-of-way for us. I have never caught you in a blunder yet. When it comes to sizing up a proposition all around I don't believe you have an equal. Now look here." With a quick movement he took a paper from a pigeon-hole in his desk and laid it before the other. The paper was a carefully tabulated statement of Jefferson Worth's financial condition at that moment. In vain the official tried to see behind that gray mask.

"Well." The word was absolutely colorless.

"Well!" repeated the other savagely, "what I want to know is this: why in hell you are bucking Green-field and his crowd to such a limit?"

"Because," said Jefferson Worth carefully, "I believe in the future of The King's Basin project, providing—" he paused.

"Providing what?"

"Providing someone bucks Greenfield to the limit."

In one instantaneous flash, the man whose clear brain directed thousands of miles of a great railroad system caught a glimpse of the real Jefferson Worth —the Jefferson Worth who was not, as the railroad man had himself said, "doing it all for a dinky little power plant."

"Jeff," he said slowly, "when you asked us to build a branch line into the Basin I told you that we couldn't do it. As I said then, we are not in the insurance business. A railroad's business depends

THE WINNING OF BARBARA WORTH

upon the actual development of a country, not upon
backing promoters who open up a new country simply as a speculative proposition. You say you believe
in the future of The King's Basin country providing
some one bucks Greenfield and you are sure giving
him a run for his money. But you have reached the
end of your pile and I know it. Now, I have been
taking up this matter with our people and we are
ready to take a chance on your judgment. Suppose
we take over your road as it stands at a fair price—
what would be your next move? Get out and leave
us in the insurance business?"

"I would build a line from Kingston to Barba,
tapping the South Central District, which is the
richest section of the Basin," came the instant reply.

"Good! But perhaps you don't want to sell the
line you are building to the S. & C.," he suggested
with a smile.

"I figured that you would be ready to make me a
proposition about the time I had it in shape for the
last shipment of steel."

Worth's bluff had won.

The railroad man said again solemnly: "Jeff, you
are a wonder!"

With the passing of his nearly completed railroad
into the hands of the S. & C. Jefferson Worth began
at once to arrange for the building of the other line
from Barba to Kingston. This new road, to be known
as the King's Basin Central, connecting with what
was now the S. & C., would give an outlet to the rich
South Central District, while the Southwestern and
Continental Company announced that its new branch

would not stop at Kingston but would build on south to Frontera.

With a main line branch of a trans-continental railroad building straight through the heart of the new country, and their town located just half way between the junction and the terminal, The King's Basin Land and Irrigation Company saw the value of their property increased many times. The day was not far distant now when every quarter section of the desert land would be filed on by eager settlers, and the once barren waste would rapidly give place to the fertile fields of the ranchers, every foot of which should yield tribute to James Greenfield and his associates. But the reclamation of the desert opened many avenues for profit other than the irrigation system.

From these also the Company, obeying the law of Good Business, had planned to take toll, but the field for investment most closely allied with the fields of the ranchers, and therefore keeping even pace with the increasing wealth of the new country, had been preempted by Jefferson Worth. The Company desired to add to their holdings those enterprises that had come to be known as the Worth interests. They had failed repeatedly to bring about a union of forces. Their only recourse then was to force the independent operator to sell to them or to eliminate him from The King's Basin project. To this end Greenfield and Burk watched and planned on the well known principle that whatever Jefferson Worth wanted was bad for the Company, until the day when the interests of Worth and those of The King's Basin

Land and Irrigation Company should be the same or Jefferson Worth should be no longer a factor in the new country.

While the Worth enterprises were firmly established in all the centers of activity in the Basin, the Company knew that his largest interests were in Barba and the South Central District. Worth must have railroad connections with the S. & C. line before he could even begin to realize on his largest investments. There was every reason why he should desire to make Kingston the junction point of the road he was now forced to build. James Greenfield was not backward in letting Worth understand that he would need to pay well for a right-of-way with terminal facilities in the Company town.

For two weeks Jefferson Worth tried to bring the Company president to some reasonable settlement but his efforts only served to make Greenfield more determined to exact royal tribute. "I tell you," said the president triumphantly to his Manager, "he's forced to build that line or go to smash with his town and district. No one will settle away off there from the railroad as long as they can locate in reach of Kingston or Frontera, and he has got to connect with the S. & C. branch at Kingston, for we are the only place between the main line and the terminal."

When Mr. Worth reminded them that the proposed road would benefit Kingston and that in view of its value to their town it would be only just for them to give him the privileges he needed but for which he was quite ready to pay a reasonable price, Greenfield declared that his Company had already given Worth quite enough. Of course, if they could find some basis upon which to unite their interests that would be another matter.

Then the evening mail brought to Mr. Worth certain legal looking papers and the next morning he called again upon Mr. Greenfield. In a spring wagon in front of the Company office Texas Joe and Abe Lee waited with a prosperous looking stranger who also had arrived the evening before.

"Mr. Greenfield, I have come for your final answer on this railroad deal."

On Greenfield's face there was a smile of satisfaction and triumph. There were several reasons why he enjoyed seeing Jefferson Worth in a corner. "I am ready to listen to any other proposition you have to make, Mr. Worth."

"You have the only proposition I shall make."

"Really, I fear that we can do nothing this morning."

The visitor turned on his heel and left the office.

Later, in describing the interview to Willard Holmes, Burk commented thoughtfully: "I very much fear your festive Uncle Jim played the game a little too fine. You can take some things and most men for granted; but a railroad, now, and Jefferson Worth——" he shifted his cigar to the corner of his mouth and cocked his head in the opposite direction. "I think, Willard, that something is going to happen."

What happened was this: When Jefferson Worth left the Company's office he stepped into the waiting rig beside the stranger. "Go ahead, Abe," he said.

Then the surveyor giving Texas the direction, the team sped away. Once in the desert they stopped occasionally while the surveyor examined the four by four redwood stakes. At a point on the S. & C. four miles north of Kingston and therefore between the Company town and the main line, Abe directed Texas to stop.

The surveyor, taking a note book from his pocket, went to a corner stake and indicated with outstretched hands the direction of the boundary lines of a tract of land owned by his employer. "Here we are, Mr. Worth."

The place was raw desert and except for the railroad without sign of life save the life of the hard, desolate land; though in the distance could be seen the improved ranches, with Kingston in their midst. Standing on the slight elevation of the railroad grade Jefferson Worth looked around silently. Then, followed by the stranger and Abe, he walked some distance west of the track.

Pausing and striking his boot-heel into the soft earth, he said with much less show of emotion than is exhibited by the average school boy in laying out a ball-ground: "We will build a hotel here; over there a bank. The main street will run toward the railroad. The Basin Central from Barba will come in from the southeast."

And this was the beginning of Republic, the town that was built on a barren desert almost in the time it would have taken to prepare the land, plant and grow a crop of corn.

The stranger was the president of a townsite company organized by Jefferson Worth while James Greenfield was congratulating himself that he at last had that gentleman in a trap. Worth had given the company the land and had entered into an agreement whereby he was to build a hotel and several business blocks and furnish them, rent free, for one year.

With the railroad to deliver material in any desired quantity, work was begun in a few days. The King's Basin Messenger and the papers in Frontera and Barba, all owned by Worth, gave full accounts of the birth of the new town and the reason why The King's Basin Central would not be built into Kingston, with glowing accounts of Worth's plans for the future of the Company's rival town. The Worth Electric Company moved its plant from Kingston to Republic; the ice-plant, the bank, the telephone office and every enterprise controlled by Worth followed; while many merchants, lured by the success of the Wizard of the Desert in every undertaking and by the promise of rent free, went with the Worth industries; and from the world outside many, who had hesitated to enter the new country before the railroad, rushed in to locate in the new town. The first building completed in Republic was a cottage for Barbara and her father.

Meanwhile the work on the road to Barba and the South Central District was begun. The "something" prophesied by Mr. Burk had happened.

CHAPTER XXIV.

JEFFERSON WORTH GOES FOR HELP.

THE winter following the birth of Republic witnessed the greatest activities that had been seen in the new country. The freighters' wagons that had once seemed so pitifully inadequate, as they crept feebly away into the mysterious silences, were replaced now by long trains, heavily loaded with building material and goods of every kind and drawn by laboring engines that puffed and roared and clanged and screamed their stirring answer to the challenge of the silent, age-old, desolate land. And still the work that had been done was small in comparison with that which was yet to do before the reclamation of Barbara's Desert would be complete. The acres of land untouched by grader's Fresno or rancher's plow were many more than the acres that were producing crops. The miles of canals and ditches that were to be built were many more than the miles already carrying water. The tent houses and shacks of the pioneers were yet to be replaced by more comfortable homes. The frontier towns—big in that new country—were yet to grow into cities. From the top of any building in any one of the four towns one could look into the barren desert.

Tourists on the main line that skirted the rim of

the Basin, from the car windows saw only the
mighty reaches of the dun plain, with its thirsty vegetation, stretching away to the distant purple mountain wall. Curiously the overland passengers looked
at the crowds of settlers waiting for the Basin train
at the Junction, wondering at their hardihood. Curiously they followed with their eyes the thin line of
rails and telegraph poles leading southward until it
was lost in the mystic depths of color. To the tourists it was a fantastic dream that out there, somewhere in the barren waste, people were building
towns, cultivating fields, transacting business and
engaging in all the Good Business activities of the
race. It was as impossible to them as it had been
to Willard Holmes when Barbara first introduced
him to her Desert and tried to make him see, as she
saw, the greatness of the work of which he was to
become a part.

The latter part of that winter found Jefferson
Worth again with his back to the wall. James Greenfield, in his attempt to hold up his rival in the matter of the King's Basin Central junction, had
wrought better than he knew. While Worth's enterprises were barely as yet paying their way, the railroad, which he was forced to build in order to protect his own interests in the town of Barba and in
the South Central District, would require practically
all he had realized on the sale of the other line that
had so nearly exhausted his resources. The Company
president, in forcing him to build the town of Republic in addition to his heavy outlay on his new
railroad, forced him to take another desperate chance.

For the first time he was unable to pay the men, and in thirty days large obligations for material would be due; while certain rumors, carefully started by Greenfield, made it almost impossible for him to raise the funds he must have.

"I'm sorry, Jeff," said his friend the railroad man. "But with present unsafe conditions we can't load up with any more property in The King's Basin. You know as well as I that if the river comes in *we* will have to get in there to protect our interests, for if those ranchers were wiped out our road wouldn't sell for scrap iron. You couldn't do it and the Greenfield crowd wouldn't. Why, that New York bunch, outside of Greenfield, don't know whether the Colorado is a trout stream or a mill pond. Their actual investment doesn't amount to half what you have put into your work, for the sale of water rights to the settlers is paying all the expense of their extensions and they won't put up a cent to rebuild their shaky old structures. And look where we stand! We have put more money into that country now than the Company and you together, and we won't pay operating expenses until the land is developed. And still the public is roaring about our rates. We don't want another desert line on our hands."

Quietly Jefferson Worth sold his interest in the banks in Frontera, Barba and Republic; and as quietly Greenfield, who was watching, set about gaining control of these institutions. His South Central District water stock was already sold and most of his property in Barba. Even his little home in Republic was mortgaged.

Thus Worth held on for a while longer. He dared not stop his work, for such a move would not only ruin his chances of negotiating the loans he needed, but by bringing upon him a swarm of creditors, would make it impossible for him ever to recover his standing in the financial world.

Another pay day passed without the men receiving their pay and the third was drawing near. Already there was grumbling and complaining among the men over the delayed pay checks. It would take but little more to start serious trouble.

There were many in the crowd at the depot that day when Jefferson Worth waited for the train to the city, who looked with envy upon the builder of towns and railroads. Horace P. Blanton proudly pointed out to a stranger "his friend, the Wizard of the Desert," with the information that Mr. Worth had cleaned up a cool million in the new country. Several went out of their way for a closer look at him or for a possible greeting. Others cursed him roundly under their breath for a hated member of the class of parasites that live on the industry of the laborer, a financier who robbed the people, a capitalist who produced nothing.

The train pulled in, and Mr. Worth, with a good-by to Barbara and Abe, who had come to see him off, stepped aboard. No one save Abe Lee, not even Barbara, knew that her father must raise fifty thousand dollars before the first of the month or suffer financial ruin. And no one—not even Jefferson Worth himself—knew where he could find the money.

Barbara, when her father was gone, though she

knew nothing of the danger that threatened him, was restless and ill at ease, beset by vague and nameless doubts and fears. The little desert town with its bustling activity, its clamorous, rushing disorder, its naked newness and glaring bareness, offended her. Nothing was completed. The streets, the buildings, the very people, seemed so unsettled, so temporary. She could not shake off the feeling that it would all vanish soon, as she had often seen the phantom cities of the desert plain melt and disappear.

The morning after her father left, as she rode El Capitan slowly along the little village streets that lay so dusty and flat and that ended so quickly in the open country, she caught herself wondering how long the dream would endure. The farms, too, with their new green fields and their primitive, pioneer shacks, tent houses and shelters and their acres of still unimproved land, all lying under the white blaze of the semi-tropical sun, were they more than a mirage weirdly painted in the air by the spirit of the dreadful land to lure foolish men to their ruin?

Near the crossing of a canal she saw a zanjero turning the water through a new delivery gate into a new ditch, and checking El Capitan, she watched the brown flood rolling down the channel prepared for it and heard the dry earth hiss and purr as it sucked up the moisture with the thirst of a thousand years. She wanted to cry out a protest. The effort was so pitifully foolish. This awful, awful land would never yield to the men who sought to subdue it with such feeble means. From the little stream of water, no deeper than would reach to El Capitan's

knees and no wider than his stride, she looked away
and around over the seemingly endless miles of barren waste.

The man at the delivery gate recorded the number
of inches in his book and, with a greeting to the
young woman, mounted his horse and rode away
along the canal. Barbara, moving on, left the farms
behind and rode into the barren waste. This at least
was real. This in its very desolation, its dreadful
silence, its still menace, was satisfying. But as on
that morning when she first rode El Capitan into the
desert from Kingston, she grew afraid. The dreadful
spirit of the land so pressed upon her that she turned
her horse and fled as one might fly from an approaching storm.

Another restless, unsatisfying day and a lonely
evening dragged by. Texas and Pat she had not
seen for a week. Even Abe had not been near her
since her father left. To-morrow, she told herself,
she would find them at their work and demand a
reason for their neglect.

The next morning she set out on El Capitan to
follow the line of her father's railroad until she
should find her neglectful men-folk. As she rode
along the right-of-way she watched the hundreds of
Mexican and Indian laborers at their work on the
grade and thought of the men who had built the
South Central Canal. Those men too had labored
for her father, but they worked also for themselves.
The canal they built was to reclaim their own land
and to make for them farms and homes. These poor
fellows on the railroad, she reflected, had no share in

that which they were doing. There was in their toil
nothing but the day's wage. She could not feel, as
she had felt in the South Central District, that she
had a part with them in their work. Here and there
she recognized a Mexican from Rubio City, and these
returned her greeting pleasantly, for they remembered the young woman's kindness to the poor. But
by far the greater number gave her only sullen
glances. She was to them only the daughter of the
man for whom they toiled and who had not paid.

Passing from gang to gang and camp to camp,
watching the dark faces of the laborers, listening to
their sullen undertone, the young woman felt the restless, threatening spirit of the little army as one may
feel sometimes the heavily charged atmosphere before
an electric storm. But she did not understand. She
had never before ridden over the railroad work alone
as she had so often done in the South Central District.

She grew a little frightened at last at the scowling
looks and muttered remarks that followed her as she
went, and she was wishing that she had not come
when she saw just ahead Abe Lee and Pat. The
surveyor was giving some instructions to the Irish
boss and both were so intent that they did not see
Barbara approaching. As the young woman drew
quite near, a low-browed Mexican who, in watching
her approach, either forgot the presence of his
superiors or, in sheer ruffianly bravado, ignored them,
uttered a coarse remark to his companions about his
employer's daughter.

The young woman heard and turned pale as death.

Pat heard and, turning quickly around, caught sight of Barbara and saw the ruffian who had spoken looking at her. With a roar the Irishman leaped forward, and with a blow of his huge, hairy fist dropped the Mexican a senseless heap in the dirt.

With cries of rage the fellow's countrymen ran toward the white man, drawing their knives as they came. Barbara sat leaning forward in her saddle breathless. Abe Lee was quietly rolling a cigarette. Pat stood motionless, his battle-scarred features set and his eyes shining like points of light.

Within ten steps of their boss the little mob stopped. Then the Irishman spoke in a voice that rumbled and shook with menacing rage. "Ye, Manuel an' Pedro—drag that carrion off the right-av-way, an' tell him when he wakes up av he values his life to shtay out av rache av me two hands. The rest av ye hombres git the hell out av here!"

The two whom he called by name did his bidding and the rest scattered like sheep. Pat turned to Barbara. " 'Tis sorry I am that ye should see ut, me girl, but ut had to be done."

"Oh, Pat! Did you— Is he—" She could not speak the word, but followed with frightened eyes the still form of the unconscious man as his companions half-dragged, half-carried him to the shade of a mesquite tree.

"There, there, don't worry," said her big friend soothingly. "He's not as much hurted as he should be. He'll have a bit av a bump on his noodle that'll maybe make him a bit careful wid his foul tongue for a while, that's all."

352

Barbara looked down into the face of the old gladiator whose eyes, as they looked up at her, were soft
as a childs. "Oh, Pat! Are you sure? He—he
crumpled up so! It was awful!" She shuddered.

"There, there; av course I'm sure. Don't I know?
Look at him; he's sittin' up now. He'll be on his
fate in a minute."

Sure enough, as Barbara looked again she saw the
Mexican rising to a sitting posture and with his hand
to his head look around in a dazed manner as though
awakening out of a deep sleep. The young woman
drew a long breath of relief and, with a faint smile,
said to the surveyor, who had drawn nearer: "I'm
sorry I came, Abe. I'm afraid you'll think that I'm
only in the way to make trouble. But I was so lonesome all alone at home."

"Why, Barbara, you know how glad we always are
to see you. You must not mind this little incident.
It's all in the day's work with Pat, you see. That
fellow there has had this coming to him for some
time."

The Irishman grinned and the young woman on
the horse, with a little laugh, said: "All the same I
don't think I would like you for a boss, Uncle Pat.
You're too—too emphatic."

And the big Irishman with twinkling eyes
retorted: "Sure av ye was boss av a gang ye wud
break more hearts wid yer swate face than I could
heads wid me two hands." Which retort effectually
closed the incident.

When the three had chatted a while and Barbara
had scolded them for not coming to see her, Abe said:

"I think you had better go back now, Barbara. But don't follow the line. Strike west over the desert until you come to the road and go in that way. We can't leave now to go with you, and some of these greasers might get gay again. I'll see you this evening."

It was after nine o'clock that night when the surveyor finally reached the Worth cottage. Somewhat awkwardly he entered and seated himself in the nearest chair, while Barbara, returning to her favorite rocker by the table, said: "It's time you came. I was so lonely I don't believe I could have stood it another hour. Really you and Pat and Tex have neglected me shamefully. You haven't been near since the day father left. Even Pablo has forgotten me."

"Pablo is at the power house at Dry River," Abe said slowly. "We've all had our hands full for the last three days. I reckon you know we have not stayed away because we wanted to."

Something in the man's tone and manner caused Barbara to look at him closely. Was it a fancy in keeping with her gloomy spirit of the last few days, or did the surveyor's tall form droop as if with discouragement? He was not looking at her with his usual straightforward manner. He seemed to be studying the pattern of the Navajo rug that lay between them, and certainly his lean, bronzed face wore a careworn look that was new. She noticed too that he wore belt and revolver, which was very unusual for Abe.

"Of course; I know!" she exclaimed. "It was childish of me to complain. Forgive me."

Abe, without answering, looked at her—a straight, questioning, challenging look that for some reason brought another flush to her cheek. Then the surveyor turned his gaze again upon the Navajo rug.

"I know you are tired," said the young woman again. "You have so much to think about with all those men to look after and daddy away. Come now; you sit right over here in this easy chair and shut your eyes and smoke and forget all about the work and everything, while I make a little music for you."

Barbara did not realize how she tried this man of the desert with a glimpse of a heaven that Abe knew could never be for him. For a moment he sat motionless without answering, his eyes still fixed upon the floor. Then with a quick, resolute movement he threw up his head and straightened himself. "I'm sorry, Barbara, but I can't stay this evening."

"Can't stay?" she cried. "Why, Abe, you just came!"

"Yes, I know. I—I just ran in to ask you—to see if you"—he hesitated and stammered, then finished desperately—"to ask you to let me send Texas to stay here to-night."

She looked at him in bewildered amazement. "Why, what in the world do you mean? Why should Texas stay here to-night?"

Then as a sudden possible explanation came to her mind—"Abe, has Uncle Tex— Is he in trouble?"

The surveyor smiled at her words. "It's nothing like that, Barbara. Tex is all right. But I don't think that you should be left alone here with only Ynez just now. Pat is at the power house and I must be at the ice plant, and Tex—" He checked himself in alarm.

Barbara's face was white and her eyes, fixed upon his, were big with sudden fear as, rising slowly to her feet, she went towards him. With an exclamation he sprang from his seat but she regained control of herself and, quietly taking another chair nearer him, said: "I think you had better tell me, Abe, just exactly what the trouble is. I know something is wrong or you would not want to send Texas here to me. You know that I have always stayed with Ynez. Why are you afraid for me? Why is Pat at the power house, and why are you going to stay at the ice plant? And why do you wear that?" She pointed to the heavy Colt's revolver.

Little by little she forced from the reluctant superintendent an explanation of the whole situation: how her father had been driven by the Company to build the new town of Republic in addition to the construction of his railroad to Barba and how conditions in the Basin had made it impossible to sell this line to the S. & C. as he had sold before. He told her as gently as he could that the men had not been paid for nearly two months, and that if her father did not succeed in raising the necessary funds quickly he would lose everything. The men had been put off from day to day with explanations that their employer was away and that they would receive their pay when he returned. But ugly rumors were afloat among them and their angry uneasiness and discontent were increasing. Threats against their employer and his property were being made by the hot-headed leaders, who always appear under such conditions, and the surveyor feared that serious trouble might start at any hour.

To Barbara the situation was almost incredible. Again and again she exclaimed with pity for her father, and demanded to know why they had all kept her in ignorance of the truth; and as she realized how lovingly she had been shielded from every worry that she might feel nothing of the burden that weighed so heavily upon them, her woman heart cried out that she had not been permitted to bear her share.

"But I know now," she said at last, brushing aside the tears that, against her will, filled the brown eyes. "I know now and you men shall see that I can do something to help." She stood before him—her strong beautiful figure bravely erect, her face glowing with the light of a determined purpose.

The surveyor smiled his appreciation as he said: "It's almost as good as money in the bank to hear you talk like that, Barbara. But you'll let me send Tex over to-night, won't you?"

"You must do whatever you think best, Abe. But you must promise me this. From now on you will tell me everything, just as you have always told me about the work."

Abe drew a long breath. "I don't know what your father will say but I'll do it. I've felt all along that it was hardly square to keep you in the dark."

"Of course it wasn't," she agreed. "And now listen! You and Pat come here for breakfast with Texas Joe and me. Come as early as you like."

He began to protest, saying that they would need to eat at daybreak in order to get back to the work by seven o'clock, but she silenced him with—"And do you think that I cannot even get up at sun-rise? You shall not lose a minute's time and it will do you good to start out with one of Ynez's good break-fasts."

So the surveyor was forced to promise this also. Then with a soft "Buenos noches, Senorita," he left her.

Later Texas Joe came to sleep in Mr. Worth's room. The night passed without incident, and when the first trace of silver gray light shone above the eastern mesa beyond the rim of the Basin Abe Lee returned with Pat to find the meal ready and Barbara waiting to pour the fragrant coffee. While the sky was still aflame with the colors of the morning and the desert lay under a curtain of fantastic figures and grotesque patterns woven by the light, the three men mounted their horses and set out for the field of the day's labors. And Barbara at the gate watched them go until, in the distance, their forms too were caught in the magic of the desert's loom and woven into the airy design.

Before noon Abe came back. The men had struck. The surveyor had already sent a telegram to Mr. Worth and in the afternoon they had his answer that he was going to San Felipe. But there was no word of hope in the message.

All that day the men from the railroad were gathering in the little town, and in the early evening the laborers from the power canal at Barba joined the throng on the streets. This dark-faced, scowling crowd of Mexicans and Indians was very different from the company of pioneers that met in Kingston to receive Jefferson Worth a few months before. On every hand they were heard cursing the man who owed them their wages and threatening to take revenge if they were not soon paid.

That night Texas Joe again slept at the Worth cottage, for Barbara stoutly refused to leave her home, and Abe and Pat, with the little handful of white men from the office force, stood guard at the power house, the ice plant and the other buildings that were grouped near the railroad on the edge of town.

CHAPTER XXV.

WILLARD HOLMES ON TRIAL.

SCARCELY had the train with Jefferson Worth aboard passed beyond the yard limits of Republic when the Manager of The King's Basin Land and Irrigation Company in Kingston was called to the telephone by the cashier of the bank in the Company's rival town. Ten minutes later a Western Union message in cipher went from Mr. Burk to James Greenfield in the city.

The afternoon of the following day Willard Holmes, at the Dry River Heading, was called to the telephone. Mr. Burk was at the other end of the line. "There is a telegram here from your Uncle Jim ordering you to go to the city on the first train. If you can make it, catch the four-twenty at Frontera. I'll pack your grip and give it to you when you go through."

Mr. Greenfield met the engineer at the depot in the city the next morning and escorted him to his rooms in a hotel. "I was almighty glad to get Burk's wire that you were on the road," said the older man. "I was afraid that he would not be able to find you in time; you go gadding about the country so. Where did he catch you?"

"Dry River Heading. My gadding takes me mostly there or to the intake heading these days.

Just now I am trying to patch up the spillway which threatens to go out at any time altogether, and the heading itself is so shaky I'm almost afraid to touch it for fear it will fall down on top of me. No one ever dreamed that these structures would ever be called upon to stand the strain they are under now. I wish—"

"All right; all right, my boy; I think I've heard you say something like that before. I called you in to help me on a little deal that will put us in shape to build all the new structures you want."

"You mean that the Company is at last going to make the appropriation I have been begging for?"

"Not exactly. They will if we can handle one individual."

"Who?"

"Jefferson Worth."

"Jefferson Worth? What under heaven has he to do with the Company's appropriations?"

"He has a lot to do with the Company's profits, which amounts to the same thing."

At this Holmes was silent and his uncle was forced to continue: "You know what Worth has been doing to the Company, don't you?"

"Yes; and I know what the Company has been trying to do to him."

"Exactly. And do you know his present situation?"

"Only in a general way."

"Well, in a definite way then: he is here in the city trying to raise fifty thousand dollars. He must have it before the first of the month or go to smash.

If he goes to smash the Company will be able to get hold of his interests, which will give us control of the whole King's Basin project as we planned in the beginning. Then we would be able to put what you want into the system. If Worth gets the fifty thousand he is safe to make a million or two that would otherwise go to the Company and we wouldn't feel justified in spending any more money on new structures."

"But Uncle Jim, what on earth have I to do with all this?"

"It happens that you have a whole lot to do with it my boy, or I wouldn't have called you away from your beloved headings. You remember old George Cartwright, don't you?"

Willard Holmes had grown to manhood with Cartwright's sons and his earliest memories were of boyish good times at the old gentleman's home. With James Greenfield, Mr. Cartwright had been one of his father's oldest and warmest friends. The engineer listened with amazed interest as Greenfield told him that his old friend was spending the winter on the coast, and that some one, the general manager of the S. & C., probably, had introduced Jefferson Worth to him.

"And," Greenfield finished, "they have him all lined up to furnish Worth with the capital he needs to go ahead. If he gets that money we will never be able to block him."

"But why don't you get Cartwright into your crowd, if he is so ready to invest in reclamation projects?" asked the engineer.

"I can't on account of White and some of the others. You know how cranky the old man is. Besides, we don't want him in the Company. What we want is to block Jefferson Worth from getting hold of that money. I sent for you because you can do more with Cartwright on this proposition than any man living."

"You mean that you have sent for me to influence Mr. Cartwright against Jefferson Worth's interests?"

"I mean that I expect you to use your influence in the interests of the Company—in my interests. Surely, Willard, that is not asking anything unreasonable."

"But Uncle Jim, you just said that if Worth gets this help he will clean up a million or two. That looks like it would be safe enough for Mr. Cartwright."

"Yes, and I said also that if Worth did *not* get that money the Company would acquire his interests in The King's Basin."

While the Company president was speaking a messenger boy knocked at the door. Greenfield read the note and handed it to Holmes, who in turn read: "Mr. Cartwright left this afternoon for San Felipe. Will probably return in a week. Worth is still in town."

"That means you must take a little vacation, Willard."

"But I can't, Uncle Jim," protested the engineer. "My work is in such shape that I—"

The older man interrupted. "Your work! You seem to think that there is nothing of importance to

The King's Basin Land and Irrigation Company but drops and headings and intakes and canals, and the Lord knows what else, you mess around with! If you handle old Cartwright in the interests of the Company it will be the best week's work you ever did. He is likely to return any day, and you've got to stay right here and see this matter through."

All that day the engineer roamed about the city, striving to find distraction in the amusements offered but feeling strangely alone and out of place. Under other circumstances he would have keenly enjoyed the brief vacation and the change from the desert life and work, but now he could think of nothing but the situation in which he so unexpectedly found himself.

Once he would not have hesitated an instant to do Greenfield's bidding. Why should he hesitate now?

Why, indeed; save for this—Willard Holmes knew that it would be better for the people in the new country if Jefferson Worth continued his operations.

Willard Holmes's conception and understanding of his work as an engineer had changed materially in the years since those first days with Barbara in Rubio City, even as, under his hand, the desert itself had changed. It may have been that in his long, lonely rides across the great plain in the white light of the wide, cloudless sky, something of the spirit of the slow, silent ages that had wrought in the making of the desert had touched his spirit as it could not have been influenced by the smoke-clouded atmosphere and crowded highways of the East; or that in the lonely nights under the stars the weird, mysterious voices of the desert had taught him truths he had never heard in the noisy cries of the great cities. Perhaps, as he had looked day after day across the wide far-reaching miles with their seas and scarfs and veils of color to the purple mountains, the very greatness of the unpeopled lands forced him to a larger thinking and planning and dreaming than would have been possible in the limited views of his eastern homeland; or that the spirit of the hardy settlers awoke the blood of his own pioneer ancestors to a feeling of fellow-ship; or his constant struggle with the river aroused the old conquering spirit of his race. Or again it might be that some powerful chord, deep-hidden and silent in his nature, had been touched by the spirit of the girl who had bidden him learn the language of her country and who had said that she could never forgive one who was untrue to the work itself.

On the other hand there was the training of his whole professional career. Up to the beginning of The King's Basin work the engineer had known no other creed than the creed of those corporation serv-ants who have no higher interest than that of the machine they serve. There was also his intimate relation with Mr. Greenfield and the debt of grati-tude he owed the man who had, in every way, been a father to him. And there was the prejudice of class, the instinct that holds a man to his own peculiar people, and the argument cleverly advanced by Green-field that the protection of The King's Basin project would be secured.

As the engineer was wandering, in the aimless and preoccupied manner of one whose mind is not on his task, through one of the city parks, he saw just ahead a man whose figure seemed familiar. With aroused interest he quickened his pace. There was no mis-taking that form, so strongly upright, so instinct with vigorous power; nor those broad shoulders and the finely poised head. It was the Seer.

Overtaking the older engineer, Holmes greeted him eagerly and the brown eyes of the old Chief shone with pleasure while he returned the young man's greeting heartily.

Had the Seer any engagement that afternoon?

None at all. He had just arrived from the North Country and was loafing a day or two. And Holmes?

The younger man laughed. He was a stranger in a strange land, forced by circumstances to do nothing.

Good. They would find a quiet corner somewhere and Holmes could tell his old Chief about The King's Basin work. Also The King's Basin man could tell the Seer about Barbara.

So they found a seat and Willard Holmes told how splendidly the Seer's dream was coming true, and in answer to many questions talked of Barbara and her life in the new country, of Jefferson Worth and his operations, and of some of his own professional diffi-culties and problems. And the Seer, as he led the younger man on and studied the strong bronzed face that was all aglow with enthusiasm over the work, smiled quietly as he remembered the tenderfoot who had once threatened to report his Chief to the Com-pany.

Brave, great-hearted, generous Seer! There was in all his questioning not a hint of any feeling against the younger man who had been given the place that should have been his. He fell to wondering if after all the Company had now in Holmes the man they thought they had, or the man they did have, indeed, when they made him their chief engineer. If the test were to come now— The Seer did not know that Willard Holmes was even then undergoing that test.

The two men dined together that evening and afterwards over the cigars in the Seer's room the old engineer talked of the progress and future of the great Reclamation work, of its value not only to our own nation but to the over-crowded nations beyond the seas, and of its place in the great forward march of the race. Then gravely he spoke to the younger man of his own efforts to bring the work to the attention of the people, of disappointments and failures, year after year, until at last the work in Barbara's Desert had been launched, and following that several other projects until now at last reclamation had become a great national enterprise. And Willard Holmes knew that out of the millions that would be realized from these reclaimed lands this man, who had seen the vision, would receive nothing. The Seer had not even a position with an irrigation company or with a reclamation project.

As he listened to the man who had literally given the best of his life to a great work, the Company engineer felt as he sometimes felt when alone in the heart of the desert itself he heard its call, the call that was at once a challenge, a threat and a promise; or as when he had felt the sweet power of Barbara's presence.

At his hotel Holmes found the president of The

367

King's Basin Land and Irrigation Company anxiously awaiting him: "Look here!" was Greenfield's
greeting. "This thing is approaching a climax."

He handed the engineer a telegram from Burk.
Willard Holmes glanced at the yellow slip of paper.

"Strike on the K. B. C. Looks serious."

"Jefferson Worth left for San Felipe this afternoon," Greenfield said quickly. "There's another
train in thirty minutes. We mustn't miss it!"

CHAPTER XXVI.

HELD IN SUSPENSE.

EORGE CARTWRIGHT, the retired New York capitalist, belonged to that older school of American financiers who, having built up large fortunes by taking advantage of the speculative opportunities of their day, look somewhat doubtfully from the pinnacle of a successful old age upon the same adventurous spirit when shown by the active younger generation. George Cartwright was ready to take a chance, certainly. He had taken chances all his life. But George Cartwright distrusted mightily what he called the "slap-dash, smash-bang" system of the modern manipulators of capital. Some day, he predicted, the manipulators themselves would go "smash-bang" along with their methods.

Though retired from the rush and drive of active business, the veteran still enjoyed taking an occasional hand in the game, though more than ever he played that hand with a dignified leisure befitting the stake. "A business transaction," said he, "was not something to be put through with a nod and wink or at most a half dozen monosyllables between as many bites of a sandwich."

Jefferson Worth was in desperate need of quick action. He was not playing a game of business for the mere pleasure of playing. He was fighting for his financial life and every hour's delay increased his peril. But Jefferson Worth did not need his railroad friend's warning that an attempt to rush George Cartwright would be disastrous. The old financier was not at all backward in making known to Jefferson Worth his opinions of Jim Greenfield and the men associated with him in the Company. He had had some experience with them not altogether satisfactory to himself. But an investment in actual improvement and development enterprises, such as he understood Mr. Worth to be promoting, was rather an attractive venture. He was going for a week's trip to San Felipe and when he returned he would take the matter up.

Barbara's father could not urge his need of immediate relief, for to do so would have been to destroy his only hope. So he was forced to await the New York man's pleasure. Nor was Mr. Worth ignorant of Greenfield's efforts as indicated by the presence of Willard Holmes in the city. He knew also the high regard that Cartwright held for the engineer and that he would place great value upon the Company man's opinion. What would Willard Holmes do?

Abe Lee's telegram announcing the strike and the critical situation in the Basin changed conditions instantly. Now Jefferson Worth's only hope was to get to Cartwright without delay and to present the urgent need of immediate action. For while the chances that the old capitalist would come to the rescue were greatly lessened, Jefferson Worth's financial ruin was certain if the critical situation at home was not relieved instantly. Sending the telegram to Abe Lee he took the first train for San Felipe. It was indeed a forlorn hope.

Mr. Worth's train arrived in San Felipe about eleven o'clock in the morning. Scanning the register at the principal hotel he found the eastern man's name, but the clerk informed him that Mr. Cartwright was out for the day sight-seeing with a party of friends from New York and would not likely return until late in the evening.

No one observing the quiet, gray-faced man who waited in the hotel lobby that evening could have said that there was more on his mind than a mild interest in the evening paper. Yet Jefferson Worth was reading an account of The King's Basin strike. Finishing the article, he dropped the paper on his knee while the slim fingers of his right hand sought his chin with a nervous, caressing motion and his expressionless eyes moved continually over the crowd in the big room. Outside, the depot 'bus had just stopped in front of the hotel and a company of newly arrived guests were entering the corridor, while the bell-boys were running forward to relieve them of their luggage and lead them to the spick-and-span clerk behind the register.

First of the group Jefferson Worth saw the portly, well-groomed president of The King's Basin Land and Irrigation Company and with him his athletic, bronzed-faced chief engineer.

Even as the two were talking with the clerk and, as Worth rightly guessed, asking for Mr. Cartwright, the old gentleman with his party of friends entered.

At a word from the man behind the desk Greenfield and Holmes turned to greet the entering capitalist and his party. They were all New Yorkers—acquaintances and friends. Coming together with the width of the continent between them and their homes, their greetings were cordial—joyful—even boisterous. And as they parted to follow the waiting bell-boys to their rooms, the western pioneer banker heard them agreeing to meet and dine together a few minutes later.

Jefferson Worth realized that a business interview with Mr. Cartwright that evening was impossible. Without visible interest in anything else he raised his paper again and continued reading.

The next morning when the New York capitalist stepped from the elevator on his way to breakfast he found himself face to face with the man who so desperately needed financial assistance. "Why, how do you do, Mr. Worth. When did you land in San Felipe?" Cartwright's tone seemed to subtly change his commonplace question into—"Why are you in San Felipe?"

Jefferson Worth's answer was straightforward. "I arrived yesterday. Conditions have arisen that make it necessary for me to see you at once."

The old veteran looked straight into Jefferson Worth's face with the understanding of one who had himself passed through many a financial crisis when the issue depended upon time gained or lost. Sometimes the wheel of Fortune turns with dizzy speed.

"Certainly, Mr. Worth. Come to my room in half

an hour," he answered quickly and as quickly moved away.

When The King's Basin man had placed the situation fairly before him and the old financier had asked a number of pertinent questions, he said: "Mr. Worth, I understand that neither the value nor the safety of my investment is necessarily impaired because you have a situation on your hands demanding immediate relief. I can see that the capital you ask me to put into your enterprise will relieve the situation at once and enable you to place the whole business upon a solid foundation. If you fail to raise this money, or if you get it too late, you go to the wall and I lose a chance for what seems a profitable investment. As I told you, legitimate promotion of actual development projects has always been attractive to me, but I want to examine into matters a little further before I give you my final answer. Frankly I want to ask the opinion of Willard Holmes. I would not place too much confidence in Mr. Greenfield's judgment, or rather, I should say, in any advice that he would give me in this particular matter. But I have known Willard from babyhood. I knew his father and the whole family, and I would be guided by his opinion as an engineer of conditions in the new country in which you are all interested. Fortunately Holmes is here in the hotel. Let me have a little talk with him and I'll give you my answer without delay."

Writing a brief note asking the engineer to come to his room, he summoned a boy and directed him to deliver the message immediately. A few minutes later Jefferson Worth, in the lobby, saw the boy approach Holmes, who was with Greenfield. The engineer took the note from the boy, glanced at it and handed it to his companion. For a moment they stood in earnest conversation; then the engineer turned and moved away.

Jefferson Worth saw him enter the elevator, saw the ornamented iron door close and the cage glide smoothly upward.

James Greenfield, confident, self-possessed, with the air of one whose position and future are secure, jovially greeted one of the New York party, who came up on Holmes's departure, and the two stood laughing and chatting over their cigars.

Jefferson Worth sat alone in a secluded corner of the lobby.

CHAPTER XXVII.

ABE LEE'S RIDE TO SAVE JEFFERSON WORTH.

THE evening that Jefferson Worth spent in the San Felipe hotel lobby, apparently absorbed in his paper while Greenfield, Holmes and Cartwright with their New York friends were enjoying their dinner, Barbara and her court had their anxious supper together in the Worth home.

The night that followed was one of wakeful readiness on the part of the men who guarded the Worth property. But the strikers seemed content to curse and threaten. Breakfast the next morning, in spite of Barbara's efforts at cheerfulness, was a gloomy meal. Worn with their anxious vigil the men ate in silence, save when they forced themselves to respond to their young hostess's attempts at conversation. They knew that another day of idleness would fit the striking laborers for reckless action.

When the meal was over Barbara insisted that they must get some sleep. They protested, but she argued rightly that there was nothing else that they could do and that they must keep themselves fit for a possible need of their strength later. So she brought comforts and blankets for a bed on the floor in the little sitting room and, drawing the shades, announced that she would take her sewing to the front porch while they slept.

Three hours passed and a boy arrived from the telegraph office with a message addressed to Abe Lee. Speaking in low tones that the tired men within might not be disturbed, Barbara said that she would hand the message to Mr. Lee, who was in the house, and signed her name in the book. Then as the boy went down the walk the young woman, with trembling fingers, tore open the yellow envelope.

The message read: "Money to-day by wire from Tenth National Bank, New York. Pay men and go on with work. I leave for home to-night ten-thirty.
Jefferson Worth."

Barbara and her Desert had won against the Company through Willard Holmes, but Barbara did not know that.

Behind her, as she stood with the yellow slip in her hand, the sitting room door opened softly and turning she saw Abe standing on the threshold. The alert surveyor had been aroused by the coming of the messenger. Even before she spoke her face told him the good news.

Abe went at once to notify the strikers that they would receive their pay on the morrow without fail. To several of the leaders he exhibited the telegram with Mr. Worth's instructions: "Pay men and go on with work," and they in turn verified to their countrymen the good news. As the word went around, the dark scowling faces were lighted with satisfaction and pleased anticipation, curses and threats were silenced in laughter and merry talk. In a short hour or two the little army of striking laborers that had for days been in a mood for any violence became a good natured crowd bent on enjoying to the full their short holiday.

Barbara insisted on serving dinner for her three friends, and with the strike practically settled and the weary strain of the situation removed the four made the meal a jolly one. When they could eat no more they still sat idling at the table, reluctant to break the spell of their companionship.

Texas Joe, leaning back in his chair, with his slow smile drawled in an inconsequential way: "I reckon, now that the financial obsequies of Mr. Jefferson Worth has been indefinitely postponed owin' to the corpse refusin' to perform, that Company bunch will wear mournin' because said funeral didn't come off as per schedule. Them roosters are sure a humorous lot."

"Of course they will be sorry, Uncle Tex," said Barbara. "It's Good Business, you know, to want your competitor to fail."

The old plainsman shook his head. "I sure don't sabe this financierin' game, honey, but I'm stakin' my pile on your dad just the same."

"Well," said Pat, "we're all glad on Mr. Worth's account, av course, that ut's over as aisy as ut is. But for mesilf, av ut was all the same to him an' to ye Barbara, I'd be wishin' the danged greasers 'd kape on a shtrikin' so long as ye wud lave me put my fate under yer table."

They all laughed at Pat's sentiments, which the other two men endorsed most heartily. Then the surveyor with his two helpers went up town.

Stopping at the bank and showing the cashier his

message from Mr. Worth, Abe asked if he had heard from New York.

Before answering, the man picked up a telegram from his desk and scanned it thoughtfully. "No," said Greenfield's cashier, as if against his will; "we have heard nothing to-day."

Just before the close of banking hours the surveyor again called at the bank. "Any news from New York yet?"

"Yes. We had their wire just after you left."

"Well?" asked Abe impatiently. "Isn't it all right?"

"It's all right, Mr. Lee, except that we were forced to answer that we could not handle the business."

The surveyor searched his pockets for tobacco and cigarette papers. "I think you'd better explain, Mr. Williams."

Again the cashier hesitated, turning thoughtfully to the telegram on his desk. Then he said reluctantly: "It is Mr. Greenfield's orders, Lee."

With a cloud of smoke from Abe's lips came the question: "And the other banks in the Basin?"

"You would only waste your time."

"Thanks, Williams. Adios."

Abe Lee walked slowly out of the building. Moving aimlessly down the street, unseeing and unheeding, he ran fairly into Pat and Texas, who were talking with a rancher from the South Central District.

The voice of the Irishman aroused him. "Fwhat the hell! Is ut dhrunk ye are?" Then, as he caught a good look at the surveyor's face—"For the love av Gawd, fwhat's wrong wid ye, lad?"

The rancher also was looking at him curiously. Abe gained control of himself instantly with an apologetic laugh. "Excuse me, Pat. I was thinking about the work and didn't see you. There's a little matter that I want to take up with you this afternoon. I'll be too busy for it to-morrow."

The rancher, with another word or two, turned away. Then Abe, in a low tone, exclaimed: "Let's get away from the crowd quick, where we can talk."

They started down the street and instinctively their feet turned toward Jefferson Worth's home instead of toward the office. As they went Abe explained the situation. Pat cursed the bank and James Greenfield and the Company with no light weight curses.

"Hell will sure be a-poppin' when them greasers don't get their pay checks, as we've been promisin' them," drawled Texas Joe, shaking his head mournfully. "For regular unexpectedness this here financin' business gets me plumb locoed. What will you do, Abe? Greenfield sure takes this trick, don't he?"

They had reached the gate of the Worth home and had paused as people sometimes will when engaged in conversation of absorbing interest. Before Abe could answer Texas, Barbara, who sat on the porch, called laughingly: "What's the matter with you men? Are you hungry again? Why don't you come in?"

In consternation the three looked blankly at each other. Pat growled another curse under his breath. Texas shook his head doubtfully. Abe groaned: "She'll have to know, boys."

Slowly they went up the walk and Barbara, as they drew near, did not need words to tell her that something seriously wrong had happened.

When Abe had explained it in as few words as possible she said: "But it will only be for a few days."

"A few days will be too late," said Abe bluntly. "We have promised these greasers and Indians that we will pay to-morrow without fail. When we don't pay, on top of all the trouble we have had, no explanation will stand. They'll go on the warpath sure. If they were white men it would be different."

"Well, why don't you telegraph father and let him bring the money or send it by express from San Felipe?"

"But he couldn't get the cash started before to-morrow afternoon. Then it would have to go around by the city and wouldn't get here until three days later. Williams didn't tell me, you see, until he knew that the San Felipe bank would be closed before I could get a message through."

They sat in troubled silence—Pat in sullen rage, Texas squatting on his heels cow-boy fashion, Abe pulling at a cigarette, Barbara leaning forward in her chair. Three hours before they had been so merry because the trouble was over; now they faced a situation many times more perilous than before.

With a quick gesture of decision Abe tossed aside his cigarette. "Tex, where is that buckskin horse of yours?"

"In Clark's stable. Want him?"

"Yes. Give him a good feed and bring him here as soon as he is ready. Bring one feed and a canteen, and while the horse is eating go around to my room and get my gun."

Without a question the old plainsman left the group and walked swiftly away.

Barbara puzzled for a moment then asked: "Are you sending Tex to San Felipe for the money, Abe ?"

"I am going myself. Tex will be needed here. He's worth three of me at this end of the game. To-day is Wednesday. That buckskin will make it to San Felipe in twenty-six hours. That will be to-morrow evening. If your father can have the money ready I should be back here by Friday night."

While speaking he was tearing a leaf from his note book. Quickly he wrote a message to Jefferson Worth. "Pat, take this to the telegraph office and make them rush it. It must catch Mr. Worth before he leaves at ten-thirty to-night."

Barbara sprang to her feet. "Oh, please let me go. Let me do something."

Abe handed her the slip of paper with a smile. "If you don't mind I will take a nap in your father's room. And will you ask Ynez to have a bite to eat ready for me with a sandwich or two that I can slip into my pocket. Pat, you stay here and don't let anyone disturb me until five-thirty. Then call me sure. Tex will be here with the horse by that time." With the last word he disappeared into the house.

When Pat called him he was sleeping soundly. Barbara had sent the telegram and with her own hands prepared his supper and a lunch. While he ate, the surveyor gave brief instructions to his two helpers.

Then Barbara went with him to the gate where the buckskin horse, one of that tough, wiry, half-wild breed native to the western plains, waited, head down with bridle reins hanging to the ground. As Abe tightened the cinch and took his spurs from the saddle horn, the girl went closer to his side. "I wish you did not have to go," she said as he stooped to put on a spur.

He straightened up and looked at her. The brown eyes regarded him seriously. "Why, Barbara! you are not afraid? Texas and Pat will be here."

"It's not myself, Abe; it's you," she answered. "You have had such a hard time since this trouble began and now this long, lonely ride. I wish there was some other way."

Stooping quickly so that she might not see his face he adjusted the other spur with trembling fingers.

"I shall think of you every minute, Abe," said the young woman softly.

The strap of the spur required several ineffectual efforts before the man could fasten it on the steel button. At length it was on and, rising again, he threw the bridle reins over the horse's head, holding them in his left hand on the animal's neck. Barbara came still closer and with her finger traced the design carved on the heavy Mexican saddle. "You will be careful, won't you, Abe?"

The hand on the horse's neck tightened on the

reins as the surveyor looked straight into the young woman's eyes a moment as if searching for something that he knew was not there. Then he held out his free hand, saying in Spanish with a smile: "Adios, sister."

Giving him her hand she answered in the same soft musical tongue: "Adios, my brother."

Turning he put his foot in the stirrup and, with the easy graceful swing of the western horseman, he mounted and the buckskin, as his rider lifted the bridle reins, struck at once into the long lazy lope of his kind.

Leisurely Abe Lee rode along the main street of the little town. The strikers, idling in front of the stores, leaning against the buildings or awning posts, squatting on their heels on the sidewalks, or sitting in rows on the curbing, saw him pass without interest. If they thought anything it was that the superintendent was going to Kingston on some business or other for their employer, Senor Worth, or that to-morrow the man on the buckskin horse would give them the slips of paper that they would take to the senor at the bank, who would give them their money.

Still riding leisurely, Abe left behind the town that Jefferson Worth had built in the barren desert and passed the newly improved ranches on the outskirts. Without hurry, even checking his horse to a shuffling fox-trot at times, he reached Kingston.

From the window of his office in the Company building Mr. Burk saw the horseman as he passed, and the Company manager, who was paid for thinking, shifted his cigar to one corner of his mouth and, tilting his head, grew thoughtful while the buckskin horse carried his rider out of Kingston toward the south.

Reaching the old San Felipe trail the surveyor swung his horse to the west and, leaving behind all that man had so far wrought in La Palma de la Mano de Dios, rode straight toward the mountain wall that in grim barrenness and forbidding solitude had stood sentinel through the unnumbered ages, shutting out from the land of death the world of life that lay on the other side. As that mighty wall had from the beginning turned back every moisture-laden cloud from the thirsty, starving land, so it seemed now to impose itself as an impassable barrier against the man who rode to save the work of Jefferson Worth.

The buckskin horse, as if realizing that this was no jaunt of ten or twenty miles, held to his steady, machine-like lope that measured the distance of each swing with the accurate regularity of a pendulum; while the lean, loose body of his rider, resting easily in the saddle, yielded without resistance to the horse's every movement so that those laboring muscles, working so smoothly under the yellow hide, might not be called upon to adjust themselves to the sudden strain of unexpected changes in balance. Mile after mile of the dun plain slipped away under those apparently slow-measuring hoofs at surprising speed. Now and then, at the slightest signal from Abe, the gait was changed from a lope to that easy shuffling fox-trot that lifted the dust in a great yellow cloud.

Straight ahead the rider saw the sun go slowly down behind the mountain wall. He watched the purple shadows that he knew were canyons deepen, and the blue that he knew to be shoulders and spurs and points change and darken until every detail was lost in the slate gray mass, while against the light that lingered in the west every tooth, knob and peak of the sky-line showed a sharp, clean-cut silhouette. He saw the colors of the desert fade and melt as the dark mantle of the night was drawn quietly over the plain. He heard the night voices of the desert awakening and sensed the soft breathing of the lonely land. And in his nostrils was the indescribable odor of the ancient sea-bed that, for uncounted thousands of years, had lain under a blazing sun and scorching wind and mistless nights, knowing no touch of human life save the passing presence of those who dared to follow that one thin trail.

And always with that dogged regularity the sandy miles were being measured by those steady hoofs. At Wolf Wells, as the last faint tinge of light went out of the sky beyond the black mass of No Man's Mountains, Abe drew rein for the first time. Dismounting, he slipped the bit from the horse's mouth and the animal plunged his nose deep into the refreshing water. The buckskin, with the blood of his wild ancestors strong in his veins, was no dainty, tenderly-nourished aristocrat that needed to be rested, cooled and blanketed before he could slake his thirst. Without pausing he drank his fill and then, lifting his head, drew one long, deep breath of satisfaction and stood ready.

In the dark Abe felt his saddle girths, then ran his hand over the moist warm neck and slapped the strong hips approvingly. "Good boy, Buck! Good old boy!" Without thought of further rest they went on—on—and on, without pause or check save the occasional change in gait from the swinging lope to the shuffling fox-trot, until they reached the line of the ancient beach, and the buckskin, with head down, labored heavily up the steep grade to the Mesa.

It was at this point, years before, that the four men and the boy had stopped to look away over the awe-inspiring scenes of wide sky, measureless plain, rolling sand hills, dream lakes and ever-changing seas of color, all hidden now in the blackness of the night.

In the dark, hall-like Devil's Canyon the sound of the horse's feet echoed and re-echoed sharply from the rock walls, while the darkness was so thick that Abe could not see the animal's head.

At Mountain Spring, where travelers into the desert always filled their water barrels, Abe stopped again. It was a little past midnight. Loosing the saddle girth and removing the bridle, the surveyor let his horse drink and, taking a sack with his one feed of rolled barley, he deftly converted it into a rude nose-bag by cutting a strip in each side two-thirds the length of the sack and tying it over the horse's head. After eating his own lunch the surveyor stretched himself out flat on his back on the ground with every muscle relaxed. The sound of the horse munching his feed ceased; the animal's head dropped lower, and he too—wise in the wisdom of the open country—relaxed his muscles and rested.

For an hour they remained there, then again the bridle was adjusted, the saddle girths tightened, and they went on. But the gait was not so measured now nor the pace so steady, for they were well into the mountains, climbing toward the summit. But still there was no pause for breath no relief for the straining muscles of the horse or for the weary aching body of the rider.

Crossing over the summit at last they were on the long western slope of the range with much better going, and the buckskin again carried his rider swiftly on while the thud and ring of the iron-shod hoofs on the rock-strewn road aroused the echoes in the dark and lonely hills.

Hour after hour of the long night passed with no sound to break the silence save the sound of the horse's feet, the rattle of bridle chains, the clink of spur or the creak of saddle leather. And when the gray of the morning came they were in the foot hills. Behind them the mountains—a bare and forbidding wall on the desert side—lifted ridge upon ridge with the green of pine on the heights, oak on the slopes and benches, and sycamore in the lower canyons. Streams of bright water tumbled merrily down their clean rocky courses or rested in quiet pools in the cold shadows. Before them spread the beautiful Coast country, sloping with many a dip and hollow and rolling ridge and rounding hill westward to the sea.

At the first ranch house they stopped. A short hour's rest with breakfast for man and horse, and they were away again. For dinner Abe drew rein in a beautiful little village in the heart of the rich farming country and at four o'clock, from the summit of a low hill, he saw the ocean, with the smoke of San Felipe dark against the blue of sky and water. There were yet three hours of riding. The tired man straightened himself in the saddle, the horse felt the motion and responded with a slight quickening of the movements of those wonderful muscles that still worked so steadily and smoothly under the buckskin coat. The animal seemed to realize with the man that the end of the journey was in sight. Yet it would take another hour and another of that steady, measured lope and the easy shuffling fox-trot.

The sun was dipping downward now toward the ocean's rim, and sea and sky were a blaze of glorious light; while on that dazzling background sail and mast and roof and steeple were painted black with edges of yellow flame. The horse, with the dogged, determined spirit of his breed, was drawing upon the last of his strength—the strength that had brought them so many miles without faltering. But still he answered gamely to the lifting of the reins with that measured, swinging lope.

But as he watched the sun go down, Abe Lee forgot his weariness, forgot his aching muscles, and stiffened limbs. He remembered only that miles away in the little desert town there was a mob of striking Mexicans and Indian laborers who, disappointed and enraged at not receiving their promised pay, would be ready now for any deed that promised to satisfy their blind desire for vengeance. He knew that no explanations would be accepted. No plea for patience would be heard. They could not understand. In their eyes they had been tricked, fooled, cheated, defrauded of their just dues. They knew no better way to redress their wrongs than the primitive way —to destroy, to injure, perhaps to kill. And Barbara —Barbara was there. If only they would let that one night pass! If only Tex and Pat and the little handful of white men could hold them off a few more hours until he could get back.

Until he could get back! But what if Jefferson Worth had not received the telegram before he left San Felipe? What if there should be a still further delay in getting the money?

Through the lighted streets of the harbor city the buckskin and his rider finally made their way. A policeman, looking suspiciously at the dust-begrimed, sweat-caked, trembling horse that stood with legs braced wide and drooping head, and at the haggard-faced rider, directed the surveyor to the hotel a block away, and then stood watching them as they moved slowly toward the end of the ride.

CHAPTER XXVIII

WHILE Barbara and her three friends at home were rejoicing over the message from Jefferson Worth telling them that he had secured the money needed to go on with the work, Willard Holmes was alone in his room in the San Felipe hotel.

Following the engineer's interview with Mr. Cartwright, he had passed through a stormy scene with James Greenfield and the words of the president of The King's Basin Land and Irrigation Company were ringing in his ears with painful monotony: "Discharged—discharged—discharged!"

For the first time in his life the engineer had heard those words addressed to himself. He could not rid himself of the feeling that he had come suddenly to the end of his career.

All his life Willard Holmes had had back of him the powerful influence of his foster uncle. Positions and opportunities had come to him from the first without effort on his part. Notwithstanding the fact that his ability as an engineer was naturally of a high order and that his training was of the best, he had never been dependent wholly upon these things. Other and stronger considerations had always given him his place. For the first time in his life he faced

390

the world of his profession with nothing but his naked ability as an engineer to speak for him, while his abrupt dismissal from the Company compelled him to realize with sudden force how over-shadowed his work had always been by outside influences and how dependent he had been upon them. He felt lost and bewildered, knowing not which way to turn. His future seemed a blank. He had been anxious and eager to get back to his work in the Basin. But he had not realized how much that work meant to him— how his plans, his dreams, his whole life work had become centered in the reclamation of The King's Basin Desert.

If his dismissal had come from anything connected with his work, he told himself, it would be different. He thought bitterly how he had struggled with insufficient equipment and inadequate makeshifts of every kind to hold the Company system together that the pioneers might have the water, without which the work of reclamation could not be done. He knew every stake and pile and plank and crack and patch in the whole system. He had learned the tricks of the river and was familiar with the conditions peculiar to the desert country. He knew the terrible danger of the flood season that was only two months away. He had planned and prepared to meet emergencies that would be sure to arise.

And now, because he had refused to deliver the settlers wholly into the hands of these New York capitalists, who cared nothing at all for the real work save as it could be made to increase their money bags, he was turned out. There was now no reason even for his return to The King's Basin. Why, he asked himself, should he go back? To see some other man doing his work? To watch as an outsider the development of the land? or perhaps—as was more likely—to stand idly by and watch its destruction?

But even as he told himself that he could not do that, he knew that he would go back; that, indeed, he must go. The desert called him—summoned him imperatively;—the desert, and something else: something that was as mysteriously impelling as the spirit of the land; something that had grown into his life even as his work had grown; something that seemed to him now a part of his work from the beginning.

All that day the engineer avoided Greenfield and his eastern friends. In the evening he dined alone and after the meal sat alone in the hotel lobby with his back to the crowd, watching through the big window the life of the street outside—watching without seeing. Moodily he pulled at his cigar, his thoughts far away in Barbara's Desert where, unknown to him, Abe Lee on the buckskin horse was riding— riding—riding to save the work of Jefferson Worth.

His thoughts were interrupted by the voice of Jefferson Worth himself, who, seeing the engineer alone, had gone to him. Holmes, drawing another chair close to his, greeted Barbara's father with eager questions. "Have you heard from home? Is everything all right?"

The older man accepted the chair by the engineer's side and answered his questions by saying: "Mr. Cartwright instructed his New York bankers to wire this money to my account in Republic. I notified

Abe to pay the men to-morrow and go on with the work."

It was characteristic of Jefferson Worth that he did not attempt to thank Holmes for his part in the transaction with Cartwright, but in some subtle way the engineer was made to feel his gratitude and appreciation. After a pause Worth continued: "I am going to start back to-night on the ten-thirty. When are you figuring on going back?"

The engineer smiled grimly. "I can't figure on anything definite just now, Mr. Worth. I might as well tell you, I suppose, that I am no longer connected with the Company."

The announcement did not appear to be unexpected to Jefferson Worth, but his slim fingers caressed his chin as he said: "I was afraid of that. Have you anything in view?"

Holmes felt that not only had Worth foreseen the situation, but that he had already set in motion some movement to relieve it. "No, sir. It came so suddenly that I have scarcely had time to think."

"I figured some time ago that the Company would not be able to hold you much longer," was the surprising comment. "The S. & C. has been looking for a good man to put down in our country for some time. Your experience on the river would make you particularly valuable to them under existing conditions. I told them about you. They have been holding off waiting developments. If I were you I would get in touch with them at once. You can go up to the city with me to-night. We will stop over and look into the proposition and then if it is all right

393

and agreeable to you we can go on home together." Jefferson Worth seemed to understand perfectly the engineer's desire to return to The King's Basin.

Before Holmes could express his delight and grati tude at the unexpected relief, a call-boy, passing among the guests, shouted: "Mr. Jefferson Worth Mr. Jefferson Worth!"

The banker opened the message, read it, then— without a word—handed the yellow slip to his com panion. The engineer read: "Banks in Basin won't accept New York business. Can't handle pay checks Abe Lee starting for San Felipe overland to-night Have money and fresh horse ready.   Barbara."

Holmes looked in consternation from the paper in his hand to Barbara's father. The face of Jefferson Worth expressed nothing. It was perfectly calm and emotionless, only the slim fingers were lifted to the chin as if behind that gray mask the mind of the man was groping, seizing, searching, examining every phase of the situation so suddenly confronting him. In answer to the engineer's questioning look he spoke in colorless words, with machine-like exactness, as if the matter under consideration were a mere mathe matical problem presented for his solution. "The Company owns the banks. Greenfield went into the telegraph office this morning as Cartwright and I came out. Abe would get my message by nine o'clock. The banks would get Greenfield's instructions the same time. Abe would at once promise the men their money to-morrow. That cashier didn't tell him they couldn't handle the business until too late for him to get me before the banks closed here. Greenfield

is playing for time so that the strikers will make
trouble. Abe has it figured out right. He can get
here and back before I could get the money to him
by train. He should reach here to-morrow night.
There is nothing to do except to see Cartwright this
evening so that he can wire New York to-night and
I can get the cash through the bank here before Abe
gets in to-morrow."

As he grasped the situation and the methods Greenfield had employed to injure Worth's interests, the
engineer's eyes flashed. "Mr. Worth," he cried,
"that is the dirtiest trick I ever saw turned."

"It's business, Mr. Holmes. Mr. Greenfield is
merely using his advantage, that's all."

The methods of The King's Basin Land and Irrigation Company in La Palma de la Mano de Dios
were the methods of capital, impersonal, inhuman—
the methods of a force governed by laws as fixed as
the laws of nature, neither cruel nor kind; incon-
siderate of man's misery or happiness, his life or
death; using man for its own ends—profit, as men
use water and soil and sun and air. The methods of
Jefferson Worth were the methods of a man laboring
with his brother men, sharing their hardships, sharing their returns; a man using money as a workman
uses his tools to fashion and build and develop,
adding thus to the welfare of human kind. It was
inevitable that the Company and Jefferson Worth
should war.

James Greenfield served Capital; Jefferson Worth
sought to make Capital serve the race. But in the
career of each of these men, who had been driven

by the master passion—Good Business, into The Hollow of God's Hand, the dominant influence was a life. In the career of Jefferson Worth it was Barbara. In the career of James Greenfield it was Willard Holmes.

In The King's Basin reclamation work, the New York financier, whose relation to Willard Holmes was a tribute to his love for the engineer's mother, felt that in some way—for some cause which he could not understand—the younger man was growing away from him. Their relation of employer and employe seemed to mar the close intimacy of the old ties, and the older man looked forward eagerly to the time when his business plans should be carried to a successful climax and they would both leave the West for their eastern home. That morning in the hotel, when he saw Holmes go with Cartwright to Jefferson Worth and by that knew that the engineer had used his influence against the interests of the Company, he was astonished and hurt. He felt that the boy whom he had reared as his own had turned against him. As the president of the Company he abruptly discharged the engineer, for he could do nothing else. As the foster-father of Willard Holmes, he was still proud of the younger man's strength of character, for under all his anger at being thwarted in his plan against Worth he knew in his heart that the engineer had done right.

As the day passed and the engineer did not seek his company, while Greenfield's own stubborn pride forbade him to go to Holmes, the older man's heart grew more and more lonely. That evening, when he saw Jefferson Worth and Holmes together in earnest conversation and through all of the following day saw them apparently associated intimately in some plan or enterprise, for the first time personal feeling entered into his consideration of the whole situation. He felt that his business rival had become his rival for the affections of the boy he loved. The business victories of Jefferson Worth he could accept without feeling; but that this man—a stranger—should come between him and his foster-son, the child of the woman he had loved with lifelong fidelity, stirred him to a vicious, personal hatred.

At dusk that evening he saw Holmes and Worth dining together. When the meal was over he sat in the lobby, ostensibly chatting with friends, but covertly watching the two who seemed to be awaiting someone. Suddenly he saw them rise quickly and start toward the main entrance. A dusty, khaki-clad man of the desert was entering the hotel. Tall, lean, bronzed, his face haggard and strained with anxiety, his eyes blood-shot through loss of sleep, his figure expressing in every line and movement deadly weariness and aching muscles, he strode forward into the hotel lobby, his spurs clinking on the white tile floor.

Greenfield recognized Abe Lee and grasped the situation instantly. The president of The King's Basin Land and Irrigation Company knew why the surveyor had come to San Felipe and he knew what he would carry back. If the money to pay the strikers reached its destination, Jefferson Worth would win; if not——

At half past nine o'clock that evening the thought-

397

ful Manager of The King's Basin Land and Irrigation Company received a cipher message from his
superior that drew a long, low whistle from his lips.
For almost an hour he considered with an occasional
quiet curse. Then, because he was a good Company
man, he put on his hat and strolled leisurely down
the street of Kingston, apparently enjoying his evening cigar. Once he stopped to greet a belated rancher.
Again he paused to chat a moment with a citizen.
Once more he halted to exchange a word with a group
of Company men, and later stopped to greet three
Mexicans who were in from the Company's camps.

The Manager asked of the work—if all was well.

"Si. Senor."

Then naturally Mr. Burk inquired for news of
their countrymen, the strikers of Republic.

The Mexicans, coming from the distant camp,
could tell him nothing. They had heard little. Could
Senor Burk tell them of the situation?

The Manager was quite sure that everything would
be all right with the men on Jefferson Worth's railroad day after to-morrow.

That was "bueno."

Yes, Mr. Worth's superintendent was starting
from San Felipe that very evening with money—
thousands of dollars, American gold—to pay the
men. He was coming alone through the mountains
on horseback. Without doubt the men would receive
their pay. The Manager was glad!

"Si, Senor."

"Gracias, Senor!"

"Buenos noches!"

"Good night."

CHAPTER XXIX.

TELL BARBARA I'M ALL RIGHT.

WHEN Abe Lee, after twenty-six hard hours in the saddle, dismounted in front of the San Felipe hotel and entered the lobby his usually perfect nerves were strained almost to the breaking point. For weeks the surveyor had carried the burden of Jefferson Worth's financial condition as if it were his own. With the prospect of seeing the work he loved better than his life wrecked and taken over by the Company, he had for days faced the critical situation of the strike. Then, in the very hour of relief, the situation had become seemingly hopeless. Abe Lee, better than anyone, knew the temper of the Mexican and Indian strikers. He realized fully how great the chances were that at the very moment when he finished his ride for relief the town of Republic was the scene of tragic violence.

If Jefferson Worth had left San Felipe ignorant of the failure of his effort to relieve the dangerous situation at home, or if by some chance the money so desperately needed was not ready, Abe knew that the cause was lost. The Company would triumph.

As he entered the hotel his eyes, searching eagerly for his employer, fell first on James Greenfield. With a movement wholly involuntary the hand of the over-wrought desert man came to rest on his hip close to the heavy Colt's forty-five. Then he saw Jefferson Worth and Willard Holmes moving towards him.

When a man feels himself hard-pressed in a fight and is struggling desperately to hold his ground, he has small thought for the trifling courtesies demanded by custom. Without returning the greetings of the two men and instinctively drawing apart from Holmes, the surveyor shot a single question at his employer. "Have you got it?"

"Everything is all right," answered Jefferson Worth, and with his words something of his calm confidence went to Abe Lee.

When the two men reached Worth's apartment the surveyor, without hesitation, began stripping off his clothes. "I want a good bath first," he said. "And while I am at it will you please have a good thick beefsteak cooked rare and sent up here? Then I'll sleep for a couple of hours. That buckskin of Texas Joe's is standing in front of the hotel. He's about all in. I wish that you would see that he is cared for."

As he finished speaking the tall lean figure of the surveyor disappeared through the bath room door. Mr. Worth sent the order for his superintendent's supper to the cook with a sum of money that insured immediate and careful attention. Then with his own hands he led the buckskin horse to a barn where the animal would have the care he had so well earned.

When Mr. Worth returned to the hotel he opened the door of his room softly. There was a tray of empty dishes on the table, an odor of cigarette smoke in the atmosphere, and in his employer's bed the surveyor, sound asleep. Abe Lee understood the value of every moment even in taking rest.

Two hours later Mr. Worth, going again to his room, found that the surveyor had just finished dressing. With a smile the financier handed Abe a slip of yellow paper. It was a message from Barbara saying that so far all was well at home, and concluded with the words: "Love to Abe."

Without a word Abe turned away to buckle about his hips the broad cartridge belt with its worn holster and his big black gun. But Barbara's father did not see him slip the bit of yellow paper into the pocket of his blue flannel shirt.

Then Mr. Worth gave the surveyor a black leather bill-book stuffed to its utmost capacity and secured with rubber bands. "Here it is," he said.

Abe stored the package in an inner pocket of his khaki coat and was ready.

At the barn they found Willard Holmes waiting with two horses. The engineer wore a new belt, holster and revolver. When he had greeted them he said: "Well, are we all ready? I have a lunch here. Is there anything else?"

Abe looked at him questioningly and turned to Mr. Worth.

"Mr. Holmes is going back with you," said the banker.

For an instant the surveyor hesitated. But something in his employer's tone caused him to withhold any objection, and with no comment he turned to inspect the horses. The animals were of the same tough breed as the buckskin. "They're all right, are they?" Abe asked of the liveryman.

"You can see for yourself," came the answer. "You know the kind. The' ain't nothin' can outlast 'em, an' Mr. Worth said that was what he wanted."

"We will need one feed apiece," said Abe. "Put it in two sacks, you know."

"Sure," returned the man. "I'd a-had it ready but this here gentleman didn't tell me."

While the liveryman was preparing the grain Abe examined saddles and cinches. "Are your stirrups right?" he asked Holmes.

"I think so."

"You'd better *know*. We don't want to stop to monkey around in the dark."

The barn man grinned, with a wink at the surveyor, as the engineer decided, after trying, that he had better shorten the straps a hole. Abe silently assisted him in adjusting them. Then—swinging into his saddle—the surveyor said to his employer as the horses moved ahead: "Good-by, sir. Wire little sister that I'm coming."

Along the lighted city streets they rode at a pace that seemed to Willard Holmes more fitting for ladies' gentle exercise than for two men bound on an errand against time. The eastern man urged his horse ahead, but his companion held back and Holmes was forced to check his speed and wait for the other to come up with him. To the engineer's attempts at conversation the other answered only in monosyllables or not at all.

There had been no opportunity for Mr. Worth to explain to Abe the engineer's part in helping him to secure the money from Cartwright and the consequent discharge of Holmes by Greenfield. To the surveyor's mind his companion belonged to the enemy. He could not understand why—with the victory or defeat of Jefferson Worth in his fight with the Company hanging upon his superintendent's mission—the Company's chief engineer should volunteer to accompany him. The presence of Greenfield and Holmes in San Felipe, the action of the banks controlled by the Company, made it clear to Abe that they understood the dangerous situation of Mr. Worth and his urgent need of immediate relief. The Company had everything to gain if the arrival of the money at the scene of the strike could be delayed even for a few hours. But Abe had seen that it was Jefferson Worth's wish that Holmes go with him and the surveyor could not, in the presence of Holmes, discuss the question.

On his part Holmes felt the antagonism of his silent companion but could not guess the reason, while Abe's attitude of aloofness prevented the engineer from making any explanation. He told himself that the surveyor was naturally over-wrought with the mental and physical strain of his long ride, and that later, at some more opportune time, when they halted for lunch and rest perhaps, they would come to a more agreeable spirit of companionship.

But he could not content himself with the slow pace when there was such evident need of haste. It was all a mistake, he thought, for the man already wearied to undertake the return trip. A fresh rider was as necessary as a fresh horse. The surveyor was evidently too exhausted to push on at the necessary speed and Holmes felt that it fell upon him to set the pace and thus force his companion to the exertion required. So he continued urging his horse ahead while Abe's mount, held back by his rider, tugged at the reins and grew restless, and the horse of Holmes, now started sharply forward, now pulled down almost to a standstill, became equally uneasy. So they rode out of the city beyond the lights and movement of the streets into the stillness and the darkness of the night.

At last as Holmes again touched his horse with the spur, making him bound several lengths ahead, and again pulled him down waiting for Abe to overtake him, the western man broke the long silence. "You'll have to quit that, Mr. Holmes," he said somewhat sharply.

The engineer did not understand. "Quit what?"

"Breaking ahead like that. I'll set the pace for this trip."

"You don't seem to be in any hurry," retorted Holmes, nettled by the surveyor's tone.

"I ain't. Not in that kind of a hurry."

"But look here, Abe. Don't you know that Mr. Worth expects us to make the trip in the shortest possible time? We've got to get that money into Republic to-morrow evening, and before if we can. There is too much at stake to poke along like this."

Abe reflected. The Company man certainly understood the situation. Aloud he said: "I think I know what Jefferson Worth wants, Mr. Holmes, and I reckon you'll have to trust me to carry out his wishes. I know the distance; I know this road; and I know horse flesh a little. At the rate you're trying to go you'll be afoot before noon to-morrow. You can ride your own horse down if you want to, but you can't hinder me by fretting mine into unnecessary exertion. He'll need every ounce of his strength and I'm going to see that he doesn't waste any of it. Either push ahead out of sight and hearing as fast as you please, or turn back; but if you ride with me you'll quit this monkey business and ride quietly at the gait I set."

Willard Holmes instantly saw the force of the western man's words. "I beg your pardon, Lee," he said. "Of course you know best. I'm so anxious over this business that I'm acting like a fool."

After that companionship was a little easier, but under the circumstances the one topic most on the mind of each was carefully avoided. At midnight they stopped at the crossing of a stream to water and feed, and Abe showed his companion how to make a nosebag out of the sack in which his grain was carried.

Daybreak found them in the foothills. At the ranch where Abe had been accommodated the morning before they again halted for breakfast. With another feed for the horses tied behind their saddles, they began the long climb of the western slope of the mountains and about four o'clock in the afternoon had crossed over the summit and reached the spring at the head of Devil's Canyon—the last water they would find until they reached Wolf Wells in the desert.

When they dismounted at the watering place some two hundred yards off the trail, the surveyor, after slipping the bit from his horse's mouth and loosening the saddle girth, moved slowly about the little glen, his eyes on the ground. Holmes, standing by the horses which had their muzzles deep in the cool water, watched his companion wearily. "Lost something?" he asked, as Abe continued moving cautiously about.

"Not yet," came the laconic reply.

"Well, what the deuce are you looking for then?"

Abe, coming back to arrange the feed for his horse, looked closely at his companion but made no answer.

When the two men had thrown themselves on the grass to eat their lunch the surveyor, between bites of his sandwich, carefully scanned the mountain side and the mouth of the canyon below. Suddenly reaching out his hand he picked up a burnt cigarette butt and regarded it intently, while the engineer watched him with curious, amused interest.

"What the deuce is the matter, Abe? You act like one of Cooper's Leather-Stocking heroes. What's the matter with that cigarette stub?"

The man of the desert, knowing nothing of Cooper, did not smile but answered shortly, eyeing the engineer as he spoke: "It ain't dry. There was a party at this watering place not more than three hours ago."

"Well, what of it? This is government property. Probably somebody ahead of us going into the new country to locate."

"There's been nobody ahead of us all day."

"How do you know that?"

Abe shrugged his shoulders. "How do I know that a party of five or six watered here since noon?"

"Perhaps it's someone going out."

"Did we meet anyone? This is the only trail."

"Well, maybe it was a party of prospectors or hunters. They would not follow the road."

"They would have pack burros or mules. Nothing but horses in this bunch. They——" The surveyor turned his head quickly to look up the hill. His ear had caught the sound of a horse's feet on the mountain road above.

Holmes, looking also, saw a horseman ride leisurely around the turn and down the grade toward the canyon. Silently they watched and as the newcomer came nearer they saw that he was a Mexican. When the traveler reached the point where he should have turned aside to the water he did not pause but jogged steadily past. "By George!" exclaimed Holmes, "I believe that's one of our greasers from the outfit in Number Eight."

"I know it is," said Abe. "Perhaps you can make a guess as to what he's doing here and why he didn't stop for water." As the surveyor spoke he was rolling a cigarette, and from the cloud of smoke he watched the Mexican ride down the mountain side and disappear between the narrow walls of Devil's Canyon.

"I'm sure I don't know what he's doing. He seems to be going toward the desert. There might be a hundred different reasons why he should have been out somewhere."

"There's only one reason why he didn't stop for water at this place."

"What's that?"

"He had already watered."

"But there has been no chance for miles back!"

"He watered here."

Holmes spoke sharply. Abe's manner irritated him. "I don't see how you know."

"Because this is the only water for twenty miles going either way."

"But you said you thought there was a party of five or six."

"I know there are five or six."

"Where are the others, then, if this man was one of the party?"

"I don't know exactly where they are, but I can guess."

By this time Willard Holmes had come to see that to his companion there was a great deal more in the common-place incident than the surveyor chose to put into words. Abe, throwing away his cigarette and rolling another with his long-practiced fingers, seemed to be striving to arrive at some conclusion about something that to the engineer was all very much in the dark.

Aggravated by the reticence of his companion, Holmes burst forth with: "For heaven's sake! Abe, open up. What's on your mind? What's the matter anyway? What's all this about?"

Abe faced the engineer with a straight, hard look. "Don't you know what it's all about?"

"So far as I can see it's all about nothing at all. Tell me."

"Well, Mr. Holmes, I will. But I'm not sure yet that it will be news to you. The rest of the gang that watered here is down in Devil's Canyon waiting for us. They were here something like three hours ago. After watering, one of them went on over the ridge to watch for us and the others went back down the canyon. They knew that we would stop here to feed and water and that the lookout could jog along past, apparently minding his own business, and tell 'em that we were coming."

"You mean it's a hold-up?" cried Holmes, in some excitement.

"That's what I would call it. Your Company would probably call it intercepting Mr. Worth's messenger."

"The Company? What has the Company to do with it?"

"Greenfield and you were in San Felipe. You knew what I went after. You know that the chances are big that Jefferson Worth will go to smash if I don't make it to Republic to-night, and that greaser is a Company man."

In a flash Holmes saw the whole situation from his companion's point of view and understood the surveyor's suspicions. At the same time the engineer realized that it was now too late for him to explain his presence or that he was no longer connected with the Company. In his perplexity and chagrin and in the suddenness of it all he said the worst thing possible. "Well, what are you going to do about it?"

Abe's voice was hard. "I'm not going to take any fool chances. This may be a plain ordinary case of hold-up or it may be a job framed up by the Company simply to delay me. It's all the same to me, but this money goes to Republic to-night. Sabe that?"

The other would have spoken but Abe interrupted. "We've palavered long enough, Mr. Holmes. The horses have finished their feed and it's time to start."

When they were mounted the surveyor said shortly: "Now, sir, you just ride ahead and you ride slow until I give the word—then you go like hell. If you lift a hand to signal or make any mistakes like stopping to fix your saddle girth or checking up to speak to that bunch or turning 'round, I get you first and you can't afford to have any hazy notions about my not wanting to kill you because you're from New York. If you're square you can make good on those Company greasers down there and I'll apologize afterwards. If you're in this deal with your damned Company, you'll stop drawing your salary right here and there won't be any funeral expenses for them to pay either! Go ahead."

"Just a word first," and Abe saw that the engineer was as cool as a veteran. "Granting that you are right about that crowd being down there to stop us, if anything should happen to you tell me how to get into Republic with the money. You will be taking no chances with that at least."

"Follow the trail to the telephone line. You know

it from there. There's water at Wolf Wells. Give your horse a drink but don't wait to rest. You can push him from now on as hard as you like. You should make it to Republic in six hours from here. Give the money to Miss Worth. Anything else?"

Holmes replied by turning in his saddle and moving ahead. Abe followed, his horse's nose even with the flank of the animal in the lead.

Easily they jogged ahead down the grade toward the narrow throat of the canyon. A hundred yards from where two points of jutting rock in the walls of the mountain hallway leave an opening not more than fifty feet wide, Holmes, with the slightest turn of his head, spoke over his shoulder. "I see a man's face looking around that point of rock on the right."

"Be ready when I give the word."

"Won't they pot us?"

"Not if they can get the drop. They'll turn us loose on the desert."

"Shall I shoot?"

Behind the engineer's back Abe smiled grimly. "When they halt us and I give the word, cut loose if you want to. I'll take all on the left."

The distance lessened to a hundred feet.

Suddenly from the left three mounted Mexicans pushed into the road and from the right two more.

Even as they threw up their guns and called: "Alto—Halt!" Abe gave the word:

"Now!"

The two white men drove their spurs deep into their horses' flanks, throwing themselves forward in their saddles with the same motion. With mad plunges the animals leaped toward the highwaymen. Even as he spoke Abe's gun had cracked thrice in quick succession—the Mexicans firing at about the same instant. Two of the horsemen on the left went down and the surveyor reeled almost out of his saddle. But Holmes did not see. His own revolver barked a prompt second to Abe's, and on his side a Mexican went over clutching at his saddle horn. The horses of the Mexicans were rearing and plunging. The quick reports of the revolvers echoed viciously from the rocky walls.

But the white men went through. Down the rocky hallway they raced, side by side now, as hard as their maddened horses could run. A moment to slip fresh cartridges into his cylinder and Holmes cried to his companion: "Good stuff, old man! Go on; I'll hold 'em." And before Abe could grasp his purpose he had jerked his horse to his haunches and, wheeling, faced back up the canyon and disappeared around a turn.

Even as the surveyor was trying to check his own horse—a tough-mouthed brute—another rattling volley of revolver shots echoed down the canyon. By the time Abe had succeeded in turning his stubborn mount Holmes re-appeared.

"All over!" the engineer sang out, as his companion wheeled again and rode beside him. "Two of 'em were coming after us. I got one and the other turned tail." He winced with pain as he spoke. "They presented me with a little souvenir, though."

Abe saw that his left arm was swinging loosely.

"You are hurt," he said sharply, reining up his horse. "Where is it?"

"Here, in my shoulder. It don't amount to anything. Let's get on to water and I'll fix it up." With the word the engineer, whose mount had also stopped, started ahead. The horse went a few steps and stumbled—struggled to regain his feet—staggered weakly a few steps farther—stumbled again —and went down. As he fell Holmes sprang clear. The animal raised his head, made another attempt to rise and dropped back. Another bullet from the last encounter had found a mark.

The dismounted engineer, who stood as if dazed, staring at his dead horse, was aroused by the voice of Abe Lee. "It looks like we'd got all that was coming to us this trip."

At his companion's tone Holmes looked up quickly. The surveyor's lips were white and his face was drawn with pain.

The man on the ground sprang toward him with a startled exclamation. "You too; Abe! Where is it?"

"My leg, on the other side."

Quickly the engineer went around Lee's horse to find the leg of the surveyor's khaki trousers darkly stained with blood. "Get down," he commanded and, reaching with his uninjured arm, almost lifted his companion from the saddle. An examination revealed an ugly hole in the surveyor's thigh. With handkerchiefs and some strips cut from the engineer's coat they dressed their wounds as best they could. When they had finished, Holmes straightened up and

413

looked around. Behind them was the bold mountain wall, grim and forbidding; on either hand the dry, barren Mesa; and ahead the miles and miles of desert.

As if in answer to his thoughts the man on the ground said grimly: "This is hell now, ain't it? Mr. Holmes, I'll make that apology. If you please, would you mind shaking hands with me?"

Willard Holmes grasped the out-stretched hand cordially. "You did just right, old man. It was the only thing you could do. But I want to tell you quick, before anything else happens that I'm not a Company man any more."

"Not a Company man?"

"Greenfield fired me because I helped Jefferson Worth to interest the capitalist who is furnishing him the money he needs."

For a moment Abe Lee looked at the engineer in silence; then his pale lips twisted into a smile. "Mr. Holmes, would you mind shaking hands again?"

With a laugh the engineer once more held out his hand. Then he asked seriously: "How are we going to get out of this, Abe?"

The smile was already gone from the surveyor's face. He answered slowly, with dogged determination in his voice. "We've got to get this money to Republic to-night. It's the only thing that will stop those cholos and Cocopahs. We'll make it to water together, then you can go on. Help me up!"

With the engineer's assistance Abe managed to gain his seat in the saddle, Holmes mounting behind, and thus they made their way down into the Basin and to Wolf Wells.

There Holmes helped his companion from the horse and to the shade of a mesquite tree near the water hole, where he stood over him as he lay on the ground, protesting vigorously against leaving him alone in the desert. But the surveyor argued him down. "I couldn't possibly make it if we had another horse," he said. "I'm down and out. There'll be hell to pay in Republic to-night, even if the boys have held them off this long. The money's got to get there this evening. You can reach there by ten o'clock and send a wagon back for me. Don't you see there's no other way?" He held out the black leather bill-book with the rubber bands. "Here, take this and go on. Go on, man! What's a night in the desert to me?"

"But those greasers may come this way."

"They won't. But if they should I have my gun, haven't I, and I'll see them before they see me. Go on, I tell you. We've lost too much time already. Think of that mob and Barbara. You've got to go, Holmes."

The engineer turned towards his horse. "Good-by, old man."

"Adios. Tell Barbara I'm all right."

Abe Lee watched the loping horse grow smaller and smaller in the distance, then watched the cloud of dust that lifted from the trail to hang all golden in the last of the light. Turning he saw the summit of the mountain wall sharply defined against the sky.

With a groan his form relaxed. He closed his eyes. He was indeed down and out.

The desert night fell softly over the wide, thirsty plain. The snarling coyote chorus came out of the gloom. Out there Willard Holmes was riding—riding—riding—along the old San Felipe trail. Away over there, somewhere under those stars, Barbara was waiting his return. He remembered her parting words and how he had failed to find in her eyes that which he had longed to see. He felt for the paper in the pocket of his shirt: "Love to Abe." She would never have sent that message had her love been other than it was. Abe Lee, born and reared in the desert, was not the kind of man to deceive himself. For his work and for the woman whose life was so strangely and closely bound up with it he had given the utmost limit of his strength. And now another man would finish the ride and go to her with the prize. Not that it would make any difference to Barbara, but somehow it mattered a great deal to Abe.

Willard Holmes, who in spite of his splendid strength had not the desert man's powers of endurance, clung grimly to one thought—the money must go to Republic. The steady rhythm of his horse's feet seemed to beat out the word: "Barbara! Barbara! Barbara!"

The trying scene with Greenfield, the long hard hours in the saddle, the excitement of the fight in the canyon, with his anxiety for his wounded companion left alone in the desert, were almost too much. Could he hold out? Could he make it? He *must.*

The engineer held his seat with the strength of desperation. He *must!* The money must go to Republic that night—to Barbara! Barbara! Barbara! The horse's feet seemed to have beaten out the word for ages. For ages he had been riding—riding—riding towards some point out there ahead in the desert night.

The engineer knew now what it was that called him back.

CHAPTER XXX.

MANANA! MANANA! TO-MORROW! TO-MORROW

HE night when Abe Lee started on his ride from Republic to San Felipe passed quietly in the little desert town. Texas and Pat with a few faithful white men guarded the Worth property lest, in some way, the news that Worth would be unable to pay as his superintendent had promised should get out and precipitate a crisis. But the strikers continued to enjoy peacefully their holiday, looking forward to the morrow when they would be enriched with nearly two months' pay. When the morrow came the laborers, their dark faces beaming with childish happiness, gathered early in front of Jefferson Worth's office. Texas and Pat, with the men of the office force who had been up all night, were sleeping, for another night of guard duty was before them.

When it was ten o'clock and no one had arrived at the office, the crowd of laborers began to show signs of growing impatience. Then someone recalled seeing Abe riding on the buckskin horse toward the south and suspicion grew. At last a few of the more intelligent went in a body to the bank.

"We come to see you about money. You sabe about money?"

"What money is that?" asked the man behind the window shortly.

"Our money for work on railroad. Senor Worth was to pay. El Superintendente say pay to-day sure. He no come. You sabe?"

"I sabe that Worth won't pay."

"No?"

"No. He has no money here."

The Mexicans exchanged glances. "No money? You are quite sure, Senor?"

"Sure."

"Gracias, Senor. Adios!"

It was a dangerous crowd that filled the streets of Republic that afternoon and evening, and all through the night that followed the friends of Jefferson Worth expected every hour the fulfillment of the strikers' threats. Soon after breakfast, which Pat and Tex shared with Barbara, the message came from Mr. Worth telling them that Abe was on his way home with the money.

Again the men were told that they would receive their pay on the morrow, but this time the announcement was received with black scowls and muttered curses of disbelief. "They make us damn fools, one time. How we know this time not the same?" asked one of the leaders, speaking for the crowd. "Mebbe, Senor Tex, you not know. Mebbe they fool you like us. We get money this day, we glad—go work. We no get money by this night——" an expressive shrug of the shoulders finished the sentence.

The attitude of the citizens of Republic was one of angry indifference. They were angry both with Jefferson Worth and the strikers because the trouble was unsettling and harmful to the best interests of all

419

the business in the town and to some degree turned the inflowing stream of settlers and investors towards other points of the new country. They were indifferent because of that underlying conviction, brought about by mysteriously authoritative rumors and whispered statements from supposed inside sources, that the cause of the trouble was a fight between Jefferson Worth and the Company. Whether capitalists rise or capitalists fall is always a matter of indifference to all who are not themselves of the capitalist class For capital continues its mastery of them just the same. No one doubted that the railroad would be finished whether Jefferson Worth failed or not. Horace P. Blanton was not backward in expressing the popular feeling, and the popular feeling often expressed grows ever more popular.

Toward the end of the afternoon Pablo, who had been mingling with his countrymen all day, came to "headquarters" to report. The strikers were planning to attack their employer's property that night. Pablo was certain that the mob would go first to the power plant and the adjoining buildings.

No help was to be had from the citizens and, save for the few white men in Mr. Worth's employ who had been made to understand the situation and the reason for the delay, Tex and Pat were alone. They knew that there was small chance of Abe's arrival until well toward midnight. For a little they considered the situation.

Then the old frontiersman spoke. "Hit stands to reason that Pablo here is right an' that the stampede will head toward the works first, an' they'll all go together. They ain't a-comin' here 'til later, after they've made their biggest play. Now Pablo, you listen. Get two horses—sabe, two—one for Ynez and one for yourself, and have them with El Capitan for La Senorita ready by the back door. You watch. If Senor Lee comes, tell him quick to go to the power house. If the men come, take the women on the horses and get out of the way. You understand?"

"Si, Senor. I will care for La Senorita."

Texas Joe turned to Barbara. "I don't reckon they'll get here at all, for I bank on Pat an' me fixin' somethin' to interest 'em until Abe gets here. But it's best to be fixed for what you ain't expectin'. You'll be a heap better off with Pablo anywhere away from here if they should come this way."

When the night fell, Texas and Pat went to the scene of the expected trouble and Barbara was left with Pablo. The Mexican prepared the horses as Texas had instructed and then took up his position by the front gate, proud and happy that they had so honored him—that they had trusted him to guard his employer's daughter. The darkness deepened. Watchful, alert—Pablo strove to see into the gloom and listened to catch the first sound of approaching friend or enemy. The white men should learn that he could protect La Senorita—La Senorita who, in Rubio City, had been to him an angel of mercy when he was lying injured—La Senorita, whom they all loved.

Behind him the door of the house opened, letting out a flood of light; then closed. In the darkness a voice called softly: "Pablo, are you there?"

"Si, Senorita. You want me?"

Barbara came quickly down the walk to his side. "It's so lonely and still in the house, Pablo; may I stay out here a little with you? We can both watch."

Surely La Senorita could stay. Why not? Pablo was to protect her, not to keep her a prisoner.

She laughed quietly. "I believe you would do anything for me, Pablo."

"I would protect La Senorita with my life," he answered simply.

"I believe you would, Pablo; and so would Tex and Pat and Abe. You are all so good to me and I— I feel so good for nothing—so useless."

In the darkness the musical voice of Pablo answered: "Our love for La Senorita is so great. It is like the desert in the gentle moonlight, so big and wide. It is like the soft night under the stars, so deep. Everybody so loves La Senorita, and anyone loved that way cannot be what you say—good for nothing. Sometime men love like the sun on the desert in day time—fierce and hot, and that is different; that makes sometimes trouble—sometime make men kill. It is not good, La Senorita, but it is so."

They heard a galloping horse coming nearer and nearer. Barbara touched her companion's arm and Pablo laid a hand on his revolver. Was it Abe? Was it someone to say that the mob was coming?

The horse and rider passed and the sound of their going died away in the stillness of the night.

"Pablo, what time will they go to the power house?"

"Any time now, Senorita."

Barbara spoke quickly—eagerly now. "Are there not a good many of your countrymen from Rubio City among them, Pablo?"

"Si, Senorita."

"And do they—do they remember me?"

"Surely no one who lived in Rubio City could forget La Senorita, who was so kind to the poor."

"Then, Pablo, I have a plan to help. I did not tell Texas and Pat, but Ynez is not in the house. I sent her away this evening to stay with a friend on the other side of town."

"Si, Senorita." The soft voice was perplexed and troubled.

"Pablo, I am going to the power house to help."

"No, no, Senorita; it cannot be."

"Yes, Pablo, I must."

"But, Senorita, that is not right."

"You will go with me, Pablo—and no one will harm me."

"But if Senor Lee comes?"

"When he finds no one here he will understand and go to us."

"No, no, Senorita; you must not! The father— Senor Texas, and Pat—they will kill me. La Senorita does not want Pablo to be hurt."

"Why Pablo, no one can blame you, and don't you see that I must do what I can? Come; we are losing time. We must not be too late. You get the horses."

She went quickly into the house and when she came out again the Mexican, still protesting, held the horses ready.

At the power house Texas and Pat sat just inside

the main entrance. In the big room beyond them the great dynamos that furnished electricity to all the towns for lights and supplied the ice plant, the shops and every enterprise needing it throughout the Basin with power, hummed and sang their monotonous song of industry. In front of the building a large arc light made the immediate vicinity as bright as day. On every side of all the buildings in the group where the little handful of white men stood guard, similar lights had been placed by Abe at the beginning of the trouble.

"Howly Mither, wud ye look at that?" came from Pat as Barbara, followed by Pablo, rode into the circle of light. With an oath from Texas Joe the two men ran forward, and as they came up to the riders the Irishman cried: "Fwhat the hell are ye doin' here? Fwhat's the matter? Did thim divils go to the house first, or are ye crazy?"

With a laugh Barbara dismounted and, telling Pablo to tie the horses to the hitch rack a short distance away, faced the astonished men. "There's nothing wrong at the house, but I knew you must be lonesome here so I came to see you. You don't seem a bit glad to see me!"

"Mither av Gawd!" groaned the Irishman.

Texas called to Pablo. "Bring those horses back here."

"Pablo," called Barbara, "do as I told you."

The Mexican leading the horses moved on toward the hitching place. Texas scratched his head in a puzzled way, while Pat grinned. "Will ye roll that in yer cigarette an' shmoke it, Uncle Tex?"

"I'll have to take a shot at that fool greaser for this," returned Texas.

"You'll do no such thing," declared the young woman. "You know he couldn't help himself."

"Be the Powers, ut's us that should know that same!"

"But honey, you can't stay here. There's goin' to be trouble—real trouble."

"I know it, Uncle Tex, that's why I came to help."

"To help!" The two men looked at her in amazement.

Before they could find words for a question Pablo came running back to them: "They're coming, Senorita! Senor Tex! They're coming!"

He was right. Texas Joe caught Barbara by the arm and with the three men she ran into the building just as the crowd of Mexican and Indian laborers reached the outer edge of the lighted space.

While still in the shadow of the night the crowd halted and the watchers in the buildings could see them across the broad belt of light—a stirring, restless mass of men, shadowy and indistinct. Now and then a single figure in the white canvas jumper, trousers and wide sombrero of the Mexicans, or wearing the blue overalls and black shirt decorated with many brightly colored ribbons and the green, yellow or orange head cloth of the Indians, would detach itself from the main company and—coming nearer—would stand out with sudden startling clearness, disappearing again as suddenly in the dark mass as it again moved farther away.

Here and there in the confusion of dusky moving

forms a face would appear as someone, looking up at the electric light caught its rays full upon his swarthy features; or the watchers would catch the gleam and flash from a weapon, a belt buckle or an ornament as the mob of men moved uneasily about. Still farther away the restless, stirring mass was dissolved in the darkness of the night.

"They're palaverin' about the lights," said Texas to his companions. "Can't jest figure the deal under Abe's illumination. They're all plumb anxious, but they's nobody wishful to make himself conspicuous."

"Oh, why doesn't Abe come; why doesn't he come?" exclaimed Barbara.

"Av the saints will only kape thim cholos considerin', the lad may git here yet."

Even as the Irishman spoke the crowd, seemingly agreeing upon a plan, moved forward slowly in a body. When they were well within the lighted space Texas drawled: "Right here's where I feel moved to address the meetin'," and throwing open the door he stepped out upon the platform, which was built to the height of a wagon-bed above the level of the ground with steps at each end.

Standing thus in the bright light of the arc that sputtered over his head, he was seen instantly by every eye in the crowd. As if by command they halted, standing motionless, their dark faces turned toward the old plainsman.

Texas spoke in their own tongue. "Good evening, men. Why do you come here at this time of the night? What do you want?"

There was an angry shifting to and fro in the

mass of men, and a Mexican standing well to the front answered: "What should we want, Senor Texas, but our pay? We have worked four—five—seven weeks without money. We must have money to buy food—clothes—tobacco."

"Do not the commissaries in the camps supply you with all that you need? Surely you can wait a few hours longer. To-morrow you will be paid every cent."

"Manana, manana; always to-morrow! The superintendent promised other time—'to-morrow.' The superintendent lied. Now we will not wait for to-morrow."

Cries of approval greeted the bold speech.

"But we cannot pay you to-night. We have not the money here."

"That is too bad for Senor Worth, then. If he cannot pay he should have told us so that we could work for the Company. The Company can pay!"

"But Mr. Worth will pay to-morrow morning."

A chorus of angry, jeering yells greeted this repeated promise, with cries of "Pronto!", "Esta dia!", and "No manana!"—"Now!", "To-day!", and "Not to-morrow!" The movement toward the building began again.

Instantly the arms of the man on the platform were extended and the mob saw in each hand the familiar Colt's forty-five of the old time West.

The forward movement was checked.

"Men!" cried Texas, in his deliberate way, "you cannot come any nearer these buildings. There are Americans here—friends of Mr. Worth, who are

427

ready to shoot when I give the word. I can kill twelve of you myself before you can get to this platform. Go away quietly and in the morning you will get your money. Come one step nearer this building and many of you will die."

The moment was intense. A shot, a yell, a sudden movement would have precipitated a tragedy.

In the full glare of the light against the blackness of the night, the crowd of dusky-faced, picturesque laborers hesitated. Standing on the platform under the arc that sputtered and sizzled—his back to the building—the single figure of Texas Joe was ready with menacing weapons. Behind the brick walls the handful of armed white men were waiting—watching. Miles away in the desert, Abe Lee was lying wounded and alone under the still stars, and somewhere in the night Willard Holmes, desperately holding his seat in the saddle, was forcing his already exhausted horse toward the end of his mission.

As the muscles of a tiger work and twitch when the beast makes ready for its spring, a movement agitated the mob, and a low growling murmur came from the mass of men. Texas spoke sharply. "Ready, you fellows in there! If they start let them have it."

·The murmur swelled in volume into an angry, inarticulate roar. The movement increased. An instant more and it would launch the mob in a mad rush.

Suddenly, as a beast checked in its spring, they were still and motionless.

By the side of the old frontiersman on the platform under the light stood Barbara.

"Let me speak to them, Tex."

Without pausing for the astonished man to reply she spoke to the mob in Spanish, her voice rising clearly and sweetly.

"Do you know me, friends?"

From different points in the crowd came the answers.

"Si, Senorita." "It is the daughter of Senor Worth." "Among the poor in Rubio City La Senorita was an angel of mercy."

"I remember many of you," Barbara continued. "Over there I see Jose Gallegos, whose wife and baby were ill. How is the little family now, Jose? Manuel Cortes, do you remember when you were hurt by a wicked horse and I would come to see the wife and children? And Pablo Sanchez, do you know how long you were without work until with father's help I found a place for you? Francisco Gonzales, I helped you bury your mother and gave money to the priest that masses might be said for her soul. And you, Juan Arguello, and Francisco Montez—I remember you all, and I am glad to see you. But I am sorry that you come to destroy my father's buildings. Why do you wish to do that?"

The Mexicans whom she called by name stirred uneasily but did not answer. Those who had known Barbara in Rubio City were few among the whole number of laborers, and to these others she was only the daughter of the man who was robbing them of their pay.

The one who had so far acted as spokesman answered angrily. "Must we say again what we want?
If you are, as they say, an angel of mercy, give us
our money and we will go away."

Cries of "Si, si!", "Bueno!", "Muy pronto!",
"El Dinero," and "Give us our money!" arose on all
sides.

"You shall have your money to-morrow—every
penny. Cannot you wait until to-morrow morning?"

The impatient cries were louder now. "La Senorita also say 'manana.' All the rich say all time to the
poor 'manana,' and manana never come. Give us
our money now." The cries were increasing in volume as man after man joined in the chorus of threatening protest.

White and trembling, Barbara realized that she
could do nothing more. Texas said, in a low voice:
"For God's sake, honey; get inside before they break
loose! Go now! NOW!" His voice rose into a
sharp command, and his steady hands again brought
the deadly revolvers into position.

The young woman reluctantly drew a step backward in obedience, then suddenly, with wide eyes
staring over the crowd into the darkness beyond and
extended hand pointing, she sprang forward to the
very edge of the platform.

"Texas! Texas! Look, he is coming! Abe is
here!"

Overcome with emotion she swayed and would
have fallen, but Texas caught and steadied her.
Every man in the crowd turned quickly toward the
rear. A horseman, shadowy and indistinct beyond

the circle of light, was riding toward them. As the newcomer pushed his horse nearer and they saw that it was Willard Holmes, Barbara uttered a cry and turned away, but the quick eye of Texas Joe had seen that the engineer's horse was staggering with exhaustion and that the man could scarcely keep his seat in the saddle.

"Wait, honey," he said, delaying the young woman. "This may pan out yet."

Barbara paused but did not turn toward the approaching engineer. Slowly Holmes forced his horse, reeking with sweat and dust, into the crowd that opened for him to pass and closed in behind him with excited exclamations as the men saw that the rider reeled in his saddle—his face haggard and drawn with pain and his useless left arm tied to his side.

But Barbara still turned away her face.

Coming so close that his leg almost touched the edge of the platform, the engineer—as though he saw no one but her—held out the black leather billbook.

"Miss Worth! Barbara!"

With a cry she turned as the rider sank and would have fallen had not Texas, reaching out, lifted him bodily from the saddle to the platform where Holmes sank unconscious.

Barbara, with wonder and horror in her face, stood as if turned to stone, while Pat and Pablo quickly carried the still form of the engineer into the building. Unable to move, the girl followed them with her eyes until Texas, who had caught up the leather bill-book, exclaimed with an oath: "Look, it's the money!"

She looked at him as though she did not comprehend and he held the bundle of bills toward her. "It's the money, the money! You tell them!"

Mechanically Barbara took the money and turned to the crowd that stood silently wondering what it all meant—waiting to learn whether the incident had anything to do with their pay.

Under the powerful light she held up her two hands filled with bills. "Look!" she cried. "Look! Here is the money for your pay. My father sent it. Now will you believe?"

Shouts and cheers of understanding burst from the crowd.

"It is for you that it is here," continued the young woman. "Will you go away now and come back in the morning—each man for what is his?"

"Si, si, Senorita! Gracias, Senorita!" Laughing, talking and gesticulating the crowd dissolved and moved away.

Before the dispersing laborers had passed beyond the circle of light Barbara was kneeling beside Willard Holmes.

And when they would have taken the engineer to the hotel Barbara said "No"; he must be taken to her home.

Texas had just finished dressing with rude surgery the wound in the engineer's shoulder, and Barbara—standing by the bedside—was looking down into the still face when Holmes slowly came back to consciousness. His opening eyes looked up full into the brown eyes that regarded him so kindly. For a moment neither spoke, but a slow flush of color crept into the girl's face.

By some strange freak of his half awakened intellectual faculties, Holmes was living over again the incident of his meeting Barbara on the desert the morning after her first arrival in Kingston. "Is it really you, or is it some new trick of this confounded desert?" he muttered. "I never saw a mirage like this before. I don't think the heat has affected my brain!"

To Barbara the words had the effect of suddenly blotting out all that had come between them and of putting them both back again to the day when they had "started square." So she answered as she had answered then: "I assure you that I am very. substantial"—and added softly, "and I am here to stay, too."

"And you would never forgive one who was false to the work," muttered the engineer, and with the words his mind caught at the suggestion of the power that had enabled him to keep his seat in the saddle through the seemingly endless hours of torture, and he remembered everything up to the moment when he had handed the money to Barbara.

With an exclamation he tried to raise himself.

"Don't do that. You must lie still, Mr. Holmes," said the young woman.

Texas and Pat in an adjoining room heard and came quickly to Barbara's side.

"I must get up, men!" cried Holmes appealingly, making another effort to raise himself. "We must go for Abe Lee. He's hurt—alone—out there in the desert. Why don't you move? Miss Worth, please——"

Texas Joe quietly forced him back on his pillow. "You've got to take it easy for a little while, Mr. Holmes. Get a grip on yourself and tell us plain what happened. We'll move fast enough when we know which way to go."

When Holmes had told them briefly the story of the fight in Devil's Canyon and how he had left Abe at Wolf Wells, Texas said: "Now Mr. Holmes, you just keep quiet right here. Barbara'll take care of you and we'll have Abe home before noon to-morrow. Also, we'll arrange for a little seance with them greasers what put you and Abe in this fix."

An hour later a light spring wagon with four horses, accompanied by a party of five mounted men, moved swiftly out of Republic toward the south.

CHAPTER XXXI.

BARBARA'S WAITIN' BREAKFAST FOR YOU.

ALONE on the desert, Abe Lee waited through the long, long hours of the night for the morning and relief.

At times the wounded surveyor sank into half unconsciousness when he would again be riding— riding—riding, toward San Felipe that seemed almost so far away that he could never hope to reach the end of his journey. Again he would be at the hotel surrounded by a crowd of people, who stared at him curiously as the clerk explained that Jefferson Worth had never been there—that there was no money—no money—no money. At other times he would be fighting desperately with James Greenfield for the possession of a black leather bill-book secured with rubber bands, or—with the Company engineer —would face a crowd of Mexicans in Devil's Canyon in such numbers that he could not count them, but could only fight, and fight, and fight. Often Barbara came to plead with him to save her from some terrible danger, and when he would struggle to go a great weight held him down and he could not—and the brown eyes looked at him full of pleading reproach. Then he would curse and cry aloud as Willard Holmes came to take her away and he would watch the two riding into the distance through the green fields and orchards of a beautiful land, in their happiness forgetting him alone in the desert.

At other times, fully conscious, he lay with aching body and that sharp pain in his leg, looking up at the stars, calculating the time and the distance Holmes had ridden since he left him—how long it would be until the engineer would reach Republic—wondering if Tex and Pat could hold the strikers or if already it was too late.

Then again, when his mind would be losing its grip and slipping away into the land of half-dreams, the sounds made by some animal at the water hole or the fancied approach of the Mexicans would cause him to start into keen readiness, to listen and watch with straining sense and ready weapon. At last all knowledge of time left him. His exhausted nerves and muscles no longer responded to suggestions of danger, his brain refused to act. A soft, thick cloud of darkness that was not the darkness of the night settled down upon him, enveloped him, wrapped him as in a sable blanket of many folds—thicker and thicker, blacker and blacker. Feebly he struggled against it for a little, then with a sigh yielded and lay still.

He did not see the stars pale and the thin streak of light above the eastern rim of the Basin widen into the morning. He did not see the hills, all rose and purple, develop magically against the sky. He did not see the sun burst into view from the world below the line of the dun plain and roll its flood of light over the wide desert. He knew nothing more until someone was forcing something between his lips and a grateful, stimulating warmth crept through his veins. A familiar voice drawled: "He ain't a-goin' out this time, boys. Hit takes more than one

greaser bullet and a little ride to San Felipe an'
back to send his kind over the line."

And a rich Irish brogue responded: "Ut's thim
black hathen that'll be goin' over the line in a bunch
av I can git widin rache av thim wid me two hands."

Abe opened his eyes with a smile. "Mornin' boys!
Did Holmes make it in time?"

An articulate yell of delight from Pat greeted
his speech. The grizzled plainsman, with a smile of
understanding, answered his question.

"Sure he made it. Everything's as peaceful as
the parson's blessin' after his discourse on the eternal
fires of torment. Barbara's waitin' breakfast for
you, son. Wake up, an' come along."

The surveyor did not need to ask why Texas Joe
had brought so large a party of mounted and armed
friends. He gave Texas and his companions all the
information he could that would help them in their
search for the Mexicans.

When they had made him as comfortable as possible on a cot in the spring wagon, with Pat beside
him and Pablo on the driver's seat, the horsemen
mounted and Texas riding alongside the wagon
drawled: "There ain't no tellin' when we'll get back,
Abe; but I don't reckon we'll be long an' there ain't
no use me tellin' you to take things easy. So adios!"

"Adios," came the answer, "and good luck!"

Pablo spoke to his team and they moved ahead.
For a moment the horsemen watched, then Tex spoke.

"All set, boys?"

"All set," came the answer.

Wheeling about, the five men rode rapidly in the
opposite direction towards Devil's Canyon.

CHAPTER XXXII.

BARBARA MINISTERS TO THE WOUNDED.

WILLARD HOLMES, after a few hours of refreshing sleep and a good breakfast prepared and served by his hostess with her own hands, announced himself as well as ever.

"But you need some fixing just the same," declared Barbara as the Indian woman entered the room carrying warm water, towels and bandages. While the young woman bent over the engineer and with firm, deft fingers removed the wrappings from his shoulder, carefully cleansed the wound and applied fresh dressing and clean bandages, he watched her face, so near his own, and wondered that he had ever thought her plain. Her skin, warmly browned by desert sun and air, was fresh and glowing with the abundance of the rich red life in her veins; her brown hair, soft and wavy, tempted him to reach up his free hand and put back a rebellious lock. He moved slightly and the brown eyes, full of womanly pity, met his.

"Does it hurt?"

He smiled and shook his head. "Not at all. In fact I think I rather enjoy it."

Her cheeks turned a deeper red and he felt her fingers tremble as she went on with her task.

"If you laugh at me I shall turn you over to Ynez," she threatened, at which he promised so pitifully to be good that she smiled and he stirred again impatiently.

"I *am* hurting you!" she cried. "I'm so sorry, but I'm almost through— There now." She finished with a last touch and, straightening, put back herself that rebellious lock of hair.

As she stood before him beautifully strong and pure and fresh and clean in mind and heart and body, her sweet personality, the spirit of her complete womanhood swept to him—appealing, calling, exhilarating, invigorating, strengthening, as he had often felt the early air of the sun-filled morning sweeping over mountain and mesa and desert plain.

The man drew a long deep breath.

"Tired?" she asked softly, looking down upon him with almost a mother's look in her eyes.

"Heavens, no!" he exclaimed, his voice ringing out strongly. "I feel as though I had been made over, ıe-created."

She laughed gladly.

"Do you know," he asked earnestly, "how wonderful you are?"

"Nonsense!" she retorted. "You are growing delirious. You must be quiet. I'm going to leave you alone for a little while now and you must sleep."

She followed the Indian woman from the room and he heard her voice speaking in soft musical Spanish as they went.

An hour later Barbara, moving quietly toward his room to see if he was asleep or wanted anything, found him fully dressed in a big easy chair in the living room.

439

"Oh!" she exclaimed, in joyful surprise. "What are you doing out here? I thought I told you to sleep."

"Your orders were inconsistent," he returned lazily. "You can't cure a patient and still continue treating him as if he were an invalid. I don't need sleep. I need— Bring your chair and sit over here and let me tell you what I need," he finished.

She did not answer, but going to his room returned with a pillow, which she arranged deftly behind his head; then, kneeling, adjusted the foot rest of the reclining chair. "There; isn't that better?"

"Bring your chair," he insisted.

Again she left the room, returning this time with a bit of old soft muslin. Drawing her easy chair to a position facing him she seated herself and began converting the material in her hands into bandages. "The men will be here with Abe any time now," she explained. "I have everything ready except these."

For a little while he watched her in silence as she tore the white cloth into long strips and rolled them neatly.

"Don't you care to know what it is that I need?" he asked at last.

She bent her head over her work and answered softly: "Whenever you are ready to tell me."

"Before I can tell you I must know something."

Carefully she rolled another white strip, her eyes on her task. "What must you know?"

"That you have forgiven me."

The color rushed into her cheeks as she answered: "Don't you know that?"

440

"But I must hear you say it so that we can start square again; don't you see ?"

"I suppose that we will be always starting over again, won't we?" Then as she saw his face she added quickly: "I mean—I—I was thinking of the Company—and—father's work."

"But you forgive me this time?" he insisted.

"Yes; I forgive you, and I am glad—so glad that I can."

"And we are square again?"

"Yes; we are square again—until next time." She added the words sadly.

"But there will be no next time."

She shook her head with a doubtful smile. "The Company will make a 'next time.'"

He laughed aloud with a sudden sense of freedom that was new to him. "But you do not know," he said, "and I would not tell you until we were square again. I am not with the Company now."

She dropped her roll of bandages and looked at him. "Not with the Company? When did you resign ?"

"I didn't resign. They discharged me."

"Discharged you?"

"Yes; disgraceful, isn't it? I felt pretty bad at first; then I came to take it as a compliment; and now—now I am glad!"

Then he told her why Greenfield had sent for him; how he had met the Seer; and how he had advised Cartwright to supply the money her father needed.

"And you—you did—that, knowing it would cost you your position?" she exclaimed. "Oh, I *am*

441

glad! That was fine; that was big—worthy your ancestors!" In her interest she was leaning towards him with flushed cheeks and bright eyes, and her voice was triumphant as if in some subtle way she was vindicated through his victory. The engineer felt her attitude and knew that she was right. It *was* her victory.

"Barbara," he said, holding out his hand; "Barbara, may I tell you now what it is that I need?"

Before she could answer they heard a team and wagon coming into the yard beside the house. Barbara sprang to her feet. "It is the men with Abe!" she exclaimed, and ran out of the room on to the porch.

From where he lay in his chair, the engineer saw through the open door Pablo and Pat coming up the steps of the porch carrying the surveyor on the canvas cot, and Barbara with mute, frightened face watching. The two men with their burden entered the room, followed by the young woman, and carefully lowered the cot to the floor. The long form of the surveyor lay motionless, his eyes closed.

With a low cry Barbara threw herself on her knees beside the cot. With one arm across the still form of the only brother she knew, and the other pushing back the rough hair from his forehead, she bent over, looking appealingly into the thin rugged face—her own face alight with loving anxiety.

"Abe! Abe! Abe!" she called softly; then again: "Abe! See dear; it's Barbara."

As if only that voice had power to call him back, the man's eyes opened, a slow smile spread over his unshaven, dust-stained features, and his voice expressed glad surprise. "Why, hello, Barbara!"

Willard Holmes, who had half risen from his chair and was leaning forward watching them with burning interest, sank back with a groan and covered his face with his hands. But they did not see.

Still kneeling Barbara took a glass from Ynez and turned again to the injured surveyor. "Here, Abe; drink this."

The Irishman lifted him in his huge arms and he obeyed. Then as he lay looking up into Barbara's face, again that slow smile came and he said: "Well, little girl; Holmes made it, didn't he? That buckskin horse of Tex's is all right, and Holmes—Holmes is a man! He sure made good! How is he?"

Holmes rose dizzily and came forward. "I'm all right, old man, and so will you be when Miss Worth has had a chance at you."

Quickly the surveyor glanced from the engineer's face to that of the young woman, whose brown eyes still regarded him with loving solicitude. "I reckon you're right," he said slowly.

Then Barbara directed them to carry him into the room she had prepared, while Willard Holmes returned to his chair to lie with closed eyes, suffering a deeper pain than the pain in his shoulder.

When his wound had been dressed and he had eaten the tempting meal Barbara brought, Abe fell asleep. But the young woman would not leave him for long, so that Holmes saw very little of her all the rest of the day. Occasionally she would run into the room where the engineer lay to ask if he needed anything, but only for a moment. Sometimes, seeing him so still, she thought that he was asleep and withdrew softly without speaking; but he always knew.

The next morning Holmes was just established in the big reclining chair in the living room when a peremptory knock called Barbara to the front door. It was James Greenfield.

The president of The King's Basin Land and Irrigation Company was greatly agitated and he scarcely noticed the young woman as he greeted the engineer with affectionate regard that was genuine; explaining how he had returned to Kingston the night before and, learning of Holmes's injury that morning, had hurried to him at once. "But I can't understand," he exclaimed half angrily, "how *you* ever came to be mixed up in this affair. When I missed you from the hotel I supposed of course that you had taken the train back to Kingston and came on expecting to find you there. What on earth possessed you to go off on this wild ride over the mountains with that man Lee? You might have been killed, and I—I—" He could not put into words the horrid thought that was in his mind—how, had the Mexican's bullet gone true, he himself would have been responsible for the death of the man he loved as his own son.

Holmes—understanding the man's thought—was touched by the capitalist's unusual agitation, and for the moment did not attempt to reply. Then with an attempt at lightness he said: "Oh, well; it's all coming out right, Uncle Jim. Thanks to Miss

Worth's care I am nearly well now. The wound really didn't amount to much."

As he spoke he looked at Barbara, and the older man also turned quickly toward the young woman who, at the engineer's words, was blushing rosy red.

"Father and I owe Mr. Holmes a debt we can never pay," she said quietly. Then, excusing herself on the plea that her other patient needed her, she left the room.

When the two men had watched her go, Greenfield said gently: "This is a bad business, Willard; a damned bad business; I'll admit that I was angry when you turned against us in that Cartwright deal, but confound it, boy! I admire you for it just the same. Your father would have done just as you did. It was that finer kind of honesty that made him a failure in the business where the rest of us made fortunes, but we all loved him for it, and your mother—" he looked away through the window toward the distant mountains. "You understand, don't you Willard, that I was forced to let you go when you turned the Company down? My directors would never stand for anything else, you know. You don't feel hard toward me, lad, because I had to let you out?"

"Certainly not, Uncle Jim. I *was* hurt just at first, but when I had taken time to think it over I did not blame you."

"You are sure, Willard?"

"Sure, Uncle Jim."

The older man was studying the engineer's face

intently. "I don't know what it is, Willard, but something has changed you since you came into this country. You know, my boy, that I have no one in the world but you. All that I have will be yours. I have dreamed and planned for you as for my own flesh and blood. I am telling you this now because I have felt that something was taking you away from me. Something that I cannot understand has come between us. I felt it the moment I met you in Kingston and it has been growing ever since. It was that that made me so angry over the Cartwright business. You know how I hate the West; you know what it cost me years ago. I feel now that in some way I am losing you too. What is it, Willard, that has come between us? Let's clean it up and get back in our relations to where we were before we left home."

As James Greenfield made his appeal the engineer's eyes turned involuntarily toward the door through which Barbara had left the room. And when he did not answer immediately the older man was sure that he understood what it was that had come between himself and the son of the woman he loved, and why Holmes had used his influence in behalf of Jefferson Worth.

"Is it that girl, Willard?"

The younger man faced him squarely and his answer meant much more to the engineer himself than he could have explained to Greenfield. "Yes sir, it is this girl."

"You love her?"

"As my father must have loved my mother."

446

At the simple words Greenfield controlled himself, but his hatred for Jefferson Worth was very bitter. That he should fail to win in the business warfare with the western man was nothing, but that Worth— through his daughter—should rob him of the son that was more than a son to him was more than he could bear.

"But, my dear boy," he said; "think what this means! Think of your family—of your father and mother—of your friends and your future back home. Who are these people? They are nobodies. This man Worth is an ignorant, illiterate, common boor with no breeding, no education—nothing but a certain native cunning that has enabled him to make a little money. We have nothing in common with his class."

"Mr. Worth is an honest, honorable man who is doing a great work," answered Holmes stoutly; "and his daughter is— Uncle Jim, she is the most wonderful woman I ever knew!"

As Willard Holmes spoke, Barbara, coming from the kitchen into the dining room, could not help hearing the words that came through the partly opened door of the living room where the men were talking. Involuntarily at the sound of the engineer's voice the red blood crept into the young woman's face and her eyes shone with pleasure. The next moment Greenfield's voice held her motionless.

"But don't you know that she is not Worth's daughter?"

"Not his daughter?" exclaimed Holmes.

"No, not his daughter. She is a nameless waif

whom he picked up and adopted. No one knows
her parentage—not even her name. She may even
have Mexican or Indian blood in her veins for all
that anyone knows."

It was not strange that Willard Holmes had never
heard the story of how Barbara was found in the
desert. In the new country, where most of the engineer's life in the West had been spent, comparatively
few beyond Worth's most intimate associates knew
that she was the banker's daughter only by adoption.
Greenfield, who had learned the story while inquiring
for business reasons into the history of his competitor, told the young man briefly of the finding of
the unknown child.

"Don't you see, my boy," finished the financier,
"how impossible it is that you should give your name
—one of the oldest and best in the history of the
country—to a nameless woman of unknown breeding, whose connection with this man Worth even is
merely accidental? It would ruin you, Willard.
Think of your friends back home! How would they
receive her? Think of me—of my plans for you!
I—I should feel that I had been false to your mother,
Willard, who gave you to me on her death-bed, if I
permitted such a thing as this. It's—it's monstrous!"

Slowly the engineer raised his head and with a
smile on his white face that hurt the older man, he
said: "I can at least relieve your mind on that score,
Uncle Jim. You need not fear that I will marry
Miss Worth."

At his words from beyond that partly closed door,

448

Barbara made her way blindly to her own room and, throwing herself face downward on her couch, strove with clenched hands and throbbing veins to keep her self control. She must not—she must not let them know, she whispered to herself—moaning in pain. She must go to them again in a moment—and they must not know.

While the woman whom Willard Holmes loved fought for strength to hide her pain, James Greenfield, in the other room, was leaning eagerly toward the engineer. "She has refused you?"

"I have not asked her. But don't misunderstand me. What you have told me—what my friends at home might think or do—could make no difference. Barbara Worth is worthy any man's love; and I love her and would make her my wife. I would give up even you for her, Uncle Jim. It's not that. It's because I know that she loves someone else too well to listen to me."

CHAPTER XXXIII.

WILLARD HOLMES RECEIVES HIS ANSWER.

WHEN Barbara returned to the living room with some trivial excuse to explain her rather long absence, she found Holmes determined to go with Mr. Greenfield to his rooms in the hotel in Kingston.

When she protested he answered: "Really, Miss Worth, my shoulder troubles me so little that I am ashamed to offer myself as an invalid; and now that Uncle Jim is with me I haven't the shadow of an excuse for burdening you any longer."

"I am sorry if I have made you feel that you were a burden," she returned with a brave smile.

He answered warmly: "You know I did not mean to imply that. I shall never forget your kindness—never."

Greenfield too expressed his appreciation of her kindness but she answered the engineer as if she had not heard the older man. "And I can never thank you for what you have done for us."

As they stood on the porch while Greenfield went on ahead to the buggy, Holmes held out his hand. "And we are square again?"

"Yes, we are square."

"Then adios, Senorita."

"Adios, amigo."

450

Bravely she stood watching until the carriage disappeared down the street. Then she went slowly into the house to Abe's room.

The surveyor lay propped up in bed with pillows, looking quite cheerful. "Well, sister," was his greeting; "you have lost one patient and you are going to lose the other one before long. I feel like a new man already."

For a little she made no answer and, as she stood before him silent, those eyes that were trained to let nothing escape their notice studied her face and noted her hands clasped in nervous pain. "Why, Barbara! What is it, sister? What has gone wrong?"

At his words the brown eyes filled.

"Barbara!"

She dropped into the chair by the bedside and, throwing herself toward him, buried her face in her arms in the pillow by his side, her form shaking with sobs.

The surveyor's face was white now under its bronze—white and set. Lightly he placed his hand upon the soft brown hair so near his shoulder and his eyes seemed now to be looking far away. When her grief had spent itself a little he said quietly: "Don't you think, sister, that you had better tell me about this?"

When she did not answer he said again gently: "Do you care for him so much, Barbara?"

The brown head nodded her confession and for a moment the man closed his eyes and turned away his face. Then: "Won't you let me help you?"

Slowly, with many pauses, she told him what she had overheard. When she had finished Abe said simply: "But he has not told you of his love, Barbara. Perhaps you are mistaken."

"No, Abe; I'm not mistaken. He has not told me—not in words, but I know; I know!"

"Then," said the surveyor, "he will tell you. Listen, Barbara. The man who went through those Mexicans in Devil's Canyon with me is not the kind of a man who gives up the woman he loves for what others think. Wait a little, dear, and you will see that I am right. You have been too quick. Be patient a little and you shall see."

"But Abe, Mr. Greenfield is right. I am a name-less nobody; and he—he is—"

"He is a man and you are a woman, and this is La Palma de la Mano de Dios where nothing else matters," said Abe Lee almost sternly.

A few minutes later, when Barbara was gone, the surveyor slipped lower on the pillows and wearily turned his face to the wall. Several times that day Barbara looked in on him and at last, when he had not moved for so long, called him softly. He answered with a smile, but when she had arranged his pillows for him he closed his eyes again with a word of thanks.

Jefferson Worth arrived that evening and with him came the Seer, who had joined him in the city by the sea. But Barbara's joy at their coming was over-shadowed by her anxiety for Abe, who seemed to have fallen into a half-unconscious condition that was alarming. When they entered his room the surveyor, who still lay with his face to the wall, did not look up.

"Daddy is here, Abe," said Barbara; "Daddy and the Seer."

Slowly the man turned toward them and held out his hand with a word of greeting for each. "I'm mighty glad you have come," he added; "Barbara has had rather more than her hands full."

But the old engineer noticed that he did not look at Barbara as he spoke.

While the three were at supper Barbara told the men the whole story, and when they had finished the meal the Seer said: "Now Jeff, I know you have important business needing your immediate attention and our girl here must have a good night's rest—she has been through enough to kill an average woman. I'm going to take care of Abe to-night myself."

When his old chief was alone with the surveyor he drew a chair to the bedside and sat for some time looking at the man on the bed. Then he said: "I think, son, that you and I had better get to the bottom of this. First, I'll have a look at that leg."

When the examination was over the big man eyed the surveyor. "Humph! This is not a scratch beside what that greaser did to you with his knife in Arizona. You didn't even stop work for that. Your ride to San Felipe and back ordinarily would call for about twelve hours sleep and that's all. Come, lad, what's the matter? Out with it."

Abe smiled. "I'm down and out, I reckon."

"Down and out, hell!" returned the big man. "That won't do, Abe. You forget that you are talking to me." Then he leaned forward and spoke in a low tone. "I know what it is, my boy. It's Barbara." By the pain in the surveyor's eyes the Seer knew that he was right.

Then the Seer in his own way did for Abe what Abe had done for Barbara.

When the young woman brought in his breakfast the next morning Abe greeted her with his old cheery "Hello!", and declared facetiously that the Seer had talked him into a sleep from which he had awakened as hungry as a bear and ready to go to work.

Two days later Texas Joe, who had ridden in from somewhere late the night before, came to report.

"We were beginning to think that you were not coming back at all, Uncle Tex," said Barbara, who with the others was curious to hear of the old-timer's adventure.

"I 'lowed once mebbe I wouldn't come back no more neither," he drawled. "You see, Mr. Worth, after we-all got Abe at Wolf Wells I figured that—bein' so far on the way—I might as well go on over to Felipe an' get that ol' buckskin hawss o' mine what Abe had left." He paused, and, turning his head to one side, looked meditatively down at the spur on his high-heeled boot. "That there buckskin is sure some hawss, Barbara; he sure is."

"Did you get him?" asked Barbara.

Texas looked up, mildly surprised. "Sure we got him. That's what I'm a-tellin' you."

Then he laughed softly as though mildly amused at some incident suddenly remembered. "Abe, you

454

know that greaser that tumbled into the Dry River Spillway when we-all was puttin' in Number Five Gate?"

"Yes."

"I 'lowed you'd know him. I heard somethin' funny about him when I was in San Felipe after that buckskin."

"What was it, Texas?"

"He's daid."

The recovery of the two wounded men was rapid. For a while Holmes came over from Kingston every day to see Lee, and the two, with the Seer and Barbara, spent many delightful hours on the big front porch.

Jefferson Worth's enterprises pushed steadily toward completion. The power plant in Barba was finished and The King's Basin Central had stretched its steel length from the junction at Republic to within three miles of the terminal.

When Abe was able to go back to his work, Holmes did not go so often to the Worth home; but the presence of the Seer still enabled him to excuse to himself his quite frequent visits. But while the young engineer continually sought the Seer, not only because of their growing friendship but because he was always sure of meeting Barbara, he avoided seeing the girl alone for he felt that he could not trust himself; and the young woman, feeling his attitude toward her, was convinced against her will and Abe's protest that the man who loved her guarded himself against her for the reasons that she had overheard Greenfield urge upon him.

455

Then Holmes received a letter from the South
western and Continental Railroad Company offering
him a position that would place him at the head of
the engineering department of the district that in
cluded The King's Basin. The letter stated that the
position was tendered on recommendation of Jeffer
son Worth and, in view of the fact that the flood
season was at hand and that conditions seriously
threatening to the Company's property might be
expected at any hour, urged him to accept by wire
and take charge immediately.

With the letter in his hand a sudden desire to go
with it to Barbara mastered him. He knew that the
Seer had planned to go that morning with Abe Lee
to Barba and that the young woman was alone.

An hour later he dismounted in front of the Worth
home. Barbara herself met him at the door. "The
Seer is not at home to-day," she said, as they entered the living room. "I thought you knew."

"I did not come to see the Seer to-day. I came
to see you," he answered bluntly.

"To see me?"

"Yes; to ask you how I shall answer this." He
handed her the letter.

She read it slowly, gaining time for self-control.
"But I do not understand why you should come to
me."

He studied her face a moment before he answered.
How could he explain to her the impulse that had
prompted him, as every man is prompted to take the
big things of his life to the one woman who—if she
be really the one woman for him—is more than all?

"I thought—I hoped that you would be interested," he said.

"And I am!" she cried eagerly, feeling that which he could not put into words. "Of course I'm interested. I was only surprised that you should hesitate a moment to accept. Don't you want to continue your work? Don't you want to stay with us?" She added the last words wistfully and the heart of the man longed to tell her that which she longed to hear.

"Yes," he said slowly, "I want to stay, but I—I am afraid." The words slipped out unbidden.

Barbara interpreted his answer in the light of his conversation with Greenfield, which she had overheard, and her woman's pride was aroused. He should be made to understand that he was in no danger from her. Her next words were a challenge. "Afraid of what?"

"Afraid of you," he burst forth savagely. "Afraid of myself. Because I love you. From the first day when you showed me the desert you have been so closely associated in my mind with this work that I cannot think of it without thinking of you. Everything I have done I have felt was done for you. I would have given it all up a hundred times but my thoughts of you would not let me. When I have been untrue to the work I have felt that I have been untrue to you. If I have accomplished any good here it has been through you. Everywhere I have gone in this country you have seemed to me to be there. Everything I see speaks to me of you. The desert—the mountains—the farms and homes and towns; it is all you—and you—and you. I did not realize it

457

at first, but I felt it, and then as I came to love my
work I came to love you. I did not intend to tell
you this. I hate myself for telling you—but I love
you. I love you! Do you understand now why I
came to you with this letter? Do you understand
why I am afraid to stay?"

At the man's passionate outburst that came as if
dragged from him against his will, Barbara shrank
back as if he threatened her. He had not asked if
she loved him; he had only spoken brutally—savagely, of his passion for her. She repeated insistently, blindly, to herself: "He must not know! He
must not know!"

The man spoke again. "Forgive me, Miss
Worth; I did not mean to let go of myself. I know
how you love this work—how hard you have tried to
hold me true to it. I could not bear that you should
think of me as leaving it without reason. But you
see—you see how impossible it is now for me to stay."

As he spoke, a running horse stopped suddenly in
front of the house and through the open door they
saw Pablo leap from the saddle and run swiftly up
the walk toward the house.

"Senorita!" the Mexican cried, as Barbara sprang
towards him; "the river! the river! It has come.
The Company works—it is all gone! Senor Worth
send me quick to tell Senor Holmes. I go to Kingston; he not there. They say he ride this way. I
come to you, Senorita; I think maybe you know
where I find him." He turned to the engineer.
"Senor Holmes, the river has come again into La
Palma de la Mano de Dios like the Indians say it

458

was long time ago. Senor Worth say you come please pronto!"

Barbara wheeled on the engineer with flushed cheeks and blazing eyes.

"This is your answer!" she cried. "Not for me; not for yourself; but for the work—*your* work—*our* work!"

For an instant he looked into her eyes, then turned and ran towards his horse with Pablo at his heels.

Barbara saw them spring into their saddles and disappear in a cloud of dust, and the engineer, as he rode, remembered what Abe Lee had once told him of Pablo's saying: "In the Company there is no Senorita!"

CHAPTER XXXIV.

BATTLING WITH THE RIVER.

OME day, perhaps, the history of that River war will be written. It can only be suggested in my story.

It was a war of terrific forces waged for a great cause by men as brave as any who ever fought with weapons that kill.

The attacking force was the Rio Colorado that with power immeasurable had, through the ages past, carved mile-deep canyons on its course and with its mountains of silt had built the great delta dam across the ancient gulf, thus turning back the waters of the sea that sun and wind might lay bare the floor of the Basin and work the desolation of the desert.

Using the Seer's open hand for his map of La Palma de la Mano de Dios, Jose, the Indian, had traced the course of the river along the base of the fingers flowing toward the gulf which lies between the edge of the palm and the thumb—this same inner edge of the hand representing roughly the high ground that shuts out the waters of the sea. The thousands of acres of The King's Basin lands lie from sea level to nearly three hundred feet below. The river at the point where the intake for the system of canals was located is, of course, higher than sea level, for the waters that pass the intake flow on southward to the gulf.

It was the river flowing thus on higher ground **that** made irrigation and reclamation of the desert possible. It was this also that made possible the disaster that was now upon the hardy pioneers, who had staked everything in their effort to realize the vast potential wealth of the ancient sea-bed. The grade from the river at the intake to the lowest point in the bottom of the Basin is much steeper than the established fall of the river from the intake to the gulf. The water in the canals on this steeper grade was controlled by headings, spillways, gates and drops, while the structure at the intake, with gates to regulate the flow into the main canal, prevented the river from leaving its old channel altogether, pouring its entire volume into the Basin and in time converting it again into an inland sea.

The dangerously cheap and inadequate character of the vital parts, built by the Company upon the usual promoter's estimates, had led Abe Lee to protest against the risk forced upon the settlers and had finally caused him to resign. Later, as the Company system of canals was extended and more and more water was needed to supply the rapidly increasing acreage of cultivated lands, Willard Holmes came to appreciate the desert-bred surveyor's view of the danger and insistently urged his employers to supply him with funds to replace the temporary wooden structures with safe and lasting works of concrete and steel.

But the hunger of Capital for profits forbade. Some day the work would be done, the directors promised. In the meantime, without increasing the original investment by so much as a dollar but with the revenues derived from the sale of water rights, they were extending the system to supply the ever increasing fields of the settlers, thus shrewdly forcing the people, who were ignorant of the terrible risk they were carrying, to supply the funds to build the canals and ditches that belonged to the Company; while for the water carried to the ranches the farmers continued to pay the Company large rentals. The original investment of the Company was very small compared with the thousands invested by the pioneers who had been induced to settle in the new country. And yet from every dollar of the wealth taken from the land the Company would receive a share.

But the Rio Colorado gave no heed to the decree of the New York financiers. The forces that had made La Palma de la Mano de Dios are not ruled by Wall street.

Willard Holmes, who had come to understand that his work was not alone to safeguard the property of his employers but to protect the interests of the pioneers as well, had been discharged because he would not deliver the people wholly into the hands of the Company. A new engineer out of the East, as faithful to the interests of Capital as he was unfamiliar with conditions in the new country, was placed in charge.

It was as if the river, in the absence of the man whose constant readiness had held it in check, saw its opportunity. Swiftly it mustered its forces from mountain and plain. Hundreds of miles away it gathered its strength and hurried to the assault. The

sources of information established by Holmes on the
tributaries and headwaters wired their reports: a
foot rise on the Gila; three feet coming down the
Little Colorado; two feet rise in the Salt; five feet
on the Grand. The New York office-engineer
received the messages with mild interest. The daily
reports from the weather bureau covering the countries drained by the Rio Colorado lay on his desk
unnoticed.

Mr. Burk warned him, but the thoughtful Manager of the Company was not an engineer. Willard
Holmes tried to help him, but Holmes had been discharged by the Company and the words of discharged
men have little weight with those who succeed to their
positions.

The daily reports from the gauge at Rubio City
showed an increase in the river's volume of twenty
thousand second feet; then thirty thousand more;
and on top of that came another twenty thousand.
The assistants of the new chief engineer tried to tell
him what it meant, but the assistants were subordi-
nates and friends of Willard Holmes. The man from
New York, who was privileged to write several letters
after his name, was supposed to know his business.

Then the assembled forces of the river reached the
intake, and the trembling wooden structures that
stood between the pioneers and ruin, besieged by the
rising flood, battered by the swirling currents, bom-
barded by drift, gave way under the strain and the
charging waters plunged through the breach.

Too late the Company's forces were rushed to the
scene. Before their very eyes the roaring waters, as

if mad with destructive power, wrenched and tore at the Company's property, twisting, ripping, smashing, until not a trestle, plank or stick was left in place and the terrific current, rushing with ever increasing volume and power through the opening, plowed into the soft, alluvial soil of the embankment, undermining and carrying it away until nearly the entire river was admitted.

As quickly as men and material could be assembled, the Company's chief engineer began the battle to regain control of the mighty stream. The warfare thus begun meant life or death to the greatest reclamation project in the world.

Millions already invested by the settlers in farms and towns and homes and business enterprises were at stake. Many more millions that were yet to be realized from the reclaimed lands depended upon the issue of the fight.

Against the efforts of the engineers and the army of laborers the river massed from its tributaries in the regions of heavy rains and melting snows the greatest strength it had assembled in many years.

Five times, with piling and trestles and jetties and embankments, the men who defended The King's Basin were in sight of victory. Five times the river summoned fresh strength—twisted out the piling, wrecked the trestles, undermined the jetties and embankments and swept the nearly completed structures, smashing, grinding, crashing, away—a twisted, tangled ruin.

While the engineers and men of the Company were waging this war with the river, the situation of the pioneers in the Basin grew daily more perilous. Without a well-defined channel large enough to carry the incoming stream, the flood spread over a wide territory in the southern and western portions of the Basin, filling first the old channels and washes left by the waters ages ago, forming next in the areas of nearly level or slightly depressed sections shallow pools, lakes and seas, out of which the higher ground and hummocks rose like new-born islands, growing smaller and smaller as the rising tide submerged more and more of their sandy bases. Meanwhile the whole flood, eddying slowly with winding sluggish currents in the shallow places, moving more swiftly in the deeper washes and channels, swept always onward toward the north where, miles away, lay the deepest bottom of the great Basin.

Many of the settlers in the flooded districts were forced to abandon farms they had won with courage and toil, for the sweeping waters covered alike fields of alfalfa and grain and barren desert waste. The towns of Frontera and Kingston were protected from the inundation by earthen levees, in the building of which men and women toiled in desperate haste, and night and day these embankments were patrolled by watchful guards, who frequently summoned the weary, besieged citizens from their rest to protect or strengthen some threatened point in their fortifications.

The eastern side of the Basin being higher ground, the settlers in the South Central District and east of Republic, with the two towns built by Jefferson Worth, were in no immediate danger, but the old Dry

River channel became a roaring torrent, bank-full; and it was only a question of time, if the river were not controlled, when every foot of the new country with its wealth of improvements and its vast possibilities would be buried deep beneath the surface of an inland sea.

The situation was appalling. The remarkable development of the new country, the marvelous richness of the reclaimed lands, with the immense possibilities of the reclamation work as demonstrated by The King's Basin project had attracted the attention of the nation. The pioneers in Barbara's Desert were, in fact, leaders in a far greater work that would add immeasurably to the nation's life—that would, indeed, be world-wide in its influence. Because of this the attention of the nation was fixed with peculiar interest upon the disaster that had fallen upon The King's Basin. Throughout the land civil engineers watched intently the efforts of the Company men to regain control of the river and to force it back into its old channel. Many declared that, because of the alluvial character of the soil, the absence of anything like a rock floor to build upon and the great volume and terrific velocity of the current, the feat was an engineering impossibility. In the eyes of the engineering world The King's Basin project was doomed. The settlers were advised to abandon the work they had accomplished and to move out. But those strong ones who had forced the desert to yield its wealth to their hands did not move. Those whose farms were in the flooded district were forced to go. There was the inevitable sifting of the timid-

466

hearted and the weak, but the great majority stood fast.

Jefferson Worth, in the face of almost certain ruin, went steadily on with his work on the railroad and continued pushing his other enterprises toward completion—making improvements, erecting new buildings, planning further investments and developments with a confidence and conviction that was startling. Not once throughout that trying period was he heard to express the slightest doubt as to the ultimate triumph of the settlers. His business friends and associates outside urged him to stop—to wait at least until the issue was certain. He answered calmly that the issue was already certain and went on with his work.

His confidence and courage were the inspiration that fired the hearts of that threatened people. Had he given ground, had he weakened and drawn back it would have started a panic that nothing could have checked and that would have resulted inevitably in the abandonment of the cause forever. The King's Basin lands with the wealth of effort that had already been expended would have been given over to the river, lost irretrievably to the race.

Hundreds went to him when they felt their courage failing and their spirits weakening under the strain. And always they returned to their farms or to their business with renewed strength to go on. As one, who passed through that ordeal, long afterwards expressed it: "In those times we all just lived on his nerve."

Through all the Company's war with the river and

its repeated defeats Willard Holmes was forced to stand a mere observer, an idle looker-on. Foreseeing the catastrophe that was now upon them, he had prepared himself by careful study of every factor in the problem and by thorough knowledge of the situation to meet the crisis when it came. With every means at his command he had planned and worked that he might be ready and so far as possible equipped for the struggle and now, when war was declared and the battle being waged, he could only watch the ruin of the work he loved while a stranger, who ignored his preparatory efforts, took the place that should have been his.

But the great man of the S. & C., with whom the engineer had many a counsel in those days, warned him always to be ready for the time when—as the western man put it—"The Company should throw up its hands."

The waters moving northward reached the lowest point in the Basin and there formed an inland sea that, without an outlet and receiving the full volume of the river, grew ever larger and larger. Flowing towards the sea the flood developed swift currents in the depressions and washes that led in the general direction of its course, seeking thus to make for itself a well-defined channel. The largest of these ancient washes, scarcely noticeable in the desert, led from the south to Kingston, passing through the edge of the town, curved slightly to the west and extended on northward, becoming deeper and more clearly defined with higher ground on either side as it neared the lowest point of the Basin. The general lay of the land drew the flood toward this channel and developed a current that moved with increasing velocity as the waters, nearing the sea, were concentrated more and more by the greater depth of the old channel and the steeper grade of the land on both sides.

Then a new and alarming phase of the river's destructive work developed and everyone saw that the war at the intake must be forced to a speedy finish or the cause would be lost. The immense volume of water, flowing with increased strength and velocity as it defined for itself a more distinct channel down the steeper grade of the Basin, began cutting in the soft soil a vertical fall that from the foot of the grade moved swiftly up-stream; a mighty cataract from fifty to sixty feet in height and a full quarter of a mile wide, moving at the rate of from one to three miles a day and leaving as it went a great gorge through which a new-made river flowed quietly to a new-born and ever-growing sea. The roar of the plunging waters, the crashing and booming of the falling masses of earth that were undermined by the roaring torrent were heard miles away. Acres upon acres of the soft fertile land fell, melted and were swept away down the gorge as banks of snow fall and melt in the spring freshets. Day and night, night and day, the immeasurable power of the canyon-cutting river drove the cataract southward toward the break at the intake through which, by this time, the entire Colorado at its highest flood stage was turned.

The imminent danger that threatened the Basin was not the danger from the ever-rising sea. Long before the waters could fill the old sea-bed, that mighty cataract, moving ever upstream, would pass the intake; and with the floor of the river lowered thus some fifty feet it would be impossible to take the water out for irrigation. The lands reclaimed by the pioneers would go back to desert years before they would be buried once more under the surface of the sea.

The complete destruction of all that the settlers had gained and the utter desolation of the land was now a question of weeks.

The Company town of Kingston was directly in the path of that moving Niagara. While the Company's men were making a last desperate effort to close the break, the great falls were eating their way nearer and nearer the little city. When the roar of the water and the crashing and booming of the falling banks could be heard on the streets and in the offices of the Company, the people left their homes, their stores and their shops; the town realizing that no human power now could avert the disaster.

Heroic efforts were made to direct the course of the new river away from the little city, but the waters with savage, resistless power chose their own way. The pioneers, who built the first town in the heart of The King's Basin Desert, saw that mighty, thundering cataract move upon the work of their hands and felt the earth trembling under their feet as they watched homes, business blocks, the hotel, the opera house, the bank and finally the Company building undermined and tumbled, crashing into the deep canyon.

THE WINNING OF BARBARA WORTH

In a few short hours it was over. The falls moved on and where Kingston had once stood was that great gorge, with a few scattered houses only remaining on each side.

That same day the last attempt of the Company men to close the break failed.

With every hour the awful ruin drew nearer the point which, if reached, would place The King's Basin forever beyond the reclaiming power of men. Frantic appeals for help were made to the government, but before the ponderous machinery of state, with its intricate and complicated wheels within wheels, could unwind a sufficient quantity of red tape the work of the pioneer citizens would be past saving.

It was at this time that a telegram from Jefferson Worth to the great man of the Southwestern and Continental brought a special train of private cars into the Basin. At Deep Well Junction Jefferson Worth, Abe Lee, the Seer and Willard Holmes boarded the train and entered the car of the general manager, where the officials representing the highest authority in the great trans-continental system had gathered to meet them in consultation.

At Republic the president of The King's Basin Land and Irrigation Company with his manager and chief engineer joined them, and the train moved on until, at a word from Holmes, the conductor gave the signal to stop. From the windows and platform of the car the party could see the water extending to the south and west mile after mile, and nearer the huge plunging cataracts with leaping columns of spray, while the roar of the falls, the crashing and

471

booming of the caving banks shook the air with heavy
vibrations and the earth trembled with the shock of
the plunging waters and the falling masses of earth.
Just ahead, where Kingston had stood, the track
ended on the bank of the deep gorge. From here the
party was driven in comfortable spring wagons to the
scene of the Company's defeat.

Save for the camps of the laborers, the boats, pile
drivers, implements and materials of their warfare
and the debris of their wrecked structures, not a sign
of their work remained, while through the breach—
widened now to nearly a quarter of a mile—the great
river poured its hundred and fifty thousand second
feet of muddy water with terrific velocity and solemn,
awful power.

When the party had viewed the situation, the rail
road men with Mr. Greenfield retired to the tent of
the Company's chief engineer.

A little apart from Jefferson Worth and his two
companions, Willard Holmes stood alone on the brink
of the broken embankment looking down into the
swirling muddy waters. He knew that his time had
come. He knew that at that moment the railroad
officials were concluding a deal with The King's
Basin Land and Irrigation Company through its
president, by which the S. & C. would assume control
of the situation and attempt to save the reclamation
work. His chief had told him to be ready. He was
ready.

In the railroad yards at Rubio City and on every
available side-track for several miles east and west
were standing train-loads of ties and rails. In the

yards at the Coast city were cars loaded with machinery, implements and supplies. In the yards at the harbor were other train-loads of timber and piling. With the readiness of a perfectly equipped and organized army the forces of the S. & C., backed by the resources of that powerful system, waited the word, while every moment the disaster that threatened the pioneers drew nearer. From the roaring river at his feet Willard Holmes turned to look toward the tent. Why were they so slow?

Then his face lighted up and he took an eager step forward as the private secretary of the general manager came out of the tent and hurried toward him.

"They want you, Mr. Holmes," said the young man. The engineer went quickly to answer the call.

When he entered the tent every man in the party turned toward the engineer. "Holmes," said his chief, "we will attempt to close the break. You will take charge at once."

Within an hour the forces of The King's Basin Land and Irrigation Company already on the ground were set to work under the Seer preparing the grade for a spur-track that would leave the main line near the river fifteen miles north of the break, and Holmes, with Abe Lee, set out on horseback for Rubio City.

With the return of the general manager and his party to their train, the movement already planned began. Without hurry but with ready promptness the orders, voiced by the hundreds of clicking telegraph instruments covering the district affected by the operations, were obeyed. Special trains carried

Jefferson Worth's force of railroad builders with
teams and equipment to the point at which the spur-
track would connect with the main line where, under
Abe Lee, they began pushing the grade southward to
meet the forces that, under the Seer, were working
northward from the front.

Throughout the Basin the call for men and teams
was issued by Jefferson Worth, and the pioneers,
answering as the Minute Men of old, were hurried
to the scene where they found trainloads of equipment waiting ready for their use, while every hour
brought reinforcements—laborers of many nationalities gathered in the cities of the coast by the agents
of the railroad company.

The waiting trains loaded with ties and steel began
to move and the construction gangs followed close on
the heels of the graders. And when the last spike in
the track to the scene of the decisive battle was
driven, the track-men with their sledges stepped aside
to clear the way for the panting engines that drew
the first train loaded with piling and timbers for the
trestle.

Hour by hour now, without pause or halt, the men
under Willard Holmes working in shifts met the Rio
Colorado in a hand-to-hand fight for The King's
Basin lands. By day under the white, semi-tropical
sun, by night in the light of locomotive headlights
that gleamed strangely over the dark swirling floods,
the trestles were forced further and further out into
the plunging current that wrenched and twisted and
tugged with terrific strength in a mad wrestle with
those who dared attempt to check its sullen destruct-

ive will, while steadily, irresistibly, the canyon-cutting falls drew nearer and nearer. It was not alone the magnitude of the task directed by Willard Holmes that made the work heroic. It was that this seemingly impossible work must be accomplished against time. In his fight with the river the engineer raced against a destructive force which, if it reached the scene of the struggle before the battle was won, would make final defeat certain and place the Colorado, so far as The King's Basin reclamation was concerned, beyond control of men.

As the engineer stood on the trestle above the mad, whirling currents, directing his men in their efforts to drive the piling in thirty feet of water that—as one veteran expressed it—"ran like the mill tails of hell," he fancied he could hear above the roar of the river against the structure, the blows of the heavy driver, the rattle of cable and chain and windlass, the grinding and squeaking of the straining timbers and the shouts of the men—the menacing thunder of that moving cataract a few miles away. While he paced the embankments, studying the set of the currents, observing the form and action of the eddies or receiving the hourly reports from the river gauge at Rubio City, and held consultation with his assistants, he often turned his head involuntarily to look anxiously away in the direction of the racing falls.

Only when his exhausted body and wearied brain refused to respond longer to his will would he throw himself fully dressed upon à cot in his tent for an hour's sleep. His face grew haggard and deeply lined with anxious care, his hollow eyes—dark-

475

rimmed—were bloodshot and burning as if with fever, his jaws were set as if by sheer power of his will he would beat the river into submission. And he barked his orders shortly in a hoarse strained voice that told of nerves stretched almost to the breaking point. In critical moments, when it looked as though the river in the next instant would reduce their work to a hopeless wreck, the engineer, standing on the trembling timbers or clinging to the swaying pile-driver itself, seemed to those who did his bidding to become the very incarnation of human courage and power.

The Seer and Abe Lee, remembering the man who had come out from the East to go with them on that preliminary survey, wondered at the transformation. Then Willard Holmes was the servant of Capital that used people for its own gain. He saw his work then only as a means to the end that his Company might make money. Now, though employed still by a corporation, he was a master who used the power at his command in behalf of the people. He had come to look upon his work as a service to the world and through that service only he served his employers. It was as if in this man, born of the best blood of a nation-building people, trained by the best of the cultured East—trained as truly by his life and work in the desert—it was as though, in him, the best spirit of the age and race found expression.

At last the trestles were pushed across the break, the track was laid and the gigantic work of filling the channel was begun. In every rock quarry reached by the S. & C. within two hundred and fifty miles of the battle, men were drilling and blasting and with steam shovels and derricks were loading cars with material for the fill. At the word from Willard Holmes these rock trains steamed swiftly to the front, everything giving them the right of way. Merchants and manufacturers east and west cursed the railroad because their shipments were delayed. Passengers, held for hours on the sidings, complained, scolded, protested and threatened. It was an outrage! declared the tourists in their luxurious Pullmans that they should be forced to give up an hour of their pleasure in order that a train load of rock might make better time. But, unheeding, the great battle-ships, each with its fifty cubic yards of stone, and the flats and gondolas, each with its tons of material, thundered away to the scene of the struggle. Every five minutes, night and day, from the moment of the completion of the trestles until the fill was above the danger point a car of rock was dumped into the break.

So the task was accomplished; the fight was won. The Rio Colorado was checked in its work of destruction and beaten back into its old channel. The thousands of acres of The King's Basin lands that would have been forever lost to the race through one corporation were saved by another; and the man, who—without protest—had built for his employers' gain the inadequate structures that endangered the work of the pioneers, led the forces that won the victory.

The afternoon of the day on which the break was finally closed three private cars came in with the rock trains. The passengers were the general manager and the general superintendent with their wives, Jefferson Worth and a small party of friends.

Leaving their cars the party walked toward a point below the rock embankment where they could look down into the now empty gorge. With this visible evidence of the river's power before them, the visitors exclaimed with wonder.

When the superintendent had explained the magnitude of the work, the difficulties encountered and how the task had been accomplished, the general manager, who—here and there—had added a word, said: "After all, friends, taking into consideration money, equipment and everything, the whole question of a work like this, or of any great enterprise, resolves itself into a question of men. It's up to the *man on the job*. We have the system, the machinery without which this work could not have been done. We have the capital to supply material and labor—but that man up there closed the break."

As he spoke he pointed to a figure standing on the upper trestle above the fill—outlined against the sky.

Then the party climbed the grade to the tracks again and walked to the end of the upper trestle. Turning, the engineer saw and came towards them. Silently they stood to receive him. From boots to Stetson his khaki trousers and rough shirt were stained with mud and grime, his eyes were sunken in dark hollows, his worn face was unshaven and his hair, when he removed his hat, was unkempt. He did not look like a hero; he looked more like some ruffian just from a prolonged debauch. But the little party burst into applause.

478

The engineer smiled as his chief went forward from the group to grasp him by the hand. For a moment they talked of the work. Then the official, placing his hand on the engineer's arm, said: "Come, Holmes, we have some women here who want to meet the man who mastered the Colorado."

The engineer protested. He was "not presentable."

"Presentable! You're the most presentable man I know of this minute. Come along, there's my wife making signs to me to hurry right now."

There was nothing for Holmes to do but to go. A moment later he was face to face with the rest of the party and—with Barbara Worth.

CHAPTER XXXV.

NATURE AND HUMAN NATURE.

WO weeks after the victory of Willard Holmes in the River war the engineer arrived in Republic on the evening train from the city by the sea.

At the hotel he was quickly surrounded by the pioneer citizens, who were eager to greet him with expressions of appreciation for his work. But it was Horace P. Blanton who did the talking.

Horace P., in his brave picture-general hat, his impressively swelling front of white vest and his black clerical tie, was the personification of economic, financial and scholastic—not to say ecclesiastic, dignity. His greeting of the engineer was majestic. But, as a royal sovereign might welcome the returning general of his conquering armies with sadness at the thought of the lives his victories had cost, the countenance of Horace P. expressed a noble grief.

"Willard," he said, his voice charged with emotion, "I congratulate you. You are the savior of this imperial King's Basin. When we saw that Greenfield's Company was not able to handle the awful situation, I told my friend the general manager and our other officials of the S. & C. that they *must* come to the rescue without an instant's delay and that you must be put in charge of the work. I knew that if any man on earth could stop that river, you could.

480

So we decided to let you go ahead. You have justified my confidence nobly, Willard; you certainly have. I'm proud of you, old man; I am indeed."

The engineer tried manfully to appreciate the spirit of the speaker's words. With that white vest and black tie before him, to say nothing of the picture hat that crowned the massive head, it was impossible for Holmes not to wish that he could appreciate Horace P. Blanton's spirit—it hungered so for appreciation.

"I am very grateful to you, Mr. Blanton," said the engineer. "But really I feel that you over-estimate my part in the work. I—"

"Not at all; not at all, my dear boy. I knew my man and I was not disappointed. But the cost—" he shook his kingly head sorrowfully and heaved a majestic sigh. "Confidentially, Willard, I estimate that the financial losses of Greenfield and myself alone are close on to a million. I haven't a thing left. Wiped me out clean."

Holmes looked really sympathetic. He knew that every dollar that Horace P. Blanton ever spent was a dollar belonging to someone else, but even mythical losses of mythical property, when suffered by Horace P., demanded sympathy. The man in the white vest felt them so keenly and strove with such noble courage to bear them bravely.

Encouraged by the engineer's interest and the presence of the little crowd of pioneers, the speaker continued: "When I saw our beautiful town—the town that we had built with our own hands—falling in ruins into that terrible chasm, I cried like a baby,

sir." Even as he spoke his eyes filled with manly
tears which he made no attempt to hide. Then he
lifted his majestic bulk grandly and looked about
with kingly countenance. "But I shall stay with it,
Willard. I shall stay and help these people to regain
their losses. We *can't* desert them now. If my creditors will give me a little time, and I am sure they
will, not a man shall lose a penny, no matter what it
costs me."

The sentence was a bit ambiguous but it was a
noble resolution, worthy of such a lofty soul.

At this moment a boy with the evening papers
approached the group. "Here son, my paper," called
Horace P.

The boy gripped his wares with a firm hand. "I
got to have my money first. You ain't done nothin'
but promise for a month."

"Boy! Give me my paper. You shall have your
money to-morrow," he thundered from the depths
beneath the white vest.

The boy backed away. "I dassn't do it. I can't
live on hot air."

With an imperial air, as if tremendous stakes hung
upon the trivial incident, the great man said to
Holmes: "Excuse me, Willard; I must see about
this," and with a firm and determined step he left
the hotel.

A hush fell upon the company of pioneers. Not
one of them but would have gladly—had he dared—
offered the outraged monarch the price of a paper.
The King's Basin settlers were proud of Horace P.

But that night Horace P. Blanton boarded the

north-bound train and was never seen in The King's Basin again. His creditors—and they are many, from the newsboy to the hotel manager, the barber, the laundry agent, the liveryman and boot-black—are still "giving him time," as he was confident that they would. The pioneers miss him sorely, but they manage to struggle along without him, living perhaps in the hope that he will some day come back.

In the silence that followed the passing of Horace P., Willard Holmes slipped away from the group of men and approached the Manager of The King's Basin Land and Irrigation Company, who was sitting alone with his cigar in a far corner of the room.

"Hello, old man," was Burk's greeting as the engineer approached. The thoughtful Manager of the Company had been an interested observer of his friend's reception and of the newspaper incident. As the two men shook hands the Manager's cigar shifted to one corner of his mouth and his head tipped toward the opposite shoulder. "How much did Horace P. touch you for, Willard?"

"I gave him my admiration and sympathy."

The other shook his head wonderingly. "A special providence watches over you, my son. After that, nothing could have saved your pocket-book if that kid had not been sent by your guardian angel to your rescue. When did you leave the river?"

"Last week. The S. & C. called me into the city. I'm on my way back to the work now. What's the news?"

Burk grinned. "The first train over the King's Basin Central went out this morning with a special party of distinguished citizens—Jefferson Worth, the Seer, Abe Lee and Miss Worth. The lady will spend a week or two in the town of Barba and with friends in the South Central District. Texas Joe and Pat left this morning in a rig, leading Miss Worth's saddle horse, El Capitan. It's all in The King's Basin Messenger." He handed the paper to Holmes who mechanically stuffed it into his pocket.

"How's Uncle Jim?"

"He is at the office, I think. You know he is winding up the affairs of the poor old K. B. L. and I."

"So I understand."

The two men were silent for a moment, then Burk said thoughtfully: "It's hard lines for the Company, Willard, but the mules, including your humble servant, don't seem to care much. That's one advantage in being a mule. I will be glad to get back to civilization and so will your Uncle Jim I fancy. Take it altogether I don't think he has enjoyed watching the success of Jefferson Worth's little experiments as much as we have. The same beneficent power that has knocked out the Company seems to have taken good care of friend Jeff."

"You are not going to stay in the West?" asked the engineer.

"I go Monday. I understand there is still a demand for good mules back home."

The president of the wrecked Company received his former chief engineer warmly, and heartily congratulated him on the success of his battle with the river.

"I suppose you know, Willard," he said, "that The King's Basin Land and Irrigation Company has virtually passed into the hands of the S. & C.? We owe them a good half million for closing the break, which means that they will have to take over the property. We knew when we went into the deal how it would end, of course. If you had remained with the Company the river never would have had a chance to get in at all."

The younger man did not remind Mr. Greenfield of the many times the Company had been urged to make the improvements that would have prevented the disaster, nor did he suggest that he would have remained with the Company had not the president himself discharged him. "Your engineer did all that any man could do after the break was made," he said warmly. "It was the equipment and organization of the S. & C. that put the river back in its channel, and no other power on earth, under the circumstances, could have done it in time to head off that back-cut."

The older man smiled. "We all know who closed the break, my boy. I suppose you are planning to stay with the railroad?"

"They have offered me the management of the irrigation work here in the Basin. They are going to put in permanent structures and reconstruct the whole system in first-class shape."

"And you accepted?" There was a note of anxiety in the older man's voice.

"Not yet. I asked for a few days to consider."

James Greenfield did not speak for several minutes, then he said—hesitating as if searching for words: "Don't do it, Willard. Don't do it, for my sake. Let's go back home. You know how I hate this cursed country. I ought never to have gone into this deal after what I had already suffered in the West. But it looked as if I could clean up a good thing and get out. Personally, my money losses don't amount to anything. I have enough left for both of us, and you know, Willard my boy, that it's all yours when I go. Come back home with me and leave this damned hole! We don't fit in here; let's go back where we belong. I'm coming along now to the time when I must begin to think of getting out of the game; and I need you, my boy, I need you."

Willard Holmes was strongly moved by the appeal of this man for whom he had a son's affection. "I wish I could say yes, Uncle Jim," he answered. "I owe you more than I can ever repay, and if it was only the work here I would go. But—there's something else—something that I cannot give up if I would—that I have no right to give up."

"You mean that girl? I thought that was all settled."

"So did I," returned the other grimly. "When I talked with you about it I thought there was no possible chance for me, and perhaps I was right. But I can't let it go now without absolute certainty."

"You don't mean, Willard, that you are going to offer yourself to a woman whose love you have every reason to think belongs to another man?"

The engineer rose to his feet and walked up and down the room. When he spoke there was in his voice a suggestion of that which marked his speech in the days of the river fight. "I mean this: that no man on earth shall take this woman from me if I can prevent it. I would deserve to lose her if I gave her up on the mere guess that she cared for another man. I am going to know from her own words. If there is still a chance for me I am going to stay and fight for it. If I have no chance"—he dropped into a chair—"then I'll go back with you, Uncle Jim."

James Greenfield's face flushed hotly at the younger man's words and then, in the silence that followed, grew pale and stern while his fingers gripped his pencil nervously. "Very well, Willard," he said at last. "You are a man and your own master. If your love for me cannot influence you—"

"Uncle Jim!" The engineer's cry was a protest and an appeal, but the other continued as though he had not heard: "I can urge no other consideration. But you must understand this. I will never receive this nameless woman of unknown parentage as your wife. If you prefer her with that illiterate, low, cunning trickster whom she calls father, you need never expect to come back to me. I have been true to your mother in my care for you. I have done all in my power to give you the place in life that you are entitled to fill by your birth and family. You have been my son in everything but blood. But, by God, sir! if you, with your breeding and raising—if you can turn your back upon the memory of your mother and father and upon me and all that we stand for— if you can turn your back upon us, desert us for these —these damned cattle, you can herd with them the rest of your life."

He was on his feet now, pacing the floor angrily. The engineer had also risen and stood waiting for this storm of wrath to spend itself.

"Understand me," the older man continued. "If she refuses you, you can come back. If she accepts you, you need never show your face to me again, and I shall take good care that your friends at home understand the reason. Probably if you let these people know what the result will be if you are accepted it will make a great difference in the woman's answer."

Willard Holmes dared not speak. Nothing but his life-long love for the man whose devotion to the engineer's mother had stood the test of years enabled the younger man to control himself. When he could speak calmly he said: "I am sorry, sir, that you said that; for you must see how you have made it impossible for me now ever to go back with you. If Miss Worth does not care for me, I would have been glad to go home with you, for next to her, Uncle Jim, you are more to me than anyone in the world. When you say that my relation to you shall depend upon her answer you make it impossible for her answer to make any difference so far as you and I are concerned. Won't you—won't you reconsider, Uncle Jim? Won't you take back your words?"

"No, sir; I have said exactly what I mean."

"Good-by, sir."

"Good-by."

When the office door had closed behind the engineer, James Greenfield stood motionless in the center of the room. Once he took a step toward the door but checked himself. Then turning slowly, wearily, he sank into the chair before his desk. For a few moments he fumbled aimlessly over the papers and documents, then from his pocket took a flat leather case and, opening it, held in his hand a portrait of the engineer's mother. As he looked at the face of the woman who had never ceased to hold the first place in his heart, his lips framed words he could not speak aloud.

Slowly his form drooped, his head bowed. Then, with the picture held close, he buried his face in his arms among the business papers on his desk.

CHAPTER XXXVI.

OUT OF THE HOLLOW OF GOD'S HAND.

HE first train from Republic to Barba over the new King's Basin Central arrived in the town by the old Dry River Crossing shortly after noon. Later in the day Jefferson Worth with his daughter, his superintendent and the Seer went to the power plant on the bank of Dry River.

When the plant was built it was placed as low in the old wash as the depth of the ancient channel would permit, so that the greatest possible fall from the Company canal above might be secured. As Jefferson Worth and his companions stood now on the bank of the river they saw the waste-way from the turbine wheel that ran the generators nearly thirty feet above the bottom of the channel. The flood that had cut the deep canyons through the heart of the Basin, destroying Kingston on its course, had worked on a smaller scale in the old Dry River wash, cutting a narrow gorge nearly fifty feet deep from its outlet at the new sea past the power plant at Barba and nearly to the spillway of the main canal.

Standing almost on the very spot where they had found the baby girl years before, the Seer asked Barbara's father: "Jeff, does your contract with The King's Basin Land and Irrigation Company call for a certain amount of water, or for water to develop a certain amount of power?"

Jefferson Worth answered in his careful, exact voice: "The first contract called for water to develop a certain amount of power. This new one is a contract for three hundred inches of water. There's nothing in it about the amount of power, but it gives me the sole rights to all the power privileges on the Company property. You see, when Greenfield tried to change the line of their canal so as to cut me out, Abe and I had begun to figure that some day the water from the spillway might cut down the channel and give us a little more drop. But we never counted on this, of course. I simply figured that I might just as well make the new contract safe."

The Seer smiled. "You made it safe all right, Jeff. Do you know what this cut means to you?"

"In a way, yes. That's why I wanted you to look at it."

"It means," said the Seer, "that you have rights here worth a million dollars at least. By lowering your turbine to the bottom of this cut you can, with the same amount of water that you are now using, develop power enough to run every electric light system and turn every wheel in all The King's Basin for years to come."

"You mean that the river breaking in and doing this has made daddy's property worth a million dollars?" asked Barbara breathlessly.

The Seer turned toward her. "Yes, Barbara. The same force that destroyed Kingston and wrecked the Company has increased the value of your father's holding to fully that amount. A million is very conservative."

491

The young woman looked down into the gorge at their feet. Slowly she said: "The Indians must be right. This must be indeed La Palma de la Mano de Dios. Such things could happen nowhere else."

She had just finished speaking when the sound of wheels behind caused them to turn toward the desert and the old San Felipe trail. It was Texas and Pat in the buckboard with El Capitan leading behind.

Catching sight of the group on the river bank, the men turned aside from the road and went to them. "Howdy folks," drawled Tex. "We 'lowed we'd jest about meet up with you-all somewhere about here."

"Sure, 'tis a family reunion we do be havin', wid no empthy chairs at all," declared the Irishman, looking from face to face with twinkling eyes. "Well, well, who'd a thought now that the little kid we found under the bank here, shcared av the coyotes an' more shcared av us rough-necks, wud av growed up like this? An' wid me a shwearin' by all the saints I knew that I wud niver set fut on the disert again. Here we are once more altogether, wid Barbara an' Abe bigger than life. 'Tis the danged owld disert itsilf that's a-lavin' niver to come back at all." He drew the back of his huge hairy hand across his eyes.

Barbara's eyes too were wet, and the others turned away their faces. Pat's words had recalled so vividly the scene at the dry water hole with the changes that the years had brought both to them and to the desert.

It was Texas Joe who broke the silence. "Mr. Worth, Pat and I would like to see you some time this evenin' if you ain't engaged."

"What is it, Tex?" As he spoke Jefferson Worth

492

looked straight into the eyes of the old plainsman.
Texas Joe, gazing steadily into the face of his
employer, drawled easily: "Jest a little matter we
'lowed maybe you'd like to know about, sir. What
time shall we come?"

Something—the memories of the place, perhaps,
aroused by the words of Pat a moment before—
caused Jefferson Worth to lift those nervous fingers
and softly caress his chin. "I guess I can go now.
We're all through here." He turned to the others.
"I'll go on to the hotel with Tex and Pat and you
folks can come along later when you are ready."

He stepped into the buckboard and with the two
drove away. At a livery barn where they stopped to
leave the horses, Texas took from under the seat of
the buckboard something that was wrapped in a sack
that had held a feed of grain for the team and El
Capitan.

When they had reached the privacy of Mr. Worth's
room, the old plainsman and the Irishman stood as if
each waited for the other to begin.

"Well, men," said Jefferson Worth. "What is it?"

"Go on, ye owld oysther," growled Pat to Tex.
"Why the hell don't ye tell the boss what we've come
to tell him. Shpake up."

Texas Joe cleared his throat and began formally:
"I don't reckon, Mr. Worth, that you-all has forgot
that outfit we left in them sand hills back yonder on
the old San Felipe trail the time we found the kid."

At the words Jefferson Worth's face became a
gray mask from behind which his mind reached out
as though to grasp what Texas would say before the

man put it into words. "Well?" The single word came with the colorless sound of dull metal.

"Also I reckon you know how them big drifts are allus on the move, so that when they covers up anything, say an outfit like that one, it stands to reason that some day they'll drift on an' leave it clear again."

Jefferson Worth's hands were gripping the arms of his chair. His gray lips could frame no sound.

"I've allus kind a-kept an eye on that there particular ridge," continued Texas, "an' so to-day me and Pat stopped for a little look around an' "—slowly he unwrapped the grain sack from a long tin box— "an' we found this." He laid the box carefully on the table before Barbara's father. "Hit was a-layin' with what was left of a bigger wooden box or trunk, which same had gone to pieces, and there was a part of that old wagon with that same piece of a halter strap you remember fastened to a wheel. There ain't no sort of doubt, Mr. Worth, that hit's the same outfit an' hits mighty likely that there's papers in here that'll tell us what we tried so hard to find out at first, but what"—he paused and looked around, then finished in a low tone—"I don't reckon any of us wants to know now."

Jefferson Worth sat motionless in his chair, his eyes fixed upon the tin box.

The heavy voice of the Irishman broke the quiet.

"Av Tex wud a listened to raison, Sorr, I'd a-dumped the danged thing into the river, sayin' nothin' to nobody. Fwhat good can we do rakin' up the past that's dead an' gone? The girl is as much

494

yers as if she was yer own flesh an' blood, an' who can say fwhat divil's own mess may come out av this thing? Lave it alone, I say; an' fwhat nobody don't know can't hurt thim. 'Twas wrong intirely to bring ut to ye afther all ye've been sich a father to the little one. Lave it to me, Sorr. Give me the word an' I'll" —he reached eagerly for the box, but Jefferson Worth held up his slim, nervous hand.

"Wait a moment, Pat. I—I don't think that would be right."

Never before had these men seen Jefferson Worth hesitate. The will of the man, whose cold decision had carried him through so many critical situations and upon which the pioneers had relied in the recent time of peril, seemed to fail him at last. The spectacle told the men more clearly than words could have done what he suffered. "I—I don't know what to do," he finished weakly. "Give me time. Let me think." He bowed his face in his hands.

Pat growled an oath under his breath and Texas turned his eyes from his companions to the box and from the box back to his friends in bewildered uncertainty. At last he said in his soft southern drawl: "Mr. Worth, hit's dead sure that me an' Pat ain't helpin' you none in this. I reckon I was all wrong to bring hit to you at all. But hit seemed like I was plumb balled up an' couldn't rightly say what was best. There ain't really no call to crowd this thing as I can see. Suppose you takes your time to think it over. Me an' Pat'll let you alone, an' if you decides to fergit all about hit, you can bet your last red we'll be damn glad to help. Nobody but us three will ever know. 'Tain't as if it was a-doin' anybody any harm."

Jefferson Worth raised his head. "Thank you boys," he said. "I'll have to figure on this thing a little."

Left alone, Jefferson Worth faced the temptation of his life. Dearer to this lonely-hearted man than all the wealth and power that he would realize from his King's Basin work was the child who had come to him out of the desert. The man knew that it was the influence of Barbara upon his life that had prepared him for that night in the sand hills and enabled him rightly to weigh and measure and value the efforts of his kind. That afternoon at the power house it had all been brought before him with startling vividness. He felt that in all that he had accomplished in Barbara's Desert he had been led by the child, who had come to him out of The Hollow of God's Hand. The desert had given her to him; he had given himself in return to the work she loved. He could not think of his work apart from her. She was his—his—his. His gray lips whispered the words as he stood looking down at the box. No one had the right to take her from him; to come into her life. And yet—and yet. He reached out and laid his hand upon the box, then, turning again, paced the room.

Suddenly he whirled about and approached the table. With cold fury he seized the box and placing it upon the floor, broke the light tin fastening with his boot-heel. Again he paused and looked dully at the thing in his hands. Then with a quick motion he threw up the cover. The box was filled with documents and letters, with four or five old photographs.

The address on a large unsealed envelope met his eye and he started back with a low cry as though he had looked upon some startling apparition.

When Barbara with the Seer and Abe returned to the hotel that evening the clerk gave her a note from her father who, the note explained, had been called to Republic on business of importance. He would be back to-morrow.

The clerk said that Mr. Worth had left only a few minutes before with the engine and car that had brought them to Barba that morning.

CHAPTER XXXVII.

BACK TO THE OLD SAN FELIPE TRAIL.

IN the office of The King's Basin Land and Irrigation Company, James Greenfield was aroused by a knock at the door. He lifted his head from his arms and looked around as if awakened out of a deep sleep.

Another knock, and he slipped the picture he held in his hand into his pocket and called, "Come in."

The door opened and Jefferson Worth stepped into the room.

For a moment the president of the wrecked Company sat staring at his business rival, then he leaped to his feet, his fists clenched and his face working with passion. "You can't come in here, sir. Get out!" he said with the voice and manner he would have assumed in speaking to a trespassing dog.

Jefferson Worth stood still. "I have business of importance with you, Mr. Greenfield," he said, and his air of quiet dignity contrasted strangely with the rage of the larger man.

"You can have no business with me of any sort whatever. I have nothing to do with your kind. This is my private office. I tell you to get out."

Jefferson Worth turned calmly as though to obey, but instead of leaving the room closed the door and locked it. Then, placing the small grip he carried

498

upon the table, he deliberately went close to the
threatening president and said coldly: "This is rank
nonsense, Greenfield. I won't leave this office until
I'm through with what I came to do. I have business
with you that concerns you as much as it does me."

"You're a damned thief, a low sharper! I tell you
I have nothing to do with you. Now get out or I'll
throw you out!"

Jefferson Worth answered in his exact, precise
manner, as though carefully choosing and considering
his words: "No, you won't throw me out. You'll
listen to what I have come to tell you. The rest of
your statement, Greenfield, is false and you know it.
It will be just as well for you not to repeat it." The
last low-spoken words did not appear to be uttered as
a threat but as a calm statement of a carefully considered fact. James Greenfield felt as a man who
permits himself to rage against an immovable
obstacle—as one who spends his strength cursing a
stone wall that bars his way or a rock that lies in his
path. With an effort he regained a measure of his
self-control.

"Well, out with it. What do you want?"

"Sit down," said Worth, pointing to a chair.
Mechanically the other obeyed. "You have no reason
for taking this attitude toward me, Mr. Greenfield,"
began Worth with his air of simply stating a fact.

At his words the wrath of the other again mastered
him. "No reason! You—you dare to tell me that?
When you and the young woman that you call your
daughter have come between me and the boy who is
more than a son to me! When you have broken our

close relationship of years' standing and robbed me of his companionship! When you have wrecked and ruined all my plans for his future! When you have defeated the object of my life! No reason? But what can you understand of us? You're a nobody, sir, without a place or a name in the world; a common, low-bred, ignorant sharper with no family but a nameless daughter of unknown parentage whom you found on the desert. How can you understand what Willard Holmes is to me?"

"I figured that you would feel this way about it," came the colorless words. "That's what I came here for to-night—to fix it up."

The angry amazement of Greenfield at what he considered the man's presumption could find no expression.

Worth continued: "I know a great deal more about you and your folks than you think. When I saw that my"—he hesitated over the word, then spoke it plainly—"my daughter was becoming interested in Willard Holmes, I took some pains to look up his history. In doing that I naturally found out a good deal about you. Later I learned a good deal more."

"It is immaterial to me what you know," muttered the other in a tone of deep disgust. "What do you want?"

Worth spoke with quiet dignity. "I want you to understand first, Mr. Greenfield, that my girl is just as much to me as young Holmes is to you. You are right; I am a nobody, ignorant and all that, but you must not think Mr. Greenfield that because you belong in New York and I belong in the West that this thing is harder for you than it is for me. You are not going to lose your boy but I"—for the first time he hesitated and his voice expressed emotion—"I am going to lose my girl."

The pathos of this lonely man's words touched even Greenfield. His manner was more gentle as he said gruffly: "It's a bad business, Mr. Worth; a damned bad business for both of us. I wish I had never heard of this country."

"You'll feel different about that. Anyway I figure that this country and this work will be here long after you and I are gone, and so will these young people." Again he hesitated and his slim fingers caressed his chin. Then from behind that gray mask he asked: "How much do you know about our finding Barbara in the desert?"

"I know the story in a general way, that's all. It does not interest me."

"Let me tell you the facts."

In his brief, colorless sentences Jefferson Worth related the incidents of that trip across the desert, and as he did so Greenfield began to realize that some powerful motive had brought this man to him and was forcing him to relate his story with such exact care for the details.

"And you never found the slightest clue even to the child's name?" he asked, when Worth had finished.

Jefferson Worth hesitated, then: "Mr. Greenfield, you had a younger brother who came West?"

The man gazed at the speaker in amazement as he

501

answered mechanically. "Yes. He died out here somewhere—in California, I believe. I was never able to learn the details. He was an adventurous lad and a good deal of a rover. But why—how—" As the full import of the question dawned upon him Greenfield started from his seat. "My God, man! You don't mean—you cannot mean that it was my brother Will who was lost in that sandstorm on the desert? That the woman you found by the water hole was his wife, Gertrude, and that—that—" His voice sank to a whisper. "Will wrote me that there was a child—that she had Gertrude's hair and eyes. I had never seen her." He turned fiercely upon his companion. "And you have kept this from me all these years? You have kept my only brother's child from me? By God, sir! I— But perhaps this is all one of your damnable tricks. What proof have you that this is so, and if it is, why have you kept it a secret?"

Jefferson Worth opened his satchel and laid the tin box on the desk before the president of The King's Basin Land and Irrigation Company. "This box was found this afternoon by Texas Joe and Pat, who brought it to me. I opened it. It is all here."

When Greenfield had examined the contents of the box—letters, some of them written by himself to his brother, papers relating to William Greenfield's business affairs and property, and photographs of the little family and of the two brothers and their parents, he looked up to see Jefferson Worth sitting motionless, his form relaxed, his head dropped forward.

Suddenly the words of the man who had been a
father to his brother's child came back to Greenfield.
"My girl is just as much to me as young Holmes is
to you. You are not going to lose your boy, but I
am going to lose my girl." In a flash the financier
saw it all—saw how Jefferson Worth loved Barbara
as his own child, as Greenfield cared for Willard
Holmes; saw how Worth might have destroyed the
papers so strangely brought to light and kept the
secret; saw and realized a little what strength of
character it had taken to overcome the temptation,
and felt what the man was suffering.

As Greenfield's hand fell on his shoulder, Jefferson
Worth slowly lifted his head. Slowly he rose to his
feet. In silence the two men faced each other. Without a word—for no word was needed—their hands
met in a firm grip.

After a little while Greenfi ld asked eagerly:
"Where is she now, Mr. Worth? Where is the girl?
Does she know? I must see her at once. Come!
And Willard—I wonder if Le is still in town. Come,
we must go to them."

But Jefferson Worth answered: "I've been figuring on that, Mr. Greenfield. You had better let me
tell Barbara myself. And if I was you, after what
you have probably said to Holmes on this subject, I
wouldn't be in a hurry to tell him. For the sake of
their future we'd better let Barbara handle that matter herself. You can easily figure it out that it will
be best for them that way."

CHAPTER XXXVIII.

THE HERITAGE OF BARBARA WORTH.

BARBARA, walking quickly, left the little village and, crossing Dry River on the bridge that now spanned the deep gorge where the old San Felipe trail once led down into the ancient wash, climbed the slight grade to the grave that was marked by the simple headstone with its one word—"Mother."

That morning Jefferson Worth had told her of the tin box found by Texas Joe and Pat. With reverent care she had read the papers and letters and had looked long at the portraits of her parents and people. She could not at first realize that the desert had at last given up the secret that she had so longed to know. It was not real to her, the revelation was so sudden, so startling. She could not think of herself save as the daughter of Jefferson Worth, whom she loved as a father.

As soon as the noon day meal was over she had left her room in the hotel, and once out of doors her steps had instinctively turned toward her mother's grave beside the old trail.

Standing before the headstone she looked at the one word. "Mother," she said softly. "Mother!" Then, still in a whisper, she repeated the unfamiliar names: "Gertrude Greenfield; William Greenfield

504

—my mother; my father! I am Barbara Greenfield
—Barbara Greenfield!"

Seating herself on the ground beside the grave, she
looked about: at the sand hills in the distance; at the
Dry River gorge and the power plant; at the canals
shining like silver bands among the green fields of
the ranchers to the southeast; and at the little town.
An hour passed; then another; and another.

Across the river she saw Pablo riding out of the
town and away along the road that follows the canal.
Then from the power house came Abe Lee with the
Seer. She watched them as they walked along the
bank of the old channel. Once she thought she would
call to them, but hesitated. If they crossed the bridge
and came up the hill they would be sure to see her.
So she waited, keeping still. They passed the bridge
and continued on down the bank of the stream.

Barbara knew instinctively that they were talking
of her and the secret that the desert had at last
revealed, for she had asked her father to tell them.
She thought of her father who had gone to Republic.
He would return that evening and Mr. Greenfield,
her uncle, would be with him. "Her uncle"—how
strange!

Then Barbara saw on the other side of the river a
horseman riding from the south toward the town.
She could not mistake the khaki-clad figure that,
while fully at home in the saddle, still lacked the
indescribable, easy looseness and swinging grace of
the western rider. It was Willard Holmes, and the
young woman's heart told her why the engineer had
come. Since that meeting at the river in the hour

of his victory she had known that he would come and she had known what her answer would be.

He had evidently ridden from the river, from his work. Did he know? No, she decided, he could not know yet. Then the quick thought came: he *must not know until*—until she herself should tell him. Quickly the young woman walked down the hill across the bridge toward the town.

Willard Holmes arrived at the hotel and, learning that Miss Worth was out, carried a chair to the arcade on the street to await her return. He had not waited long when a voice at his shoulder said with mock formality: "I believe this is Mr. Willard Holmes."

The engineer sprang to his feet. "Miss Worth! They told me that you were out. I was sitting here waiting for you."

"I was out when you arrived," she confessed; "but I saw you coming and hurried back pronto. I knew you had just left the river, you see. And of course," she added, as though that explained her eagerness to see him, "I wanted to hear the latest news from the work."

"There is no news," he answered, as though dismissing the matter finally.

"And may I ask what brings you to Barba?"

He looked at her steadily. "You brought me to Barba."

"I?"

"Yes—you. I stopped in Republic on my way back from the city the evening of the day you left. I was forced to go on to the river, but took the first opportunity to ride out here, for I understood you expected to be in Barba several days. Surely you know why I have come. The work I stayed in the Basin to do is finished. I have another offer from the S. & C. which, if I accept, will keep me here for several years. I have come to you with it as I came with the other. What shall I do? Please don't pretend that you don't understand me."

The direct forcefulness of the man almost made Barbara forget the little plan she had arranged on her way to the hotel to meet him. "I won't pretend, Mr. Holmes," she answered seriously. "But—will you go with me for a little ride into the desert?"

Her words recalled to his mind instantly their first meeting in Rubio City, but Holmes was not astonished now. The invitation coming from Barbara under the circumstances seemed the most natural thing in the world.

The young woman went to her room to make ready while the engineer brought the horses, and in a very few minutes they had crossed the river and were following the old San Felipe trail toward the sand hills.

Very few words passed between them until they reached the great drift that had held so long its secret. Leaving the horses at Barbara's request, they climbed the steep sides of the great sand mound. From the top they could see on every hand the many miles of The King's Basin country—from Lone Mountain at the end of the delta dam to the snow-capped sentinels of San Antonio Pass; and from the sky line of the Mesa and the low hills on the east to No Man's

Mountains and the bold wall of the Coast Range that shuts out the beautiful country on the west.

The soft, many-colored veils and scarfs of the desert, with the gold of the sand hills, the purple of the mountains, the gray and green of the desert vegetation, with the ragged patches of dun plain, were all there still as when Willard Holmes had first looked upon it, for the work of Reclamation was still far from finished.

But there was more in Barbara's Desert now than pictures woven magically in the air. There were beautiful scenes of farms with houses and barns and fences and stacks, with cattle and horses in the pastures, and fields of growing grain, the dark green of alfalfa, with threads and lines and spots of water that, under the flood of white light from the wide sky, shone in the distance like gleaming silver. Barbara and the engineer could even distinguish the little towns of Republic and Frontera, with Barba nearby; and even as they looked they marked the tall column of smoke from a locomotive on the S. & C. moving toward the crossing of the old San Felipe trail, and on the King's Basin Central another, coming toward the town on Dry River where once beside a dry water hole a woman lay dead with an empty canteen by her side.

Willard Holmes drew a long breath.

"You like my Desert?" asked the young woman softly, coming closer to his side—so close that he felt her presence as clearly as he felt the presence of the spirit that lives in the desert itself.

"Like it!" he repeated, turning toward her. "It is my desert now; mine as well as yours. Oh, Barbara! Barbara! I have learned the language of your land. Must I leave it now? Won't you tell me to stay?"

He held out his hands to her, but she drew back a little from his eagerness. "Wait. I must know something first before I can answer."

He looked at her questioningly. "What must you know, Barbara?"

"Did you ever hear the story of what happened here in these very sand hills? Do you know that I am not the daughter of Jefferson Worth?"

"Yes," he answered gravely. "I know that Mr. Worth is not your own father, but I did not know that this was the scene of the tragedy."

"And you understand that I am nameless; that no one knows my parentage? That there may even be Mexican or Indian blood in my veins? You understand—you realize all that?"

He started toward her almost roughly. "Yes, I understand all that, but I care only that you are Barbara. I know only that I want you—you, Barbara!"

"But your family—Mr. Greenfield—your friends back home—think what it means to them. Can you afford—"

"Barbara," he cried. "Stop! Why are you saying these things? Listen to me. Don't you *know* that I love you? Don't you know that nothing else matters? Your Desert has taught me many things, dear, but nothing so great as this—that I want you and that nothing else matters. I want you for my wife."

"But you said once that you would never *marry me*," persisted the young woman. "What has changed you?"

"*I* said that I would never marry you? *I* said *that?* That cannot be, Barbara; you are mistaken."

She shook her head. "That is what you said. I heard you myself. You told Mr. Greenfield at my house that morning he came to see you when you were hurt. I—I—the door into the dining room was open and I heard."

The light of quick understanding broke over the engineer's face. "And you heard what Uncle Jim said to me? But Barbara, didn't you hear the reason I gave him for saying that I would not marry you?"

"I—I couldn't hear anything after that," she said simply.

At her confession the man's strong face shone with triumph. "Listen, dear, I told Uncle Jim I would never marry you because you loved someone else and that there was no chance for me."

Barbara's brown eyes opened wide. "You thought that?"

"Yes. I thought you loved Abe Lee."

"Why—why I *do* love Abe."

The man laughed. "Of course you do; but I thought you loved him as I wanted you to love me; don't you understand?"

"Oh-h!" The exclamation was a confession, an explanation and an expression of complete understanding. "But that"—she added as she went to him—"that *could not be.*"

And then—

But Barbara's words, rightly understood, mark the end of my story.

Rarely is it given in the story of life, to those who work greatly or love greatly, to gather the fruit of their toil or passion. But it is given those others, perhaps—those for whom it could not be—to know a happiness greater, it may be, than the joy of possession.

THE END.

Printed in the United States
74706LV00004B/15

9 781417 941162